THE DOLL

Taylor Stevens has a remarkable life story – raised in a religious cult, the Children of God, she was denied basic education, her storytelling quashed by cult leaders, and her writing confiscated and burned. When she finally broke free of the movement, she was determined to write a novel – and she has now written three, *The Informationist*, *The Innocent* and *The Doll*.

Taylor Stevens has lived in central Africa but now lives in Dallas.

http://www.taylorstevensbooks.com/author.php

Facebook.com/TaylorStevens

Twitter.com/Taylor_Stevens

Praise for Taylor Stevens

'Munroe is a sensational character and
Stevens is a sensational writer'
Lee Child

'One of the best thrillers of the year!'
Tess Gerritsen

'The world may have found its next Lisbeth Salander'
Sydney Daily Telegraph

Also available by Taylor Stevens

The Informationist
The Innocent

THE DOLL
TAYLOR STEVENS

arrow books

Published by Arrow Books 2014

2 4 6 8 10 9 7 5 3 1

First published in the United States in 2013 by Crown Publishers, an imprint of the
Crown Publishing Group, a division of Random House Inc., New York

First published in Great Britain in 2013 by
Arrow Books
Random House, 20 Vauxhall Bridge Road,
London SW1V 2SA

www.randomhouse.co.uk

Addresses for companies within The Random House Group Limited can be found at:
www.randomhouse.co.uk/offices.htm

The Random House Group Limited Reg. No. 954009

A CIP catalogue record for this book
is available from the British Library

ISBN 9780099588795

The Random House Group Limited supports the Forest Stewardship
Council® (FSC®), the leading international forest-certification organisation.
Our books carrying the FSC label are printed on FSC®-certified paper. FSC is the only
forest-certification scheme supported by the leading environmental organisations,
including Greenpeace. Our paper procurement policy can be found at:
www.randomhouse.co.uk/environment

Book design by Elina D. Nudelman

Printed and bound by CPI Group (UK) Ltd, Croydon, CR0 4YY

With love and gratitude to the other Bradford. Always.

one

DALLAS, TEXAS

Palms to the glass, watching the lot from his office window, Miles Bradford saw her topple. The fall was a slow-motion sort of thing, the type of tilt and drop that made him hesitate, unsure for a long second whether to laugh or worry. He held his breath, urging her up. Any second now, knowing he was there, she'd turn toward the building and wave. They'd laugh about it later.

But she didn't move. Made no attempt to edge out from beneath the motorcycle that pinned her leg to the pavement. Didn't even raise her head.

Seeing though not understanding, moving as if treading water, Bradford backed away from the window. Then turned and bolted out of the office, down the hall, and past reception. Bypassed the elevators for the stairs, took the five floors at a run, and emerged from the stairwell into the lobby, where he pushed through the big glass doors only to find an ambulance blocking the northern lot access and Munroe on a stretcher, being lifted into its interior.

Bradford yelled, swung his arms to attract the attention of the paramedics so they would wait a moment longer, and allow him time to get across the lot so he could ride with her. But they never turned, never looked. The stretcher slid inward, the doors shut, and Bradford ran again, racing the distance, arriving seconds too late.

The ambulance, siren blaring, pulled out onto the service road.

The Ducati lay on its side, shoved slightly from where she'd been pulled from underneath, engine off and keys still in the ignition. He stooped and heaved the bike upright. Straddled the machine, hit neutral with his foot, punched his thumb into the starter button, and compressed the clutch handle only to find that the impact with the pavement had snapped it off.

He swore and stared in the direction the ambulance had traveled, frustrated and motionless, catching his breath, processing, while the wail faded and traffic began to flow again. Had he run directly for a car instead of the ambulance, he might have had a chance to chase it down, but he was too late for that now. Bradford glanced back toward the building, where the small crowd of onlookers had already begun to disperse.

Two decades of working in the line of fire, of watching his back and chasing images from shadows, and he still had the tendency to think like a civilian on his home turf. What were the odds that one of the people on the ground floor had made the call and an ambulance had been close by? Not impossible, but not highly likely, either.

Bradford dismounted and rolled the Ducati to the garage, to the out-of-the-way nook Munroe typically stashed it, and then jogged back to the lobby with the mental tape of her fall playing inside his head. Watched her jerk and then glance down, saw her pause and the way her left hand had wandered over her thigh, the long hesitation before she slumped and toppled. Hers weren't the motions—the sudden drop, the collapse—of someone passing out.

At the elevator he jammed a finger into the up arrow and ran through a list of possible alternatives—allergies, medical conditions, recent sicknesses—and drew one blank after another.

By the time Bradford returned to his floor, he'd gone through the replay a dozen times, more frustrated with each rewind. He pushed through the wide doors that separated Capstone Security Consulting from the hallway, crossed the plush reception area with its rich furnishings and oversize logo—corporate tokens that implied something other than the blood-and-guts outfit beyond the wood-paneled wall—and came to a full stop at the reception desk and Samantha Walker who sat behind it.

She stared up at him with her big brown eyes and the same

give me the sitrep look she always got when his stress level soared. "What the hell was that all about?" she said. "You look like death paid a visit. Talk to me."

Bradford ignored her with a vacant half-smile and leaned across the desk for the Post-it stack. What else could he do? Tell her that based on his gut and a ten-second memory loop that wouldn't stop, he was pretty sure the woman he loved had just been tranqued and shoved into an ambulance?

He scribbled the few digits he'd caught off the plates when the vehicle had peeled out onto the service road and, with eyes still on the pad, said, "Where's the closest emergency room?"

"Medical City and Parkland."

"Call them, will you? Find out if Michael's there?"

She gave him that look again, then reached for the mouse and her monitor came alive. "Am I calling about Michael or some other name?" she asked.

"Michael," he said. Because unless Munroe was working, that's who her ID said she was, but the inquiry sent his mind bolting in two directions, and while Walker searched for numbers, he forced thought fragments and scattered images into a coherent question: He'd watched Vanessa Michael Munroe being lifted into the ambulance, but to those who'd done the lifting, was it Michael they'd taken or another of her incarnations?

He struggled to draw from the ether some sense of why, of who would have had the means and motive to put her into that ambulance, and, more important, how she'd been traced. Munroe had surely made enemies in her life, trading secrets and buying souls, but she'd worked with disguises and aliases, had stayed away from home for so many years, that there were few who knew who she truly was or how to find her.

Walker cleared her throat, picked up the phone, and gave Bradford a decided stare that said she'd make the calls but not while he stood there listening and micromanaging.

He moved to get out of her way, swiped a key card through a scanner.

A segment of wall to the right of the desk clicked open a sliver. Bradford pushed against it and stepped through. Beyond the paneling, the interior hallways and facing walls were glass, with privacy blinds kept open, giving the entire floor a sense of light and space.

He moved past the offices to what most businesses would consider a conference area but which was to Capstone the war room, the nerve center, the place from which the business tendrils reached out for thousands of miles to support and supply the private security gigs running at any given time.

There was no door, only a frame where one used to be, and at one of the desks facing a wall of oversize monitors, Paul Jahan swiveled away from a keyboard.

Bradford nodded, said, "Hey, Jack," and handed him the Post-it. "Dallas Fire-Rescue plates. Can you run them?"

Jahan took the purple square with its three handwritten digits, gave it a look, and then stuck it to the nearest monitor. "Give me a minute," he said. "I'll see what I can get."

In the ensuing silence, Bradford strode to the marked-up whiteboards that functioned on the right wall as the monitors did on the left. He followed the note changes, minor updates on the two-man team in Peshawar, but read them without really seeing. His mind was elsewhere, still running, still torn in the two directions Walker's innocuous question about Munroe's identity had sent him.

Having nothing to answer the first, he shifted to the second: If something happened to Munroe, Logan's number was the emergency contact in her wallet. No first name, no last name, just Logan. He was her surrogate brother, soul mate, partner in crime, the man whose history was nearly as convoluted as her own and who guarded her back as fiercely as she guarded his.

Bradford checked his watch. Checked his phone. Ten minutes, if that, since he'd watched Munroe take the bike down with her fall. Still early if he meant to start tracking, but that didn't matter. He pulled from speed dial the number known to few, the phone Logan always carried and almost certainly answered.

Called and was sent directly to voice mail.

Bradford hung up without leaving a message.

Thumbed through the contacts for Tabitha, Munroe's eldest sister, hit call, and then ended it before the dialing began. No one in Munroe's family had any idea of the life she led off the grid and she took care to shield them and leave nothing that would trace back to them. It was still too soon for this kind of call, and he wasn't ready to step into the resulting quagmire of explanations if Tabitha should happen to pick up. Needed to script a plausible cover story first.

From across the room Jahan said, "Looks like those digits belong to valid Fire-Rescue plates. I can't say for sure with only half of them, but they seem to check out."

Bradford turned from the whiteboard wall. "Is it a stolen vehicle?"

"Not that I'm showing, although it might not have been reported yet."

"What about a trace on the GPS? Can we figure out where the ambulance ended up, maybe where it's been?"

Jahan swiveled his chair around to face Bradford and then shifted a couple of inches to the right, then left, and back again in a maddening fidget. "I *might* be able to do that," he said, and stopped. "When do you plan to let us know what's going on?"

Bradford sighed. Walked to the nearest blank spot on the whiteboards, picked up a red marker, and drew the beginning of a diagram. Wrote: *Michael—passed out or taken down?*

He turned. "That's all I've got."

Jahan's mouth opened for a full second before he spoke. "You've gotta be kidding." And a beat later: "What did you see?"

"Not enough."

Jahan's index finger moved toward the whiteboard. "But enough for that?"

Bradford's posture sagged and he glanced again at the diagram.

Given Munroe's lifestyle, it was more than enough, but there was nothing he could point to for confirmation. The nine months since the infiltration in Argentina had been quiet, her initial week in Dallas had turned into months, the occasional overnight stay at his place lengthening into more, until she, who had no home of her own, gradually grew comfortable in his. He'd offered her security contracts as a way to delay the inevitability of her leaving, but they'd been small and relatively inconsequential—the longest had been a month in Abuja, Nigeria, which had evolved into an adult baby-sitting gig—definitely nothing to write home about, nothing he could connect to today.

The intercom crackled. Walker said, "I've got a Michael Munroe at the emergency room at Medical City."

Jahan raised his eyebrows; Bradford shook his head.

"It's too soon," he said.

Jahan's head tilt was subtle, an acknowledgment of trust rather than agreement. Bradford reached for the key rack, lifted off a set, and moved toward the door space. "Keep an ear for the phones, will you? I'm closing down the front and taking Sam with me."

Bradford and Walker took the elevator down to the ground floor and crossed to the parking garage, to an Explorer, one of three vehicles Capstone kept on hand. Bradford got in behind the wheel. Walker slid into the passenger seat, buckled up, and kept her focus beyond the windshield, biting back, he knew, questions she wouldn't ask.

Her silence now was part of the same dance of avoidance that had descended on most of the team when Munroe had first come onboard. Suspicions of preferential treatment tainted the waters. Bradford had brought Munroe into the company, it was no secret that he was sleeping with her, and he'd already dropped everything once before to watch her back. Until proven otherwise, this little jaunt to the hospital was Bradford's overly paranoid, overly protective private mission, and as such, a waste of company resources.

THE EMERGENCY ROOM at Medical City, like most emergency rooms, was harshly lit and filled with depression. Seating took up the bulk of the waiting area. The next-of-kin story got Bradford and Walker beyond the wide swinging doors that divided the helpless from the helped and into the hallway, where the smell of antiseptic filled the air and the glare of fluorescent tubing illuminated nothing Bradford wanted to see and everything he didn't.

He found the room and passed through the curtained entry, only to back out as quickly as he'd gone in.

Walker, close behind, nearly collided with him in the process. She jumped sideways to avoid impact.

"What the hell?" she said, and when his only response was to search out the room number again, she gave him *that* look and continued past.

The room held one bed, an assortment of medical equipment, and a small space to move about. Bradford joined Walker beside the bed, where, expression clouded over, she stared down at a stranger, bloodied, stitched up, and doped.

"You want me to check with the nurses?" she whispered. "Find out if there's been some mistake?"

Bradford drew the curtain fully around, and motioned for her to keep watch. Belongings lay to the side of the bed and he searched through them, rifling through clothing, shoes, and purse until he found a wallet.

Munroe's wallet.

There was nothing else to indicate who this person was—no notebook or gadgets, no phone or identifying items. Only the folded leather that had, until this morning, been in Munroe's back pocket. Bradford flipped through it and pulled out the ID, turning it toward Walker long enough for her to get a good look, then nodded his head toward the exit.

She turned and left.

He continued past the driver's license and credit cards, which were still there, searching for the emergency numbers and the cash, which should have also been there but were not. Bradford pocketed the wallet, lifted the sheets slightly to see what lay underneath—a violation of privacy to whoever was in that bed, but he needed to confirm what he already suspected—and then having done so, slipped out.

Walker waited for him at the Explorer, arms crossed and leaning against the hood, and when he was within hearing distance she straightened and said, "The woman was brought in at about ten-twenty this morning. Michael didn't leave till eleven-thirty. The timing doesn't work."

"Except Michael got to the office around ten," he said. "The timing works if they were waiting for her to arrive, if they knew they'd get her on her way out."

"They'd have to be watching your place," Walker said.

"Maybe they are."

Bradford opened the doors and slid in behind the wheel, a hundred questions charging through his head, all of them superseded by guilt. Munroe would never have been found if she hadn't been in Dallas, and she'd stayed in Dallas for him.

two

Samantha Walker was five-foot-two, brunette, buxom, wide-smiling, and naturally tanned. She was the type of inviting cliché that men in bars mistakenly groped and called "honey," only to later call "bitch" after she'd broken their nose.

Walker was a military brat: an only child, a dual citizen with a U.S. Marine sniper for a father and a Brazilian exotic dancer for a mother. At twenty-six, she was not only the youngest member of Bradford's nine-man team but also the only woman, besides Munroe, who was temporary.

It was easy to mistake Walker for Capstone's mercy hire—the token female brought into a man's world to appease civilian work-force standards—or for eye candy, especially when she sat behind the front desk, but those were ignorant assumptions based on not knowing Walker—and on not knowing Bradford. At Capstone, where an assignment often meant life or death, egoism, sexism, and racism were wastes of time. If you could do the job, you got the job, end of story. This was the internal culture that kept the team tight, and as far as Bradford was concerned, Walker was one of his best—which was why he'd brought her with him to the hospital.

She sat in the Explorer, eyes closed and thumb pressed to the bridge of her nose, doing that thing she did: remembering, retracing steps, imprinting details that meant nothing in the moment but which she might need later. Bradford took the Explorer out of the parking lot, pulled the phone from his belt clip, dialed Logan, and was once more connected to voice mail.

On an average day, Logan not answering would be an understandable oddity, but today the silence screamed of complications. Bradford tossed the phone onto the front console, yanked a hard left on the steering wheel, and swerved. Cut across two lanes to pull a U-turn. A lady in a red Mazda hit the horn and let it blow. The guy behind her was more explicit and gave Bradford the finger.

Walker grabbed the hand bar for support and through clenched teeth said, "Where are we going?"

Bradford swung tight and punched the gas. The Explorer lurched forward just fast enough to keep from being rear-ended. "Logan's not answering his phone," he said, and though Walker wouldn't fully grasp the implications, she knew enough to save him an explanation.

When they were once again moving with the flow of traffic, Walker said, "Why the body double in the hospital? Why'd they even bother to plant the wallet?"

Bradford looked away from the road and stared at her a second too long. Shifted his focus back to the traffic and answered with an audible growl. Twice now, so intent on getting to Munroe, he'd run in the wrong direction, hadn't seen the maze before Walker asked him to.

She answered for him. "They knew we'd come looking and gave us a distraction, not for long, just long enough, because they had to know as soon as we got to the hospital the ruse would be up." She paused. "You asked Jack to run plates, right?"

"Yeah."

"What'd he get?"

"Valid Dallas Fire-Rescue," Bradford said. "Nothing reported stolen."

"But your gut says the paramedics weren't the real deal."

Instinct told him many things, none that he wanted to articulate. He said, "At this point, it's all conjecture."

She was quiet for a moment, then said, "If they were real, we'll find her eventually, so let's agree they weren't and that Jack is right. Where'd they get the ambulance? Emergency vehicles aren't exactly easy to drive off with, not without causing a commotion we should be able to pick up."

"I'd use an out-of-service unit," Bradford said. "The city's got to keep them stored somewhere."

"It's a lead."

He reached for the phone and tossed it to her. "Get Jack on it," he said, and swung the vehicle down a semideserted industrial strip.

FAR ALONG THE street on either side and in both directions were squat block buildings, businesses divided one from the next by narrow windows and truck bays. The signage on one, scripted in large metallic block letters, read LOGAN's, and Bradford pulled to the front of it.

The parking area was empty, and from the ground level the building appeared quiet, if not deserted. Concrete steps under a roofed walkway led up to a mostly glass front door. Beyond the entry, all was dark, and daylight reflecting off the glass created a mirrored effect. The door's latch rested against the frame as if someone in a hurry hadn't realized the spring was broken.

Bradford reached for the weapon holstered under his arm and toed the door open. Walker, following suit, went in behind him.

The hallway was a straight, empty shot forty-five feet back to another door, which led to the warehouse area. Off the hall on both sides were the four rooms that made up the entire office—two in the front for workspace, two to the rear that had been used as a kitchen and a bedroom for as long as Logan had leased the place. At the moment, the only light was what filtered through the front door.

The interior was silent, the floor littered with glass shattered from one of the large framed posters that had once hung high and now lay disjointed at the base of the wall. Bradford stepped beyond the shards, moved from one room to the next, staying in each just long enough to confirm it empty.

The primary evidence of a struggle was in the kitchen, where the table was broken and dishes lay shattered on the floor. Dried blood streaked across the floor and counters. He found a light switch and elbowed it on, adding a garish illumination to the mix, and then, seeing what he needed to see, backed out, nodding for Walker to take a look.

She stopped just before the chaos, and after a moment her eyes cut to his. He continued down the hall to the door that led to the warehouse and the restrooms, though he knew he'd find nothing out there. Whoever had done this had come for Logan, found him in the kitchen, taken him, and left.

The warehouse, double the width of the front office, was spaced with machines, tools, and storage. Bradford stood in the oversize area listening to the buzz of electricity that ran through unseen wires to powerful lights. In the silence, he holstered the weapon, then turned a slow circle and willed the facts to come to him.

The events of today were too connected to be coincidence, were too well informed to be new. There was a history that pulled everything together, something from their past, someone who would have known where to look and who to grab, and somehow all of this tied in to today. The events of Argentina tumbled inside his head.

He pushed past Walker, who guarded the egress.

In Logan's bedroom, he dug through dressers and drawers, scanned the walls and surfaces, added almost as much to the mess as those who'd come before him, searching for photographs, artwork, personal touches, anything that would lead from Logan to Hannah, Logan's daughter, who'd been the catalyst for Munroe's infiltration in Buenos Aires.

He found nothing. Like Munroe, Logan was careful not to leave anything that traced back to the ones he loved, and this one relief was drowned out by several more destructive possibilities. Bradford paused, then looked up to find Walker studying him. He straightened, ignoring what she left unsaid. No matter how it might appear to her, his weren't the actions of a man who'd witnessed the abduction of his girlfriend. Walker didn't know Munroe's history, didn't understand how Logan factored into the equation, and without having seen it, lived through it—survived it—she could never understand the place from which his fear was born.

Vanessa Michael Munroe was a killer with a predator's natural instincts; she could take care of herself. What scared him—terrified him—was what would happen if she was pushed too far. He'd seen that place of destruction, had witnessed firsthand what the darkness could do to her mind, and if whoever had taken her had also taken Logan . . .

Bradford let the thought die and cut off the murky places to which it led. He stood in place, deliberating, analyzing, then whispered, "Surveillance footage."

Walker's head tipped up and around.

He said, "Fiber optics."

They found the security system racked inside the kitchen's closet, the miniature cooling fans still blowing and signs of hurried disturbance along the walls.

The recording tray was empty.

Bradford scanned behind the equipment, where clusters of wires fed to and from machines through the wall. He used the closet walls to brace himself and shimmied up to the faint outline of a cutaway. Pushed up, and the segment of ceiling lifted and slid away on rollers.

The area above the kitchen was clean, had been decked, and the heating and cooling air vents redirected to include this small area—everything opposite what one might expect in an unused crawl space. A foot away from the opening were two servers and next to them a small rack of jacketed DVDs. He punched the button to open the recording tray, ejected an unmarked disk, slid it into a sleeve, and dropped it down to Walker.

They moved from the kitchen back to the front area, where the computers had been destroyed and the hard drives removed. Hunted for logs, journals, notations on paper, anything that might direct them to Logan's last visitor, but what they were searching for, if it had ever existed at all, had probably ended up on a scrap of paper tossed out with yesterday's trash.

They didn't speak again until they were back inside the Explorer and Bradford had found a random pay phone from which he made an anonymous call to 911.

"What's the connection?" Walker asked. "Michael and Logan?"

Bradford, eyes fixed on the road ahead, didn't respond. He didn't have the words to articulate the jumbled confusion of experience and history, the obscure paths Munroe had trod, from them the murky depths they were about to wade.

Walker sighed and turned back to the window. Said, "You know things I don't know and I can't help solve this thing if you insist on playing the role of grieving boyfriend."

Bradford stole a glance in her direction. Said, "Whoever did this came after Michael and took Logan as collateral, as a hostage." Paused. "Either that or they took him as a setup to a revenge killing—for Michael to witness before they kill her, too. One of those two."

A long, heavy silence filled the car and eventually Walker said, "Wow."

"It's all just conjecture," he said, "but you wanted to know."

She shifted in the seat so that she faced him. "I don't understand. Logan races motorcycles for a living. Why the hell does he need his place wired like that?"

"He races, he retools performance engines, but he's also got a supply business that has nothing to do with his machine shop. Logan's kind of a go-to guy. If you need something military-grade and difficult to get, he'll do the getting."

"But no alarm system?"

"Nothing that would bring law enforcement to his doorstep."

"And you don't think what happened today might possibly be because of him and"—Walker air-quoted—"his supply business?"

Bradford shot her another glance and turned back to the road. Whoever had done this had taken Munroe clean while Logan's place was trashed and bloody. Even without knowing the history, it didn't take a genius to follow the logic. He waited until he'd exited the freeway and stopped at a traffic light before answering. "It may be intertwined with his business somehow," he said, "but ultimately this is about Michael."

"And you know this how? More gut instinct?"

"Stop sniping at me," he said. "I know you see it. Whoever did this grabbed Michael in public and in broad daylight, went through a hell of a lot of effort to create a diversion. This is not an amateur, so let's just assume that if all he wanted was her dead, Logan would be here grieving over her body with us, but instead he's missing, too. The only reason to take Logan is to control Michael."

"Fine for a theory," she said, "but why take Logan specifically? Sure, he's her friend, but if the idea is some sort of hostage situation, why not take you? Why not me for that matter, or some kid on the street?"

Bradford waited again before speaking. How to explain who

Logan was to Munroe? "Holding Logan hostage is the best weapon they could have come up with," he said. "She's tighter with him than with any blood bond."

"Someone knows this?"

Bradford nodded. Someone knew. *Who* was the big fucking question.

three

Down the hall and through the glass walls, Jahan shifted away from the monitors, watching their approach, swiveling the chair back and forth until Bradford entered the war room.

Before Bradford spoke, Jahan said, "Confirmed the VIN numbers to the ambulance. Found the service depot and am working on tying in to Dallas Fire-Rescue records and GPS systems so we can figure out where it came from and where it's been." He paused. "News on Logan?"

Bradford shook his head. "He's missing, too."

Walker handed Jahan the disk. "Don't know if it's current, but we pulled a surveillance backup."

Jahan stared at it for a moment, then turned to the computer and inserted the disk into a DVD tray.

Bradford and Walker leaned in closer.

At their crowding, Jahan put his palms against the desk and rolled the chair backward. "Please," he said.

They both straightened, then took a step back. Jahan waved them on farther. "Go do what you do and let me do what I do." When neither of them budged, he slid lower in the chair, stretched his legs, and tilted his head upward. "I've got all day."

Walker glanced at Bradford, and when he offered no reassurance, she took another step in retreat, headed for the hall, and paused in the door frame just long enough to lean back in. Said, "You'd better call me if there's news, Jack—you leave me out of this and I swear I'll find a way to make the rest of your life fucking miserable."

The click of the wall segment followed a half-minute later.

Jahan muttered under his breath, his right hand making a talking motion, "As if she doesn't trust me!" When, after a long silence, Bradford didn't move, Jahan glared up at him.

"I need to watch," Bradford said.

"No, you don't. I know you think it'll help you feel better, keeping busy, being up-to-the-second on what's going on, and all that. But standing there breathing in my ear while I pull this apart is only going to give you anxiety—is going to give *me* anxiety. There are new notes on the board and you have a business to run." Jahan motioned across the room toward the whiteboards. "Go that way."

Bradford sighed, shifted away from the computer and everything he hoped, and fought against hoping, to find.

Hope. The activity of the impotent. His was a world of action, of relying on his own wits and ability to create the luck that kept him alive, and yet here in a moment of weakness he was a mendicant *hoping* for alms.

He turned away, a concession to a friendship with Jahan that went back far enough that privately they still called each other names earned during rougher and cruder times.

Jahan's career path had taken him from army intelligence into Bradford's mercenary fold. At thirty-seven, he was a second-generation American, semi-attached to an extended family in Mumbai, and having spent the predominance of the last eight years working private security in the Middle East, he could now, at least on the surface, as easily pass for Pakistani, Saudi, Persian, or Syrian as he could Indian—sometimes Mexican or Colombian, depending on a person's prejudice, and there always seemed to be plenty of prejudice to go around.

Jahan had a snarky way of bringing bigotry to the fore, and as it wasn't easy to argue with a smartass who had a penchant for mockery and an IQ of 152, his words often provoked blows. Dodging, mocking, he would laugh and taunt, claiming that jacking with intolerance was the best free entertainment around. It didn't take long for the Capstone term of endearment to follow.

BRADFORD FACED THE whiteboards and the diagram he'd put up this morning when the image of Munroe toppling off the motorcycle was still fresh and raw and hadn't felt like two weeks of decay smothering his airway.

He rubbed out his previous words and replaced them simply with *Michael*. Then, as if on autopilot, filled in the blanks with what little he knew: They, whoever "they" were, knew Michael was in the country, knew where to find her, knew she was a woman, knew who Logan was to her, and knew how to find him and that his place was wired. In the heaviness of the unanswerable, Bradford's eyes wandered along the boards to Jahan's latest updates on the team in Peshawar. The satellite phone bill on that job alone was going to bankrupt him.

Seven of his core team were currently out on assignment—the two in Pakistan, plus four in Afghanistan and one in Sri Lanka. With the exception of himself, who as boss and owner got to cherry-pick for his own schedule, the overseas assignments were rotated with homebase operations and factored by time and expertise.

Home was nice, but the big money was in the hazard pay. It took a certain mentality to sign on for something that meant more time living rough in shithole situations than with hot water and clean sheets. The job was difficult on relationships, if you were lucky enough to have them, and it seemed at times that a good portion of running the business involved weeding out the lunatics.

Dozens of others worked under Capstone's umbrella, foot soldiers who came and went, but like partners in a law firm, these nine—ten if you counted Munroe—were vested: they were Bradford's people, tried and proven, a breed apart from polite, or even impolite, society. Their motives for staying with the company varied, but one thing was consistent: They were each very good at what they did because the incompetent didn't live long.

VIABLE FOOTAGE WAS sparse, but not for the reasons Bradford had expected. Though the intruders had grabbed the original disk, they'd still taken precautions against being recognized. They were a pack of three, with a leader who had let himself in with a key, followed by two accomplices with baseball bats, their faces shielded from the camera by caps and lowered heads. The fight, which had taken place in the kitchen, was off camera but had lasted a painful four minutes.

Three against one. For four minutes.

When they'd hauled Logan out, his right leg appeared to be broken. He was cut and bleeding, but so were two of his assailants, and he still fought, still took a beating, all the way out the front door.

The final scene was cued at 10:13 A.M., minutes after Munroe had arrived at Capstone, and for a long while the war room was cocooned in stunned silence. Almost simultaneously, Bradford let out a stream of expletives and Walker went off in Brazilian Portuguese. Jahan remained quiet, his fingers tap-tapping against the desk. Finally he said, "Did they take out Michael to get to Logan, or take out Logan to get to Michael?"

The question was more or less the same line of inquisition Walker had raised in the car and Bradford didn't want to run through it all over again. "Put out a run for information," he said. "See if Logan owes anyone money or if there are any jealous lovers in recent history. My bet is he's clean. He's got too much to lose, is too focused on living life and reconnecting with his daughter."

Jahan said, "But—"

Bradford cut him off. Said, "Michael is the target, Logan is the collateral."

"Collateral for what?"

Bradford closed his eyes. Pressed the base of his palm to his forehead. Another go through the same information. "Collateral to save their own lives. Protection. They just grabbed Michael," he said. "Michael." He paused for emphasis. "Assuming she's tranquilized now, what happens when she wakes up? Logan is the cage, the shock collar, the shackles . . ." He stopped. This was pointless. A waste of time.

In his peripheral vision, he saw Walker shush Jahan. She'd tell him later. They would hash out reservations and alternate theories on their own. At the moment the motive didn't matter half as much as moving quickly with what little they knew.

Bradford paused, waiting for argument, for contradiction, and got nothing. Said, "Besides those of us here in this room, those on our team, how many people know the role Logan plays in her life?"

Walker shook her head. Jahan turned palms-up.

"There can't be many," Bradford said, "and that does us some pretty big favors in narrowing the playing field."

Jahan stood and strode to the whiteboard. Added notations to Bradford's scrawl. He turned to the others. "Where do we go with this?"

Bradford said, "Find Michael, find Logan," and turned back to the screen, where the image of the intruders stood frozen in time, two heads down, the leader's tilted up just enough that the side of his face showed to the camera. There was a look of youth in his posture, an arrogance that hadn't yet dimmed through time and experience. "That son of a bitch knows it's there," Bradford said. "And he's smirking."

Walker came to stand beside him, then drew closer and also focused on the image. Jahan said, "Perhaps we're giving them too much credit for sophistication. Maybe they're bumbling idiots, figuring it out as they go along."

Bradford and Walker stared at him.

"Or maybe not," he said. "But while I have your attention, and without intending to sound callous or change the subject, with Michael out of the picture and our available resources put toward finding her, what do you want me to do with the Tisdale assignment?"

Bradford paused and blinked, a long, slow open-and-shut, then turned to look at his office, where, although he couldn't see it, the Tisdale folder still sat on his desk and the signature page Munroe had signed this morning waited to be faxed. Tisdale. The reason she'd come into the office today.

Tisdale wasn't a security gig or one of the peace offerings Bradford handed Munroe to entice her to hang around longer. This was different, a request for her services, though it hadn't named her specifically, and it hadn't arrived through normal Capstone channels.

The plea had come to Bradford personally from two frantic, desperate parents in California, in the hope that he might know where and how to locate Munroe. They might not have known her by name, but anyone who was anyone within the upper social strata knew the story of Emily Burbank, missing for four years in Africa and presumed dead, and how Munroe had found her. Bradford was still connected to the board of trustees that had bankrolled the search. Henry and Judith Tisdale, one a Silicon Valley giant, the other a United States senator, with their combined power and influence, hadn't needed much time at all to track him down.

Neeva Eckridge.

Missing person.

Could Munroe find her?

Bradford had made no promises, given no indication that he even knew *how* to locate Munroe, told them he'd see what he could do. And now Munroe was missing, too. If the Eckridge kidnapping had been a ruse to pull her in, it was a goddamn masterpiece of ruses, because the whole world was looking for Eckridge and nobody could find her.

Two weeks ago, the girl had been an up-and-coming B-list Hollywood starlet and now hers was the most recognizable face in the country. Amid a busy schedule and a flurry of appointments, she'd vanished in the only one-hour window that she would have been unaccounted for. No signs of foul play, no eyewitnesses, no details: It was as if she'd simply vanished.

What started out as sensational gossip soon turned into a media feeding frenzy, because until Neeva Eckridge had gone missing, nobody, not her agent, not her boyfriend, not her Hollywood friends, had had any idea that the Tisdales were her parents. Speculation buzzed as much over Neeva's true and fabricated pasts as it did in regards to what could have happened to her, and regardless of the angle—sensational, fearmongering, alien abduction, or otherwise—Neeva's picture, and her parents', were everywhere.

Bradford continued to stare at his office, toward the documents. Munroe had wanted the assignment, had been eager for it, but if she was the Tisdales' best hope for finding their daughter, then at the rate things were going today, it was a lost cause.

Walker drew near and stood beside him, the top of her head reaching his shoulder. When he'd shifted straighter, taller, and had obviously returned to the present, she spoke.

"Do you think they're connected?"

"I can't see how," he replied. "But the timing is freakishly coincidental."

"We have Michael taken down," she said, "Logan being held as a hostage, and all of this possibly connected to Neeva Eckridge, who also disappeared with no witnesses. What thread draws them together?"

"I wish I knew," he said. "Because if I had that piece of information, I'd find the bastard who's behind this that much faster." He turned to her and she looked up to meet his gaze. "I will find him," he said. "And I will destroy him."

four

Valon Lumani looked down at the woman lying on the bench seat, so docile, so relaxed. Studied her face and tracked the length of her long body, and as he'd done the first time he saw her, he scoffed.

Because she was a woman. *This* was the solution he'd gone through such effort to secure on behalf of his uncle.

Lumani understood the need for expertise and the need for a stranger, but not why so much energy and expense had been put toward this one in particular, even if the nonsense was true—and really, maybe half was about right.

She was even less worrisome up close than she'd been from a distance, dressed in black on that black motorcycle. Even so, he'd used a heavy dosage calculated for her height and estimated weight, and he'd give her another during the trip to keep her unconscious until it was safe. But the rest of it? The rules and the talking—so much talking? Bah. Superstitious nonsense.

Do not let her hear your language, the source had said, she will use language as a weapon. *Keep the area around her free of objects,* everything will be used as a weapon. *Stay clear of her reach,* she doesn't need a weapon to kill you. *Don't use restraints,* she will find a way out of them, and they will only give a false sense of safety. *Do not touch her,* the source said. *Leave her in peace, and treat her re-*

spectfully, only then will the violence stay muted. Disrespect these and make no mistake, she *will* kill you.

Lumani smiled and made his fingers into the shape of a gun, placed it to her forehead, and pulled the imaginary trigger.

Bang.

In the end, this woman was no different from any other piece of merchandise. Disposable. He patted her face, the way he would a dog, as if to say Sleep well, little animal, until you are needed. And then he straightened and moved to the fore of the cabin, where a drink waited for him.

He took no alcohol today because until he delivered, the job wasn't complete, and because once started there would be no stopping until his own inner carnival ran dead. There would soon be time enough for private celebration.

Lumani took a sip of the soda and checked his watch. They flew against the sun, seven time zones east, on a Gulfstream G550, an extravagant expense toward speed and flying range that nudged the overhead for hunting down this one woman to the same level as for a run on merchandise, maybe more.

Who could say if she would be worth it? He was only the right-hand man, the doer. Extract, Uncle had said, and so Lumani had performed, and perhaps in having executed this job so perfectly, he'd achieved enough to earn a smile, or a *Well done,* or something, because to solve the problem would bring enough to lease this jet outright for years, if that's what Uncle wanted—although he wouldn't. Only idiots kept toys that attracted such attention.

Another glance at his watch.

Once beyond U.S. airspace, he would notify the pilots of the change in plans: They would land in the Dominican Republic to refuel and then continue on to Tenerife, where he had connections and could charter something smaller and more affordable—something European, less ostentatious and easier to hide.

Not that he really worried. He'd taken precautions within the United States to buy time, and once they were international, he might as well have become invisible. The switch in the Canary Islands was one last precaution in case the pilots talked when they returned, because someone highly motivated would come looking for this woman, and Lumani knew better than to lead a straight path to her.

five

DALLAS, TEXAS

Palms against the glass, Miles Bradford stood precisely where he'd been when Munroe had toppled. His eyes roamed from the frontage where she'd fallen to the neighboring buildings and then over and across the Dallas North Tollway, up one office tower and down the next, creating a mental map, searching out the several positions a shooter could have used to make the hit.

The fear was gone now. Shut off, tamped down, and replaced with the same emotional detachment that kept him alive in combat, allowed logic to replace panic, and made it possible to block out the anguish of holding a bleeding friend to the last breath, in order to go on to fight and survive.

This was a war in which the fight had been brought to Bradford's doorstep, and in place of fear sat only the mission: track the enemy, find him, destroy him, and take back what had been stolen.

From behind, Walker said, "If it was me, I'd be perched over there."

Bradford turned and watched, silent, as she strode across his office to stand beside him. Paul Jahan had come with her from the war room, but he remained in the doorway, arms crossed and leaning against the frame.

"Or there, or there, or there," she added.

Bradford followed the line of her finger as it jumped from building to building, returning finally to her original target: a twelve-story at ten o'clock, with an attached parking garage.

"It's a clear line of sight," she said. "The garage offers a place to stash a vehicle during the wait without worrying about it getting ticketed or towed, and it's close enough for a half-assed shooter with a decent rifle to guarantee a hit. Even if he's an expert marksman, if he tranqued her, then he's using something special, something modified, and that's going to affect the calculations, maybe limit distance, so he's going to want to get in as close as possible for accuracy. If it had been me set up there, I'd be gone before the ambulance even got here."

Bradford nodded and returned to staring out the window. Out of the many points from which to choose, Walker had singled out the same location he'd zeroed in on. He pounded the glass, a brief hit of frustration, and then straightened, took a calm step back, and said, "Go find me my building, Sam. Call me when you've got it, and we'll pick up the leads from there."

He would have preferred to work with her directly, hunting clues, staying updated to the instant, but Walker would find what they searched for more quickly than he could and he needed to see what had become of Logan's place after the call to 911. She lingered at the glass and Bradford waited until she turned and passed by him into the hall, watched her go and then moved to head out.

Jahan stepped into his path.

Impatient, Bradford attempted to brush past, and Jahan shifted fully into the doorway. Bradford said, "Get out of the way, Jack. Don't make me knock you on your ass."

Jahan put a hand on Bradford's shoulder. Maneuvered so that Bradford couldn't avoid his eyes. "Listen," he said, "I know you've gotten a lot of flak from all of us for bringing Michael onto the team, but we've got your back on this, okay? She was ours, too."

Had the words been said yesterday, Bradford would have countered wiseass to wiseass, but at the moment he had nothing but a desire to get out the door, to keep moving, so he nodded a silent thanks and gave Jahan's shoulder a jab of camaraderie.

Jahan caught his fist. "You'll feel it eventually," he said. "You know you will, and when that happens, don't take it out on someone else or get yourself killed or arrested; you come to me."

Bradford held his place, kept silent, until Jahan released his hand, and then continued to the exit without a word. The concern was warranted, but getting killed or arrested wasn't on the agenda, he was smarter than that.

By making the call that he hoped had turned Logan's place into a crime scene, Bradford had added manpower and resources to the task of solving, at the least, Logan's disappearance. He wanted latents that might lead to whoever had taken Munroe, and there was no point in doing what local law enforcement was better equipped to handle. He made the trip to confirm the level of interest in the broken and bloodied office, a shortcut to figuring out whom to pressure, where to start calling in favors—or, as the case may be, discover where new friends needed to be made.

The parking area in front of Logan's building was busy, as much a result of the morbidly curious as from city vehicles and the official personnel. The crowd was a good sign, meant crime scene techs had been called in, and if anything was worth having inside that building, he could eventually get to it.

Bradford drove to the end of the block, parked in front of an upholstery wholesaler, and walked the slow trip back to the yellow line—just one more face in the gawking crowd—until seeing all he'd come for, he made the return trip to Capstone.

Three blocks from the office, his phone chirped.

On the other end, Walker, excitement in her voice, said, "I've got it."

Bradford checked his watch. If she'd truly found what they wanted, she'd done it in under two hours: fast, but not surprising. Walker wasn't shy about utilizing sexism's dirty flipside, casually oozing sexuality and preying on hormones and the stupidity they induced to get what she wanted. He expected that right about now, in a building somewhere along the tollway corridor, a security guard was hiding a hard-on and jumping all over himself to get the lady whatever she wanted.

He'd never asked that behavior of her, but if that's what she chose to do to get the job done, then like an exotic weapon used in battle, he was glad it was on his side.

The address came by text and Bradford swung a right to accommodate it. The building wasn't the one they'd originally targeted but the one next door, of the same height and with access to the same garage.

He found her exactly as he'd expected: holed up in a room the size of a large walk-in closet, surrounded by closed-circuit monitors, and with two guys in uniform trying, and failing, to avoid staring at her chest. When he stepped through the door, the room fell silent.

She waved a cursory greeting in his direction and leaned across the desk to control one of the machines. Jeremy Justin, according to his ID, slid out of her way, just enough to avoid appearing rude but not enough to avoid her brushing against him.

Walker, oblivious, said to Bradford, "You've gotta see this."

Her fingers flew across the machine's controls to rewind a recording, her explanation a staccato faster than the grainy video, until she froze the process, leaving on the screen the image of a late-model Impala.

The face of the driver was blurry and he wore sunglasses, but the license plates were clear. "I've been running time stamps," she said. "Searched for ins and outs based on our estimates. We know he was holed up before ten but have no idea when he got here. Better, we know when it happened. I figure our guy would want to get out as fast as possible. He'd be an idiot to stay on foot, so for now I've focused on parking. For most of these buildings, free visitor parking has a time limit, and"—Walker paused, and in an instant personality shift, smiled kindly at Justin, whose face reddened at the attention—"Jeremy here tells me visitor parking is patrolled hourly and violators towed. This garage is gated and vehicles need a pass card. No cards reported lost or stolen, so . . ."

She scanned backward, running the machine at high speed, and pounded the stop with a force that made Justin twitch. "There," she said. "Tailgating into the garage. One other car did this in the same time period, so I ran through the interior cameras. There's not a lot we can use, nothing that takes this guy up to the roof, but look by the elevators." She hit the stop again.

"The time stamps coordinate, the tie and pattern on the shirt match the person in the first car. Briefcase," she said. "Check the size of that thing."

Bradford leaned in closer. "Can you zoom in on his face?"

Walker stepped back and to Justin sweetly cooed, "Can you zoom?"

Justin leaned forward and handled the controls, maneuvering the image to capture as much of the face as possible. "That's the best resolution we can get," he said.

There were similarities between this face and the one they'd captured on Logan's surveillance disk. Walker reached for the control again, brushing her hand over Justin's in the process, and went back to the original image of the driver in the Impala. "Check the time stamp on the exit."

The driver had headed down the ramp and out toward the street at the same time Bradford had run for the office door.

Justin said, "What about the briefcase?"

Walker smiled. "It's awesome, isn't it?"

Bradford said, "You have the plates?"

Walker handed him a piece of paper.

"How many sites did you visit?"

"Three so far."

"It's good work," he said. "I'll get Jack on these, but let's assume we missed something, okay? Keep looking."

Walker nodded.

Justin said, "What about the briefcase?"

Bradford headed to the door, and behind him, Walker, full of sugar, said, "I want one for my birthday."

FROM THE VISITORS' parking area, Bradford called Jahan with the plate numbers and then dialed the first of several contacts within the Dallas Police Department. If this request didn't stick, there were other possibilities. Favors begat favors, and Bradford, in this world of walking the gray lines of the law, had done many. A return back-scratch like this was easy to put out, and if there were prints, if the police had any suspects or leads, he'd eventually get the details, although not nearly soon enough.

It was a seven-minute drive to the office, and when Bradford got there, he knew Jahan had worked his magic. Leaning back with his palms behind his head and grinning like an idiot, Jahan swiveled his chair. When Bradford stepped into the war room, Jahan said, "Plates go to Enterprise rental, and I've traced the ambulance."

Bradford paused midstep, then continued to the board. This was good. This was progress. But it had also been five hours since Munroe was taken, and if his and Walker's earlier conclusion was correct, if the entire ruse was only intended to be a temporary distraction, then Munroe and Logan could be anywhere by now and every piece the team uncovered might come too little, too late.

Bradford studied the Michael diagram, mentally placing the surveillance footage of the parking garage.

The chair squeaked.

Bradford said, "Talk."

"You were right about the out-of-service depot. Getting into the GPS system was easier than pinpointing the ambulance, but no question, that's where it came from and where it returned. I've yanked chains to see what we could flush, but far as I can tell, everything we're looking at there is low-level: misplaced paperwork, dubious signatures—hallmark signs of a few well-placed Ben Franklins—no masterminds or anything."

Bradford turned. "The paramedics?"

"Nothing."

"So the ambulance is a dead end."

"We could go digging," Jahan said, "but I don't think it's worth our time. Not if we've got the plates on that rental."

"We could be wrong on the rental."

"Could be," Jahan said. "But the way Sam tells it, it's pretty convincing, and she's bringing over the footage for me to analyze. Where there's a rental, there are credit cards."

"Can you get them?"

"Yeah, eventually."

"I guess that's our focus." Bradford paused. "Where did the ambulance go between Michael and the depot?"

"There's an unexplained four-minute stop," Jahan said. "Then Medical City, then back to the roost." He fiddled with the keyboard and pointed to the screen on his right. "*X* marks the spot. What do you have on latents?"

"I've got calls in," Bradford said, and walked to the street map. Stared. The stop was a parking lot, of all things, as if the fuckers didn't even care if they were observed.

Jahan followed Bradford's line of sight. "You've gotta admire their balls."

Bradford turned just enough to glower at him.

"Or not."

"Zoom this thing out," Bradford said, and when Jahan had enlarged the surface area of the map, Bradford studied it for a long while, processing. He had the what and he had the when. If he could trace the how or even the why, he could find the who and take this fight to a whole new level. Finally he straightened and swore under his breath. "The airport," he said.

He reached for the phone and dialed Walker. "What've you got?"

"So far, that parking-garage footage is the best lead we have. I could go further on the search, take it to fifteen hundred yards, but I dunno." She paused. "To make a hit like that from that kind of distance . . ." She let the sentence fade.

"You did good," Bradford said. "Come on in, I need you."

SIX HOURS SINCE Munroe's take-down, and with the critical time window to manage a speedy find-and-rescue fast closing, the airport was another hunch that might just be more misdirection. But it also made perfect sense. If the shooter had been prepared, then Addison Airport was, quite literally, the fastest route out of town. A small head start would have been enough.

Bradford pulled to a stop outside the administration building.

The bulk of the complex lay in the tarmac of the seventy-two-hundred-foot runway and its smaller twin. Straddling these sister strips were more than one hundred fifty hangars in a range of sizes, hundreds of thousands of square feet of office-related facilities, an FAA tower, and a lot of open field.

He stepped from the vehicle and tossed Walker the keys. What he hoped for were flight records to point him in the right direction—everything and anything that had departed out of Addison since ten that morning, more specifically between eleven and one, but if the shooter hadn't wanted to be traced, pulling these records would mean throwing around a lot more weight than a phone call or two, which was once again why he'd brought Walker.

The main office was quiet, most of the staff already gone for the day, and Bradford waited a full ten minutes before a well-kept woman, who introduced herself as Beth Evans, operations manager, greeted him. He handed over a private investigator badge, opted for a simplified version of the truth, and when he had satisfied Evans's questions, she offered to take him into the hangar area as soon as she'd finished what she was doing.

Walker was waiting when they stepped outside, leaning against the hood of the Explorer, the same position she'd been in when they'd convened outside the hospital. She held a sheet of paper.

Bradford introduced the two, then to Walker said, "What'd you get?"

"Not much," she said. "Most of what comes in and out are prop planes. Little. And most are private. I figure we're looking for something a bit bigger, a little more charterable." She handed Bradford the page. "Within that range, eight flights left between ten and three. I think we should start with the larger hangars."

They rode with Evans in her car and she took them to where the lights were brightest and the highest number of employees congregated, but even with her guidance, it took showing Munroe's and Logan's pictures to the employees of three hangars before they scored a hit.

One of the ground crew picked up Munroe's photograph, and Evans kept by the car while Walker and Bradford moved in closer.

Like Evans, the man hovered close to either side of fifty, balding and heavy around the middle, and he lit up in Walker's presence. "I think I saw her," he said. Paused to catch Walker's eye and then skimmed over her chest to stare at the photo again. "Yeah, I guess that was her. Hard to say, really, because she was sick or asleep or something. She was in a wheelchair."

From a few feet away, his workmate put down a wrench and wiped his hands on a rag. "That was the wheelchair flight?" he said. "Let me see that."

Walker handed him the photograph. He smiled at her and she smiled back.

He glanced at the picture for a moment and returned it. "I guess that was them."

"Were there men with her?" Bradford said.

The first guy said, "Just one. Clean-cut, dark hair, about your height, maybe. Young."

"Did he have a briefcase?" Walker asked.

"Yeah, a big one. Almost looked like a suitcase."

"What about other luggage?"

"I think they had a couple of carry-ons. I wasn't really paying attention, you know, so I can't say for sure."

"Any idea where they were headed? Tail number, maybe?"

"Bahamas, I think. Not sure about the tail number, but it

shouldn't be too hard to get from the office. Was a G550; don't get as many of those passing through."

Bradford peeled off a hundred and shook the guy's hand. Not five feet away, heading toward the car, Walker said, "That's our plane."

"Yeah," Bradford said. "I want you back here first thing in the morning. If they're flying international, then it's possible they dealt with immigration, which means they've got a passport for Michael. I want names—especially what she's traveling under. And there's no mention of Logan," he said. "What's that tell you?"

"The condition he's in? He's still here."

THE WAR ROOM was empty when Bradford and Walker returned, but on the desk were two copies of the transaction record for the credit card that had been used for the rental car.

Walker picked one up, looked through it, and said, "Nice."

At the end of the hall a toilet flushed.

Bradford picked up the second copy, got to the first page, and stared, stunned. Fought for air. And for the first time since he'd shoved it away this afternoon, he felt the fear. He had no words, no voice, and struggled to remain standing.

Walker paused from leafing through the pages, turned to him, and then seeing his face, retreated a step. "Miles?" she said.

He held up a finger and closed his eyes. Pushed the panic back, stomped on it, shoved it away to where it couldn't touch him and he could think again, rationalize again. He drew a breath and felt the cold.

Jahan entered the room and stopped midstep. He looked first to Bradford, then to Walker, and back again. "What?" he said.

Bradford tapped the pages, and the words came mechanically. "I know this name," he said. "This company." He turned toward the window, stared out at the darkening sky, and after a long moment turned back. "Fuck!"

He moved toward the doorway and then his office, where he turned a slow circle, trying to decide where to start. Walked to the fireproof cabinet in the far corner and dug for the key on his key chain. Unlocked it. Flipped through the hanging folders until he found a manila envelope and pulled it out.

He straightened.

Jahan and Walker blocked his exit.

"War room," Bradford said, and wordlessly, they turned, Jahan following Walker, Bradford following Jahan.

Bradford opened the envelope, took out the documents, and tossed the contents onto Jahan's desk. Searched through the stack of papers until he found what he was looking for, a spreadsheet and an old newspaper article, and shifted both of them to face Walker and Jahan.

"This is who we're hunting," he said. "This is our shooter."

The collected papers from the envelope were over an inch thick: bank records, company records, notes, and threads that detailed a web of evil that wound out of Europe and across the globe. After a moment of flipping through them and scanning the data, Jahan paused and stared at Bradford. "Where did these come from?"

Bradford tapped the pages in his hand. "About two years ago," he said, "Michael took a missing-person job in Central Africa. Was the first time I'd worked with her and the case took us places we had no idea we'd go. These came out of the aftermath."

"You were dealing with this?"

"No, I discovered these at the end, here in the U.S. in the safe of a guy who died."

Walker said, "If this had nothing to do with Michael, why would people like this come after her and Logan?"

Bradford moved to the door. "I don't know," he said. "But I know where to dig."

six

ZAGREB, CROATIA

The only source of light was a sliver beneath the door, but that was enough to make the headache worse. Vanessa Michael Munroe shut her eyes against the pounding beat and returned to darkness, to the words and sounds that echoed along the walls.

Not real speech, a recording. She could tell that even from this drug-induced haze. She stretched fingertips to the wall and heard from touch the same story told by the smell of this place. Dank. Damp. Buried.

Her leg was stiff and tender, her shoulder badly bruised. Mental nudges took her toward the last thing that she remembered: The tollway. The bike. The hit to her thigh. Falling into darkness and into pain.

Beyond the door came footsteps. Voices, real voices—occasionally screaming—while the steady pattern of language played on and on, masking and muting the sounds of the world beyond the walls and providing a strange sense of continuity in this dungeon of a place.

Munroe breathed a slow, deep in-and-out, and sank fully into the mattress with its stench of mold and grime and human sweat, floated in the vibration of the language, drowned in it until the lock clanked metal against metal and the door slid to the side and the room went blinding white.

The pain returned with the light and she squinted at the shadow that stooped and filled the doorway. The intruder was followed by another, and the two kept a cautious distance until they were joined by a third, who moved in closer. "You are awake now," he said, and there was a familiarity to his voice, as if she'd dreamed him or this was déjà vu. "That is good," he said. "You eat, then you come with us."

His English was accented and clearly enunciated—perhaps from an education in England or even in Canada; he wasn't a native speaker. But he'd stopped talking and Munroe's mind, still numb from the drugs, worked too slowly to capture what she should have known. Knowledge was there on the edge and then it vanished, and she sighed and let go again, into the peace.

The shadowed voice spoke to the two behind him, words that fractured and spun inside her head. Meaning, but not exact, a language familiar, although not perfectly so.

"Let her sleep some more," he'd said. "She's not ready."

Yes, that was the meaning. And then they were gone and she was left with the silence and the voices, always the voices, and the darkness, and the passage of time.

Then awareness.

Her eyes snapped open to blackness, her mind fully awake.

Munroe flipped to her stomach and into a crouch.

The sliver of light was gone and the Hungarian recording still intruded into the silence.

She slid from mattress to floor, followed the wall to a corner, taking minutes to explore through touch what sight would have told her in seconds, tracing along the perimeter of a cell that she guessed at seven feet by about six, with a ceiling so low it occasionally snagged her hair.

Near the door she knocked into a metal tray, paused in reaction to hunger, then continued past because nourishment wasn't worth the risk of being drugged again. Returned to the mattress, and there, seated with her back to the cold stone, she let her mind meander in slow soft circles—puzzle unfolding, questions forming—timed to the rhythm of voices that imitated the language immersion she would put herself through before entering a new country or new assignment—as if they—whoever they were—*knew*; knew of the inexplicable ability that had been with her since childhood, the ability to assimilate language with nearly the same speed others processed what they saw, a poisonous gift that had defined every moment of her life and brought her to the place that had created what she now was.

HE RETURNED AT last, the articulate one with his silent companions. Forearm to her face, Munroe shielded her eyes from the light that shadowed the men in silhouette. The English speaker put a packet on the floor. Used his foot to slide the bundle toward her.

"Clean clothes," he said. "Put them on. I'll be back in fifteen minutes." He glanced at the tray. "The food?"

"I'm not hungry."

He shook his head. "There are no drugs."

"All the same," she said, leaning forward to reach for the package. His response to her movement—their responses—gave her pause.

They stood there, three against one, blocking the exit to a prison cell built for miniature people, and twitched when she'd shifted toward them.

"Can you turn it off?" Munroe said, nodding her head toward the strongest source of sound.

"It's not possible," he said, and she knew then that whoever this young man was, and whatever role he played in what happened to her, he wasn't the final authority. "I apologize for this treatment," he said with a cursory wave toward the mattress, the walls. "We'd been told you might not come willingly and felt it best to take precautions. You understand, I think."

She didn't reply, just stood, and in a space small enough that she could have simply reached out and taken the package, stepped forward. Microsecond gaps of instinct measured their body language, reported back with clarity and understanding: They'd come three against one into this cell because all three were unarmed—brute force in place of weapons.

The articulate one watched her with curious eyes, as if like the others he knew she had the potential to be dangerous, but like a child waiting for the snake to strike just to see what happened, he doubted.

"Won't you open it," he said, eager, she supposed, for her reaction to the clothing in the package. She slipped her finger into a crease and tore the paper.

Inside were men's clothes. Pants. Shirt. Shoes. Undergarments. Elastic bandage. The hair on the back of her neck raised slightly. These people, whoever they were, knew far more about her than was comfortable.

"Fifteen minutes," the young one said. He nodded toward the larger of the two flanking him, a man with scars and disfigurement that spoke of fighting that had been close and personal. "Then Arben will cut your hair."

Munroe returned to the mattress. Placed the wrapping and the clothes beside her and, with hands relaxed on her thighs, looked up at the young one. Said, "If he touches me, I'll kill him."

Rattle on a snake, a dog's growl to prevent a bite, her warning was meant to avoid unnecessary bloodshed and the burden of taking life, because as surely as the earth turned, if that man put a hand on her, instinct and history would overwhelm reason and she would destroy him or die trying.

The young man choked back a cough and followed it with a snicker.

Arben and the nameless third showed no reaction; the guards spoke no English.

Fingering the collar of the new shirt, her eyes deliberately avoiding the English speaker, Munroe said, "Get me clippers. I'll cut my own hair."

"I will consider it," he said.

THEY LEFT HER to change, although she needed a shower: hot to the point of scalding, to rid herself of her own smell, the sick of this place, and the remnants of the cotton-headed fog of whatever they'd used to put her under. But there was no water. Only the mattress, the cold concrete floor, and the drain in the corner that she'd noticed once the hallway light had filtered in.

She stripped down and put the new clothing on.

Their charade, their rules. For now.

Slipped back into the leather jacket and zipped it closed.

The men came again, fifteen minutes as promised, although she had only an internal clock to gauge the truthfulness of time. They waited for her at the cell opening; didn't approach, didn't attempt to cuff or touch her, nor did they move to force her to rise when she remained seated on the filthy mattress staring blankly at them. Curiosity dared her to test their resolve, to see how hard she could push before they reacted, but the desire to escape this dank hellhole was stronger.

She rose to follow.

In the doorway, the English speaker stared at her jacket as if demanding she remove it, as she had the rest of her clothes. She shook her head, a slow no. The man-boy paused and, in an act of maturity that belied his youth or ego, half grinned. "We take care of the hair later," he said, and stepped out of her way.

Munroe ducked through the opening. Squeezed by him into the narrow corridor, where fluorescent bulbs, crudely daisy-chained along the ceiling, made the hallway institutionally bright. The sting of bleach smarted in her nose, masking more of the moldy wet damp that had filled the cell.

The sight, the scent, hit her with the full impact of a brick to the head: memories of violence and retribution still fresh from Argentina. And although the events that had previously drawn her into the arms of evil had been random, because of them she knew what this place was and what being here might mean, and for the first time since she'd been awake—for the first time in a very long time—bloodlust, immediate and feral, burned up from inside and crept toward her fingertips.

Munroe clenched her hands and glanced down the hall.

To the right stretched the length of two more cells, and near the end, drowning out the Hungarian, came another scream, carrying with it not pain but all the primal vibration of animal rage.

Munroe turned in the direction of the cry. Flanked fully in the narrow hall, two in front and one behind, she would have had to move through the men to get anywhere. They paused because she paused, did not touch her, and offered no explanation. After a long wordless standoff, the young one finally motioned her to the left, in the opposite direction of the screams.

She followed down a seeming dead end that cornered to face steep stairs beckoning with fresh air and natural light. A thick metal door separated the world below from the living above, an otherwise impenetrable barrier, that at the moment stood open and inviting. Still flanked and guarded, Munroe stepped through to a high-ceilinged room, where light from transom-style windows bathed her and the workers' whispers flowed around her in a mixture of words; some Slavic—not identical to the Macedonian she already spoke, but familiar—others the language of the silent ones, a language she hadn't heard in years. In response to the multiple conversations, as naturally as breathing, intrusive and invasive, without work, without effort, flashes of illumination set off inside her brain.

They walked the corridor of the stone-floored room, a path formed between smaller offices off to one side and the oddly spaced desks and cluttered tabletops that filled the open-spaced area. Munroe's eyes roamed from ceiling beams to floor, from wall to wall, searching out routes of escape, scanning for improvisable weapons.

Employees were busy over mounted magnifying lenses and small Bunsen burners, wax molds and scalpels: gold-crafting in all its stages. No one paused when they passed, and in the apparent nonchalance Munroe sensed a mixture of fear and commonplace experience, as if a dirty prisoner of war being marched along a goldsmith's workstation was a normal course of events in this place.

The scene, surreal as it was, ended as quickly as it had begun.

The scarred man whom the articulate one had called Arben and his still nameless partner took up sentry positions outside a door; he opened it and nodded her inside. She paused. The young English speaker continued past her without a backward glance. Munroe stepped into the room, the door shut behind her, and she stopped.

Filling the room, floor to ceiling, on shelves along each wall, in glass cases, resting on chairs, and standing on credenzas, were porcelain dolls: small and life-size, hand-painted and air-brushed, richly clothed with waxen hair, curled and styled. They stared out at her—more lifeless eyes than she could count—each doll in perfect condition: items a collector had doted on and cared for, with not a speck of dust to tarnish them.

The rest of the office resembled any other random business, although from the fixtures, the window, and the radiator beneath it, she was clearly not in Texas—or the United States for that matter. Europe. She suspected the Balkans based on the languages she'd heard in the big room and the old stone architecture and the impression of a courtyard beyond the window—beyond the man who partially blocked her view.

He sat behind the desk, hands folded upon it, head haloed by the morning light that left his face in shadow. Munroe nodded an acknowledgment. He nodded back, and if she guessed correctly, he was smiling.

He stood and reached for the vertical blinds. Tilted and pulled them across the window so that Munroe no longer squinted at his shadow and in English without any trace of the young one's accent invited her to sit. His smile was genial, his manner gracious, and while Munroe tipped her head again, matching geniality for geniality, the primal side of her brain calculated the odds of the window frame having been reinforced, the glass replaced with shatter-proof, the difficulty with which she might plunge into him and take them both out the window to the cobblestones below.

He followed her eyes as they wandered from the dolls to the window and back again and, as if reading her reaction upside-down, said, "They are beautiful, aren't they?"

Munroe offered a half-smile in answer.

The Doll Man stood and walked to the shelf on her left; starting near the window, with hands behind his back like a general surveying troops on parade, he worked his way along the wall, pausing to admire and occasionally reach out and touch a lock of hair or rearrange a dress.

He was five-foot-six at the most, and small, not just in height. Had he been a woman, petite would have been a better description. He was immaculately clothed in a suit, surely custom made, his tie perfectly knotted, his shoes at a high shine. Thinning hair and hands with ample sun spots put him in the upper range of sixty-plus, though from his posture and controlled energy, it would be a mistake to think of him as aging.

"Perfection," he said, his fingers to lace, his voice soft and full of admiration. "They have no flaws, only beauty." He paused and, still gazing at the dolls, whispered, "Only beauty."

The man turned toward Munroe and his voice returned to room volume. "I have others," he said, "but these are my treasures. I keep them close; they bring me joy." He stopped to stroke a porcelain cheek and then with a sigh walked back to the desk and returned to his chair.

"But I am rude," he said. "And you have questions."

Munroe waited a beat, allowed silence to engulf the room while she studied him and he studied her. "Where am I?" she said finally. "And why am I here?"

"You are in Croatia for an assignment," he said, and punctuated the statement with a dismissive wave. He shifted and crossed his legs. "To repay the debt."

Munroe held back a snort. It would be reasonable to ask for clarification in order to understand this obligation of which he spoke so casually, as though he took for granted that she was familiar with the matter, but instinct told her to hold back. "Most people simply request my help," she said. "No matter what it is you want, kidnapping me, putting me in a cell, and keeping me under guard is the worst kind of way to get it."

"Yes," he replied. "Most people would ask, I suppose. But I expect this job falls beyond what you consider acceptable. Why bother with the opportunity for you to say no? That would only make me angry."

Munroe kept quiet while thought unspooled in an attempt to apply logic to madness. Her inner danger reading snapped like a Geiger counter to radiation, warning her not to press, prompting her to play his game. She leaned forward, matching him posture for posture. Folded her hands on the desk and said, "What can I do for you?"

The Doll Man shifted back and smiled as if he were breathing the victory of the moment, making a memory of a battle won before it had started, even though he'd known he would. His smile told of power and control in a world where he ruled supreme, a sadistic smile Munroe had seen before, that declared he owned her, and what lay beneath that smile ticked up the tempo of her heartbeat.

Motionless, expressionless, she waited until he finally leaned forward and spoke again. "You will deliver a package," he said. "Transport from point A to point Z, so to speak."

The words were no surprise—not given the underground from which she'd just come. "Is the package alive?"

"Yes, very much alive," he replied, eyes lit and dancing as if he'd finally found a worthy playmate.

Munroe leaned back, slow, casual, deliberate. She studied his face, waited for cues, then continued on. "Transport a live package," she said. "I could probably do that, although it would depend on the package and the location. I assume that since no isn't an acceptable answer, I'm also not getting paid?"

The man's expression clouded. The brilliant playmate had turned into an idiot after all. "You repay the debt," he said. "That should be more than enough."

"What if I disagree? And what if, after all your trouble, I still say no?"

"I have ways to insist."

"I have ways to decline."

"You'll pay one way or the other," he said.

"In euros? Dollars? How much do I owe you?"

If he registered the sarcasm, he didn't react to it. "You pay in the only currency that holds value to you," he said. "You pay in innocent life."

The words stung like a hard smack across the face and her eyes smarted as if she'd been physically struck. He should not know these things.

Casual indifference remained plastered on her face while deep below, in that hollow crevice where madness had lain dormant these last nine months, the slow, steady percussion of war tapped out, faint but perceptible.

"Which innocents?" she said.

He waved his hand with that dismissive gesture. "Innocents are innocents," he said. "Is one life really valued higher than another?"

From the fear bubbling to the surface, she instinctively knew. Knew that the only way a man in his position could gloat as if he owned her was if he held what she deemed most priceless. She said, "Millions of innocents die every year, nobody can save them all."

"Then allow me to show you."

He reached for the phone and pressed the intercom button, and when the speaker came alive with a voice, he spoke in a language he assumed she didn't understand summoning the person who'd answered. In the resulting wait, the Doll Man leaned back, hands folded in his lap, observing her with his sly smile.

Munroe studied her nails while the inner anvil pounded plowshares back into swords, and with deep and measured breaths she braced for what was to come.

seven

When the office door opened, Munroe didn't turn. Her focus remained on the Doll Man, whose expression shifted with a fleeting glimpse of pleasure that passed as quickly as it had arrived.

"You've met Valon," the Doll Man said, though he wasn't looking at Munroe. The newcomer was the English speaker from the dungeon, the one important enough that he'd needed bodyguards, the one still more boy than man. Valon Lumani greeted his elder with reverence, then turned to glance at Munroe, studied her until the Doll Man arrested his attention.

Their exchange was in Albanian, and elation threatened to creep out from under Lumani's skin as he basked in the sparse words of commendation offered by the old man. And then the Doll Man's tone changed. "Show her," he said, and Lumani responded by pulling a phone from his pocket. He thumbed the controls and with video playing and volume turned up, put it in front of Munroe.

Her body screamed in rebellion. Her lungs seized, the percussion beat harder, faster, while Logan, battered and bloody, refused to speak when ordered, refused to cry out when struck. The world turned a hazy black and white that blocked out everything but the man behind the desk.

The anvil hammered out the order to kill.

Blinded, unable to focus, Munroe pushed the tumult into silence, forced herself to watch the clip, to truly grasp beyond Logan to his surroundings—searching out clues to his location and finding them in split seconds of shaky footage that encompassed a table and window in the background.

A Ziploc bag and two-inch horizontal wooden blinds. Mainstays of American culture, available elsewhere but not with the convenience and price of the United States—certainly not in Europe.

In a house or an office somewhere in the U.S., Logan took another hit. More blood, more broken cartilage. A gun to the back of his head. Munroe gave no outward reaction. Inside, the pressure struggled to break free, to pull her out of the chair and over the desk, to wrap her hands around the Doll Man's neck until his face changed color and his tongue lolled lifeless, and she stole from him his final breath the way he was stealing hers.

Lumani turned off the clip and tucked the phone away.

Munroe let air seep into her lungs in measured portions, afraid to breathe, afraid to betray the pain and fear that burned through her veins; guarded against showing the rage and hatred she felt toward this man and his protégé.

Debt.

Package.

Transport.

To kill the Doll Man now would pull the trigger of the gun at Logan's head. She was too far away to save him from the repercussions before they exploded outward. Her mind reeled, searching for answers, searching for a way out. Munroe pointed toward the pocket in which Lumani had stashed the phone, turned to the man behind the desk, and said, "So I deliver your package, and you pay me by returning the life of that guy?"

A half-beat of disappointment registered on the Doll Man's face before the sly smile returned and he said, "Yes, you will have repaid the debt, and I will exchange it by returning that life."

Which was bullshit, of course.

There was no way a man with the power to find her, kidnap her, and transport her across the ocean, a man who had a dungeon hollowed out below his building, would allow her to see his face, this hideaway, one of his businesses, if he intended to let her—much less Logan—walk free. But the illusion of his control, and the appearance that she accepted the lie, was all that mattered. She tipped her head in silent acknowledgment.

"We might have an understanding," she said, and the Doll Man's smile widened into a look of contentment and his body visibly relaxed.

"I'm so glad," he said. "I much prefer to do business with a rational person. It keeps the mess to a minimum."

A slow smile of agreement forced itself across her face. Given the state of Logan's abused body, it would seem he didn't dislike the mess too terribly much. "I should probably see the package," she said.

He motioned toward the door. "Valon will show you," he said, and then to the young man, disdainfully in their own language, with none of the passing tenderness he'd previously shown, "Bring the doll transport to me when you're finished."

Lumani nodded, his earlier elation replaced by something hard and expressionless. He turned to the door and, barely glancing in Munroe's direction, nodded her forward and waited for her to move.

She stood, slow and languid.

Stepped across the floor in no obvious hurry, thoughts jumping and hopscotching from one random piece of information to another, scrambling to assemble a composite of the present and make sense of the unexplainable.

The two sentries still stood outside the office door, and with Lumani leading the way, they followed Munroe back down the gold-worker-flanked pathway, through the metal door, to the underground again, beyond the cell in which she'd been kept, all the way to the end, while the same Hungarian voices droned on as background noise.

Against the far wall of the narrow hallway was yet another guard, who rose from a metal folding chair as the small group approached. With a flick of a finger, Lumani ordered him to unlock the last cell, and the man withdrew a chain from a pocket and from the chain a key.

Clanking metal reverberated through the tight space and then the door slid open. Munroe leaned forward to enter the low doorway and Lumani put out a hand to stop her. She paused, and in that pause a spoon flew past her leg followed by a rush of garbled slurs.

The voice was female, the accent West Coast USA, and as Munroe saw and smelled when she ducked to enter, the holding cell had the retching stench of a pigsty.

Lumani didn't enter. Like the guards, he remained poised to allow Munroe to go in alone. Behind her, he flipped a switch and the dim light cast a macabre glow over the bedraggled creature that had retreated against the wall. Filth and rot overpowered the permeating wet of damp mold. Whatever food this girl had been given, she'd flung rather than eaten, mostly in the direction of the door. Munroe moved closer to get a better view.

The girl was shackled, one foot chained to a metal ring in the wall like a prisoner in the goddamn Dark Ages. She couldn't crawl far off the pad that worked as her bed and had been forced to soil herself. Her clothes were filthy, stained, and torn; her hair matted, her face and arms so streaked with grime, it was impossible to see what color her skin had originally been.

Eyes adjusted against the light, the girl moved toward Munroe in a crawl, spewing creative profanity. At her approach, the stench grew stronger and Munroe fought the urge to vomit. The girl lunged, then jerked, caught by the chain. Munroe remained just beyond her clawing reach, the creature cursing and screaming, straining at her bonds with all the anguish and rage of a wild animal taken into captivity.

In response to this, tears of anger and powerlessness welled hot beneath Munroe's surface. Under other circumstances, violence would have erupted on behalf of this girl, whoever she was, and Munroe, unable to fight back the urge as she had in the hallway prior, or in the office upstairs, would have struck out to destroy the men who had done this.

Innocent life.

To save Logan would be to abandon this girl to whatever fate the Doll Man prescribed. To save the girl was to abandon Logan. The first wave of defeat crept toward the edge of Munroe's soul, tugging at the upturned corners of thought, begging to be let in. She was a prisoner of the same story, her own chain just as solid, her walls equally thick.

Munroe turned. She'd seen what she'd come to see.

Outside the cell, where the air was bleach-tinged and free of the nausea-inducing, fetid, sick stench, she could breathe again. No words were exchanged in the hallway, not between the guards, not between Lumani and her. He simply nodded once more in the direction of the stairs and Munroe moved toward them.

From behind, the thud of a hose hitting the concrete floor was followed by the squeak of an unwilling tap and a rush of water. And then the girl's scream again—that gut-piercing, wailing scream.

IN THE LARGE room, Lumani directed Munroe away from the doll office to a smaller room that turned out to be a bathroom with only a toilet and a sink with a speckled and aged mirror. With yet another flick of a finger in place of speaking, Lumani summoned and a young boy approached with a cardboard box.

Lumani took it and glanced at the contents, then held it out to Munroe.

She didn't move.

"For your hair," he said.

He paused, then pointing toward the bathroom added, "In your hands, that mirror is a dangerous weapon, yes? You could kill me. Kill a few others. I take this risk. You understand that anything you do will come back to hurt Logan?"

Munroe, eyes steady on his, nodded.

"My uncle deals harshly with failure," he said. "You understand?"

This young man, Lumani, this *boy,* had no right to Logan's name, to spit it out so casually, with such familiarity, as if he were some long-lost acquaintance.

Munroe took the box, turned her back to him, and shut the door.

Slumped to the floor. The pit of blackness welcomed her to let go and fall into the murky depths where conscience and pain ceased to exist.

Hands to her head, face to the stone, screaming without sound, she pushed back hard. For nine months she'd tasted happiness, a chance at the closest thing she'd known to peace and a real life. For nine months the rage and violence that had defined so many of her years had finally ebbed, and now those who had no right had come with impunity to rip her out of this newfound calm, throwing her into an impossible situation where no matter what she did or what she chose, the end result would be a return to madness.

She breathed in rapid gulps. Needed time to think, to sort

through details that made no sense; needed to find a way to reach Bradford and tell him to find Logan, to unloose her shackles, to buy her options, to buy her time.

Lumani pounded on the door.

"A minute," she said. "Toilet first."

She stood and flushed. Opened the box and found hair clippers. Located an electrical socket and plugged in the appliance. These people knew what drove her, knew what mattered, appeared to know everything there was to know about her, yet strangely they didn't suspect she understood their language. How could they not? Albania and Macedonia shared a border—Albanian was frequently spoken in Macedonia, especially among the border cities. It was an oversight so basic that no one from this part of the world could have made it unless everything they knew about her had been fed secondhand from someone who wasn't fully aware of the geographical implications of wars and borders and centuries of conflict.

Munroe flipped on the buzzer and stared at the broken, chipped reflection in the mirror. With hands skilled from practice and familiar with routine, she ran the buzzer from forehead to back, side to top, changing and adjusting blade guard heights as needed. Strands of dark hair fell away, shed into the sink. In the mirror's reflection a young man with a military buzz cut and civilian clothes stared out with bloodshot eyes.

To create the gender roles and slip between them was a tool of the trade so long utilized in her working life that it had become as natural as blinking, and like her gift for language, was a skill with which her captors were familiar and clearly intended to put to use.

They *knew*.

Munroe straightened and tucked the clippers away.

Box in hand, she still studied the image in the mirror when Lumani opened the door. He hadn't bothered to knock. She turned toward him, her eyes the last part of her face to leave the reflection.

He hesitated. Surprise faded into a grin that surfaced and spread slowly while he scanned her with the same blatant curiosity with which he'd first watched her in the cell. Finally he nodded, apparently satisfied.

"The clippers," he said, and Munroe handed the box to him.

"You go to my uncle," he said, and she understood then that in the twisted way of this crazy world, the creature in the cell below was the doll of which the Doll Man had spoken.

Arben and his nameless counterpart flanked her again for the brief journey across the work floor to the office, a journey that mentally slowed while Munroe absorbed the details of the workstations, the miniature torches, the pointed tools, and the furniture pieces, each calling out to be put to use in the way of salvation. But this instinct toward survival and its rush to violence was futile, because choke chain to the junkyard dog's neck, there was Logan. Always Logan.

THE DOLL MAN stood when Munroe entered, and once more, with the geniality of an age gone by, offered her one of the high-backed chairs facing his desk. He waited until she sat before returning to his own.

He motioned to her hair. "Very nice," he said. "The illusion is better than I had anticipated." And then he smoothed his tie and placed his hands on the desk. Folded them. "You've seen the package," he said.

"Yes," she said. "I have questions."

"Let's take coffee, and we can discuss."

He picked up the phone. *"Mala, donesi nam dvije kave, brzo. I to u najboljem porculanu kojeg imaš, čuješ?"* Not English, not Albanian, not Macedonian, but close. She ticked more information off a mental checklist. Like her, this man spoke many languages, and as it was with her, language had nothing to do with his place of origin.

There was a knock and then a slight creak as the door opened. The Doll Man motioned curtly and a young woman entered carrying a silver tray with full china service. Munroe and the Doll Man stared at each other without breaking eye contact, while the woman laid out piece by proper piece, as if this was the end of a meal at the Ritz instead of some alternate universe where Logan had been kidnapped by a madman and to save him Munroe would violate every sense of self and self-preservation by delivering that girl downstairs to . . . Where exactly?

Alone again, the Doll Man, poised and proper, poured cream and sugar and when Munroe made no move to do likewise, he poured a second cup and took a sip from it before placing it in front of her. "There are no drugs," he said. "And, please, what are your questions?"

"Where do I deliver the package?" she said. "And through what means?"

"You will travel by car. It's a hard one-day drive, two days, perhaps, depending on circumstances."

Circumstances. Like dodging borders, outrunning authorities, and trying not to attract attention to the animal in the front seat. Or did they intend to use the trunk?

"Tomorrow you receive details," he said. "And the rules, and then the package will be your problem."

"You have men," she said. "You've got guns. You don't need me to do this. Why go through the trouble and expense—and risk—of kidnapping me and bringing me across the ocean just so I can deliver that girl—the package—to some location that's only a two-day drive from here? You've already got what you need to do the job yourself."

The Doll Man put down his cup and sighed. "Such trouble I've had, my friend, such trouble. Issues with the delivery. Issues with the client. Issues with the package. Far, far too many complications and too much attention. I won't risk myself or my operation, so you will take her."

Munroe picked up the cup that had sat cooling and, with elbows to the table and eyes over the rim, glanced at him. He'd had her shot, drugged, and abducted, held Logan hostage to guarantee compliance, then served her coffee in a fucking china cup and called her "friend." This was like waking up in a Dalí painting of porcelain dolls.

She blew on the liquid. "I can't transport her in her current condition. Not even locked in the trunk."

The Doll Man smiled, his expression both chiding and tolerant. "She is custom ordered," he said. "We would never send a doll to a client looking as she does now. These details are our problem. When we have solved them, then the package is your problem."

"Who is the package?" Munroe asked.

"Neeva Eckridge," he said.

Munroe sat silently for a long while, mulling irony and cursing fate. To protect the one person who meant more to her than life, she would be forced to betray the one person she was contractually and morally obligated to save.

"Human trafficking is a serious crime," she said. "The whole world is looking for her. If I get caught, I will kiss away years of my life. What if that person in the video doesn't mean enough? What if that girl in the dungeon doesn't mean enough? What if I don't fucking care?"

The Doll Man's smile faded only a little. He said, "Hmm," then stood and walked to a table behind her and picked up one of the dolls. He carried it back to the desk, holding it in the crook of his arm the way one might hold a cat. "You'll care," he said. "If not for him, then for another, and then another."

He sat again. Stroked the doll's hair and brushed his fingers along the dress with its intricate lacework. "She's very beautiful, isn't she?" he said. "She is perfect to me. I had her made to order. Like the package downstairs, made to order. I'd no idea the problems this girl would cause. I'm late in delivery. You'll fix it."

"You don't need me to do this job," Munroe said.

The Doll Man's smile remained though his eyes never left the toy child. "You won't like the mess," he said. He raised his eyes to hers. "Let's avoid the mess. It keeps things pleasant for everyone."

"Why me?" she whispered.

"I've already explained this," he said. "You owe a debt, and so for you this is a fair exchange. Your difficulty in understanding baffles me."

"I might be more compliant if you'd go over the details of this debt."

"What more details do you need?" he said. "Because of you my American facilitator is in jail." The Doll Man paused, shifted forward, and began again slowly, as if trying to explain quantum physics to a four-year-old. "First the facilitator goes, then the logistic problems begin. After that, the money loss follows. It's quite simple, really. So I leave it to you to earn the money back. This package is a high-high-dollar shipment. You deliver, we call it even."

Munroe sighed and allowed him the visible triumph of her defeat. "Okay," she said.

Very few knew who she was or how to find her. Fewer still knew of her attachment to Logan or had the balls to come after her, but throw a facilitator into the mix and only Katherine Breeden came to mind. In that instant of understanding, Munroe connected this crazy man to Bradford's files, to the trafficker who made dolls of women; understood now that everyone she cared about was at risk, that agreement was the only way to purchase time, and on behalf of Logan and the treacherous waters they'd now tread, her soul grew heavy.

eight

The door slid open, a hollow metal clank that let in better air, way too much light, and set Neeva's pulse racing. It couldn't have been five minutes since that . . . that person . . . he, she, "it", whatever, had come to gawk, and visits were never this close together.

Teeth clenched, she positioned to a crouch, waiting for whatever would happen to happen: *Bring it on, fucktards, and get it over with.* Bunch of freaking perverts all of them. Carry in a tray of food and then drop your pants, stare at the chick in chains, and jerk off before you go. Reasoning, questioning, none of that seemed to matter here. Even pitiful tears hadn't worked. And, anyway, these assholes didn't speak English.

No matter how many vile names she called them, they never reacted—except for the pretty boy. He'd smiled once when she'd been exceptionally creative, but that was sixteen meals ago and she hadn't seen him again until today, when he'd brought that . . . person.

Maybe that person was the one running things.

Maybe that person knew the whole point of why she was here.

Maybe they'd explained the reasons in their gobbledygook and she just hadn't understood, although that was pretty unlikely. Men didn't do a whole lot of talking when they were getting themselves off, and whenever one of these Neanderthals did speak, it was only to grunt commands she didn't understand or to swear at her, which she didn't need to understand to know.

They couldn't have brought her here just to feed her crap food and touch themselves, not even if they knew who she was. She'd dealt with crazy fans, even psycho fans—it's wasn't as if she'd never gotten sick stuff in the mail. But no matter which way she strung it, and she'd had plenty of time to think it through, this just didn't fit the psycho-ax-murderer-stalker-total-creep-fan concept.

She'd kicked, fought, bit, and screamed, and not once had they hit her back. They wanted to—she could see that—sometimes it even seemed as if they would—but instead they'd retaliated by taking away the bucket that functioned as a toilet and tightening the chain so that she couldn't reach the drain in the corner.

She hadn't seen that one coming.

Then they took the blankets and without them she shivered constantly.

The only good thing, if there could be a good thing, was that the worse the smell grew, the more they left her alone. It had been five meals since the last gorilla had dropped his pants. Oh, sure, they could get off just fine staring at her chained and degraded body. But now that she stank? Not so much.

Assholes.

A shadow filled the doorway but didn't enter.

Neeva waited. Eventually he'd come closer, they always did.

With the door open, the incessant talking in the hallway was even louder. The noise was a lesson or something. Words in English and then in some other language, trading back and forth with the same blah-blah-blah that had been going nonstop at least four meals back, and which was a whole lot better than the sporadic crying she could hear before. Crying and screaming. Little girls, it seemed, or maybe teenagers. Sometimes the screams seemed older, crying out in a different kind of protest than the hell she was living here alone: hurt, desperate, hopeless. The words were never in English, and with the crying, they came and went, came and went, usually spaced between every five or six meals, until eventually there was nothing but the language lessons and what seemed like just one person down the hall.

The guard's silhouette filled the doorway again, and in his hand was a rope . . . a lasso. No, a hose. Neeva waited for him to come closer, but he wouldn't. They'd grown wise to her tactics, knew what she would do, and he wouldn't make himself a target.

With a flick of the wrist, the shadow man raised the hose and an unexpected wave of water hit. The cold brought shock and pain, and Neeva screamed. The water hit her full in the face. He aimed not only at her but at the walls and the floor, as if he intended to flush the filth and smell down the grated drain in the corner, the same way a zookeeper cleaned the cages of his keep.

She gasped and choked, and when the stream moved to her chest, screamed again, and still it didn't stop. Not until the walls were wet, the floor was wet, her clothes clung to the shape of her body, and the pad she'd been sleeping on was thick and heavy.

The water shut off, and the shadow left with the hose. He returned to the doorway, then entered and came close, and although she clawed to get away from him, she was chained and hurting, shivering, and had nothing to throw. He grabbed her head. She fought him. He pried her jaw open. She tried to bite. He squirted liquid down her throat and in a moment the strength went out of her.

He stood looking down at her as she lay shaking on the waterlogged mattress, staring up at him while the world tilted at long angles. With disgust in his voice he spoke, and although she couldn't understand his words, she grasped the intent: *Not such a tough one are you now, you filthy animal?*

nine

GATESVILLE, TEXAS

It was nine in the morning when Bradford drove into the parking area of the Mountain View prison unit. He had no legitimate reason for being here on such short notice, much less on a weekday and outside of visiting hours. It had taken an hour and a half on the phone during the drive down, and two hours this morning, asking favors and pulling strings, to make certain he'd get this far.

He'd rolled into town at ten last night and spent the remaining hours between dark and dawn at a nearby hotel, grabbing what little rest he could from a mind that wouldn't shut down. Replays and guilt. Possibilities and connections. Questions that didn't have answers, until after a while it had all run together in a muddy pool and the sun began to rise.

Bradford switched off the ignition. Before stepping out, he emptied his pockets, dumping everything, phone included, into the console. He repocketed his ID. None of the rest was allowed into the visitation area anyway, and the unnecessary clutter would only slow things down during the security screening.

He paused before shutting the door, hesitant to move forward. Not because of what he might find, but for what, even after coming all this way to reach, he might not yet acquire. There were answers here, he was certain of it, but even after the warden had granted the exemption necessary for this visitation, he still didn't know if Katherine Breeden would see him.

Breeden was a lawyer, a damn good lawyer—thorough, clinical, brilliant, warm, and ruthless—a lawyer in prison for a murder she didn't commit. She was there, not because she wasn't smart enough to disentangle herself from the corrections system as quickly as she'd been dumped into it, but because Bradford had seen to it that she wouldn't try.

His success had taken ten minutes from start to finish, a conversation that had wrapped his metaphorical arm around her neck and put her in a choke hold, back when she'd been sitting behind bars in county, with bail set so high she couldn't post a bond and flee, awaiting a trial being pushed through with impossible speed. Bradford hadn't seen her since and it was difficult to know what to expect, what angle of approach would get what he wanted from a woman he was blackmailing into silence.

She had to know he was coming.

What was the point in being diabolically brilliant if there was no one around to admire the effort? Even if Breeden hated him, he was one of the few to whom she could gloat, perhaps the only one who could appreciate the endurance and tenacity necessary for a woman in her position to exact any form of revenge—assuming she'd had anything to do with Munroe's abduction.

But she had to have.

Breeden had taken the fall for a crime that wasn't hers because, to paraphrase a man Bradford had once known, she was risking her life to save it from a greater fear. Based on what he'd seen on those credit-card receipts, the people Breeden had kept silent for, the people she'd feared, were the kind of men who minced bodies into pieces rather than risk the repercussions and sting of betrayal.

Out of the aftermath of Munroe's Africa assignment, in the last pages of that story, had come the documents that outlined corporate shells, legal structures, and the mechanisms through which a criminal organization run by a man known only as the Doll Maker moved, transported, and sold human souls.

Here, in the United States, Breeden had made it possible.

Bradford had stumbled upon the connection shortly before she'd been arrested, the same papers he'd shown to Walker and Jahan the day before, and used that information to control her. The dossier of investigations and dirt digging had uncovered what Breeden had created on American soil, and then in the threads of splotchy documentation went further, tracing back to Europe, drawing connections between the apparently legitimate businesses in the United States and a worldwide market that sold girls into sexual slavery.

None of the information Bradford held was specific enough to be provable, but it *was* enough to call attention to an organization that had thus far operated across borders invisibly and with impunity. He had taken the information to Breeden and threatened to make it all public in her name, knowing Breeden understood that if he did, these same men would guarantee her permanent silence.

Blackmail was as close to a death threat as Bradford could offer, and it had done the job. Breeden had kept silent, and he still didn't know if she'd been aware from the beginning who her clients were and of the tender life they sold, or if her choice to facilitate these crimes had been accidental and he'd been the one to bring her the news.

At the time it hadn't mattered. Breeden's hands were certainly dirty in other affairs, and though she may not have been guilty of the murder, she wasn't innocent, either.

Bradford shut the vehicle door and made his way inside, to face the screening procedure and the metal detectors and to move on finally to the common room, where those not on offenders' visitation lists had through-the-glass, noncontact visits with inmates.

He was here because, despite what he still didn't understand about Breeden's prior involvement with the Doll Maker, the events of yesterday had been too precise to have been random, too accurate to have been accidental. Someone was feeding information to high-level filth, and Kate Breeden was the only possible pivot upon which all the pieces turned. Assuming he'd put the puzzle together properly, she would want to see him, if only to feel the triumph of his pain, and perhaps from this weakness he would learn what he wanted.

Bradford was directed to a chair by a prison guard, and waiting for him on the other side of the glass was Breeden. She smiled when she saw him. Not happiness, per se, or gloating. Something closer to the relief of seeing a face from beyond the walls, no matter how much she hated it, because that was better than nothing at all.

She didn't wait for him to speak or even allow him a chance

to fully settle and put the phone to his ear before she said, "Miles, what a pleasant surprise. I expected you eventually, of course, but certainly not so soon."

Her words, the first third of which he'd lip-read, took the wind out of him. He'd come to find out what she knew—what she'd done—had tossed around opening lines and approaches, hoping to explain his presence without showing his hand, and she'd shut him down before he'd started.

His face must have registered surprise.

Breeden laughed.

"Oh, Miles," she said, "don't be such a douche. If you've been clever enough to come to me, then surely you had to know I'd be waiting for you."

He swallowed bile and waited a half-beat. "What have you done, Kate?"

She smiled, Cheshire cat–like. "That's such an open-ended question with so many potential surprises. Let's be more specific, shall we, darling?"

"We both seem to know why I'm here, and we both know what I hold, so let's just get on with it, okay?"

Her fake smile faded. "Well," she said, scooting back. "Obviously, cordiality is not your forte. As glad as I am for company, if you can't be polite, if you can't at least pretend to drag the conversation out with flattery or talk about the weather, I think I'm quite finished here."

Phone still pressed to her ear, she moved to stand.

Bradford said, "How's the food?"

Breeden laughed again. "That's much better," she said, and returned to the chair. "The food fucking sucks, thank you very much."

"I like your choice in clothing," he said. "It suits you."

"Now you're pushing your luck."

"Do you like your roommates?"

She sighed and exhaled toward the ceiling as if she was blowing cigarette smoke. "College was worse."

"Where's Logan?"

She turned her eyes to his. "Things were going so nicely, and you're ruining the fun." She paused and then, as if the idea of Logan bored her, said, "I haven't the foggiest clue."

"But you knew they'd take him?"

"Oh, please," she said. "Me? Locked up in here?"

"Look, Kate," he said. "I'm not here to prove or disprove anything. I don't have a recorder on me, I'm not taking notes, I'm not going to quote you, I'm not here to make your life difficult. I just want to find Michael. The men who took Logan have already broken bones, he's cut and bleeding bad, and I've got it on tape. I need to find him before they kill him. Do you know where he is?"

"I don't," she said.

"Nor do you care."

"No, not really."

"And you had a hand in this?"

She shrugged. "Wouldn't matter either way, would it? I'm already locked up, aren't I?" She smiled again knowingly, teasingly, and Bradford understood then, ran the numbers, the timing, and it made sense now how it was that those who had taken Munroe had known where to find her. "You pointed the Tisdale family toward me to get to Michael, didn't you?" Breeden didn't answer, but her smile widened, as if it pleased her that at least he grasped her brilliance.

"They're going to kill her," Bradford said. "You know that, right?"

"Maybe," Breeden said. "And maybe you should have thought about that before you put me in a room with no way out as a way to protect her."

"I didn't put you here."

"Well, you made damn sure I wouldn't get out," she said, and then let out another long exhalation of imaginary smoke. "Someone always loses, Miles, and this time it won't be me."

"The information isn't going to go away."

She smiled once more, this time witheringly. "That's the problem with men like you, all tough guy and bang-bang," she said. "You're stupid and short-sighted. Honestly, I don't know what Michael sees in you—you don't exactly play in her league." She leaned back, phone placed on the desk, and stared at him a long while before returning to the handset and speaking again. "Do you know why Michael partnered with me?"

"Yeah, I do," Bradford said.

"She didn't allow me close because I was a lawyer, or even a friend or surrogate mother figure—"

He cut her off. "I know why she partnered with you, Kate. Does it make you feel good to say it?"

Breeden continued as if he'd never spoken. "I am as tough and devious as she is, Miles. You'd be wise to remember that." She paused. Turned her eyes directly to his. "There's not a thing you can do to me now," she said. "If that information leaks, they'll know it didn't come from me."

Bradford leaned toward the glass. "If that's true, then there's no harm in telling me where they've taken her."

She rolled her eyes. "You really aren't the brightest bulb in the box, are you? You have the information. You've always had it. Go be a good little boy and figure it out for yourself."

He waited for the sting of frustration to pass and then, calm, emotionless, said, "You're right, I'm not the smartest man. Perhaps I should ask for help in figuring this thing out—maybe from the media and law enforcement."

She laughed once more. "Oh, Miles, darling, such pleasant entertainment you provide today. You already had your shot at trying to destroy me," she said. "You're good, but you aren't that good. I'm free of you now and I do find your myopia pathetically amusing, running here and there, so focused on Logan that you can't see the bigger picture. Even if I wanted to, I couldn't possibly help someone so hopelessly obtuse." She paused, nodded knowingly. "Don't waste what precious little time you have." And with that she put down the phone, stood, turned, and walked toward the guard on the other side.

Bradford watched her go, and when she was fully out of sight, he, too, stood. On his way out, he detoured for the additional hassle and bureaucratic aggravation necessary to gain access to Breeden's visitor records. Pinpointing who she'd been talking to was easy considering there was only one name on record, though not one he recognized.

In the Explorer, Bradford shut his eyes and ran through their conversation, making mental notes and jotting words down on paper so as not to forget them. Lack of sleep and twenty-four hours of stress was starting to take a toll and irritation was setting in, made worse because he was now uncomfortably into his second day in the same set of clothes.

He pulled his phone from the console. Missed call from Samantha Walker. No voice mail, just a text asking him to get back to her. And a missed call from Alexis, Tabitha's daughter, which got his mind churning. He waited until he was on the road, heading east on 84, before he returned Walker's call.

"What did you get?" she asked.

"Enough to know we're moving in the right direction," he said, "but not enough to take a shortcut. You at the office?"

"I'll be there in five," she said. "I'm on my way back from Addison Airport. Why?"

"I've got a name for Jack to run, can you pass it along?"

"Yeah. And I've got a name for you," she said.

"Who?"

"Michael Munroe."

"You're shitting me."

"Nope. They had docs in her name—or I should say *his* name. And the guy accompanying her—him—is Valon Lumani."

Bradford swore under his breath. The name Lumani was familiar to him from the blackmail pages. He was a kid, trained monkey and right-hand man to the Doll Maker, an orphaned nephew who had been under the Doll Maker's wing since he was in diapers. That Lumani had been personally sent to collect Munroe was telling, as was the fact that he'd come prepared with documents for Munroe's male persona. But the detail that put Bradford's foot to the floor and sent the Explorer surging was that Lumani had traveled under his own name.

If the profiles assembled in the documents were accurate, the Doll Maker was a perfectionist, a stickler for detail, a man who lopped off fingers and toes, sometimes arms and legs, to punish those who failed to meet his expectations. If the nephew wasn't worried about putting his real name on the line, then they weren't worried about Munroe coming back after them.

He said, "Off the top of your head, who do we have on reserve?"

"Adams and Gonzalez."

Men that didn't get a lot of hazard time but were kept on call in case personnel was needed on short order. They weren't vested as part of the core team but had been with the company long enough to step in just about anywhere when needed. "Bring them both in and set them up for surveillance," he said. "I'm going to need them for round-the-clock tracking."

"For how long?"

"As long as it takes. I'll pay the bill out-of-pocket, so don't harass me about the resource expense, and I need you and Jack to start breaking down threads from that dossier and see what you can pull."

"We've been on it all night," she said. "I'll call the guys in as soon as I get back to the office."

"Listen," he said. "I need you to do me a favor and swing by a couple of places—just drive-by stuff, see if you spot anything out of place: surveillance, odd activity, that type of thing."

"Okay," she said, but he could hear the sigh in her voice. "Where to?"

"Michael's sister's place. I just need to be sure we're not overlooking anything."

"More hostages?"

"Yeah, exactly. I'll text you the details."

He sent Walker the information, set down the phone, and stared through the windshield at the three hours of road ahead. He didn't have the manpower, the resources, to protect everyone. His mind churned over what Breeden had said, and more specifically what she hadn't. She'd pointed the Doll Maker's men toward Munroe and Logan, but the why escaped him. What need did a man like the Doll Maker have that he would send his nephew to collect Munroe? Certainly not as a favor to Breeden. If this was meant to avenge the business lost since Breeden had been in prison or to release the choke hold and allow Breeden to work again, they would have simply killed Munroe and come after Bradford. Instead, Munroe was missing and they'd abducted Logan.

They needed Munroe for something, but that on its own made no sense. Her skills were overkill for the type of operation the Doll Maker ran, and bringing her on against her will meant absorbing an enormous risk. You brought Munroe in when the job required stealth and brains and a chameleonlike quality, a job where a strategist, tactician, and linguistics expert was your safest bet. You didn't bring her in to do a job your men had been doing on their own for a decade, you brought her in when the stakes were high, when you were moving something that . . . And then it hit him.

Neeva Eckridge.

He saw it now, the bigger picture, how Katherine Breeden the facilitator had offered Vanessa Michael Munroe as a fix to the Doll Maker's problem of transporting the most sought-after face in the world. Breeden, who, outside of Logan, knew Munroe better than anyone.

Breeden was no longer afraid because she'd brokered a deal in exchange for her own life. If the Doll Maker should fail, Munroe's only option would be to destroy him, and Bradford's blackmail would be useless. If the Doll Maker succeeded, Munroe would die, and because of the brokered deal, Bradford's blackmail would be useless. No matter the outcome, one of Breeden's enemies would fall. No matter the outcome, Kate Breeden had already won.

MILES BRADFORD WALKED through the doors of Capstone Consulting to the sight of Samantha Walker in the middle of the reception area, sorting through a pile of boxes that were part of the steady stream of mail received on behalf of team members stationed abroad. She looked up when he entered, nodded an acknowledgment, and said, "Drove by both places, and everything seems to be normal. For now. Reserves will be here in thirty minutes. Jack's in the war room. I'll be there in just a sec."

He swiped his key card, the door buzzed open, and he stepped through. Beyond the dividing glass walls, Jahan's head shifted up from the keyboard toward one of the monitors, which displayed a rapid database scan that paused occasionally to ping information.

Jahan didn't turn when Bradford entered the war room, so Bradford let him be and instead stepped to the left side of the whiteboard, which was now heavily marked with fresh diagrams and notes, details his home team had obviously been puzzling over for far too many hours. The Doll Maker documents had been deconstructed and scrutinized, each thread of a potential trail broken down into further paths with dead ends crossed off and possible leads highlighted.

Names.

Companies.

Purchases.

Vehicles.

Properties.

Bradford wasn't the only one running on lack of sleep.

With his back still turned, he said to Jahan, "These guys actually own stuff here in Dallas?"

A long pause and many keystrokes later Jahan answered. "Not sure yet," he said. "We're running into dead ends, a few red herrings. Not everything's as accurate as we'd hoped. We're still trying to sort the valid from the rest."

Considering the original information source, the news wasn't entirely surprising. "Did the papers exaggerate?" Bradford said.

Jahan shook his head. "If anything, they undershot by a wide margin."

"How wide?"

Jahan shrugged and returned to the keyboard. Bradford didn't press. How did one quantify the degrees of horror in human trafficking? Young girls lied to, bullied, bought, or kidnapped; children and teenagers transported and isolated, raped and beaten into submission, and then inducted into a life where the control wasn't chains but abuse and fear.

Like Jahan, Bradford wasn't ignorant on the issue. It was impossible to spend time in shithole locations without being touched by the plight of the victims and the helplessness of it, but until now most of what he'd encountered were child brides and the accepted domestic slavery of the cultures, not this, this barbarianism that took enslaving women one level deeper and preyed on the most basic of human drives.

Bradford knew what Jahan meant by "a wide margin." The organization was farther-reaching and more deeply entrenched than they'd believed.

Bradford drew his finger along the California thread.

Jahan and Walker had seen it, too: Neeva Eckridge.

Too many threads, too many possible paths, and no time to trace them all.

Time.

How much time did they have? How long would it take Munroe to do the job they'd snatched her for? A day? Two? A week? God, it was impossible to know.

Time.

He followed the threads down into Texas. Mentally cut off ninety percent of the diagram. Turned to find Jahan staring at him.

"Texas," Bradford said. "They had Michael out of here within an hour of take-down. They didn't pull Logan—and he's in no condition for them to move far. He's still here. In Texas. Probably still in Dallas. We need to find him."

"Before Michael?"

Bradford drew a deep breath and stared at the ceiling. There was far more behind Jahan's question than a matter of logistics. After a long exhale, he turned his eyes to Jahan. "Yes," he said. "Before Michael."

ten

ZAGREB, CROATIA

Munroe sat on the mattress, back to the wall, eyes closed, forearms resting against her knees. To wait in darkness was familiar from long ago, to allow the night to swallow her and take with it the fear of helplessness and the impatience for action.

One breath followed another while inside her head countermove played against counterstrategy, and she ordered and reordered, ended and started over in an attempt to see past the ruin, until noise in the hallway pulled her from her trance back to the madness.

The door slid open. She opened her eyes.

Arben filled the space, his body a silhouette against the hallway light, and he didn't say anything, as if his presence was all the order she would need. Beyond him was another shadow—most probably the nameless guy, Arben Two. Neither man entered the cell, and this time the big man didn't flinch when she stood and walked toward him.

Munroe followed Arben down the narrow hall, up the stairs, and through the gold-working room, which was now dark and deserted. Artificial light from the outside filtered in through the windows, casting just enough of an ambient glow on empty workstations that flashlights weren't needed, and up ahead yellow light and muted conversation filtered out of the Doll Maker's office.

Arben rapped on the door and opened it without waiting. Nodded Munroe inside, and for the third time that day she found herself in the presence of the crazy man. This time he sat on the edge of his desk, assessing a life-size doll seated on a chair in the middle of the room. Lumani was to the right, standing military at-ease. He turned toward her only long enough to acknowledge her presence and then, expressionless, returned focus to his uncle.

Munroe stepped into the room and the creases in the Doll Maker's forehead relaxed. He smiled and motioned her closer. "Come, come," he said. "She's here for you to see, your package."

Munroe moved to the center of the room and circled the chair, speechless, tempted to reach out to touch the soiled, matted blond hair that had been transformed into perfect silky ringlets.

Hair, makeup, clothes, Mary Jane shoes—Neeva was an exact replica of a doll, every aspect perfect and convincing down to the bright blue eyes, which were glazed, heavy-lidded, and staring straight ahead in a drugged stupor.

The Doll Maker said, "She's beautiful, yes?" and Munroe nodded, because in truth Neeva took her breath away. Here it was obvious why the screen came to life when Neeva was on it, why the world raced to find her, and most important, why it would be impossible to hide her in transport.

The Doll Maker straightened, and while Munroe continued to study the girl, he passed to the shelves behind her. "My client has rules," he said.

Munroe turned to face him.

He pulled down a smaller version of Neeva, who, like the living girl, was dressed in green velvet. "No bruises," he said. "No scars. No drugs. She must remain perfect and undamaged, and any deviation is considered failure."

He cradled the doll. "Rules," he said. "How to control an animal with such handcuffs, I don't know, but she's your problem now." He looked up and smiled. "This one comes from Italy. Not custom-made, but beautiful nonetheless." And then, as if there had never been an interruption or a derailed train of thought: "My customer grows impatient, especially considering the news and the attention.

The price is good, but nothing is worth the scrutiny this brings on us."

Munroe turned from him back to Neeva, whose eyelids drooped and opened again. To the Doll Maker she said, "You said no drugs."

He shrugged. "It couldn't be helped. It was the only way we could get her cleaned up, but it will be out of her system soon and no one will know. It's our secret and we can't repeat it. You'll have to find another way to control her."

"No bruises."

"Yes, yes," he said. "It's tedious, but the merchandise must remain undamaged, those are the instructions."

"Why?" she asked.

The Doll Maker shrugged. "Who can say, and who cares? For a good customer that pays, we do what we do and ask no questions."

"So this is not the first?"

The Doll Maker cooed slightly, fingers resting on brunette curls, lifeless eyes to lifeless eyes. "Not the first," he said. "And if you succeed, not the last."

Munroe continued her way around Neeva, one in a line of stolen lives.

She said, "And if I fail?"

"No failure."

"Ever?"

"Not without a price."

Completing another circle, focus always on the girl, she said, "It's a lot that you expect of me. You with your guns and your men have had to drug her to control her. I'm but one person and you want me to do what you can't."

"It's not my problem anymore," he said. "You do it. You fix it. You follow the rules. If you break them, if you fail, the innocent suffer. When you've delivered and I'm paid my money, I let your friend go."

"And me," Munroe said. "Let's not forget that I'm also your prisoner."

"I let you go, too," he said. He still stared at the doll in his arms, and Munroe's eyes left his face, for the walls, for the ceiling, for the reason that not one blink or blush, not one muscle in his body had betrayed his lie.

"I'll need your plan," she said.

"Through Italy and into France," he said. "The two days to allow for any possible delays. One day straight if the package behaves."

Not highly likely.

"The easiest way to deliver would be to fly her," Munroe said. "The same way that you got me here, probably the way you got her here, and you really don't need me for that."

"You can transport her any way you wish," he said. "She's your problem and your responsibility. But you will have to provide your own jet and pilots."

Munroe walked yet another slow circle around the chair, analysis disguised as interest in Neeva's doll-perfect clothing. Inside her head the permutations of getting airborne played against the odds of making a break with Neeva and rescuing Logan before the crazy man and his minions caught on and killed him first.

No matter which way the pieces moved, Logan was always too far away.

She needed time. Needed to drag this out as long as possible. To the Doll Maker she said, "If I drive?"

"I'll provide a car."

"Is it a stolen car?"

"The plates are good," he said as if that was all that mattered, and then added, with a toying smile, "and I will pay for gas."

"Tomorrow, so that the drugs have time to flush out of her system?"

The Doll Maker nodded.

Munroe pointed to Neeva. "Are you taking her back to the cell?"

"Yes, of course," he said. "Until we are ready for transport."

"She'll get dirty again."

"The mattress has been changed," he said, "but still, such a waste." He took the doll from his arms to rest her on the desk, then walked to Neeva. Ran his fingers through her curls and along the outer seam of the lace and velvet dress. "It would be so much more pleasant if we could keep her like this. She is a true doll. Made to order. A collector's item. It's no wonder she fetches such a high price."

The Doll Maker nodded toward Lumani, who called the Arbens inside. Together, they lifted Neeva by her elbows and instead of dragging her out the door they worked her nearly useless legs forward.

Upright, Neeva was even more childlike than she'd appeared while seated. Tiny and slender, she stood five foot two at the most, probably closer to five flat—everything opposite to the larger-than-life personality, the image on the big screen that created something much greater out of this little person.

"What will they do with her?" Munroe said.

"Undress her and put her to bed."

His words and the nonchalance with which he spoke them sent blood rushing to her head. Munroe took a step in Neeva's direction, to block the way. An involuntary movement, an urge to protect and intervene so strong that it overcame reason and took her by surprise nearly as much as it did the Arbens, who paused in their exit. She took another step, this time deliberate, and another until she was solidly between Neeva and the door.

The Doll Maker smiled as if reproving a young child. "It won't do to become attached to the merchandise," he said, and when Munroe didn't move, he added, "She is worth more to me whole than whatever temporary use the men might make of her."

Slow and hesitant, she stepped aside and the Doll Maker smiled, triumphant, wordless in his gloating, while the Arbens walked Neeva out the door and Munroe stared after them.

When the door had shut, the Doll Maker said, "You will stay in the holding area. We'll leave your door open, but if you attempt to climb the stairs, we will take measures against your collateral. You understand this?"

Munroe nodded, still moving with the trancelike tempo of the conversation, navigating around the chair so that this time her path took her in Lumani's direction.

Throughout this entire exchange the young man had remained silent and motionless, his gaze following his uncle like that of a loyal dog waiting for approval, waiting for orders. Each measured step brought her closer to him, though her attention remained entirely on the Doll Maker, who continued in his smugness.

In a movement both sudden and violent, Munroe turned mid-step and in the heartbeat of Lumani's delayed reaction, she punched fingers to his trachea and grabbed his wrist.

She jerked his arm behind his back and shoved him, gagging, to his knees. Lumani's free hand flexed and reached for his shin, and she, knowing that in his moment of panic he would attempt to access any weapon he carried, moved faster than he did, finding and unsheathing his knife.

The handle connected with her palm like a creation returning to its mold, metal against skin, familiar and soothing, calling out to be used, begging to shed blood. She pressed the flat of the blade to Lumani's throat and held it there.

At the desk, the Doll Maker picked up his doll and, ignoring Munroe and Lumani, cradled her again. In his indifference, as in his lies, no tell of betrayal marked his face, no body language spoke his hidden thoughts. The Doll Maker smiled at the porcelain face that stared lifelessly at him. Without looking up, he said, "You'll pay for this failure."

Lumani twitched and Munroe drew the flat of the blade across his neck to prevent instinct from slitting his throat. "Is it worth the price of this one?" she said. "Or the destruction of the package?"

"I'll get what I need with or without you," the Doll Maker said.

Munroe pulled Lumani to his feet and stepped back from him. Slid the knife along the floor in his direction. "I also have a choice, and I think we've both made our points," she said. "I want to see Logan, video streamed live so I can confirm his current condition."

"I can arrange that," the Doll Maker said.

"By tonight?"

"It'll be done," he said. "Tomorrow."

"I'm going downstairs," she said. "You don't need to guard me. Leave me alone and let me know when the girl is awake."

eleven

Miles Bradford stood in the middle of the war room and dumped two Kevlar vests on the floor. Jahan and Walker stared at him, both silent and sullen. "Fight it out between you," he said. "I'll be in my office."

More specifically, he'd be on the floor in his office, beneath the desk, grabbing a moment of sleep before heading out again. He turned from the room, and the heated whispered exchange started once more behind his back. Someone had to stay behind and there were no volunteers.

It was nearly one in the morning, technically into day three of the hunt for a trace on Munroe and Logan, and they were running on empty: nerves strung a little tighter, edges a little sharper. Bradford's body couldn't handle this lack of sleep crap the way it could eighteen years ago when he was twenty and king of the world. He needed five minutes, ten, if he was lucky.

For a full day they'd stalked information, putting aspects of running Capstone on temporary hold to pore over gigabytes of data, tracking leads and cutting off dead ends—tedious brain work, numerous phone calls, and the occasional in-person visit to pull records—until what they had now was a short list of four valid possibilities, four locations where if Logan was being kept in Texas, they might actually find him: a residential home, an office condo, a warehouse, and a transport company, all within the Dallas metro area.

Might find him.

At this juncture, everything was a crapshoot, and this was the best they had.

Bradford threw a bedroll under the desk. Lay feet to the window, head to the darkness, and before closing his eyes, he checked his phone, the same flick of the wrist he'd been making at ten-minute intervals throughout the day, hoping against hope that either Munroe or Logan might have gained access to a phone, might have called, texted, or emailed, and somehow he'd missed the alert.

But nothing. He closed his eyes and opened them to Sam Walker's feet.

From where she stood, he could see the bottom of the vests, one draped over each shoulder, and gripped in her right hand a backpack that held the war room's ready stash of tracking and surveillance equipment.

The clock on his phone said fifteen minutes since he'd blinked.

"You awake?" Walker whispered.

Just enough of a hiss to ensure that even if he hadn't been, he would be now.

"Yeah," he said. "What'd you get?"

"Jack stays, I go."

Bradford scooted out from under the desk. "That so?" He turned his back to roll up the bed. "How'd you manage that?"

Walker sighed. "Two on, two off, and we break after dawn."

Bradford nodded. "Does he have a shopping list?"

"He's good with whatever we get."

He handed her the Explorer keys. "You drive," he said. "I'll sleep."

THE ARMORY WAS a war-room legend, on par with Bigfoot or the whispered rumors of Munroe's ability to absorb languages. Only a handful knew of its confirmed existence, and of those only Bradford and Jahan knew where it was or how to get inside. The armory was just in case; it was hell-in-a-hand-basket, old habits die hard: a collection that had steadily grown over the years in anticipation of a scenario in which he with the biggest guns wins.

Walker pulled the Explorer out of Capstone's garage space, and Bradford recited the address. She glanced at him with that look of hers but said nothing until they were off the 8o, east of Dallas, a full thirty minutes from where they'd started. She pulled off the access road to stop in front of a twenty-four-hour storage complex and nudged Bradford awake.

The cluster of cinder-block buildings sat back off the feeder road in an area of used-car lots and bodywork and pawn shops—an area just derelict enough that the razor-wire fencing, powerful lights, and security cameras would have been necessary if they hadn't already come as part of the package.

Bradford leaned over Walker, half planting himself in her lap to enter the gate code. She held her breath. It seemed unfair that after days of burning the midnight oil, she still smelled human and lightly floral.

The fenced gate rolled open, and Bradford directed Walker through the maze of alleys between buildings to the rear of the complex and the front of a cinder-block ten-by-twenty leased in a fake name and registered to a fake business.

Bradford stepped out, keyed the padlock open, and lifted the reinforced door up on its rollers to the midpoint, then went in under and moved through the darkness to the left wall. By touch he deactivated the alarm on a pad without a backlight.

If the door had passed the three-quarter mark, if he'd taken longer than forty seconds to get to the numerical pad, the storage unit would have filled with smoke and CS gas, and the war room, so many miles away, would have been notified that the cache had been compromised and to stay the hell away.

Bradford raised the door the remaining distance, and Walker backed the Explorer as close to the opening as the limited width of the alley allowed.

The unit housed seven fireproof gun safes, chained together and lag-bolted to the concrete. Bradford unlocked two. The fragrance of gun oil and metal overpowered the musk of dust from the storage space. He paused to scan the contents, and Walker, guiding the flashlight for his benefit, let out a low whistle.

"Armageddon, much?" she said.

"Grab that duffel bag to your right, will you?"

She swung the beam just long enough to snag the canvas and toss it in his direction. Paused and then also toed an empty plastic foot locker toward him. In the silence, it groaned, loud against the concrete. Bradford stared at her. Shook his head and returned to a safe. Pulled the door wider so that she had a clear view of the inventory.

"Pick your flavor," he said.

Walker pointed with the light. "One for me, one for Jack."

Bradford unracked an MP5, ran the bolt, and handed the weapon to her. Did the same for the two he placed in the locker. "And that sniper," she said.

He followed the light to the lone M2010, his newest addition to the cache, a tool that in the right hands had an effective range of 1,200 meters: agent of death from three-quarters of a mile away.

Walker didn't have traditional military training, hadn't gone through a conventional war that might look good on a private contractor's brag sheet, or give him cause to hand over such a piece. Instead she'd had her overly protective father who'd lived as a shooter for nearly two decades and treated her as if she was his only son. Walker knew more about the art of sniping than some men who'd been hunting their entire lives, and although Bradford wouldn't risk putting her up against elite military, the jobs he ran typically didn't require that level of skill.

She slid from the tailgate to take the rifle from him. Handled the piece with the same tenderness and admiration a mother would show a newborn.

Bradford collected the scope and bipod and passed them to her, then shut that safe.

Walker said, "What about plastics?"

She wanted controlled explosion. Bradford reopened the safe, grabbed several C4 bricks and the detonators. He raised them to her.

"Good enough," she said.

He added the explosives to the duffel bag, then locked the safes. She helped him lift the supplies into the Explorer.

Against everything his heart wanted, he would use what was left of the morning's darkness to track Logan—not Michael, Logan. Because Logan was here and Munroe was not, and if they were successful in rescuing Logan before the Doll Maker's men finished him, it just might also be enough to save her.

Valon Lumani stood in front of the wall of dolls, hands behind his back and his focus entirely on Uncle, who sat studying papers. In the thirty minutes since he'd been summoned, not once had Uncle acknowledged his presence.

He would stand here for a touch of acceptance, *something* to show that he had value in the eyes of the only father he could remember. And he would stay silent, because to speak and be ignored, as if he was a ghost passing unseen and unheard among the living, would only reconfirm his worthlessness, and in that lay infinitely more pain.

So Lumani stood and waited, while the events of last night became his private movie and the whispers among the men the sound track, words that filtered back to him as resentfulness, as accusations of favoritism, because for failure Uncle punished him with silence instead of taking flesh.

The men would never understand.

For physical pain there were painkillers to last until the torment faded, but for emotional pain there was only the perpetual numbing of drugs and alcohol: a weakness that served to emphasize his defects and bare the humiliation in his lack of perfection. Physical pain would be preferable—far easier to block out and endure.

Time passed, Uncle shuffled more papers, while the actions that had forced Lumani to his knees rewound and played again. Even after all his training, she had used him like a puppet to make a point to Uncle, had moved with speed so stunning he'd had no time to brace for it, utilized surprise to lead to the hidden weapon that if he'd followed the warnings, he wouldn't have carried.

In front of Uncle's eyes, he had been humiliated, and he had failed. The successful completion of his latest mission, the orchestration of perfection in Texas, all the history of success was now so far away—nothingness, erased like marks in sand on the beach. The only thing that mattered was the moment, and the moment for him was failure.

Uncle paused from his papers to pet the silky hair of a nearby doll, his action distracted and peaceful in the same contented way an old woman might stroke a cat. This had always been the way of the old man: love and attention lavished upon nonliving things while breathing flesh and blood held no space in his heart.

The door reverberated with a knock, and Lumani's heart answered with its own beat. He had been humbled last night by a woman, outsmarted in a way that none of Uncle's men had ever managed. He wanted what she had, even if she was only a woman, and that realization brought a touch of fear, and more, the rush of feeling alive.

The door opened.

Lumani didn't turn.

The Michael woman stepped inside and Uncle glanced up from his papers, his expression transforming from indifference to a welcoming smile.

"My friend," he said, and motioned for her to sit.

Hatred and jealousy crested over Lumani's rush. She, through no good thing, she, this woman, this disposable commodity that would be used and destroyed, had earned another smile that should have been given to him.

The woman sat, then slow and deliberate turned to look in his direction. Without words she spoke to him, and without words said that she knew his thoughts, his prison. He focused on the desk to ignore her, though his heartbeat quickened again. If he could have, he would have gone to her now and forced her through her pain to allow him her secrets.

Instead, frustration and resentment seeped through his pores.

The movements of Uncle and the Michael woman seemed to set out in slow motion. Uncle reached into a drawer for the car keys and GPS system, the map, the passports and car papers: as transport, she was given full responsibility for the package, would be alone in the car with it. More conversation until Uncle's voice cracked through the mirror of oblivion and Lumani raised his eyes to find both Uncle and the woman staring at him.

His face flushed. He hadn't heard the words, but he knew their intent, the purpose for which he'd been summoned, and so he straightened, pulled the phone off his belt, and approached the woman. Offered her the phone, careful this time to keep a safe distance.

He would have liked to have read from her body posture that no strike was imminent, but he hadn't anticipated the attack in her last night and did not trust himself to properly gauge her now. She took the phone and stared at him again, as if attempting to read him the way he had tried to read her.

Lumani, offering nothing, stepped back; she glanced at the phone and tapped the screen to play. She wanted proof of life and they were happy to make sure the evidence was plenty, but no matter what Uncle had promised, live streaming wasn't going to happen. There was too much risk that Logan might, in some coded language, give away information that would aid her in circumventing well-laid plans, even from half a world away.

Lumani studied the woman for reaction, and as he had done, she offered nothing. Unreadable. She raised her eyes to his when the clip ended and handed back the phone. Uncle pushed the supplies in her direction and she considered them a moment before speaking. "I want duct tape and a blanket," she said, and when Uncle protested because none was at hand, she replied in his own words, "No drugs, no bruises."

She would get what she wanted because Lumani would be tasked with making sure of it, though nothing in that regard was said here in this room. The client was impatient and demanding. If they couldn't deliver on his schedule, he would rescind his order, or worse, up the stakes and create more hoops for them to jump through, else the doll would have to be terminated. Uncle risked losing his investment, so therefore Lumani would provide and they would leave today, even if it meant this afternoon, which would turn this delivery into a minimum two-day event.

Uncle spoke again, words of control, words of deterrence, to keep this woman from straying from the plan; every action had consequence, each delay a price. He offered her another smile, a smile that made Lumani's insides burn. The Michael woman stood and Uncle handed her a cell phone. "This phone is your life," he said. "Don't lose it. Keep it on always."

The phone was the line of communication through which they were tethered, the means through which she would receive instructions for each leg of the journey. It was also bugged for sound and tagged for location so that they could electronically see and hear her always. Should she choose to risk damage to Logan by pulling the battery, the car held similar equipment.

But these things Uncle never mentioned.

Lumani, with his rifles, with his training, would be the one to ensure that she didn't deviate from the plan, the one to report the moves upon which Logan's life depended.

twelve

Veers Transport was first on Bradford's hit list for finding Logan because it had everything he looked for: Trucks. Office. Warehouse. Seclusion. Red flags.

On the surface, the company was legitimate and profitable, and if not for the information found in the Doll Maker files, there would have been nothing about the business to have drawn the war room's attention. Even Katherine Breeden's name was no longer connected to the company, although it had once been. Only by following Breeden's trail, as the dead man had, and working backward, could the connection have been made.

Veers Transport owned a fleet of fifteen trucks, most of them class-six commercial vehicles with a couple of eighteen-wheelers thrown in for good measure. State filings were up-to-date; there was no pending litigation; the company properly paid income, sales, and unemployment taxes; it provided health-care benefits to full-time employees, of which it had eighteen; and none of the directors or officers of the closely held corporation were connected to the names on the Doll Maker's roster.

It had taken digging into the personal lives and histories of the primaries to sniff out the hole in the facade, because there was just no explaining how those who owned the company didn't also own or rent property, own or drive vehicles, or how as recently as last month one of the men had listed a homeless shelter as his permanent address.

Bradford drove by for a visual first pass.

They were off Loop 12 in a commercial area dotted with importers and wholesalers spread among parking lots and wide single-story office complexes. The depot was directly off the road, surrounded by a chain-link fence, with a separate prefabricated building near the front and a two-bay warehouse toward the rear. There were six trucks in the lot, and if the entire fleet ever came home to roost at the same time, it would be a tight squeeze.

To the casual observer, security was lax if not nonexistent, but to well-trained eyes, the cameras and motion detectors were easy to spot. Walker said, "You'd think in an area like this they'd flaunt the security."

"Maybe the low-key approach is for the benefit of law enforcement."

"Perhaps," she said, and Bradford continued down the strip, far past the depot, to a smaller street and from there to the first right, which was an alley along the other side of the ten-foot wall that separated the residential area from the commercial complexes.

Here, streetlights dotted the alley and backyards stretched from clapboard siding to chain-link fence, and faded and cracked plastic toys littered patchy lawns, occasionally joined or replaced by a car up on blocks.

Satellite images had pointed to this route as the least intrusive form of access to the transport company, and Bradford kept the vehicle creeping along the narrow pitted road until the roof of the warehouse settled into position ahead. He stopped in what shadow existed and allowed the length of an office complex to separate the Explorer from their target. Walker snapped a magazine into an MP5, and they stepped into the night.

ZAGREB, CROATIA

Flat on her back, arms to her sides, Neeva stared at the ceiling. The metal door was open and had been ever since she'd woken: open and wide like a tormenting bully who offered something just to take a swing if you accepted. Chained to the wall, ankle trapped inside the rubber-coated metal ring, the tease of escape was far worse than being locked away in darkness. She yanked the chain in frustration, felt the solid tug, and deflated. She'd no energy left to scream and fight.

The guard who usually sat outside her door was gone and the language recordings had stopped. She didn't know if this was bad or good, because in this place change meant something worse was coming.

She'd been bathed or showered since the water attack, because she was clean and the track suit smelled freshly laundered, and her hair was really weird. Shirley Temple weird.

A shadow filled the doorway. Neeva jerked upright and backed up against the wall. There hadn't been any footsteps to announce the person, not even in the silence. She fingered the chain, which had enough slack in it to use as a weapon if the shadow got close enough.

The person ducked to enter and then moved out of the doorway so the light wasn't directly behind, and Neeva could see the face—definitely the mystery person from yesterday, although the hair was different and the person now wasn't so much an it as a he.

"May I come in?" the person said, and Neeva stared, blinking, not because of the polite nature of the request but because this was the first real-life English she'd heard in so long she'd lost track, and it was real American English, not all accented and stilted as if one of these animals had learned it in school.

"You're already in," Neeva said, and he smiled, kind of sad.

"Michael," he said, and stuck out a hand.

Neeva didn't move and after a while the hand withdrew.

"You speak English," Neeva said finally.

"Apparently, so do you," the Michael person said. "Very color-fully."

Neeva snorted, and Michael stepped closer. About halfway into the cell, he sat on the floor with his back to the wall and tipped his head toward the ceiling. Neeva waited for him to say something, but he didn't. Didn't even look at her, which was more out of character for this place than anything else so far.

"What do you want?" Neeva asked.

His face shifted toward her. "To talk with you, if you don't mind."

Neeva let out a bark of laughter. Chained to the wall, she wasn't exactly going anywhere, and until now what she did or didn't want had meant nothing. "Sure, talk," she said. "But don't you need to drop your pants and whack off first? That seems to be the order of things—that is, if you skip talking altogether."

Almost as if to himself, he said, "You're lucky."

The words were like a smack in the face. "Yeah, for sure," Neeva said, "I'm so lucky. That's exactly what those pervs are thinking when they honor me with their presence."

"They're trying to degrade you," he said. "That's the best they could do without touching you. If you were anyone else, they would have beat and raped you. To humiliate you. Break you."

The honesty of the explanation left Neeva without a retort, without any sense of up or down, and all the questions that had no answers came back again until Michael spoke once more. "I'm being forced to do a job that I don't want to do," he said. He turned to look directly at her. "I just want you to know, no matter what happens, this isn't what I want."

"I don't see you in chains," Neeva said. "So don't talk to me about want."

"I'm a prisoner here just as much as you are, wearing chains, even if you can't see them."

"Excuse me if I'm all out of sympathy."

"I wanted to say it before the insanity starts," Michael said, then stood and turned for the door. Neeva fought for a reason to keep him there. He was American. He was English conversation. Possibly he had answers to the big why and what. "You're the person in the cell down the hall?" she said.

Michael nodded.

Neeva pulled her knees to her chest, wrapping her arms around them. "Can you answer the questions that nobody else will?"

Michael stopped and turned. "I don't know," he said. "I can try."

"Why am I here?" she asked. "What do they want with me? Is it for ransom?"

He studied her as if plotting things in his head, maybe weighing answers or trying to find words, then said, "This is a holding place, a waiting area. Someone put a purchase price on you and the people who control this building, the ones who kidnapped you, they've made it my responsibility to get you to the person who bought you."

The words brought clarity. Neeva drew in a sharp inhale and said, "Knowing this, you're going to just hand me over?"

Michael moved toward the door, looked back, and paused. "I don't know you," he said, "but I know who you are, and if I could find a way to save us all, I would, but I can't. I have a gun to my head, and the more you fight me, the harder I will have to fight you back to save my own life. You understand?"

Neeva refused to justify the pitiful excuse with a reply. Instead she crossed her arms and glared.

Michael nodded. "I'm truly sorry."

From down the hall came the sick thud of boots against the concrete. Michael's head tipped up and then, as if Neeva ceased to exist, he straightened and walked out.

She tugged on the chain. Wiped away tears she didn't even know she'd cried. In a fit of futile desperation she yanked harder and more frantically on metal that refused to give, while the anger and fear and frustration; the urge to destroy that had been building and building through the passing days; the want, the desperate want to hurt and maim and kill and exact revenge on anyone who'd had anything to do with this state of helplessness, came out in a curdling scream.

thirteen

Munroe could count them by the footsteps, time them by the pace; she stepped into the hallway and stood in Lumani's way before he reached her cell.

He breached her personal space, smiling slightly as if her antics amused him. Behind him were the Arbens, bullies waiting for the fight. One held a hanger festooned with the lace and velvet clothes that Neeva had worn previously. It would appear that the Doll Maker, in his fanciful wisdom, would have the girl travel in the costume—as if avoiding attention wouldn't already be difficult enough—and had sent his men to dress the merchandise.

"Your tape and your blanket," Lumani said, extending the items in Munroe's direction until she took them. "Now you should move out of the way."

She didn't. Wouldn't. Even if the girl at the end of the hall was nothing more than a barrier standing between her and Logan's freedom, she couldn't abide these men defiling the helpless with their eyes or their touch. "Let me have the clothes," she said. "The package is my responsibility, I'll see that she's dressed."

In the language he wrongly assumed she didn't understand, Lumani instructed the man to pass over the clothing. Munroe took the hanger and turned toward Neeva's cell, and behind her a hushed argument erupted, which ended with Lumani's clipped instruction.

Munroe draped the dress across the empty chair at the hallway's end, placed the blanket on the seat, and carried the tape into Neeva's cell, where the screams of animal fury that had followed her out into the hall were now silent. Neeva was backed up against the wall, positioned in a semicrouch with a play of chain held tightly in her hand, blond ringlets a jarring, comical contrast to the primal nature of the moment.

Munroe neared and Neeva shifted, tightening her grip and maintaining position even when Munroe stopped beyond lunging distance. Munroe knelt so that she was at eye level. "Please don't try to fight me," she said. "I'll be forced to hurt you, and that's the last thing I want."

Neeva didn't reply, didn't lower her eyes, and Munroe's stomach churned. The rules said no drugs and no bruises, but there were plenty of ways to create pain that left no visible evidence—her own suffering had taught this lesson well.

"We need to change your clothes," Munroe said. "You can do it yourself if you want. I'll give you privacy and leave you alone, I just need to know that you'll cooperate."

Silence.

"Will you?"

Neeva stared blankly, posture still tense, a jungle cat waiting to pounce.

Munroe tried again. "If you keep your hands and feet to yourself and do as I tell you, I'll be nice, but if you fight, I'll be forced to retaliate. You only get one warning, understand?" She waited for a reaction, any reaction, and when Neeva continued to eye her unblinkingly, she added, "Please don't test me."

Neeva breathed a slow and focused in and out, not the shallow quickening that would be spurred by adrenaline and produced by fear. Munroe had already seen the fight in the girl, and no matter how tiny, no matter how outclassed, she wouldn't make the mistake of underestimating the human spirit fueled by the desire to win. Still kneeling, still holding eye contact, she called for Lumani, choosing the language she'd been force-fed to make a point, knowing that Hungarian wasn't his mother tongue any more than English was.

Munroe counted seconds and, without turning, knew when he stood behind her; held out her hand for the garment he surely carried.

The weight of the hanger tugged on her fingertips.

Again in Hungarian, she said, "I need the chair," her sentence clipped short because although the words were inside her head and she understood their meaning, she'd not experienced the absorption of real-life interaction that allowed for her own fluency.

She didn't turn when he dragged the metal chair, scraping it against the concrete, into the cell. Didn't flinch when, mouth inches from her ear, he whispered, "Don't push your luck, I'm not your errand boy."

"I need a few minutes more alone," she said, and waited until he'd fully left before slowly, theatrically, redraping the clothes across the back of the chair. With one last attempt to mitigate the inevitable fight with Neeva, she said, "I know you understand my warning." Shifted the chair so that the clothes were within reach. "Take the dress. I'll turn if you want privacy, but I can't leave until you've changed."

Nothing.

"Thirty seconds before I make you," she said, and still Neeva didn't react.

Munroe's anxiety welled. This was a fight she didn't want, one Neeva couldn't win, yet a fight necessary to save Logan.

"Time's up," she said.

Still Neeva didn't move.

Munroe set the roll of tape on top of the seat, stepped around the chair, and placed herself within reach of the inevitable strike. She stretched for the girl's wrist and it was then that Neeva lunged, fist and chain swinging toward Munroe's face, as if the chain was meant to go over her head like a hood.

Hand out, Munroe snagged the snaking metal. Twisted. Wrapped. Pulled Neeva off her feet.

In the delayed hesitation of Neeva's shock, Munroe yanked again, drawing Neeva toward her, and elbow into the girl's stomach, knocked her to the mattress. Neeva fell hard. Munroe dropped a knee into her and took the chain behind the girl's head, winding it around her neck in the same choking move that Neeva had intended: tight enough to constrict air but not enough to crush her windpipe or leave bruises.

Neeva's body writhed to get away, hands stretched and flexed, attempting to fight the chain. Munroe leaned in harder, pinched the girl's nose with one hand, and with the chain wrapped around the other wrist to keep it tight, placed that hand over Neeva's mouth.

Neeva grew frantic. Clawing. Kicking. Bucking. Only when Munroe felt the strength begin to leave the girl's body did she let go. Neeva gasped for air and lay limp long enough to take in oxygen. Then, like a battery suddenly recharged, she went at it again, clawing for Munroe's eyes, tearing at her skin.

The ferocity of Neeva's fight, her struggle for survival—to live, to wound, to maim and kill an opponent—if only to wake tomorrow and do it again, was a vivid flashback. Under other circumstances, Munroe's conscience would rise in pride and camaraderie, would turn to fight beside this girl while they dug their way to victory. But circumstance had turned solidarity into a hollow void and Neeva, this feral, fighting animal, into an object to be subdued in order to set Logan free.

Munroe drove a fist into Neeva's stomach, and when the girl gasped and again struggled for air, Munroe took Neeva's arm so close to snapping that had Neeva not screamed and frozen in the struggle, her shoulder would have gone out of joint. There were tears in Neeva's eyes, and Munroe recognized in them her younger self. Not tears of self-pity or pain, but of rage and frustration.

"I warned you," Munroe said, releasing the chain but keeping Neeva's arm in place. "And I will hurt you more if you don't stop."

Neeva nodded. And Munroe, in another reflection of years gone by, understood the gesture. Not a concession or submission but unbearable physical pain. The nod was a way to buy time. This fight wasn't over.

Straddling the girl, Munroe summoned Lumani, who arrived in the doorway so quickly that he had to have already been nearby, listening and possibly watching from beyond the corner. "Your knife," Munroe said, again in Hungarian, and when he hesitated, she added, botched and incorrectly, "I know you have it. I won't cut the girl."

He bent to retrieve the blade, and when he drew closer and

Neeva caught sight of him and the object in his hand, she began to struggle again.

Munroe increased the pressure and the girl screamed. Munroe reached for the handle of the knife Lumani held in her direction.

The cold metal connected with Munroe's hand, and her sight grew dim with the rush of expectant euphoria. The cell faded to gray and the lust for blood rose inside, a response to the blade and the history the metal represented, an unbearable urge that screamed to be let loose.

"Leave," Munroe said, because if he didn't, she'd not have the control to finish what had to be done here and would instead turn the knife first on him and then on the Arbens, to force an escape for herself and this girl, and in the end, Logan would be lost.

Lumani didn't move. With a knee pressed into Neeva's chest, and gripping the knife in one hand and still twisting the girl's arm with the other, Munroe turned her eyes to him. Teeth gritted, she said in English, "Leave *now* or there will be consequences."

Lumani's lips parted with unspoken words, and without breaking eye contact, he backed away as if encountering a mad dog. Not even waiting for him to fully exit the door, Munroe turned the knife toward Neeva and, with the blade tipped away from the girl's throat and into the collar of the shirt, sliced through the fabric down to the elastic of the pants, and farther to the crotch. Then Munroe flicked the fabric away with the blade so that Neeva lay chest naked to the ceiling.

"I can get off you now," Munroe said, "and allow you to dress yourself, or we can continue to do this the hard way."

Neeva's face twisted to hold back the tears. "I'll do it," she whispered, and her voice rasped thick and dry in response to the struggle and the pressure the chain had made against her windpipe.

Munroe backed off, a slow, staggered process of first releasing the arm, unwinding the chain, and then removing her knee and standing up. With each phase, Neeva lay completely still, as if she had finally understood that any movement might undo this little progress and that to concede now meant a chance to fight again later.

When Munroe was upright and had once more stepped behind the chair and the dress, she said, "I don't want to hurt you."

Neeva said nothing but stood and stared defiantly at Munroe for a long moment, and then, dramatically, every bit the actress before an audience, loosed the sliced clothing and let it drop to the mattress. Naked, never breaking eye contact, she reached for the dress and with some struggle slipped into it.

Clothed, she stepped barefoot and cocky off the mattress, to the floor, exaggeratingly tugging on the chain with her left leg as if to say *Now what?*

Munroe picked the roll of tape and the blanket off the chair, grabbed the back of it, and dragged it, the metal scraping across the floor, out into the hall, hating herself, hating the Doll Maker and the man-boy and the thugs and the perverse underbelly of human nature that cloaked base desire in goodness and pointed fingers and created scapegoats.

She stood in front of Lumani and, before the urge to put the blade to further use could be fulfilled, dropped the knife on the floor at his feet. Were there no market, no buyers, and no men willing to pay for sex, organizations that fed off human misery and criminals like the Doll Maker who stole and cashed in on the value of the female body would cease to exist.

"I want to kill you," she said.

He smiled. Picked up the knife. "The feeling is mutual."

"I need the key."

"Have you damaged her?"

"I'm not stupid," Munroe said. "So get me whatever else you want her to wear, shoes perhaps, so that we can be on our way."

Lumani didn't turn from her. Studying her face, searching her eyes in a way that betrayed more of himself than he might imagine, he gave the order to Arben Two in Albanian. The man turned and went up the stairs, and as the echoed thuds played out in the enclosed underground, Lumani's unabashed study continued until the man returned and handed over a box.

Without conceding the stare-down, Lumani gave the box to Munroe and handed her a key. Only then did she avert her eyes, and that only because she had to. In the entirety of the alpha chest-thumping exercise, she'd read him, he'd read her, and without a word they understood each other just fine.

fourteen

IRVING, TEXAS

Samantha Walker laddered over Bradford's body, from knee, to shoulder, to wall, and then settled, balanced, at the top and belly-crawled in a slow move toward a better view. She'd gone up instead of him because she was the smaller and lighter of the two, and her whisper fed into his earpiece: Equipment. Camera positions. Distance.

If they'd been planning to play it safe, to run conventional surveillance, this would have been the place to set up shop, but they didn't have the time or the resources for smart or safe. Saving Munroe meant finding Logan, and tonight that meant kicking down doors.

After a long pause, Walker said, "Window. Second floor of the warehouse, north side. A yellow light just switched on."

Bradford heard the snag in her thoughts, felt it, too, as it charged down his spine. Until now, the property had appeared empty, but where there were lights there were people, and people meant guards, and guards meant prisoners.

"Come on down," he whispered. "Let's go in through the front door."

Walker slid backward, hung off the wall, and dropped the remaining four feet. "Drunk and angry?" she said.

He nodded. "Should work."

Should. On a run like this, everything was guesswork.

While Bradford drove, Walker stripped out of her overshirt, leaving just the tight-fitting cami to conceal what little it could of her chest. They were possibly walking into a line of fire without protection, but they'd never get through the front door dressed for war. She pulled her hair out of the ponytail and ran her fingers through it. Thick black waves dropped over her shoulders.

"You sure you want to do this?" Bradford asked.

She rolled her eyes, and he said, "Okay then."

From the end of the alley, he headed back to the main road. Stopped just before reaching the target, beyond the range of the cameras, and stayed only long enough for Walker to step out.

Bradford continued one complex south, parked where he could keep an eye on her while she meandered to the front gate, steps uneven and exaggerated. She pulled on the chain-link gate and shook it. Attempted to climb, one clumsy boot toe that couldn't gain purchase. Slid down in an incoherent stumble.

Additional security lights powered on.

Once more she shook the fence, shouting. Paused to wipe her nose against her arm. On the northeast corner of the warehouse, a camera shifted. Her performance kicked up a notch, and she continued, dragging her fingers along the loops of the fence, a slow stumble in Bradford's direction, while occasionally attempting another unsuccessful climb to the top.

A side door to the warehouse opened and a solitary male stepped out. He was bulky, though not from fat, and short enough to look like a brick in rumpled clothes, shirt half-tucked into jeans. If he was carrying a weapon, he was smart enough to keep it out of sight. The closer he got, the softer his expression became, until, right in front of Walker, he almost looked compassionate.

Walker staggered some more, rubbed her eyes, and swiped at her nose again. Held a conversation that Bradford couldn't hear because with Walker so scantily dressed there'd been no place to safely stash a wire, but he got the general idea. The man gestured. Walker nodded and ran her palm over her eyes, wiping away tears. In her lifetime, she'd taken more than one poker pot with that same act of drunken, pitiful helplessness that wrenched male heartstrings and tugged at their zippers.

The man pulled a key ring from his pocket and opened the lock to the gate. Walker slipped inside. The man made to relock it, but Walker's drama started again and she strode in the direction of the door he'd exited so that he had no choice but to leave the lock and follow her.

No further camera movement, no light flickering from the few warehouse windows, no backup personnel. The entire response seemed to be a solitary watchman pulling night duty and sleeping on his shift.

Bradford waited until Walker was halfway from gate to building, and then moved out of the vehicle and into the night. Slipped through the opening.

Ahead, Walker stumbled slightly, and when the man dropped an arm around her and stooped to help, she glanced over her shoulder, noted Bradford, and continued on. The two reached the door, and as Walker passed inside, her right hand transferred from her back pocket to brush along the door frame.

The door shut.

Bradford fought the urge to rush in ahead of plan to watch the back of a partner who had just broken every rule in the live-long playbook.

He'd known it would happen and still bristled.

Counted seconds.

And then hand to handle, he tugged on the door. The latch, depressed by a strip of tape, opened effortlessly. Bradford listened, scoped out what he could, and then slipped inside.

The warehouse was truly that, a large and mostly empty building lined with industrial shelving that bore empty pallets. Forklifts slept nearby. Near the truck bays at the front stood a minimal amount of freight, stacked and ready for loading. The legitimacy took him by surprise.

There had to be a holding place, a way station, some soundproof location to keep the trafficked women, and it made sense that if such a place existed, it would work equally well for keeping Logan. Everything they had learned about this warehouse, about this company, screamed that what they looked for must be here. But this place was all wrong.

To Bradford's right, metal stairs ascended along the inner wall to the second floor, to offices apparently, which occupied only the back quarter of the building and hung over pilings and empty space, and from where voices now carried, one of them distinctly Walker's being drunk, which was good.

Bradford traced the ceiling, searching out cameras, and found nothing. For all the electronic eyes pointed outward, security on the inside was sparse. He moved along the perimeter, from shelving to pallets to forklifts, and found nothing that might indicate a false-paneled room or even a hiding place beneath his feet.

The conversation upstairs continued, still only two voices. Men weren't often silent around Walker, which meant that Warehouse Man was alone, and without more men, Logan, if he had ever been here, was not here now.

The office door opened, and Bradford retreated to the shadows beneath the stairs. Walker teased and stumble-walked her way down with the guy close behind. Fiddled with the keys to a forklift. Warehouse Man tried to take them from her and she slipped beyond him laughing, plugged them into the ignition, and ran the engine. The noise, however long it lasted, was a perfect cover for footfalls against the metal stairs. Bradford hurried now. Warehouse Man would only endure so much teasing and forklift play before the situation turned nasty.

The upstairs was as Bradford expected, two rooms and a rest-room area the size of a small closet, the latter with a small outside ventilation window, which was where Walker had spotted the light.

Half of the first room was allocated for security monitors, the other half to a desk with two computer towers, one without a monitor. On the desk in front of the security cameras, a handgun lay naked and exposed.

A nice Walker touch.

Bradford reached for the weapon, then stopped. Taking it would only alert the Doll Maker's people to their movements. Bradford turned to the second room, in which was a conference table, several chairs, a coffeemaker, and a couple of filing cabinets. No Logan.

Then, even from this far back in the office he could hear the change of tone downstairs. The forklift had been silenced. Walker was shouting. Bradford headed out the door.

Downstairs, Walker shook a fist in Warehouse Man's face.

He tried to grab her hand, to grab her.

Bradford started down the stairs.

Warehouse Man lunged at Walker and she scooted around a pallet, a lot less drunk and a lot more angry. The man swore at her, and with an accent thick and foreign called her a bitch and a whore.

Bradford made it to the bottom of the stairs and hesitated.

Walker screamed, "Get the hell out of my way," and Bradford bolted for the exit knowing that the message had been intended for him and not the cur that stood between them.

In the parking lot he checked his watch, anxiety rising. To be on the outside while a partner was still within those walls was wrong on every level.

Half a minute and the noise moved in his direction. Bradford retreated toward the shadows, mindful of the cameras and of the distance yet to cover. Louder it came: Walker close and moving quickly.

Bradford bolted for the gate and reached it just as she came barreling out the door, running full out with Warehouse Man not far behind. Bradford faced the two, waited until Walker blew past, and then, in character, charged toward Warehouse Man. "What the *fuck* are you doing with my girlfriend?"

The man slowed, his hands forward indicating caution, but before he'd fully stopped, Bradford collided into him, palms to chest, instep to knee. The guy staggered at the shock of the first hit, buckled with the second, and attempting to right himself, swung wildly in defense.

Bradford ducked, moved into his personal space, chest to chest. "Keep your filthy hands off my woman," he said, and drove forward, forehead to nose, breaking cartilage and drawing blood.

Warehouse Man reached for his face and, smearing red, howled a smarting rage. Right hand went behind his back to draw the weapon still sitting on the desk upstairs. Swearing, he threw himself at Bradford.

The guy was wide and his bulk ungraceful.

Bradford sidestepped. Used the man's weight and momentum to continue his top half forward, used a leg to keep his bottom half in place. The man hit the pavement hard.

Bradford began to walk away. Paused long enough to point a

finger at the man crawling to his knees. "You touch her again," he said, "and I'll kill you."

WALKER WAS IN the Explorer, seated and buckled in, when Bradford returned. He slid behind the wheel, put key in ignition and foot to gas. Peeled out into the deserted street with far more noise than was prudent and ran a red light in the process.

Damn adrenaline.

"I hope you broke his nose," Walker said.

"Taken care of," he said, then glanced in her direction.

Arms crossed and fists clenched, she glared through the windshield. "When this is over, when we have Logan and Michael," she said, "I'm going back in."

"Fair enough," Bradford said. "Why?"

Walker turned toward him. "Because that man's a lunatic psychopath. I swear to God, there's a body count somewhere, and if I don't get to him first, another woman somewhere is going to get hurt bad."

"The stuff he promised to do to you, huh?"

"Among other things."

Bradford turned focus to the road. "Michael and Logan first," he said. "Then we take out the trash."

fifteen

ZAGREB, CROATIA

For the first time in three days, Munroe breathed outside air: late morning and early spring air, colder than Dallas and filled with the must of old stone and wood. Smelled faintly of diesel or oil, the way an old barn might, and after endless hours among the rot and mold and bleach of prison, it was a sweeter and cleaner high than mountain wind.

Slung over her shoulder was the backpack she'd been given, stuffed with the blanket and tape, passports, car papers, maps, and GPS from the Doll Maker. Neeva was still down in the hole, chained to the wall with the rubber-coated cuff and the stupid clothes the Doll Maker and his minions insisted she wear. Munroe would retrieve her when she was ready, but for now her focus was on the car parked inside the courtyard.

The ground was cobblestone and the walls on three sides formed part of the building she'd been in—the gold workroom and the windows to the Doll Maker's office were directly behind her, and in front of her was she knew not what. The exit from the courtyard was blocked by a massive arched wooden door or gate, quite possibly centuries old, and definitely the source of the barnlike smell.

The vehicle, an Opel Astra, was a good eight or nine years old, dull gray with half-worn tires and Slovenian plates; a basic model, five-door hatchback, with door locks, windows, and transmission all manual, no air conditioner. The radio had been ripped out and the body had seen a light pole or two in its time. The Doll Maker wouldn't cry if he never got this piece of property back.

Munroe circled the car, taking in the details, then stopped in front and popped the hood to check the fluid levels. She wiped the oil dipstick on a rag that lay to the side under the hood, checked again, then removed the brace and let the metal drop with a thud.

Lumani stood off to the side, arms crossed and leaning against a stairwell arch, and as had been his way thus far, he studied her as if she were a bug under a glass or an exotic caged animal, as if he expected to learn something from her. So she lingered, drawing out each movement far longer than she should have, attempting to provoke impatience in him, but he gave her nothing and finally said, "It's time."

Neeva was sitting on the mattress when Munroe came to collect her. The Doll Maker and his henchmen didn't want the wild animal soiling her new clothes, so for the sake of cleanliness, the girl hadn't been fed since she'd been dressed and wouldn't be unless Munroe decided it was worth the aggravation.

Drugs would have made this entire venture a breeze—pop a sedative in the girl's drinking water, say nighty-nighty, and put her in the trunk. For that matter, drugging the girl would have made Munroe's involvement completely pointless, and were it not for this strange requirement from the Doll Maker's client, there was a chance Munroe would still be in Dallas right now, probably on the Ducati, burning fuel under the Texas dawn.

But the customer had rules.

No bruises. No drugs.

Prerequisites that made no sense.

Most traffickers kept their women doped and dependent, not only for the sake of dulled compliance but also for control. A stable of heroin addicts was far easier to maintain than one filled with fighters and screamers like Neeva.

No bruises. No drugs.

Why?

A thousand possibilities could lay claim to the answer, and Munroe pushed away the desire to know. No matter the reason, it wouldn't change the facts.

Munroe said, "Let's go."

Neeva lifted her head and said, "Where are you taking me?"

Fight-or-flight reflexes long honed during Munroe's own captivity of sorts had heightened her sensitivity to tone, body language, and expression: instinct that picked up nuance with radarlike clarity and in the moment set off a warning sensor. "I don't know yet," she said. "They only give me pieces of the journey, one step at a time."

"Where do we go first?"

"Ljubljana."

"What's that?"

"The capital of Slovenia."

Neeva stared back at her blankly.

Munroe pulled the roll of tape from the backpack, and going for conversation, for distraction and something familiar, said, "We're in Croatia, Slovenia is one country west."

Eyes to the floor, Neeva was quiet as if running numbers or trying to recall why she recognized what she recognized, and said, "I've been kidnapped into a war zone?"

Munroe shook her head. Slovenia and Croatia were splinters from the same origin, but Croatia, far more familiar to most Americans than Slovenia would ever be, meant that those who did recognize the country's name often associated it with the destruction that took place in the nineties—frozen in time and recategorized as one and the same as the mass genocide and wholesale slaughter within Bosnia and Herzegovina.

Neeva was too young to have the collective consciousness. Maybe her awareness was the result of political parents. Either way, there wasn't time for a geography lesson, much less a history one that covered the various Yugoslavian wars. "No war zone," Munroe said. "At least not for almost twenty years. Stand up, please."

Neeva stayed seated. "We're crossing a border?"

"Yes."

"You have my passport?"

"Doesn't really matter, does it?" And she repeated the request. "Please stand up, Neeva."

Neeva nodded. Stood. Stepped off the mattress. Munroe's internal alarm ticked up another notch. She loosed the edge on the roll of tape and pulled it upward. "Hold out your wrists."

The girl did as requested, hands forward, fingers bent into relaxed fists. Munroe moved forward, took Neeva's right wrist in her left hand, felt no twinge of caution, no indication of warning. Leaned in closer to wrap the tape to the girl's skin, and in that moment, Neeva's other fist rushed toward Munroe's eyes, a jagged edge of metal protruding, piercing upward.

Munroe jerked backward.

The improvised blade missed her jawbone by a hairbreadth. Scraped air and came back down again in an attempt to connect with her cheek, and then as quickly as the strike had come, Neeva was on her back, struggling to breathe, trying to scream, and Munroe, on top of her, stared at her own hands on Neeva's throat.

Slowly, deliberately, making her fingers move by force of will, Munroe released Neeva's windpipe, while every nerve and primal instinct cried out to win and finish the kill.

Munroe drew back.

Plucked the three-inch slice of metal from Neeva's hand and mechanically examined what appeared to have once been part of a bed frame. "The last person who tried that is dead," she said.

Munroe tucked the piece of metal into a pocket, pulled herself off Neeva, and with the girl still flat on her back, tears sliding from eyes to mattress, Munroe bound her wrists in a tight figure-eight that wouldn't allow for slippage.

Using the center of the tape as a handle, she pulled Neeva to her feet, mind replaying those fast few seconds again and again, searching for the place to fit the puzzle piece that didn't belong: This strike, like the previous fight, hadn't been the random work of panic or adrenaline or merely the actions of a girl struggling for survival. Neeva controlled her body with the assurance of someone who'd studied for years, maybe even competed professionally, but who hadn't had much of the kind of real-world experience where instinct and speed and the ability to outthink an opponent made the difference between bleeding under the blade of a sadist or not.

"I warned you not to fuck with me," Munroe said. "Even if I don't want to hurt you, I will. You should have listened."

In place of words, Neeva nodded, and Munroe patted her down, hands running underneath clothing and along seams in tempo with her irritation. She should have seen the strike coming long before it had happened, but although she'd sensed the warnings, she'd missed the signs, and this irritated her more than the strike itself. Munroe pried open Neeva's mouth, searching for any other hidden weapons. Perhaps the actress in the girl had blinded her, playing the role, not unlike Munroe's own chameleon nature that allowed her to become what people needed in order to get what she wanted.

Finding no other weapons, Munroe put fingertips to the girl's chin and, without resistance on Neeva's part, raised her head so that she could better view her neck and the aftermath of those few seconds.

For now, the damage was internal. With luck, there'd be no outward sign.

"I'm going to unlock you," Munroe said. "If you move, we'll end up playing on the mattress again and I don't think that game is very fun for you."

Neeva avoided eye contact, staring straight ahead with her jaw working back and forth as if she was grinding her teeth or readying to spit. Munroe said, "I'm doing everything I can to avoid hurting you—protecting you when I can—don't make me regret it." Then she knelt to release the shackle that secured Neeva to the chain.

Pieces of the restraint separated and dropped off, and Munroe pressed Neeva's foot. "Keep still," she said. She prodded the flesh and bone that had lain beneath the shackle. "Does it hurt?"

More than two weeks, maybe, of tugging and yanking were ample time for Neeva to bruise, cut, and harm herself—damage for which Munroe would be held responsible although she'd had nothing to do with the cause.

"It's sore," Neeva whispered, "but doesn't really hurt."

Munroe pressed once more, waited for a wince or a twitch, and receiving none, stood. The rubber coating appeared to have done its job. As the Doll Maker had said, Neeva wasn't the first to be delivered under these strange requirements. He'd had plenty of practice keeping his merchandise damage free.

Munroe picked up the backpack and led Neeva by the elbow from the cell to the hall. The girl didn't resist, but her reluctance to leave this prison was there, and why not? This was a world she'd learned to understand, if not navigate, and how much better the devil she knew than the one still to come.

In the hall, Arben blocked the path to the stairway. Neeva stiffened when she saw him. Without letting up on the pressure that moved them forward, Munroe said, "Do you know him?"

Neeva nodded.

"He doesn't speak English," Munroe said.

Neeva's voice came in a hoarse whisper. "He came into my cell most often."

"He won't hurt you as long as I'm here."

Neeva's resistance lessened some, and Munroe guided her forward, single file, past Arben, who in a show of dominance refused to move, forcing them to squeeze by to get to the stairs. He was not subtle in his groping of Neeva, and the girl shied away from him.

There were rules about not bruising the girl, but nobody had said anything that put the big tough guy off limits. Opportunity would arrive eventually, and when it did, Munroe would take it and Arben would die.

Up the stairs Neeva went, with Munroe following.

When they had passed, Arben kept close behind—far too close—so that Munroe felt his heat along her spine, felt him crawling up her neck all the way to the top of the stairs and into the main room where the gold workers toiled.

Neeva moved awkwardly, feet shuffling forward while her head turned up and to the sides, as if seeing humanity for the first time. Munroe, in no hurry, allowed her to take her time.

Arben pushed them forward. He'd stopped long enough to shut and bolt the metal door, the first that Munroe had seen or heard it close, and then coming near again, used his bulk and the invasion of space to drive Munroe faster.

With his breath once more hot against her neck, her insides rebelled; her choler rose and with it came the color change of rage.

The light of the room shifted to dull gray.

Munroe let go of Neeva's elbow.

Stopped short.

Turned as if to ask a question and brought her forehead into the right side of Arben's jaw. The crack of the hit and the hurt that followed brought on a touch of catharsis. She yearned for more, craved release in the soothing balm of pain, longed for the fight and the euphoria that a kill would bring. Even a boot to his scarred and angry face and the crunch of bone against flesh would suffice, but that would have been too obvious, and would force an immediate retaliation.

Munroe put her hands to her head and staggered slightly, every bit the apologetic player in an accident. *"Bocsánat,"* she said, backing away.

Lumani had seen the hit and he stared past Munroe with a poorly concealed grin. Arben, whatever he did or whatever his reaction, kept back far enough that Munroe couldn't feel him. The man would want to kill her now, and this was good. Rage clouded reason, hate distorted logic.

They reached the Opel, and seeing the car, Neeva stiffened.

"Don't fight it," Munroe said. "I don't want to have to hurt you again." She could feel the self-defense response running through the girl's head: *Never get in the car. Better to run. Better to scream fire and call for attention. Better to fight where there are people around.* She felt Neeva's body expand with an inhale and slapped a hand over her mouth. "I warned you," Munroe said. "And I can fix it so that you don't scream again, ever."

Neeva deflated.

Progress.

To Lumani, she said, *"Nyisd ki az ajtót,"* and he stepped toward the car and opened the passenger door. Her hand on Neeva's head for protection, Munroe helped the girl settle. With Lumani still at the door, Munroe knelt with the roll of tape and wound around Neeva's ankles the same figure-eight she'd used for her wrists, then passed the tape up between the restraints, connecting them so that the girl couldn't lift her arms to the window. Package secure, Munroe shifted the seat back to an incline so that one of the most recognizable faces on the planet couldn't be seen from outside the car. Then draped the blanket across Neeva's lap and feet, hiding what bound her.

Munroe stood, and closed and locked the door.

Lumani stepped back and grinned approval—possibly respect—killer to killer, professional to professional. Behind him Arben glared, and Munroe paused to send a smile in his direction, nothing toothy, just a taste, enough to needle and inflame his rage.

sixteen

The courtyard wasn't large enough to swing a three-point turn, so Munroe took the Opel out in reverse through the thick, gated arch while Lumani stood to the side, his eyes tracking her.

The first address, with an estimated time of arrival of less than ten minutes, had already been entered into the GPS, but she wasn't meant to stop, merely arrive, plug in the next address, and continue onward. In this way, she was forced to travel the exact micro route that Lumani had plotted. According to the GPS, they were on the outer edge of Donji Grad, old-town Zagreb, one district in a city of 800,000 that bowed outward into a mix of functional, if not aesthetic, buildings and high-rises.

Standing beneath the arch, Lumani watched the Opel pull out onto the street and then shut the oversize gate. The Doll Maker's lair disappeared, blending into a facade that was nearly identical to those on both sides of the street, one corner of each long block followed by the next, where solid walls of three- and four-story stone buildings, sidewalks, and parallel-parked cars were interspersed with ancient doors that presumably led to similar courtyards.

To the sides of the archway were window displays of two jewelry shops, gold wares on show for pedestrians passing by, each shop a different face on the Doll Maker's die. As best as Munroe could tell, he controlled the buildings on either side of the courtyard, and the only way in was through the archway. Perfect cover for moving his merchandise—once beyond the gate, what went on behind his walls was for his eyes only.

On the road, away from the building, away from Lumani and the rest of the madmen, Munroe picked up the Doll Maker's phone and turned on the screen. Neeva tilted her face toward the seat belt and closed her eyes.

Munroe's focus shifted from the road to her hand and back again, navigating traffic while flipping through text messages, scanning each and moving on through to the end of an in-box already filled with a series of addresses meant to be her immediate dot-to-dot travel instructions.

ZAGREB TO LJUBLJANA should have been a straightforward trip from one country's capital, along well-maintained highways, across green-forested countryside, over the border, and into the next country's capital. Traveling the route of a sane person, the trip would have taken two hours, not counting delays for immigration and customs purposes. But just as the last few days had resembled a paranoid's darkest delusion, so, too, did the Doll Maker's travel plan. Munroe followed farther and farther along a patchwork of roads and townships that doglegged between neatly kept fields and chalet-cum-farmhouses with laundry lines, groomed gardens, and geranium-filled window boxes.

The Doll Maker hadn't provided a reason as to why making a straight cut across borders was out of the question, but it didn't take much to figure it out. Slovenia was part of the European Union's Schengen Area, one of twenty-something countries that operated as a single state insofar as immigration control was concerned, and Croatia was not.

Inside the Schengen Area, border posts were rarely manned, and in some cases only local knowledge and a change in language or street signs indicated having passed through one country to the next. Among Schengen countries were no visa forms or passport stamps, no customs procedures or waits in line to continue beyond uniformed officials with the power to say no. But crossing from a non-Schengen country into the Schengen zone, similar to traveling between Mexico and the United States, was a different story.

Slovenia, like Hungary, Slovakia, and Poland, lay at the perimeter of the Schengen Area. Their territorial boundaries held the line, and on behalf of the entire zone, their major checkpoints were charged with the responsibility of filtering out the illegal for the rest.

Another address retrieved and entered, Munroe slid the phone into a holder on the console and reached for the backpack on the rear seat to pull out the map. Eyes shifting from road to hand, she searched until she found.

They were meant to enter Slovenia at Krasinec—barely a dot on the map—a hamlet south of Metlika, which on its own was barely a town. This far down the checkpoint food chain meant that they were certainly headed for a remote and isolated crossing: an entry point intended only for locals who lived near both sides of the border and had the plates or stickers to show for it.

The cell phone rang.

Munroe stopped at an unmarked junction, conferred with the GPS, and then picked up the phone and answered it. Lumani said, "Find a place to stop, something out of the way, and wait until I call again."

Munroe said, "Why?"

"That I said to do it should be reason enough."

"It's not."

"You have no choice."

"In that you are very mistaken," she said. "Every move I make in the next twenty-four hours is a choice. Choice, Valon, that'll affect the rest of my life. At any moment I can choose to walk away, and you know it, so if you want my cooperation, you'll give me what I want."

A hesitation, and then he said, "We have friendly eyes in Krasinec. Eyes that may or may not care what car you drive or what papers you have, but those eyes are delayed in getting to work, so as I instructed, find a place and wait until I call." Lumani hung up.

Neeva said, "What's going on?"

These words in a raspy whisper were the first she'd spoken since they'd been on the road. Munroe zoomed out on the navigation, looked at the map. "They're coordinating something," she said. "We need to pull over and wait."

She headed back in the direction of a wooded area and took

the car up a suspension-damning dirt track, caked hard with ruts left after a previous rain. Two hundred meters into the dimming shroud of forest, the track widened slightly, so Munroe turned the car, hood pointing back the way they'd come, then shut off the engine and reclined her seat.

"Now what?" Neeva said.

"We wait."

"I'm thirsty."

"I'm sure you are," Munroe said.

"Hungry, too." Neeva's words were a plaintive whisper. "But even more than hungry, thirsty. I lost track of time in the darkness, but I think it's been at least a day since I've drunk anything."

"Put yourself in my shoes," Munroe said, and turned to look at the girl. "By not feeding you or giving you anything to drink, I only have to put up with your whining and a strip of tape over your mouth deals with that. Your clothes stay clean, you can't try to bite me, and I don't have to drag my ass out of the car to hunt through whatever food they put back there."

"I promise not to spit or throw it," Neeva said.

"Oh, I know you won't throw it," Munroe said, "because I'm not cutting you loose. If you eat, it's because I put the food in your mouth. I really don't feel like fighting with you right now."

"I'll behave."

"I doubt that."

Neeva looked up, a tear of precious water trickling down her cheek. "I promise," she said.

Munroe stared at her a long while, trying to discern the girl from the actress, the truth from the lie, then sighed. She ripped a strip of duct tape, placed it over the girl's mouth, then opened her door and stepped out. She'd pawed through the ratty duffel bag on the backseat before setting out, just to confirm that she wasn't transporting drugs in addition to human cargo. Lumani had arranged for drinking water and packaged food: pretzels, candy, and the like. Nothing satisfying, just enough to push back against excuses for stopping. Munroe would get to them eventually, but Neeva had provided an opportunity to step out of the car without arousing suspicion.

She opened the hatchback, and hands roaming, measuring every lost second, searched side compartments, floorboard, and under the rear seat, hoping that unlike the radio, the emergency supplies had been left untouched.

One by one she recovered the pieces: reflective triangles, empty first-aid box, cheap-ass tire jack, and finally, what she really wanted: a lug wrench. Not as good as a crowbar for thug weapon of choice, but it would do. Munroe pulled the wrench and with some maneuvering got it beneath the front seat.

Then she grabbed a pack of crackers and a bottle of water from the bag in the back and climbed in behind the wheel. Opened the package. "Don't say a word, behave, and you can have this," she said, and Neeva nodded. Munroe inched the tape off her face.

The girl didn't fight, didn't spit, and, more important, didn't talk. The new version of Neeva made Munroe uneasy, because whatever the girl was, she wasn't broken. She drank the water in deep gulps and took the crackers in steady bites, avoiding Munroe's fingers, and when both were consumed, Munroe crumpled the packaging, tossed it into the backseat, and leaned against the headrest, hands to the base of the wheel.

Twenty minutes since the order to wait and still nothing.

Her fingers tapped out a steady Morse code of phrases, random words, a habit of deep thought that went back years, all the while wondering if Lumani, or whoever was on the other end of whatever listening devices were in the car, was wise to the patterns and if he'd understand the construct.

After another thirty minutes, the phone rang again.

"Continue," Lumani said. "After you are across the border, you'll receive new coordinates."

"What about the rest of the points toward Ljubljana?"

"Change of plans. We bypass the city."

"Why?"

He hung up and Munroe swore under her breath. If she had any hope of establishing contact with Bradford, she needed access to civilization, had to have some idea of where they were headed in the short term so that she could project forward, strategize, figure her way out of this nightmare. In one swipe, Lumani had taken away what little she had counted on.

Munroe turned the ignition key and moved the car forward, back toward Pravutina, the closest dot on the map, and the border.

The crossing was a two-lane road that spanned a bridge, Croatia on one side, Slovenia on the other: one picturesque postcard village separated from the next by a band of water and two guard posts, one on either side, each attached to the equivalent of a carport.

Neat. Clean. Quaint. Quiet.

There were no questions when they left Croatia, not even a second glance. If the border guard had gotten closer, had seen Neeva in the car, there might have been issues. Maybe. But they were leaving Croatia for Slovenia with Slovenian plates—what was there to see?

Across the bridge, Munroe stopped beneath the carport roof, and the young man in uniform stepped from his office, glanced at the car, and without pausing, turned and went back inside.

The phone rang.

Munroe answered.

"Continue on," Lumani said.

Munroe checked the windows, checked the mirrors. He was out there somewhere, he had to have seen—*someone* had to have seen—for him to have this kind of timing. "Now what?" she said, but he'd already hung up, and a few seconds later the phone began to vibrate with the alert of incoming texts.

MUNROE EASED THE car forward, and for another hour and forty minutes they drove terrain that wound over hills and occasionally through tiny postcard-perfect towns. Continued in silence until Neeva said, "I have to use the bathroom."

The words set off a wave of strategy inside Munroe's head, pieces shifting, move against move, probability played against death.

When she didn't say anything, Neeva added, "Really, really badly."

Aside from the crackers, Neeva hadn't eaten anything since she'd been doped up in preparation for the trip, and although she may have been given something to drink, it would have been minimal. Neeva knew it. Neeva knew that Munroe knew it and so had chugged an entire liter of water. One didn't have to be an actress, didn't even have to watch TV, to know that the bathroom ploy was the oldest escape tactic in the book, so either Neeva took her for a fool or she believed her acting ability trumped logic.

Munroe said, "You should have gone before we left."

Neeva's voice, still raspy from the beating her windpipe had taken earlier, went up a notch. "Please tell me you're kidding," she said. "One of the perks of being a kidnap victim in transport should be the right to use a real toilet, right?"

Munroe didn't respond.

Within Neeva's plotting was opportunity. Unless Lumani would have his precious package use a field and risk messing up her clothes, this was a legitimate reason to stop the car within at least a touch of civilization. Navigation said they still had several kilometers until the next town, and the speed limits kept the going slow. Neeva said, "Anyway, they took the bucket away again, so the only way I could have gone was in these clothes and I didn't want to stink them up."

"I can't do it," Munroe said.

Neeva drew a deep breath. "I've gotta go," she said, "and if you won't let me stop, I'll use the seat of this car. Trust me, after the crap I've put up with these past few weeks, it won't bother me one bit."

"It's not my car," Munroe said, "and I don't have to wear the clothes, so suit yourself."

It was another long minute before Neeva spoke again, this time quieter, and once more it was difficult to tell where the actress ended and the real person began. "The clothes must be important," she said. "Otherwise they wouldn't have starved me and taken the bucket away and wouldn't have gone through all the trouble to doll me up and put me in them." She paused. "Are you really sure you want me to pee in them?"

Munroe said, "If we stop, if you try to run, if something happens to you, someone I love will die and you will have been the cause of that."

"My bladder just wants a toilet," Neeva said.

Munroe took her eyes off the road and glanced at Neeva. "If because of your actions you're responsible for a killing, then I'll have no reason to keep you alive."

"Just a toilet."

Munroe reached for the phone. Dialed one of the only two numbers the phone was permitted to call and in English, though she would have preferred to avoid it and thus keep Neeva on edge, relayed the conversation.

"Can you control her?" Lumani asked.

"*That's* something over which I have no choice," Munroe said. "But if it's wiser not to stop, I don't have a problem with her using the car seat for a toilet. It's the smell I'm unsure about. Even if you have a change of clothes, only you can say how your client will react to stinking merchandise."

A long pause and then: "I'll call you back."

The mental gamble shifted chess pieces, conscience against conscience: Munroe's instinct for survival drawing on Neeva's determination to fight as a method toward her own means. If she timed it right, the immediate might save them all in the long run, painful as it would be.

Munroe put down the phone and Neeva said, "And?"

"We drive and we wait."

Neeva turned to stare out the window, and Munroe checked the navigation. Less than half a kilometer to the next town. And then the phone rang.

seventeen

DALLAS, TEXAS

Bradford pulled the Explorer into Capstone's parking spot, a haphazard straddling of the line that welcomed someone to ding his doors. Adrenaline rush followed by adrenaline dump and around again, sleep deprivation, caffeine and sugar crashes, one after the other, combined to bring him to the point he was at now: a danger on the roads and virtually worthless for making rational decisions, much less the quantitative leaps necessary for pulling together and putting sense to the massive amount of information that had been coming at him over the past days.

Walker wasn't doing a whole lot better.

Time was fleeing, and hope fading just as quickly.

By all accounts, the last hours had been a bust, a wasted opportunity and time lost for nothing except to mark two properties off their list of potential hiding places and prepare to move on to the next. From the transport depot they'd driven another thirty-five minutes to a warehouse, only to once again find no Logan, no clues, nothing but a black and deserted property without security, without vehicles, and without any sign of life.

Now, within the haven of Capstone's reception area, he buzzed the panel door open and then pointed in Walker's direction. "Office. Sleep," he said. "It's an order. We'll reconvene at eleven."

Walker deflated but didn't argue and, head hung low, followed him into the hall. She bypassed the war room for the closet to stash the vests.

Jahan turned when Bradford entered and, making eye contact, shook his head.

"I need to sleep," Bradford said. "Unless it's an emergency, I'm not available. Sam's headed to the back office, same story for her. Did you pull all night?"

"I stopped at two," Jahan said. "I'll be ready to roll whenever you are."

"Give me four hours," Bradford said, and walking away added, "Put in another call to Robertson for latents, will you? See if there's something new on the prints and samples they took at Logan's. The guy owes me, he's gotta have something." He paused, then returned to the war room and hung back in the doorway. "Anything on the lines?"

Jahan shook his head once more.

"You've confirmed they're all operational? Nothing's down?"

"Everything's working. I'll let you know if something comes. I swear."

Bradford nodded, turned again. Exacerbated by the sleep deprivation, waves of anxiety rolled in, and the first touch of fear licked his skin since the morning of the take-down, when he'd so thoroughly pushed it back.

Seventy-two hours and they still had nothing to go on but hope and fumes. If Logan was alive, they had no proof. If Munroe was pursuing whatever had brought the Doll Maker and his men calling, he'd no indication of it. And Neeva Eckridge? Time to shred the Tisdale contract, and say he'd been unable to reach the tracker the parents were after.

Bradford checked his phone again, a nervous answer to the same question he'd asked Jahan. Capstone, international as it was, had voice-mail drops on six continents and in nearly twenty countries, phone lines that would record and digitally transfer information to the war room, a fail-safe or backup for operatives who might fall into trouble and not have international phone access.

Bradford untied the strings of the bedroll and let it loose beneath the desk.

Munroe would call. If she was alive, if she needed help, if she could get to a phone, she would call, and this thought cycled through his mind as the darkness of sleep descended.

JAHAN WOKE HIM in what felt like two minutes later, and Bradford struggled to lift eyelids secured shut by grappling hooks and weighted by sandbags. He finally resorted to manually opening them with his fingers, squinting against the oxygen burn. Too many hours awake, too few asleep, and he was too fucking old to keep up a pace that had been hard enough ten years ago.

Jahan was a couple of feet from his head, squatting low and holding forward a cup of coffee.

"It's been four hours," he said.

Bradford groaned.

"You want me to come back in ten?"

Bradford reached for his phone and with eyes still half-shut checked against hope. Another sixth of a day gone without a smoke signal from her.

"Getting up," he said, and reached for the coffee. "Anything new?"

"Only that Walker's already in the war room. Unless you want to be the girl here, you best get moving."

Bradford scooted out from under the desk, juggling the coffee with balancing upward, and left the roll on the floor.

"You look like shit," Jahan said, and smiled.

"Thanks," Bradford said. Took a sip of the coffee. Winced.

Jahan studied Bradford's face, his smile morphing into something closer to that of a psychiatrist observing a man on suicide watch.

Bradford held out a palm toward him. "Enough, Mommy, I don't need this from you right now."

Jahan said, "You have a visitor."

"Visitor."

"Yeah, some girl who won't give her name or say why she's here, just asked for you, says she knows you and that you'd understand. She's got a baby with her."

"Baby."

"Kid in a stroller, maybe two years old."

The lightbulb went on.

He'd missed a call from Alexis, Tabitha's daughter, when he'd been visiting Kate Breeden in prison. Had sent Walker to check up on her but hadn't bothered to return the call, needed to do damage control and keep her as far away from this mess as possible.

She was waiting for him on the sofa in Capstone's reception area, stood and smiled when he walked through the door. Not so much happiness as relief. "I tried calling," she said.

It was easy to see Munroe in Alexis, although the hair was lighter and at closer to five foot eight, Alexis didn't quite have the height. The lanky frame was the same, as were the high, angular cheekbones and especially the eyes, and because of the similarities, at the moment it hurt to look at her. But physical was where the comparisons ended. In contrast to Munroe, who lived on the edge, off the grid, and had killed men on at least four continents, Alexis was soft and sweet and in some ways still naive.

"I've been working a tough job, missed a lot of calls," Bradford said. Knelt in front of the stroller, tickled Preston and got him laughing, then stood and guiding Alexis toward the door said, "Let's talk out in the hall."

Most who knew Munroe socially assumed from her evasive answers, and at times outright denial, that she was an orphan, or at best estranged from anyone who should matter—and for years that had been true. She still hadn't spoken to either of her parents since leaving the Africa of her birth, but during the months since Argentina, she had made the effort to reconnect with siblings she barely knew. Bradford was short on the details, but he did know that for Munroe, Alexis was a tender bond, the only one of her near relatives for whom she cared deeply.

"I can't get in touch with Essa," Alexis said. "We were supposed to have lunch day before yesterday, but she never showed and her phone goes straight to voice mail. She told me once that if I ever couldn't reach her, I should contact Logan or you, but nobody's answering. Do you know where she is?"

Bradford drew down his sigh and through the mental maze searched for the right words, the right *lie*, that would give Alexis the warning without terrifying her. "I haven't heard from her for a few days," he said, "but I'm sure she'll turn up."

"You think?"

"She's pretty badass, I think she'll be okay."

Alexis smiled, almost blushed. "I thought maybe I'd upset her, that she didn't want to talk to me anymore."

Bradford nudged her toward the elevator and pushed the call button. "Well, at least I know for sure that that's not true."

"She was very unclear about why I'd ever need to contact you; it makes me nervous now. I know there are things I don't know."

Bradford dug a business card out of his wallet and handed it to her. "I don't know how good I'll be about answering my phone during this next week," he said. "This is the office number. You think you could give a call a few times a day?"

She took the card and studied the logo, but he didn't need to be a mind reader to know that she did it as a way to buy time, to figure out how to word the questions running through her head.

"Not to sound all paranoid," he said, "just a better-safe-than-sorry-type thing, is there any way you and Preston could get out of town for a week or so? Anyplace you could go?"

The elevator arrived and Alexis didn't move, just stared at him. The doors began to close. Bradford caught them. Held them open.

"What kind of trouble is she in?" Alexis said.

Bradford inched the stroller into the elevator. She followed.

"I don't know," he said. "I really truly don't, but I am a bit concerned, and it doesn't hurt to play it safe, right?"

He stepped back and Alexis, arms crossed, glared at him until the doors began to close.

"Remember to call," he said, and when she was gone, his shoulders sagged. Because it had been Kate Breeden who'd fed information to the Doll Maker, the issue of Alexis troubled him greatly.

Jahan was waiting when Bradford returned to the reception area. "Who was it?" he asked.

"Michael's niece."

"Looks like she could have been her sister."

Bradford nodded, swiped his card to buzz the paneled door open, and said, "They're a couple of years apart or something," and Jahan cocked his head as if doing sibling math, then followed him into the interior.

IN THE WAR room Samantha Walker sat in Jahan's chair, one hand on the mouse, another around her own cup of coffee, while her head tipped up toward one of the flat-screen monitors. She scrolled through Veers Transport freight manifests.

They stood behind the chair and watched her work. From the

data she scoured, she'd clearly spotted the same incongruity in the Veers Transport warehouse that Bradford had.

"What's your analysis?" he asked.

Without turning or breaking rhythm on the mouse, Walker said, "If we discount the trafficking, it has all the earmarks of a healthy money-laundering setup."

"They do have to have a way to funnel and legitimize the payments for the girls," he said. "Freight transport is the perfect cover, especially if they're making the trip anyway."

"But *this* much traffic," Walker said. "They couldn't possibly be moving that many out of the country. Our missing-persons databases would be burning up over numbers like this. Someone would notice patterns, similarities, and begin poking around. And what we're looking at here isn't the kind of operation that throws a bag over someone's head and drags her over the Mexican border. This is serious organization and serious investment."

Jahan, who had until now remained silent, said, "No freight at the depot?"

"Not a lot," Bradford answered. "Not as much as you'd expect given the manifests, not even if they skipped the warehouse and delivered door-to-door for ninety percent of the stuff."

"The amount of traffic may be cover," Jahan said. "They may be transporting girls, but probably not on every trip. They need the miles, logs, and manifests to build the documents for a legitimate business and then to infuse the cash into the company—to wash it. Maybe some of those manifests are legitimate."

Walker said, "That just seems so clunky. Inefficient, you know? To keep an operation like this running just to cover the trafficking."

"Yeah, but it's perfect," Jahan said. "Who would look hard at something like that? Even we wouldn't have if we hadn't been pointed to it. This is the kind of thing that can operate out in the open for decades without drawing attention, and it probably pulls in enough from legitimate business to break even on its own."

Bradford shrugged. "It's a good setup for money laundering. It's a good setup for transporting human cargo. Probably both." He rested his arms on the back of the chair, his focus switching from one screen to the other. If he was right about Logan being held hostage in order to control Michael, then she was going to demand proof of life along the way. To release the choke hold so she could save herself, they needed to find Logan, find the safe house, and they were running out of time and options. He said, "Legitimate business or not, the question remains, where's the human cargo?"

"There's still the business office and house."

"I have a hard time seeing it. We're missing something."

Jahan said, "We're searching for a needle in a goddamn haystack. I'd fire myself if I even faked confidence in having found everything."

A buzzer interrupted—cue that someone had crossed the threshold of the reception area. Walker turned, began to stand, and Jahan said, "I've got it."

He left the room. Walker, returned to the monitors and Bradford shut his eyes, pulling in the essence of the conversation. Jahan returned with two bags of takeout that left the room smelling more of deli than coffee or electronics. Nodding at Walker, he said, "That's my desk, I want it back." He handed her a bag. "Get off, go eat."

He handed the second bag to Bradford.

"Talk faster than you eat, because I need to know everything you know, how it went down play by play, and then we need to get moving."

They took turns, Bradford and Walker, reliving for Jahan the details of the early morning, half-speaking suppositions and theories between shoveled bites, while Jahan recorded the facts as they knew them in threads along the whiteboard, threads that led nowhere specific and everywhere vague, threads that wound around and around until the food was finished and Bradford stood. To Jahan he said, "Suit up."

AS PER PUBLIC records, the office condo was owned by Akman, LLC, although the company's actual business purpose was as nebulous as its name. Import/export was the war room's best guess, although *of what* was still open for debate. None of the names of Akman's three primaries were connected to any of the supposed owners of Veers Transport, though according to freight manifests, Akman did considerable business with Veers and not a whole lot else.

If that on its own wasn't enough reason to go poking around,

Katherine Breeden's name was buried within old corporate records, making the general consensus that Akman was just another face to the same money-laundering and human-cargo operation.

Akman's office was in Las Colinas, on the north edge of Irving, twenty minutes up from Veers Transport, but for all intents and purposes, on the other side of the tracks, if not in another country completely. Here, stone masonry walls bordered neatly kept patches of grass, widely set apart from mirrored office towers, divided and plotted between golf-course-quality lawns and man-made ponds, with pristine strip malls and business complexes competing as prime office real estate.

Las Colinas was clean, structured, cutting-edge, respectable.

Definitely respectable.

A block before their destination, Jahan, behind the wheel in a suit and tie, nudged Bradford out of the inevitable sleep of a combat vet who'd learned to take whatever he could when he could because it was impossible to predict when there'd be more. He was awake as soon as Jahan touched his shoulder. Reached for the backpack and stepped out.

Jahan idled at the curb, waiting a few minutes to give Bradford a head start. An earpiece kept them connected, and Bradford continued on with the eyes of the world staring at his back, car after car flying by in an area where a man walking was about as common as a stray dog.

THE OFFICE COMPLEX was shaped like a digital figure-eight made out of single-story buildings, connected in units of three, and gapped by manicured hedging and driveway. Akman's unit was in the back right corner, and although the spaces fronting the business were empty, Jahan had parked two doors down.

Bradford continued the stroll forward, approaching from the far side, backpack unzipped, MP5 inside, the butt sticking out. Reached the go point. Jahan stepped from the vehicle and approached Akman's door.

Tried the handle.

Knocked.

Waited.

No response, so Bradford slowed.

Jahan returned to the vehicle, shut the door, and held an imaginary conversation on his cell phone.

Bradford continued to the business that shared wall space with Akman. The door sign said INTELISET, with office hours scripted beneath.

Bradford opened the door and went inside.

The interior was one large room with a shallow hallway off to the left that appeared to lead to a second smaller room. Five desks occupied the floor space; two were in use: one man, one woman, both young and in casual attire. Both looked up from papers and keyboards when he entered.

"I'm trying to find Akman, LLC," Bradford said.

"Next door," the guy said, head tilting toward the wall with more emphasis than volume.

"Yeah, I tried them. Door's locked and no one answers. I wasn't sure if I had the right place."

"Oh, you've got the right place," the guy said. His tone carried all the disdain and scorn of a home owner toward the jerk who let his dog crap on the lawn. "That's Akman."

"I've got a courier envelope to deliver and need a signature," Bradford said. "Any idea how they get packages?"

"Usually just collects on the doorstep," he replied, and the woman added, "Gets cleared away about once a week, supposedly by the owners. I've never actually seen them."

"Thanks," Bradford said. The guy already had his face reburied in paperwork before Bradford turned to leave. The woman offered him a smile. "Good luck," she said.

Even from InteliSet's front door, Bradford could see Akman's doorstep was free of mail, which meant either nothing had been recently delivered or someone had been by to pick it up.

Bradford bent down to tie a shoelace.

In response, Jahan stepped out of the vehicle and passing Bradford returned to Akman's door. He reached for his pocket. Bradford stood and strode in his direction. Another few seconds and Jahan had opened the door, and Bradford was beside him, then past him, first into the building, weapon drawn, scanning quickly for threat, then alarm systems, then cameras, and found nothing.

Bradford tapped on the slightly open door and moved inward

enough for Jahan, still the suited businessman waiting on the outside, to slip in beside him.

The interior was nearly identical to the office next door: one large room and a shallow hallway to the left, which intimated at a second room. There were extra windows along the right wall, a bonus of being a corner unit. The place was trashed in the way of a quickly abandoned campsite: opened food containers, used plastic utensils, a cardboard box filled with half-empty chip bags and drink bottles, and an as-yet-unopened two-liter bottle of Coke.

Furniture was sparse: a couple of floor lamps, window blinds, and a folding table to the right of the room near the windows. Laid on it were a heat lamp, duct tape, and a box of Ziploc bags, but what caught Bradford's attention, and jacked up his heart rate, was the baseball bat propped against the wall next to the table.

He nodded toward the piece of wood, and Jahan acknowledged it. Coincidence, maybe, that a bat had featured in Logan's surveillance footage.

If one was inclined to believe in coincidence.

Fuckers.

On the carpeted floor, small spots of brown flecked the multitoned Berber in a nearly invisible trail that led from the doorway toward the table. Bradford followed a few steps inward and the trail ended abruptly, about ten feet from the wall. More of the tiny flecks speckled the white walls on an area just beyond where, according to telltale streaks, a sponge, rag—*something*—had wiped the rest of it down.

Bradford signaled, finger toward the hall, and Jahan moved to the second room, using his elbow to nudge the open door farther inward. Nodded Bradford in for a look-see. Here again no furniture, only a set of copy machines. Jahan backed out, and Bradford continued to the end of the hall, to the last door, which opened to a bathroom. In the sink, bloody and torn, a match to what he'd seen on the captured surveillance, were Logan's pants.

eighteen

Through the rifle scope, Lumani tracked the gray car's approach.
Kept the crosshairs on the windshield, on the driver, as the vehicle
pulled from the road into the small gas station. Within the limited
parking area the car waited for another vehicle to move, and when
it finally did, the Opel took the empty space. Perfectly, as Lumani
had instructed: at the far edge of the building, as far away from the
fuel tanks as was possible to go, and to where, as a shooter, he could
cover the widest area.

Inside the vehicle, the occupants shifted. The Michael woman
bent and, from what movement he could see, appeared to use a tool
or a piece of metal, maybe a handmade knife, to slice the tape and
work it off the ankles of the doll package.

Inside Lumani's head sparklers tickled.

The unexpected was always part of the delivery. He planned on
it. Counted on it. Made contingencies against the unknown many
moves in advance based upon the certainty that any man skilled
enough to be pulled in for this job would inevitably believe in his
own skill enough to try to disrupt it. Lumani had never managed
a failed delivery because, in the end, no matter how skilled or how
hard they fought back, pressure applied in the right places caused
even the strongest men to fracture.

But this one? He'd watched her. Studied her. Observed what maybe even Uncle, the reader of people, had missed. This one was already fractured, and the lines between her broken pieces were not fissures but scar material stronger than whatever had once filled those spaces.

Finger resting outside the trigger guard, one eye to the scope for detail, the other pulling in the surrounding picture, he waited. Had the choice been his, Lumani would have said no to the stop, would have kept the convoy moving across the border and through Italy as quickly as possible. It was Uncle's insistence upon maintaining doll-like perfection to fulfill the wishes of an exacting client that granted this pause—a decision that ignored the inevitability of an escape attempt.

And why not? What had Uncle to lose? Lumani was on location to ensure a job well done: here to clean up whatever mess this lack of reason caused. And as always, Lumani would bear responsibility for whatever failure might spawn from the decisions of a man who took success for granted and punished for infractions that were inconsequential.

Inside the car, the Michael woman tossed the blanket to the backseat, and in anticipation of what would follow, Lumani's tension mounted, slow and steady, into low-grade anxiety, thick and sticky, coating each thought and pasting his gut. Against this he controlled his breathing and pulled into the focus of the moment.

She opened the driver's door. Put foot to pavement and turned back to the interior. Through Lumani's headpiece her voice was clear. "Don't move," she said. "Not a muscle, until I open your door."

The high-powered magnification allowed him to run along the contours of her body. He spotted the outline of the phone in her rear pocket, car keys in her hand, and although he would never be certain, it appeared she'd left all the documents inside the car, which was good. She was planning to return to the vehicle, and this meant one less uncertainty accounted for.

The Michael woman opened the passenger door, cut the tape at the doll girl's wrists, took her hand, and pulled her upward. Once the girl was standing, she wrapped an arm around her shoulders, every bit the protective boyfriend to his sickly girlfriend: a smooth strategy as far as controlling a package without drawing attention was concerned.

Together, stride linked to stride, they walked toward the rear of the building. Lumani angled, following with the rifle, waiting for the first indication that the Michael woman had chosen wrong. He'd not yet had to kill a driver before job completion and preferred this high-risk delivery not to be the first to force him to deliver the merchandise in the driver's place.

Halfway to the building, she stopped and, with her arm still tight around the doll girl's shoulders, turned so that they both faced in his direction, and with her mouth moving slightly, spoke words too low for the cell phone in her pocket to pick up. The doll girl looked up at his perch and, he could have sworn, directly at him.

Lumani froze. Movement, any movement, would only confirm what their eyesight might doubt. And then subtle, or perhaps not, the Michael woman nodded in his direction, as if affirming she understood, but more, that she accepted and approved. Against instinct, against reason and a life of service and training, against hatred and jealousy of this woman, thief of Uncle's smiles, he was pulled like a rope into the warmth of that acceptance and approval.

And as quickly as it had come, the warmth was gone.

She turned the girl, and with their backs to Lumani, they continued toward the side of the building where the restroom doors were marked, where he had told her to go. Together they entered the door to a single windowless room, the door Lumani knew would be unlocked because he'd made certain of it.

He counted time, impatience growing with each long minute of disconnect. Women always took longer in the restroom, he knew that, but this long? Sound, amplified and echoing in the small tiled room, carried back as unintelligible garble. This would have to be corrected by a new rule: Phone always on and phone always *out*.

Down the block and around the corner, Arben's car idled, waiting to follow again when the convoy started up once more.

Lumani instructed him to pull in closer.

The restroom door opened.

Lumani killed the order.

The Michael woman exited the restroom first, arm around the doll girl's shoulders as before. Together they walked toward the car in a stride that had already become routine. Lumani waited for them to look up again, almost begged for it, craving to be seen and accepted once more, but she pushed the doll girl forward.

And then it happened: a movement so quick Lumani only understood it in mental replay. Not the driver making a rush for freedom, but the doll girl.

She jerked.

Threw an elbow into her captor's face.

Knocked herself free and in the second it took for the Michael woman to recover, the doll girl was already running. Away from the gas station. Picking up speed. While the Michael woman went after her, keeping up, but not gaining. The doll girl was fast.

Lumani followed with the scope. He couldn't shoot, couldn't damage the merchandise, not as long as she was still recoverable, and he breathed against the anxiety, the mantra of imperfection, of failure and worthlessness, all winding through his head.

The doll girl changed course, down a smaller connecting street that led away from Arben, and would soon be beyond the range of Lumani's vantage. Lumani reversed out of position and, with the rifle slung across his back, hand-crawled across the clay tiles to another rooftop valley, and up again, to a perpendicular crest for an altered viewpoint.

The doll girl ran full out, hair flying, dress billowing, the Michael woman still several long paces behind. Lumani called Arben in for an intercept, gave the coordinates, and then the doll girl changed course again, another street, this one more populated, heading now toward a small restaurant patio, where groups of three and four had gathered to enjoy the late-day sun.

Too much attention.

If Arben closed in now, the focus would turn to Uncle's operation. The doll girl was the driver's problem. She would capture and control this wild animal, who, worth so much money, had caused no end of trouble. The decision was made in a half-beat of analysis, instant, decisive: strategy underscored by years of molding at Uncle's hand, and for the second time in as many minutes, Lumani killed the order to Arben. "Let the girl run," he said.

The doll girl was tiring. The Michael woman, motivated, was gaining, though at this rate and this speed there would be a full-on collision at the restaurant. Lumani began to descend, then hesitated. He needed to witness this last, because Uncle would want to know all.

The restaurant patrons turned toward the motion and the noise, jaws slackening, eyes widening as the doll girl plunged toward them, yelling—in English, of course. Lumani didn't need to hear it to know that's what the language was—stupid Americans, so big in their world dominance that they rarely had the capacity or the need for more than one language. And yet, of course, with English so universally spoken, it would be just her luck and his misfortune that someone in the crowd of this small village would understand.

The Michael woman yelled now, too, and this Lumani could hear in spite of the muffle of clothing and the overlying thud of each step against pavement.

She yelled in Italian.

The tension in Lumani's chest eased back slightly.

The chance of Italian being understood, here in this town so close to the border, was much better than English.

The collision happened in an instant and in slow motion.

Patrons struggled to stand, both petrified shock and wanting to get out of the way written on their faces. Chairs moved. Tables jerked. Beer and wine glasses fell, wetting clothes, distracting from and adding to the chaos.

The doll girl stumbled and collapsed onto the open patio, taking a table down with her. And the Michael woman was there beside her, fast enough to catch her and prevent her from falling completely.

The driver cradled the merchandise, held her tightly in spite of the thrashing, and spoke to the crowd clearly, calmly, above the girl's yelling. The audience, at first frozen and horrified, began to thaw and soften. Expressions shifted. Mouths moved. She had been understood by some who translated for the others.

Space was made. Water was brought.

The doll girl still thrashed and fought and screamed in English, begging for help so loudly Lumani could hear the pleas without the bug, even from this distance; sound, if not exact words, bouncing off walls, carrying far in the relative silence. The Michael woman leaned forward and put her mouth to the doll girl's ear, and after several seconds the flailing and the noise stopped. She stroked the doll girl's hair, held her tightly, whispering and consoling. Offered a glass of water that had been handed over, and then, gradually, tenderly, with the audience as accomplice, stood the doll girl upright and led her away.

The structured perfection in the midst of chaos heated Lumani's anxiety and sweated his body, spreading another layer of emotion inside his mind and stomach, a second coating of fear and hope: He wanted those words, whatever the Michael woman had said to pull the flame out of the fire and control it as her own.

He sucked air in greedy gulps, aware now that, mesmerized by the magic, he'd been holding his breath. With the inhale came the moldy, earthy scent of old clay tiles inches from his face, an unmistakable fragrance: same smell, other rooftops, and happier memories—if memories could ever be happy—when he'd been free to roam the streets of Dubrovnik. Idle time, an anomaly in a childhood he'd otherwise spent being handed off from one training master to the next: a chance delay, which, because Uncle didn't want him around, had meant staying with an acquaintance who didn't much care what he did with his time.

He'd run the streets in the early-morning dark with older boys, after the city with its perpetual summer party went to sleep. They'd scaled ancient walls within the coastal fortress, hopped rooftops to slide into the Franciscan courtyard and steal forbidden fruit from trees. Lumani was younger and smaller, and the teenagers allowed him to tag along because he was also faster and more nimble. They affectionately called him "Shipak." Pomegranate. Croat teenage humor that played off *Shiptari*, what the Albanians called themselves, and he, overjoyed at the acceptance, at having some label attached—any sense of belonging—whether real or not, had never bothered to correct them.

When the hours deepened and even the boys had gone to bed, Lumani had become one with the narrow alleys, wandering like one of the city's many feral cats, peering into windows to observe the intricacies of nuclear families, and at other times grabbing toeholds from stone to stone to climb into upper-story households to steal from them. Those two months were the first and only time he'd understood what it was to be a child, yet even then, at nine years old, at one with the quiet in the early-morning streets, he was already an adult in a child's body.

Lumani breathed in the clay once more, then closed down the memories.

That taste of freedom was a long time ago.

On the patio, where just a minute earlier panic had ensued, the guests reset furniture. Some returned to drinks and food, others continued in animated conversation, but all was still status quo and so Lumani skirted out of position, down and up again to where less than five minutes earlier, though it might as well have been three hours, he'd originally rested with his rifle.

He moved calmly, assuredly, to keep his breathing and pulse rate in check. The driver knew he was on the rooftop. Knew he would have had to move to follow the commotion, and if she was planning to bolt and leave the package behind, now, with the distractions and break in routine, would be that time.

He would never allow that.

She was smart. She was devious. She was talented. But not so much as he.

He raised the rifle to his shoulder for the better view and studied her face as she walked the doll girl nearer the car. Her expression shifted, as if a mask of tenderness had fallen away only to be replaced by rage and anger. By the time the two approached the gas station, her forced long-legged stride had quickened to the point that the doll girl was nearly running to keep up.

Then the driver stopped short and knelt, forcing the doll girl down with her. Picked up a shoe and handed it to the doll girl before moving on to collect the second.

Lumani noticed then that no matter that the rest of the outfit had been spared, the tights were shredded—ruined completely— large holes and lines traced from the doll girl's soles upward. They had replacements, but that would be beside the point as far as Uncle was concerned. Failure, no matter how great or small, no matter the circumstances or what successes had come with it, was still failure.

Lumani sighed and his stomach roiled while he debated, for a half moment, withholding this detail from Uncle.

There was no point to an omission.

When Arben or Tamás reported, the truth would be made known and Lumani would suffer for his silence. Better to tell now and get it over with.

Strangely, inexplicably, he hurt, and for the first time in memory, the pain was not for himself but for another: for the Michael woman whom he both hated and from whom he'd felt acknowledgment. Hurt for the agony she would surely suffer in retribution for her failure.

nineteen

LAS COLINAS, TEXAS

Physical confirmation that they'd finally picked up Logan's trail brought on the same adrenaline rush as the first crack of weapon fire in a combat zone.

Miles Bradford backed out of the bathroom doorway.

Jahan's head ticked up in acknowledgment, and they tag-teamed the return, left everything undisturbed, and didn't bother relocking on the way out.

In the vehicle, moving away from the office as quickly as was legally permissible, Jahan said, "What the hell? Why go through the trouble of wiping down the walls only to leave the pants in the bathroom?"

"Hurry, maybe. Or because they can come back and get the pants without worrying about leaving permanent DNA evidence."

"Maybe they forgot them," Jahan said. "Incompetent idiots, although they took whatever they'd had covering the floor. Tarp, I think, from the size of the area."

Bradford rubbed palms over eyes. While he and Walker had been scoping out Veers Transport and the nearby warehouse, chances were Logan had been stashed at the office, and they'd missed him by only a few hours. "Bread crumbs," he said. "A nice little fuck-you gift because they know someone's coming after him."

"You?"

"Yeah, who else?"

Jahan said, "If he's being kept on the move, we could play musical hiding places for days and still not catch up."

Bradford drew a breath and mentally rewound. Started from the beginning. Tore at the facts, the threads, allowed them to unspool and haphazardly pile. After a long while he said, "Based on the video footage, he's not in any condition for them to keep moving him. I think they just held him at the office temporarily."

"How so?"

"That wasn't the way station," Bradford said.

"Why take him there at all, then?"

"I don't know. Logistics, maybe?" Bradford pointed right. "Stop at that gas station, will you? There's a pay phone." Pay phones: In a world of cell phones and wi-fi, they were a whole hell of a lot harder to find than they used to be.

Same as he'd done after finding Logan's place trashed and bloodied, Bradford called in an anonymous tip. The chance of latents getting pulled out of Akman was definitely higher than in Logan's place, but still iffy. At the least, the blood should match—assuming that with no obvious sign of foul play in the Akman office, the two city police departments would connect the dots in the first place.

Jahan, as if reading Bradford's thoughts, said, "One of us could lay the map out for them, take the heat to see what they come up with."

Bradford shook his head. "I can't afford to lose anyone right now, and even if the prints do ping back, knowing who they belong to isn't going to get us any closer to Logan."

"We try the house?" Jahan said.

Bradford nodded. Last of the possible places to find Logan was the four-bedroom house, another fifteen minutes north. His gut told him going there would be a waste of time, because wherever the trafficking victims were stashed between buyers, it wasn't going to be a house—at least not in the kind of neighborhood they were headed. But riding one wave of burnout after another meant he wasn't thinking straight and so the need to be thorough overrode instinct.

Valley Ranch was to residential what Las Colinas was to business: a master-planned development, new and clean and cookie cutter, further up the tracks and a continent away from the bare and toy-strewn yards that had backed onto Veers Transport. Jahan navigated turn by turn through streets of two-story brick facades, and tightly clipped lawns, yards treed with young switches that might, in a decade or two, provide some relief against the searing summer heat.

A block from their target, Jahan slowed. "Think they're in?"

"Doubt it."

Jahan said, "Front door, back door?"

"You're in a suit," Bradford said. "You get front. You can be Jehovah's Witness."

Jahan stared at him for a half-beat, turned back to the road, and said, "That's fine, but you wear the tutu if we get anywhere near a dance studio."

In response to the imagery, against his will, against the pressure inside his chest, the corners of Bradford's lips turned up.

Jahan stopped the vehicle at the alley entrance. Bradford got out. "Meet you halfway," he said, and stared after the SUV just long enough to ascertain where it went so he could find the getaway car in a hurry if needed. Then he turned and jogged the length of the alley to the back of the house, where an eight-foot board-on-board shielded the yard from prying eyes.

Bradford tapped randomly on the fence, testing for a bark, a growl, something to indicate a guarded area, but as expected, he was answered by silence. Veers Transport. Akman. Trucks. Slave trafficking. Not a whole lot to point to the kind of people with lives stable enough to provide even the basic nurturing needed to keep a yard dog alive, and there was nothing like a starving animal left outside, howling from hunger, to draw unwanted attention from the community.

Bradford tried the gate.

Locked.

No trees or shrubs peeked out from behind the fence planks, and the two-car garage door was shut. Using the back fence as leverage, he pulled himself eye level to the narrow slits of glass that functioned as garage windows. The inside was bare. No storage. No vehicles.

From his ear piece came Jahan's voice, confirming approach.

Bradford waited for the knock, and when it came, hoisted up

over the fence, using notches in the gate for footing. Dropped into a crouch and waited again. The yard was overgrown grass with a weather-worn umbrella table and two chairs on an uncovered patio. Cigarette butts littered the area. Windows and a back door faced the yard and were covered by closed blinds.

Another knock in Bradford's earpiece.

Silence.

Doing this the right way, he should have done more than put his ear to the glass to check for occupants, but hyped up, brain fried, running against the clock, and taking Logan's bloody pants as a deeply personal insult, Bradford moved as quickly as possible, out of the gray area of trespassing into full breaking-and-entering.

He tried the door.

Secure.

Waited for Jahan's third knock, and when it came, with no sound or response returned from inside, aimed boot at door, and kicked it in.

He didn't have Jahan's skill in scrubbing locks, and what the hell, whoever had Logan knew he was on the hunt, so it was no big secret there. He moved into the house a second before Jahan opened the front door.

Weapon drawn, Jahan cleared the foyer as Bradford took the den.

Somewhere in the house a chime beeped, signaling an armed keypad waiting for input. Forty to sixty seconds tops before the master alarm went off. At best, another two minutes after that before the alarm company sent the police to the house.

"Your left," Bradford whispered. "I'll take the right."

Jahan stepped out of view.

Door by door, Bradford moved through the house.

The place was lived in, every room used, the whole of it functional and perfunctory, missing a touch of permanence in the transient home-but-not-really of a dorm. Bradford made it down the hall and through two bedrooms before the alarm screamed, an ear-splitting howl that would surely be heard several neighbors down.

Most would be at work.

Through the master and into the bathroom, Bradford continued, and then the house phone rang: alarm company call number one. He backed out the way he'd come, scanning floors and walls, eyes roaming over the few furniture pieces, counting seconds in his head.

Didn't want to be anywhere near the place when the patrol car arrived.

Here, like at Veers Transport, nothing pointed to Logan or a way station, and Bradford, brain in the overdrive of frustration, said, "Let's move." Was on his way to the rear of the house as Jahan's footsteps worked toward him; out the back door at the same time Jahan closed the front. Outside, the house alarm was audible but not as ear-shattering as it had been.

Door to patio to yard to fence, Bradford went up and over the gate and then strolled down the alley, the opposite of run, head down, as if not seeing his face would make any difference if one of the neighbors was asked to point him out of a six-pack.

At the road he turned away from the house, kept walking, eyes to the pavement, until the rev of the engine caught up with him. Bradford climbed into the SUV and latched his seat belt. Jahan tossed a lump of leather into his lap. "They seem to like wallets," he said.

Bradford flipped the billfold open and, seeing Logan's ID with the one-of-a-kind first and middle name combo, shut it again.

Sherebiah Gospel Logan.

"Everything's there," Jahan said. "Except for the cash if there'd been any, and I figure there was—probably why they brought it back in the first place."

"They always take the cash," Bradford said. "My guess is the smirking guy went out on the plane and we're dealing with a few levels down. Thugs more than thinkers."

"You still think they'll keep him in one location?" Jahan said. "Because if he was my trophy and I knew someone had the drop on me—and I would have known about four minutes ago—I'd already have him on the move again."

"What if you had him in a place you were certain he wouldn't be found? Certain because you'd been hiding in plain sight for years and nobody had noticed?"

Jahan shrugged. "That might be different. Would depend on the place. So far we haven't come across anything like that."

"Because we're still shooting in the dark," Bradford said. "I don't think he was ever at the house. Just the wallet." He shook his head, trying to shake the fog, feeling instead the same itching frustration that had been tugging at him since the early-morning foray, something he'd overlooked and couldn't quite pin—a very clear and simple unknown inside a big red circle, tapping at the periphery of his consciousness, waiting to be noticed, but which he couldn't find through the haze of exhaustion.

Bradford reached for his phone to reactivate sound and vibration before checking in with Walker but instead gaped at a list of missed calls and texts from the war room. Fighting back the rush of panicked excitement, voice strained and with far too much vibrato, he said, "The phone drop in Italy triggered."

"When?" Jahan said. "Is it her? What's the message?"

Bradford brushed him off in favor of dialing Walker. "Drive," he said, "to the office." He was connected to the war room before Jahan had time to punch the gas.

Thumb to one ear, phone to the other, Bradford blocked out Jahan's surge into traffic and the resultant horn blasts. Somewhere in the distance, police sirens wailed.

"Slow the fuck down," Bradford said. He'd meant the instruction for Jahan, but Walker slowed as well, and struggling as he was to make sense of her garbled talk, he was glad for it.

She was speaking English, but the words were crazy. He had her repeat everything and said, "We'll be there in thirty minutes." Before his thumb even reached the end button, Jahan said, "Was it her?"

"The recording ran for a full three minutes," Bradford said, "and then shut off. There's no talking, just ambient noise."

"But the digital transfer came through?"

Bradford nodded. "Seems like. She said there didn't appear to be any technical problems."

"Ambient noise?"

"Yes."

"She describe it?"

"Yeah, wind and humming, and occasionally arrhythmic thumping, like going over speed bumps. She thinks the call was dialed from inside a moving car."

Eyes to the road, Jahan said, "Speed bumps." Paused. Smiled. And then he chuffed. Gurgled a choking sound, the beginning of one of his suppressed laughs, as if he was in on a private joke, a slap-happy sound that wouldn't have been nearly as infuriating if they weren't both so drunk on caffeine and adrenaline burnout.

Bradford glared. Oblivious, Jahan chuckled again. When there was a break in traffic, he turned to catch Bradford's eye and instead caught the mood, and the laughter stopped. "You don't see it, do you?"

Silence.

"Oh, man." Jahan sighed. "You need sleep. Okay, think," he said. "You put Michael at a table and you give her a problem. Something to chew on, what does she do?"

When Bradford didn't answer, Jahan tapped the steering wheel with his thumb. *Thump thump* pause *thump*.

"Aw, shit," Bradford said and, unable to help himself, smiled—almost laughed. He picked up the phone again and said to Jahan, "You're a fucking asshole. You know that, don't you?"

Jahan nodded. "You're welcome."

Bradford redialed Walker.

"Morse," he said. "The rhythm is Morse. No, I don't care if it's difficult to distinguish from the background, that's what it is. Break down the recording, filter through the elements. Do what you can, Jack will take over as soon as we get there."

PAYING MORE ATTENTION to his phone than to where he was going, Bradford stumbled and nearly tripped over two days' worth of boxes sitting in the middle of Capstone's reception area: just another day in the endless slew of mail delivery for his boys abroad. However sexist it might be, Walker was way better at keeping the front office organized than any of the guys, and that she was pulling double duty elsewhere was showing here, big-time.

Bradford shoved the largest offending box with his foot and moved beyond it to the wall opening Jahan had already passed through.

The door closed behind him with a solid click.

Walker was waiting on the other side, in the hallway, a piece of paper in her hand, nervous energy buzzing around her, bouncing on her toes in a way that made a mockery of her unwashed, unruly hair and the dark circles under her eyes.

"It's her," Walker said. "It's gotta be. If I captured it right, it's Michael, for sure, for sure."

Bradford took the paper. "Coffee much?" he said, but his heart pounded so fast and heavy he felt his skin might burst, and his hands shook with the effort to hold himself together. He leaned into the wall, was forced to hold the note with both hands to keep steady enough to read Walker's block printing: ALIV FND LOGN IN OFC R HSE FND LOGN SAV LOGN

Bradford took in air, slow and steady, until no more would seep in. Stared at the paper. Saw through it, past it. Held that breath until his lungs burned, then gradually let it out. Jahan reached for the note, took it from him, and gave Bradford's shoulder a gentle jab. Then together, without a word, he and Walker turned and wandered toward the war room, leaving him standing there alone, staring at the reception wall, his mind replaying the words on the page over and over.

The last three crazy days tumbled headlong into a long stream of movement that blended one moment into the next and made a laughingstock of time. It wasn't until the door blurred and Bradford ran his hands over his eyes and pulled them back wet that he realized he was crying.

Pressure release.

Relief in knowing she was alive.

That she'd found a way to communicate.

That there was still hope and the clock was still ticking.

That she'd seen proof of life.

That he'd been right to focus his energy on tracing Logan.

Bradford dragged his shirt across his face, blew imaginary cigarette smoke toward the ceiling, waited awhile for the nausea to settle, then straightened and followed the others to the war room.

Jahan was at the desk, headphones to his ears, and Walker, arms crossed, stood beside him. Pen in hand, Jahan juggled jotting notes on a pad with tweaking settings with the mouse. Another notation, and Jahan put down the pen, handed the pad to Walker, and taking notice of Bradford, took off the earphones. "We're good," he said. "There's other stuff, but I can't make it out, either."

"Can you trace the number?"

"Yeah, but will it do us any good? She's obviously not in a place where she can talk, so there's no reason to call back. And it's safe to assume she's in Europe."

Bradford shrugged. "Just in case," he said, then he sighed, sank onto the sofa, and stared at the whiteboard while Jahan and Walker and their hushed discussion became white noise in the background.

Find Logan. Save Logan.

Office or house.

Munroe was handcuffed by Logan, as he'd expected, but her proof of life hadn't come within the last three hours. Not if she'd seen him in a house or an office.

Office.

Akman.

Had to have been.

With the table and the duct tape, the wooden bat and the Ziploc bags.

Which would have explained why they'd taken him there in the first place. They'd needed a place to film without giving away anything that would lead to the way station.

Way station.

Logan.

Bradford lay back on the sofa, head to one side, feet to the other, willing himself past the exhaustion, trying to grasp that intangible thing he'd missed, the nameless thing that whispered taunts inside his head.

Warehouse.

Transport depot.

Office.

House.

None of their digging had turned up anything else. Was it possible that the way station was buried so deep that Kate Breeden had never touched it, that because of its disconnect to everything else, it essentially became invisible to the war room?

Invisible.

Bradford swung his legs off the couch, sat upright.

Visible.

Walker and Jahan stopped talking and turned to face him.

"The cameras," he said.

Jahan's face creased with the same psychiatrist-to-suicide-patient expression he'd worn this morning.

"The only place there were cameras or any kind of semi-serious security setup was at Veers Transport," Bradford said. "And the cameras didn't point in, they pointed out."

Walker's mouth had opened and shut again. Arguments were already tumbling and readying for formulation, but she held them back.

"The way station," Bradford said, and he stood and strode to the board. Tapped the thread for emphasis to explain his train of thought. "We weren't able to turn up anything else because there isn't anything else. We still haven't found their hiding spot, because it was right in front of us—but not really."

He was talking nonsense. He could see it on their faces.

"Look," he said. "The only place we've seen the potential for any serious form of security is at Veers, and there the cameras point out, not in. There's nothing on the inside, everything's out. The security isn't there to keep an eye on the freight, it's there to watch the lot. We haven't found the way station because it's mobile." Bradford grabbed a pen. Erased a thread on the board. Filled it back in. "We're looking for at least one special truck, maybe more. The lot had a few, but security was lax because *the* truck wasn't there."

Walker uncrossed her arms.

Jahan leaned back in the chair and, with his feet solid on the floor, began the swivel. He was thinking. Processing.

Walker said, "If Logan was there, if anything contraband was there, we would have seen a whole lot more people. Tighter security."

"Exactly," Bradford said. "He wasn't there, they had him at the office. We've got proof he was at the office, we just don't know for how long or when they moved him." He paused. "I'll put money on it," he said. "We go back to Veers and there's going to be another truck in the lot. That's our target."

Jahan said, "And if it's not there?"

"Then it's mobile and we need to pull vehicle records. Everything they have, and then we need to track down each and every one of them, because one of those trucks is the way station."

The room was silent again but for the squeak of Jahan's chair.

Walker, in her own form of agreement, said, "The gates and

wire fencing alone would be enough to keep vandals off the trucks. There's no other reason for them to put security on that lot unless they keep something on it worth protecting."

"It works for me," Jahan said. "And it's not like we have any other tails to chase."

"Who goes?" Bradford said.

Walker looked toward Jahan, and he back up at her. To Bradford she said, "We all do."

twenty

PROVA, ITALY

Hands on the wheel, stolen phone hidden beneath her thigh, Munroe tapped her thumbs in random rhythm to thought, parsing kilometers, counting minutes through the silence while the sun made its final stretch across the sky.

Inside the Schengen zone, they'd transferred from Slovenia to Italy, one country to the next without a hiccup of notice, winding a sort of parallel to E70, the intercontinental route that began in Georgia, paused in Turkey at the Black Sea, picked back up again in Bulgaria, continued on past Croatia and Slovenia, into Italy, through France, and finally Spain.

Whatever the highway might have been, the trip she was confined to consisted of country roads, two-laned and often empty, except when they passed with irregularity along the edges of, or completely through, small towns: a dot-to-dot that had put her once in the path of *carabinieri*, military police, and once the *polizia*, state police, both of whom, submachine-gun-toting, were known for pulling cars aside at random. For now, there was no point in worrying over it. If disaster struck, then she would face it, not before.

Countryside, fields, hills, and townships came and went, street signs and license plates had long since transferred from Slovenian to Italian, architecture and landscaping subtly changed in ways that spoke of new borders and new territory, all of it a peripheral blur while memory loops of Logan, surrogate brother and star-crossed soul mate, morphed into images of him beaten and bloody: a consuming nonstop replay against the windshield that poked and prodded at nightmares, threatening to awake from sleep the whispered voices she thought she'd silenced.

Munroe glanced at the GPS.

Soon enough there would be another junction and the female voice, bossy and knowing, would kick in with instructions and provide another opportunity to mask the dialing on her stolen treasure.

They were now two hours inside Italy, and although Munroe had made several attempts, it had been a half hour since her last successful connection. The battery would eventually die, the theft would eventually be discovered, the tenuous link to Bradford permanently severed, and she hoped only for time, that one luxury of which she had so little.

She'd managed five messages so far, all of them explicit if the Morse could be deciphered through the background noise: She needed the choke chain off her neck, needed Logan found and freed, and had warned the war room against trying to return contact unless Logan was safe. But everything became pointless if Bradford wasn't able to discern her message from the noise.

From the backseat, Neeva said, "I'm hungry," and Munroe ignored her as she had since shoving her into the car at the gas station those few hours earlier. No matter that Munroe had the phone now, or that she'd allowed Neeva the opportunity to run so as to obtain it, the girl was not blameless in whatever punishment would surely follow.

It had been risky to let her get so close to a crowd, but being kept away from the cities as they were, it had been the only way to get hold of a phone. Munroe had counted on human nature, that desire of the mind to believe what was most palatable, the capacity to block out and then fill in the blanks and more readily accept a story about a grieving sister just receiving word of a lover's suicide, than that the screaming woman in front of them, comforted by the nice young man, was a sex-trafficking victim.

Human nature had come through, but one escape was all she

could bear. As a message intended to prevent another run for freedom, Munroe had put a knee to Neeva's stomach and, against her struggle, pressed thumbs to carotids until the girl had passed out.

To fight, to go down swinging, afflicting damage, however small, in recompense for your own suffering, was one thing; it was another entirely to be forced into the helplessness of oblivion. The difference, psychological and terrifying, was a lesson in survival Munroe had hard-earned. She had re-bound Neeva, put her on her side, and tucked the blanket tightly around her, all of it fixed within the time it took the girl to fully regain awareness.

Hours since, and there'd been no word from Lumani, not even after she'd pointed him out on the rooftop to Neeva, and additionally, only silence from the Doll Maker—she didn't know when, but the promise of retribution in return for her supposed failure would certainly be fulfilled.

In the hypnotic hum of wheels against the road, Logan moved across the windshield again, picked up a cue stick, smiled, and pointed to an empty pocket; stepped through the door into the night and mounted a Ducati; plunged beside her in a BASE jump off New River Gorge Bridge; and wrested the oxycontin pill bottle out of her hands when self-medicating seemed to be the only way to deal with the trauma that had sent her running from equatorial Africa to the United States, those many years ago.

Against the glass, battered and bleeding, in a living mirage that refused to plead or beg, Logan nodded, confirming the bond that tied one outcast to the other, and with her eyes roving among GPS, the road, and the small town on the near horizon, Munroe slipped fingers between thigh and seat for the phone.

The first car in several kilometers approached and passed with headlights on. Dusk was fast approaching. Unless word from the Doll Maker's people came otherwise, they would push through the night to wherever the final destination might be.

Munroe gauged distance on the navigation screen and took her foot off the gas to time progression toward the approaching traffic exchange. Nudged the phone from beneath one leg to the V between them, waited for the mechanical female voice, and when it came, punched the digits she'd been required to memorize as part of Capstone's induction process. She worked by feel more than sight, taking her eyes off the road only for an occasional stolen glance and to confirm she'd entered the numbers correctly.

Munroe hit send and shifted her leg back over the phone long enough to mute the short recording that would answer, counted seconds, and then nudged the phone out and tapped her fingernail against the side of the casing in the same deliberate shorthand she'd used for each call. The precautions were tedious and time-consuming, but in these hours of intermittent dialing they'd appeared to prevent detection.

From the back Neeva said, "I really am hungry. One pack of crackers in over a day is a starvation diet." Munroe had positioned the girl with her head directly behind the seat so she couldn't see the phone, and as such wouldn't—through ignorance or petulance—blow what little chance they had for survival, and this had also made it easier to ignore the occasional requests for food and water.

Munroe paused in the tapping and glanced at the phone. "I can't feed you," she said, though she spoke for Bradford's benefit. "We can't stop without approval, and in case the sniper on the rooftop didn't tell you anything, we're being followed and guarded."

In response, silence.

Hands tight on the wheel, Munroe willed Neeva to continue the conversation, to say something, anything, to provide a background of normalcy that would allow her to articulate more detail.

Instead there was a sniffle.

Munroe ran a mental reconstruction, prepared her own backup, readied to speak it, but Neeva started first. Tears in her voice, the girl said, "Can you at least ask?"

Actress or not, it didn't matter, the words were perfect.

"A little fasting won't kill you," Munroe said. "I don't expect it will be more than five or six hours if we continue to push through the night, midmorning our time if we stop for rest. After that, you're no longer my problem and you can whine for food from whoever takes you next."

Munroe stole another glance at the phone. Two minutes and fifty seconds. The voice drop would allow recording for three minutes and then cut off. She killed the connection and slid the phone back under her leg. Everything she would have articulated on her own through more hours of dialing had been covered by those minutes.

This would be her last attempt at contact until Logan was safe or the girl delivered, and that would certainly help extend battery life.

From behind, Neeva's hushed crying picked up intensity, the first true tearful breakdown since the beginning of the ordeal, every bit about it genuine and heartrending. Empathy threatened to well from within and overcome reason. Munroe punched the emotion down, fist to rising dough, until the compassionate lump was small and easier to control.

Neeva's sniffles grew louder, more frantic, and in counterpoint Munroe more frustrated, more angry. This journey was *that which must be done to stop the hurting.* Eyes ahead, she held her silence. In order of priority, there was Logan, and that was all.

Neeva's crying went up another notch. Munroe reached for the phone—Lumani's phone—and dialed.

He picked up on the first ring.

"I'm stopping for five minutes," she said. "I need to shift the package to the front seat and give her food."

Lumani said, "No."

"Don't push me."

"If you do this," he said, "and she runs again, Logan will die." His voice had an edge to it that under other circumstances she would have marked as concern.

"She won't run," Munroe said.

A long pause, and Lumani said, "It's on your head."

"Understood," she said, knowing more from Lumani's words than anything he could have consciously allowed: The best of the Doll Maker's men was the weakest link in the chain.

Neeva continued to sniffle the stuffed-nosed, puffy-faced sound track of tears. Munroe slowed and pulled off to the side where field met road-fill, which in turn met road. Hit the emergency lights, then stepped out and around the front of the car to the passenger's-side rear door.

She tugged the blanket off Neeva and said, "Show me your hands."

Neeva shifted, struggling against the odd angle, and with one shoulder twisted, held her wrists forward and as high as possible.

With the improvised scrap of metal blade, Munroe cut her loose, reached for a hand, and pulled her upright. "Scoot over," she said, "don't move, and whatever you do, don't wipe your nose on your sleeve."

Wordless, still sniffling, Neeva nodded. Munroe handed her the blanket. "Use that," she said, and Neeva reached for it, rubbed it along her face, and in the process of drying her eyes and blowing her nose, smeared and smudged mascara and took off most of her makeup.

Munroe sighed.

One more arbitrary act of failure for which someone would pay a price.

She fished along the floor for the items she'd thrown aside during the tussle and snagged the strap of the bag with food and water, pulled it out of the car, reached a hand toward Neeva, and said, "Come."

Hobbled, and with the blanket clutched tightly and trailing behind, Neeva slid along the backseat bench to the door and swung her legs to the ground. Munroe helped her into the front seat and handed her the food bag.

"Help yourself and don't get dirty," she said. "And don't drink anything because there's no way we're making another bathroom stop."

Neeva nodded, still sniffling, though the tears had mostly stopped.

Before Munroe had shut the door, the girl was already digging through the bag, pulling out a packet of dried fruit. Once more behind the wheel, Munroe checked the rearview mirror. Faint in the twilight, forty meters back, without headlights and almost to the point of being invisible, another car had pulled off the road.

They'd been stopped for four minutes.

She studied the reflection, searching out shape, begging for make, model, and color. Instead she found only shadow.

Emergency flashers off, Munroe pulled back onto the road. In the rearview, the second car vanished completely; headlights never powered on, she never found it following.

Neeva finished the bag of fruit, fished out crackers and ate those, too, and kept going until the bag had been mostly emptied. She took a swig of water, just a swig, recapped the bottle, put everything back in the bag, and shoved it down on the floor beside her feet.

"Thank you," she said, and Munroe nodded.

Hands folded, demure and ladylike, in her lap on top of the blanket, which had absorbed the crumbs and spills, she said, "How much longer?"

"I don't know," Munroe said. "If we stay on these roads we've got about another hour until we reach Verona, but after that I'm not sure."

"You know," Neeva said, and her voice dropped an octave into that same husky whisper that had become her trademark on film, "maybe we could run away together." She ran her fingers caressingly over the blanket and then readjusted the top of her dress, smoothing out the wrinkles over her chest. "Or, you know, at least we could make a pit stop—something that would take the edge off. We've been driving for an awfully long time—they should let us have that at least, right?"

Had the situation been anything else, Neeva's antics would have been funny. "I'm not here to be your friend," Munroe said, "and put your boobs away, I'm not interested."

"You don't find me attractive?"

"You're a stunning girl, Neeva, but no, I'm not attracted to you."

The navigation kicked in turn by turn as they passed through a small village and continued along a road that would have surely been scenic in daylight. Eventually, Neeva broke. "Are you gay?" she said.

Munroe checked the rearview. "No," she said. "Not gay."

Neeva reached toward Munroe, traced her index finger along the back of Munroe's hand. Munroe resisted the urge to smack her away, and with the lines of her mouth set grimly said, "Cut it out, Neeva, I'm not interested."

Neeva batted her eyelashes with the look of a wounded child and, with Munroe's refusal to acknowledge the display, crossed her arms and huffed back into her seat. Arms tight against her chest, she tipped her head against the window and finally said, "What is it about me you find unattractive?"

Munroe forced back a bark of laughter. She wanted to dislike the girl. Would prefer to see her as weak or stupid because that would make resentment more emotionally palatable, but she couldn't find it in her.

"You're just not my type."

Neeva sulked. "I've never heard that one from a straight guy before. What's your type?"

"Tall, dark, and handsome," Munroe said, and turned from the road just long enough to catch a glimpse of Neeva's scowl.

"You said you're not gay."

"I'm not." And then with a smirk that welled from an evil sort of satisfaction, Munroe said, "I'm a woman, and I like guys."

The girl's hands dropped to her lap and she stared, mouth formed into a tight O, while behind those baby blues the world appeared to shift. Like a snake uncoiling, everything about Neeva relaxed, as if, in spite of herself, she wasn't able to see a woman as the enemy, as if what she now knew changed *everything*—almost as if because of this one revelation the fight had left her.

After several kilometers of silence, Neeva said, "Why?"

"Why what?"

"Why everything."

"I don't have the patience for games," Munroe said. "Say what you want or, better yet, don't. I like the quiet."

"Why are you dressed as a man?" Neeva said. "Why do you act like . . ." She paused. "Why do you act like . . . like one of them?" Her voice rose, challenging and accusatory. "*Them*," she said again. "Where women aren't human, aren't people, just things—objects. *Them*." She jabbed a thumb toward the rear window, where surely one of the Doll Maker's men followed unseen. "Oh, they'll show you a real man. They'll turn you into a real woman. They'll fuck you hard, you'll *want* it, but what you want never actually matters because everything is about their own ego. *Them*." Neeva stopped for air; a long, greedy inhale. "Why?" she said. "Why would you—a woman"—she spat out the word—"you who should know what it feels like to be called a cunt and a bitch and a whore just because you voiced an opinion, to be told you're fat or ugly as a way to make your argument worthless, that you're stuck-up, repressed, and in denial of your true feelings when you find *them* repulsive. Why would you be one of them? What's *wrong* with you?"

Neeva's words added weight to a history of scars the girl would never know, and cut deeply across time and continents, dragging Munroe in the emotional direction she wanted least to travel. When she didn't answer, Neeva turned away toward the window.

Another few kilometers down the road, Munroe said, "I'm not one of them. I never have been, never will be. I'm only here to save a life."

"I'm a life."

"It's a fucked-up choice, isn't it?" And then, to change the subject before the conversation went any closer to that long-dormant mental place where the lines between want and savagery blurred Munroe said, "Why don't you get some rest?"

Neeva didn't bite. "What about the man disguise?"

"A man and woman traveling together doesn't attract the same attention as two women," she said. "As a man, I make us less visible."

Neeva faked a laugh, folded her hands in her lap, and head still tipped against the window said, "In that case, why not just send a man?"

Munroe smiled. To herself. Humorously. Regretfully. At the history of survival and instinct that had made her who she was, and the unique set of skills both inborn and man-made that, once combined, had both blessed and very nearly destroyed her life. "None of their men can do what I can do," she said.

twenty-one

Under the fluorescent lights of the gas station overhang, Munroe refilled the Opel's tank. The proprietor stared out from beyond the glass of the mom-and-pop-style convenience store with arms crossed, as if he was prison guard and she the only convict in this otherwise empty station.

She had no cash, no credit, nothing with which to pay for the fuel she was taking, only the word of Lumani and the instructions he'd given when he'd called ahead. She followed the details exactly, certain from the moment she'd reached the location and had kissed the lips of the nozzle to the mouth of the tank that the man-boy was out there, perched somewhere in the dark with the scope to his eye, watching through the crosshairs.

Munroe turned from proprietor to pump and, seeing without really seeing, watched the numbers on the display click upward. Neeva, who'd drifted off an hour earlier, hadn't woken when they'd stopped, making it possible to handle the refueling without having to also guard against another episode of violence. The girl had slept a good deal since her failed bolt for freedom, and with any luck, she would stay under for a while.

The shut-off kicked in and, the tank full, Munroe replaced the nozzle.

In the window, the station owner still stared. Munroe tightened the gas cap and then stared back. He uncrossed his arms and waved her on. She knew the look: He didn't want her inside, didn't want to risk conversation or questions; wanted her gone as quickly as possible; a man caught up in the machine, blackmailed and browbeaten into submission just as she was.

She stepped around to the driver's door and, once more, traded the cool of outside air, the taste of freedom, for the stale of the four-wheeled prison. Made yet another turn of the ignition, and Neeva slept on; another return to the dark and the roads and the trance-like hum of wheels against the pavement.

Along the empty kilometers, routing from one address to another, one random sleepy town after the next, Neeva's words returned.

The rant about the *them*.

The obvious self-defense training.

The vicious refusal to quit even when she was outclassed.

The complete change when the girl realized she wasn't dealing with a man—all of it part of a history that hadn't shown up in any of the documents the Tisdale parents had forwarded to Bradford's office, and Munroe puzzled over whether the catalyst had happened when the girl was still Grace Tisdale or after she'd become Neeva Eckridge.

Then she pushed aside the thoughts. Didn't want to know, didn't want to care.

The primal urge to fight, to win, to survive, was alive and well, but so was the darkness, licking at the edges, begging to come out and play again.

She really, really, didn't want to care.

The emotional waters were muddied enough as they were.

Munroe reached for the Doll Maker's phone, flicked on the screen, glanced at it, and shut it off.

Still nothing.

In the hours since Neeva's run to the restaurant, the only contact from Lumani had been instructions for refueling, and although Munroe had listened for some hint in his voice, some betrayal of what retribution she might expect, there'd been nothing on which to draw.

The jolt, when it finally arrived, came not by way of a phone call but as an image downloaded to the phone. An alert so jarring that Neeva twitched awake when it sounded. Munroe took her eyes off the road longer than they'd any right to be, eased off the gas, and stared at the backlit screen. Neeva, yawning, shifted, turning first to look at Munroe's face and then, following Munroe's gaze, to the glow of the phone. Munroe reached for the vibrating piece, bracing for what the damage to Logan might be. She stared at the picture that filled the screen, stared at lifeless eyes. Two shots to the head, little red rosebuds an inch apart, flowers of death that never blossomed but instead trailed threads of color down the placid face.

Time imploded.

Then stopped completely.

Darkness descended.

The air trembled.

Ruptured.

And the inner voices, symbols of a vicious past that had been silent for nearly two years, violent pressure that had been tamped down and muted, came rushing forth in a torrent of madness. Somewhere in the distance, car headlights penetrated the blackness and beside her came screaming, loud and feral, and claws like a cat's pulling and tearing at her right arm.

And then no movement whatsoever.

Munroe scratched at the door, the handle, until the barrier gave way to the cold of the night and she tipped out to the asphalt. Stumbled around the hood to the other side of the car, where her knees gave out. She heaved in rapid convulsions, an empty stomach offering up nothing but bile, and words, meaningless words, jumbled and collided inside her head, until after a time they re-ordered into form and shape and substance.

According to what they have done, will he repay.

The car door behind her opened.

Munroe didn't open her eyes. Heard Neeva's footsteps as one and, even in far-off awareness, knew the girl was still hobbled.

Inner darkness continued to swirl and, eyes shut, Munroe turned her face toward the car only enough for her voice to carry. Said, "If you run, I will kill you."

Neeva didn't answer. Clothing rustled and the girl's hands touched the ground behind Munroe's feet.

The way of peace they do not know; there is no justice in their paths.

Neeva sat beside Munroe, her breathing a shallow pant, the smell of fear on her skin. Munroe opened her eyes long enough to note the phone in her hand and her gaze fixed upon the image that remained on the screen, then she shut her eyes once more.

Neeva said, "Is this what they threatened?" and her voice shook, as if in spite of everything she'd endured thus far, only now had she grasped how tightly the puppeteer controlled the threads of life. "Is this the blackmail?"

Munroe, hands on her thighs, face toward the dirt, shook her head. No. This was a death she hadn't seen coming, couldn't have imagined or possibly foreseen when calculating what pawns could be manipulated in this madness.

Noah Johnson. A Moroccan-born American and chance encounter two years earlier that had turned into a six-month relationship, tender until the end. A lover she hadn't seen or spoken to in nine months, a death far enough removed from her present life that she had no way to steel against it the way she could against Logan's, against Bradford's, or any of her family.

Crooked roads. No one who walks along them will know peace.

Unspeakable pain.

Justice is far from us, and righteousness does not reach us.

"Who is this man?" Neeva whispered.

"He was my friend," Munroe said, and wiped her sleeve across her mouth. "I loved him."

Whatever Noah's flaws, he'd been a good man, had loved her as intensely as she'd loved him, and she'd left to protect him from herself. He'd moved on and found another, and still, he was dead.

The shock of it wouldn't leave her, was a truth she couldn't acknowledge.

Munroe struggled to stand, and Neeva, beside her, stood also.

Among the strong, we are like the dead.

Munroe reached for the phone, took it from Neeva's hand.

We look for justice, but find none.

Shut off the screen and handed it back.

"Why did they kill him?" Neeva said.

The image burned inside Munroe's head: *Double tap to the head.*

Blood trickling from the wounds. Body abandoned on the concrete pavement. "To control me," she said.

They couldn't kill Logan yet, because they needed the package delivered. But they could provide ample pain as punishment and motivation to comply. So they'd gone after others she loved, targets that mattered.

Innocent life.

Who else were they tracking?

If Kate Breeden was the one who'd charted this course, if she still fed them information, they would find Munroe's entire family no matter how careful she'd been over the years.

Their deeds are evil deeds, and acts of violence are in their hands.

They'd hunt out everyone she cared about, move fastest against those she loved most. Kate had been her friend once. She should have put a bullet in her head when she'd had the chance.

Bradford not attempting to return the coded calls, a silence that had until now been reassuring, turned to death and coldness, to the sickness of the unknown. Had they gotten him, too? With the fear, the darkness swirling inside her head thickened into a suffocating blanket. Munroe hooked an arm around Neeva's neck and drew her close. Kissed her forehead. Whispered, "Forgive me," and before Neeva had a chance to react, jerked the girl forward.

Somewhere in the darkness beyond the mind, rage- and adrenaline-charged strength turned Munroe's fingers into vises, her own body into a machine controlled by the monsters inside her head. Munroe neither felt nor acknowledged Neeva's clawing or screaming while she dragged the girl, with her bound ankles, from the dirt across the asphalt, to the middle of the road.

Munroe stopped and held Neeva's arm high. Pulled from a pocket the strip of metal—the improvised knife with which Neeva had once tried to cut her—and held it to the girl's arm.

Into the night, where surely Lumani lurked and certainly he listened, Munroe screamed for proof of Logan's life. "Give it to me," she yelled, "or I swear to God I will slice your precious package here and now and let her drain dry."

Headlights down the road flashed on, then off. Just once. And then the phone, still clutched in Neeva's hand, the hand to which Munroe controlled the wrist, began to ring. Without relaxing her grip, Munroe took the phone and placed it to her ear, aware now that the claws had stopped and so had the hitting, though the tears and the body trembling continued.

"Logan is alive," Lumani said. "I can assure you no other has been killed. Get off the road. Return to the car, continue the journey."

"Not without proof of life. No exceptions, no excuses."

Munroe ended the call before he could say more. The phone rang again. Munroe placed it in her pocket. Neeva's stifled tears and shaking body returned her fully to the moment, and aware now of the strength with which she still gripped the wrist, consciously and with almost reverent tenderness, she loosened her fingers. "I'm sorry," she whispered, and she kissed Neeva's hand and let go.

Neeva took a trussed step backward and Munroe caught her for balance. Guided the girl's elbow gently. "I'm sorry," she said again, and there, in the middle of the road, staring at Neeva's flawless skin reflecting milky white in the moonlight, looking at the long line of where she would have cut and allowed the liquid of life to trail into death, she wished for all the heartache, for all of the pain and suffering of this one drive, that against the stupid, stupid rules and client demands, against the horror of everything this trip represented, that Neeva could have been drugged and thus spared them both the long torment.

And in that heartbeat of thought, that one second of darkness-induced clarity, staring at Neeva's beautiful skin, smelling the fear on her breath, and seeing the terror in her eyes, Munroe understood the reason behind the rules.

No drugs. No bruises.

Another wave of nausea overtook her.

A client who merely wanted to own, to possess a woman like Neeva, would be content to have her gagged and drugged to expedite delivery. He wouldn't mind if the package got smacked around a bit, softened up ahead of time. For that kind of depravity, bruises healed.

These rules, these instructions, had a common ancestor to Munroe's own history, stemmed from the same sadistic psychopathic urges that had, through systematic brutalization by her own tormentor, turned Munroe into the predator she was now: hunting, always hunting, disconnected from and indifferent to most of humankind, allergic to all but the rarest of human touch.

Impossible choices. Impossible burdens.

No drugs. No bruises.

She now knew well the why behind every rule, and what had driven each step of the journey thus far: The client fed on fear, wanted Neeva to understand her life was his and so had instructed she be kept fully awake, fully aware; wanted the canvas clean and unmarred, so that when he sculpted, his tools would be the first, would be the only.

Munroe stared at the sky. Cursed her weakness, her inability to block out what it would mean to knowingly deliver the innocent into the same hell that had birthed her to life. In this moment of decision she condemned to death the one she would risk anything to save. To the night, Munroe whispered good-bye. Opened the floodgates to Gehenna—that place of the wicked, that place of the dead—and here in this deserted spot, she buried her soul.

Munroe took Neeva to the car and waited until she was seated, then reached for her legs and sliced through the tape. Balled the sticky mass and tossed it into the dark, and when she was once more behind the wheel, Munroe reclined her seat and cracked the windows to counter the stale air.

To Neeva she whispered, "When did it happen?"

"When did what happen?"

"You know what I'm talking about."

Neeva stared at her hands, thumb massaging the wrist Munroe had crushed. "When you look like I do, sometimes guys obsess," she said. "They're convinced there's something going on—see things that aren't there—read meaning into things they shouldn't, project on to you and then expect you to reciprocate. They get mad and take it personally when you don't."

"How old were you when it turned violent?"

Neeva was silent a long while. "Fourteen," she said finally.

"Do your parents know?"

"Yeah," she whispered. "We've always been close. I was never afraid to tell them anything, not even when he threatened to kill me if I did."

Fourteen. The same age Munroe had been when she'd maneuvered herself into the arms of a gunrunner and set into motion the chain of events that would, like a river diverted from its course, forever alter her perception of the world and mold her into the hunter—the predator—she'd become.

"My parents—" Neeva said, but before she could continue, Munroe held up a hand and stopped her.

Noise and movement beyond the vehicle had arrested her attention, but even with the windows cracked, she'd sensed, more than heard or seen, whatever was out there; intuition amplified by years of hunting and being hunted in the jungle dark.

A moment passed.

And then Arben's face pressed up against the passenger window and Neeva screamed. He laughed, vicious and sadistic, and made a lowering motion.

Munroe caressed the dull edge of the tiny blade held tight between her fingers. "Don't let it down more than a quarter," she said.

Neeva lowered the window several inches. Stopped.

Arben waited, motioned farther down, and when Neeva shook her head, he stuck his hand inside and tossed a packet and a bag onto her lap: new tights and a small makeup kit.

"*Szed össze magad,*" he said. "Try not to look like a filthy pig for your big day." And then he laughed again.

This was the first Munroe had heard him speak, and she understood now why Hungarian had been chosen for her language immersion and not any of dozens of other languages. His words had been intended to provoke a reaction in her, but Neeva reciprocated as if she'd understood, gave him the finger, said, "Suck it, jerkwad," and moved to close the window.

Arben, arm still inside the car, struck fast.

Grabbed Neeva's hair before she'd moved the glass an inch, took a fist of it in his meaty hand, and yanked her toward him, pulling her head into the window with a thud.

If Neeva cried out, Munroe didn't hear it.

Blood pounded in her ears, a rush drowning out all else. Pressure and agony and desire for the catharsis of pain all spilled from the fractured dam that had until now held them back.

She was out the door, over the hood, and in Arben's space before he'd fully let go of Neeva. Collided with him by the time he'd backed away from the door, rage and madness working their way from inside her head to her hands and limbs.

Arben was large. Strong. Armed. And these, his strengths, were his greatest weaknesses. Brute force and the ability to control others through fear and intimidation made men lazy. Overconfident. Slow.

She would never be as fast as a bullet, but in close contact, would always be faster than the hand that drew the gun. Speed was life. Speed was survival. Speed born from the will to live, from the necessity of staying one move ahead, speed carved into her psyche one sadistic knife slice after another. That which hadn't killed her had made her faster.

Flesh against flesh, Munroe connected with Arben's throat, and in response came a crack of pain across the side of her head, and with the pain, release. Catharsis. Laughter.

Blow for blow, Munroe fought, not with the burning, insatiable passion to kill, which so many years before had, night after night, meant the difference between bleeding to death or living through to another dawn, but to make him suffer. She wanted this man alive in the way they wanted Neeva alive.

Along the steep incline beside the road, attuned to his breathing, her instinct and hearing filled in the gaps left by limited sight. She moved one step ahead, one step aside, hunting openings at his most vulnerable points: jaw, knees, eyes, groin, each movement made in vented hatred toward the poison Arben was.

He connected with her chest. Knocked her back several steps. With the pain and the loss of air, she laughed again. Shifted before he could follow through and traced his breathing and footfalls, fingered the makeshift blade.

Taunting and singsong, she called to Arben in the same Hungarian he had used to her. *"Gyere ide,"* she said. "Show yourself a man."

He spun toward her voice, struck out.

His fist connected with her cheekbone, as did her blade to his forearm, a long jagged cut while her head rang from the blow.

Arben bellowed, the fury carrying loud in the night. He lunged, fists swinging and finding air. Training pushed her to incapacitate by any means necessary, to force him into a defensive position.

Arben swung again, and where she should have taken him down with a joint break, she backed off and cut the other arm.

He spun to face her and, swearing, reached for the weapon he should've known better than to draw. Munroe shifted in toward him, but before his hand returned, and before she connected blade against throat, the report of Lumani's rifle cracked against the night, creating an instant pause to a fight barely begun.

twenty-two

Bradford navigated the streets toward Veers Transport, head in the zone, that place where the plan of action and the action itself joined into a single point of focus.

Jahan and Walker followed in the Trooper several blocks behind and out of sight. As a team, they knew nothing more at this moment than they had when Bradford had first moved off the sofa to the whiteboard and followed the tenuous thread of logic from parking lot to security cameras to trucks.

The trucks were all they had left.

They'd strategized, stretched possibilities, prepared for the worst, and abandoned the Capstone office for this Hail Mary foray. Punctuating every decision tonight, every move, was the knowledge that if they failed here, Logan was lost forever and, by implication, so was Munroe.

Reflections from amber street lamps dotted the roadway, light mirrored on streets still slick from a downpour that had blown through, typical of Texas weather: in, out, and gone, with only the aftereffects as evidence—a feat Bradford planned to mimic tonight.

Another intersection and the transport depot would be within spotting distance, and then there it was, on the right, with the lot lit up in a way it hadn't been before. The smaller trucks had been rearranged to accommodate a semi backed into the middle. Two men strode across the pavement from the rig to the warehouse door, one leading, the other following like a hungry dog, and another two pairs of legs sprouted toward the rear of the truck.

Battle strategy churned and muscle memory amped in anticipation.

If fortune smiled, he would find Logan still alive, would bring him safely home and in his place leave behind a mess of untraceable destruction.

Just like the weather.

Bradford passed the depot, pulled into the office complex next door. Parked in shadows, turned off the ignition, grabbed the overstuffed backpack, and stepped into the night.

Strategy for tonight had amounted to two very general scenarios: If there wasn't any activity on the lot, they'd slash tires, knock down doors, and cut into truck bodies until they found what they were searching for, and if there was activity on the lot, they'd go after whatever target was the most highly guarded.

That meant the eighteen-wheeler.

He continued through shadows in its direction, skirting between buildings to the back of the complex, where one series of offices abutted the darkest side of the transport depot. Wire cutters were Bradford's key through the chain-link.

On his own soil he worried less about bad guys and things blowing up in his face than he did about being destroyed by those at whose side he served. His own country would crucify him if they traced tonight's events back to him, and yet Bradford felt no qualms about taking the matter of Logan's kidnapping into his own hands. Years spent navigating shithole situations, years surrounded by poverty and corruption in countries where life and death were ruled by the law of survival and justice was arbitrary at best, of never knowing if this was the day life would be cut short, had a way of changing how a person viewed the world.

He paused. Listened. Continued on.

Flattened along the windowless length of warehouse wall and measuring off paces, moved in the direction of the prefab office. Knelt and pulled one of the bricks of C-4 from the pack. He formed the explosive on the wall and jabbed a charge into it. Without enough primer cord to sufficiently run the building, he was limited to the handful of remote-activated detonators he'd taken from the armory.

The plastics had been Walker's call. He hadn't planned on blowing up a building, on drawing a big arrow above his head that said *Hey, guys with the power to lock me up, look here,* but now that things had come to this, he wished he'd taken more of everything: more explosives, more det cord, more charges, enough to make a proper job of the destruction instead of merely providing distraction.

In Bradford's earpiece Walker whispered, "Big guy, you coming?"

"At the party," he replied.

Jahan said, "Wingman at the party."

And then Walker again: "Music is ready."

Bradford crept forward another several yards and worked the next block of plastics to the wall. Set the detonator and headed on. No matter what happened tonight, he'd blow the charges. A little parting gift and an up-yours to the assholes who, a bit too comfortable on American soil, had failed to fully think through the repercussions of stealing from a group of trigger-happy gunslingers who got depressed if they went too long without an adrenaline kick.

And maybe that was part of the Doll Maker's plan: entice and destroy.

The eighteen-wheeler could just as easily be sitting on the lot as a trap as it could be a target—or something else altogether. But there was only one way to discover if Logan was there, and that was to take the bait.

Another several yards forward, Bradford placed the last of the explosives and Walker said, "I think the engine on the wheels is running."

Bradford said, "Wingman?"

"Two minutes," Jahan replied.

Two minutes before the phones and the Internet went down and Walker killed the street and security lights. They would have taken out the electricity and saved the rest of the hassle if they could have gotten to the connections without drawing attention, but for that they had been out of luck.

Bradford moved faster now. If the truck engine was running,

whatever was here wouldn't be staying long. He was at the corner of the warehouse, rounding onto the lot itself, when Jahan said, "Ready to party."

So came the *spit-pop* of the sniper rifle and the beginning of the carnage. Cameras on the warehouse went first, mini-explosions of glass and metal that sprinkled the area with sparkling confetti, followed by the halogen security lights, and finally the streetlights, one after the next, in a steady pattern that eventually plunged the entire lot into relative darkness.

The Veers response came swiftly. The men toward the rear of the eighteen-wheeler, in an automatic reaction to the gunfire, dropped and reached for their handguns. They twisted and shifted in a hunt for the direction of the firing—not the response to ambush or rapid deployment but of those who'd been warned against potential activity and not really believing, had only halfheartedly prepared.

The moment following darkness brought total silence. No weapon reports. No shouting. No cars on the roads. No movement at all. As if in acknowledgment of the attack, the entire world had frozen to regroup. And then the warehouse door opened, and one of the two men who'd gone in came out again, as if he'd been the one to draw the short straw and been pushed out. The man was in jeans and T-shirt, heavy in the middle, maybe in his early thirties, and because he was the only one without a weapon, Bradford pegged him for the truck driver.

Bradford skirted from the cover of one truck to the next in another surge toward the eighteen-wheeler. Tires on the perimeter vehicles hissed, flattening, in a steady procession, the way the lights had blown prior.

Beside the rig, shadows on the ground, with accents thick and foreign, yelled for the man at the warehouse door. They wanted him in the truck. They wanted the truck gone now.

At the near end of the warehouse a bay door slid partially open. Two men rolled from beneath and dropped off the platform to the ground. The escaping light stretched their shadows against the pavement and added the silhouette of assault rifles to lengths of limbs and distorted heads.

Walker said, "Big man, party guests coming at nine."

Sniper on the roof with an infrared scope meant that had they been willing to take life, this sequence would have been over in minutes. But the conundrum within vigilante justice was differentiating between employees and criminals. The immediate goal was to grab Logan without killing innocent people or tacking homicide charges onto everything else. Cold-blooded vengeance could wait.

Across the lot, the men on the other side of the truck continued to yell for the driver, and Walker took potshots at his feet every time he moved. To Bradford's left, the men with the rifles crept from the warehouse toward the perimeter, slipping out of sight and presumably continuing in the direction of the sniper fire.

With five enemy on the ground, breaching the eighteen-wheeler and getting inside would be noisy, messy, and risky, but whatever was in it clearly mattered most to the Veers people, and Logan or not, the contents could be used as a black eye and a bargaining chip.

Within the blind urgency of the Doll Maker's people to get the eighteen-wheeler on its way, Bradford formed an alternative scenario, and set out strategy change in clipped commands.

The sniper fire stopped.

The driver, still rooted to the spot and afraid to move, refused to respond to the men on the ground and so his own people turned on him, shooting in his direction to force him into doing what they wanted.

Bradford crab-walked around the last of the trucks to the open space between him and the rig. Inched forward, and the crack of a rifle split the night. The windshield above his head shattered, and the sides of the truck dinged with hits of metal on metal.

Ignoring the instinct to dive for cover, he rushed the cab.

Each step brought another series of rifle reports, short bursts fired in his direction, interrupted by a scream, then silence, and finally strafing from both rifles in the direction of the property next door.

Introduction of the automatic gunfire created confusion on the ground by the truck. Bradford didn't pause when he reached the semi, didn't climb so much as jump the laddered steps, yanked the cab door outward, and threw himself forward.

In the open hole of the door opposite, the truck driver, seeing him, froze.

Bradford leveled his weapon at the man and said, "I'm your best friend right now, just get in the truck and get us off the lot and I swear to God I won't hurt you."

The driver's mouth opened as if to say something, but he didn't move.

twenty-three

OUTSIDE MONTEBRUNO, ITALY

Neeva stared out the car window. Struggled to make sense of the shadowy movements, arms and blows and strikes that blended into one another while slipping farther away from the car, until, in the darkness, she couldn't tell who was who or what was what.

Her palms were damp and heat prickled at her hairline.

Everything had happened fast. Stunned by the speed of the violence, she strained to see outside the car and then, in a rush of panic, closed the windows, locked the doors, and checked the ignition in the hope that maybe, just maybe, in the hurry, Michael had left the keys.

But she hadn't.

In the terror of the moment, Neeva had lost time, and now her heart beat heavily, urging her to flee on foot. Fear alone kept her anchored to the seat. Down the road, in both directions, was only darkness punctuated by pinpricks of light, almost as if someone had chosen this precise location for a stop exactly because it was as far away from anything as Neeva could remember since they'd started the trip, and out there, somewhere in the empty night, was the big creep from the cell.

She didn't know which direction to run to stay away from him, but she knew his type—the kind to get his kicks from hurting other people. If he was the one to find her, there was no telling what he would do. Visual possibilities danced inside Neeva's head, fodder for a slasher film, while the image of the dead man and Michael's vomiting played out in a background montage, heightening her fear.

That man was dead because Neeva had run. If she actually escaped, what would they do? For sure they'd kill someone she loved, maybe they already had.

Her heart hurt.

Her stomach hurt.

Neeva swallowed back the pain and strained to see out the window. Saw nothing but black and then a blur of movement. She would have to run. Hands shaking, she reached for the dome light and moved the switch so that when she opened the door, the light wouldn't turn on, then eased from the passenger seat to the driver's, head low, movements small just in case. Someone outside yelled.

Neeva twitched.

Gunfire shattered the silence and Neeva fumbled for the door lock.

Michael was the only one without a gun, which meant Michael was the only one who could have been shot, which meant Michael was dead and now the creep would come for her.

Door unlocked, Neeva tried for the handle. Missed it and then like magic the door opened of its own accord.

Neeva stifled a scream.

Her eyes tracked up from the ground, searched out the face of whoever stood outside, and like some miraculous apparition, Michael spoke from the darkness. Said, "Get out of my seat."

Fear and relief and tension, and anger mixed into an emotional cocktail so overwhelmingly powerful that Neeva laughed. Nervous laughter. Crazy laughter.

Michael squatted so that their faces were level and close. From here, even without the dome light, Neeva could see Michael's eyes and the way they scanned her as if searching for evidence of damage; she could also see that Michael's lip was swollen and cut, and the skin on her left cheekbone split and bleeding.

"You're not dead," Neeva said, and her mouth felt as if it was stuffed with cotton.

"Not dead," Michael said, and reached for Neeva's hair. Neeva flinched, deflected Michael's hand with a smack, and then, realizing in horror what she'd done, braced for a retaliatory strike that never came.

"I'm not going to hurt you," Michael said. "Put the light back on, will you?"

Neeva paused.

This wasn't the same Michael from before the dead man's picture and definitely not the Michael who had dragged her screaming into the road. The voice was the same monotone calm, but something was different in a scary sort of way. Wary, and keeping her face forward, Neeva reached behind, felt for the nub, then found and pushed it, and the dim light came on, painful against the darkness.

This time, when Michael moved her hand toward Neeva's face, Neeva kept still, guarded and cautious, while Michael reached for the hair at her neck and lifted it, examining the area where the creep had slammed her into the window. "Does it hurt?" she asked.

"No," Neeva whispered, body still rigid, eyes searching Michael's in a desperate attempt to discover what was different—something about the face, the eyes—a glaze, maybe, or hollowness, like Michael saw without seeing: alive on the outside but dead behind the eyes.

Michael let the hair drop and nudged her gently. "Move over," she said, and Neeva, her mind juggling between the danger of Michael in front of her and the creep in the darkness, worked backward to the seat she'd just crawled from.

"If you're alive," Neeva said, "is the guy out there dead?"

"Eventually," Michael said, and reached behind the seat for the blanket.

"So he's still alive? Still out there?"

"For now," she said.

"I heard a gun fire."

Michael nodded again, and dabbed at the blood that trailed beneath her chin. "A warning," she said, and slid in behind the wheel. She shut the door and the light turned off. Then tipped the seat back as far as it would go and closed her eyes.

"What do we do now?" Neeva said.

"We wait."

"For what?"

"I want to know that my friend is alive," Michael said, and those words burned hot up the back of Neeva's neck. The *friend* was the reason Michael was here, and even a fool would know that if the *friend* was still alive—Neeva shut off the thought. Michael's head turned and her eyes, open and unblinking, stared at her with that same scary-dead gaze, like there were a hundred years of things to say and she had no life left to say them. Neeva said, "I thought maybe, you know. I mean, realizing you're a woman, I just . . ."

"I don't want to do it," Michael said. "I have to choose. I don't know how many people will die by me not doing this." She faced the ceiling again and closed her eyes. "It's not just the ones I love. I'm surprised they haven't threatened you with your family, too."

"They have," Neeva said, "but I didn't believe them."

"You don't strike me as stupid."

"My parents are powerful people," Neeva said. "They're hard to get to, and they're looking for me, they have to be."

"They are," Michael said, "and these guys"—she ran her finger in a circle in the air—"they know that now. I doubt they did at the beginning, which is why I'm here." She paused and opened her eyes. Looked directly at Neeva. "You pulled a fast one on the world, what with changing your name and burying your past. That's probably what has saved you now, everyone speculating about you and why you did it. But none of that makes much of a difference anymore. If you don't do what they want, they'll still find someone to kill. Maybe not your mom or your dad, but your sisters, your cousins."

Neeva tried to push back all the nightmare and the crazy, the confusion and the words that made no sense. "Saved me now?" she said. "*Saved* me?" Her voice went up a notch. Then, even more bewildered, she added, "You know about my family?"

"You can trust that if I know, they know," Michael said, and then sighed. "You have no idea, do you? What's been going on these past few weeks?"

Weeks.

Neeva mouthed the word. Pressed her palms to her head and pushed against the walls that were closing inward. She'd lost track of time holed up in that cold stone prison with no concept of day or night, hours parsed by the spacing of sleep and meals and guard changes and assholes who'd arrived to assault her. So much precious time stolen.

Weeks.

She had no words, no voice, no ability to articulate the sickening angst. Her parents would think she was dead, maybe, would have no closure, no way to know—no last words or good-byes or I love yous. Just this. This grab-and-run and cut off from the world with no way to send a message that she was alive and fighting to get back to them. There was no possible civil response, so all she said in answer to Michael's question was "I've been locked away, so how could I know anything, really?"

The minutes ticked by and the longer the silence grew, the more Neeva's anxiety increased. Unsure of what she could say or how hard she could push before Michael's hard-assed captor persona returned, she finally whispered, "What exactly *has* been going on?"

Michael just shook her head and said, "You should put the tights on and get your face cleaned up. Don't give him an excuse to come back."

Neeva kicked off her shoes, as close to venting frustration as she dared in the moment. Reached for the packet that had fallen to the floor, snatched it up, and tore at the plastic. "Seriously," she said. "I want to know."

"Doesn't matter," Michael said, and put a finger to her lips, pointed at the dash, ran her finger in a circle around the air again, then pointed to her ear, and Neeva understood then, that for all of this time, not only were they being followed but their conversations were monitored.

MUNROE DOZED FITFULLY, an hour, maybe two, of silence and downtime and decompression during which it was almost possible to tamp down the fear of retaliation, the guessing game of who, out of the few people she loved, would be next on the list of Doll Maker targets, to pretend that having been snatched away from the first true peace she'd found in the last ten years hadn't just thrown her back to the edge of the abyss, that place of madness she'd spent the entirety of her adult years trying to avoid.

The fight with Arben and the ensuing pain had been a release valve, a temporary calm from the pressure cooker of violence and voices, but they were back again, feeding off the rage, driving and relentless.

The shrill alert of the phone jolted through the quiet and Neeva jumped, then muttered, "No, not again."

Munroe picked up the phone, checked the display, and in response to Neeva's panicked deer-in-the-headlights stare, whispered, "We should be okay for now."

The number showing on the screen was not Lumani's, which left only the Doll Maker as the caller, and if what had happened over the past few days was any prediction of how things would continue, even though this call might be the harbinger of another battle, it wouldn't likely announce another death because the Doll Maker preferred to send his minions and foot soldiers as the bearers of bad news.

Munroe answered the phone with silence and after a long pause the Doll Maker said, "My friend, you are there, are you not?" His voice was warm and friendly and infused with the same fractured sense of reality that had permeated his every move within the office of the dolls.

"I'm listening," Munroe said.

"I cannot give you what you want."

"Then I see no reason why I should continue."

"As expected," he said. "It's the time frame at issue. Your friend, he is alive, this is for sure, the problem is in the timing of getting you your proof. Continue the journey. A little farther down the road, a little later, and you will have what you want."

"You killed a man for arbitrary reasons," she said, "you lost nothing and still took his life."

"Words like *arbitrary* are meaningless," he said. "The responsibility to meet each outcome is yours. No matter how failure arrives, the price for it is yours to pay. I made this clear from the beginning."

Failure.

Because Neeva had run.

Noah's life had been taken to compensate for tights and mascara.

"The dead man," Munroe said. "What was his failure?"

"It was your failure, your punishment, and so the answers are your problem to deal with as you see fit. You were given a task and failed, so there has been suffering. You can correct it now and spare further pain."

Mental disconnect filled his answers. Her response was about the value of human life, his was about damage to a costume. "You said this task is about me and my debt to you. You already hold

Logan as collateral, but instead you took the life of someone who has nothing whatsoever to do with any of this."

"Truly unfortunate," he said. "You must continue the journey now."

Munroe drew in a breath, fought the timpani inside her head, and said, "If you can't prove to me Logan is alive, then I have nothing left to lose, so no, I won't continue. Not without proof of life."

"There are others," the Doll Maker said. "There are others who matter to you, so you would be wise to follow through and avoid further failure."

She could hear the smile, the smirk, the gloat in his voice, and his threat was another punch to the head.

Jolting.

The strategy was there, amorphous, intangible.

There were others, as he said, and they would be used to manipulate her all the way until she had reached the end. Nothing would stop until he had what he wanted, and when he had won, she was destined to die, as was Logan, and eventually Neeva, and God knew who else.

The voices rose, chanting, calling.

This is a day of vengeance, that he may avenge him of his adversaries.

No matter how many moves she played out in her head, the outcome was always death. Jumping through his hoops, sacrificing one piece to save another, she would lose everything. He controlled the elements, the power, and the board. The only way to end the madness was to upend the game and let the pieces fall.

"I have nothing left to lose," she said, "and no fear of what you'll take or what you can do to me because I am already dead."

"The innocent will suffer."

"Then let them suffer," she said, and hung up.

twenty-four

The truck driver stayed motionless in the space of the open cab door, the dilemma clear on his face: return to the men on the ground who might shoot him if he jumped, or deal with the gun pointed at his head and the stranger who might shoot him when the driving was finished.

Bradford repeated the instruction, a slow and clear demand to get inside and get the rig moving, and when the response in those long, drawn-out seconds was a continued hesitation, he repeated the promise. "Best thing to happen to you all day."

The driver shifted his focus from the front to the side and turned his head back as if preparing to jump, so Bradford lowered his weapon. Without taking his eyes off the driver, he reached inside his vest for the remote and punched in to trigger the detonation.

The warehouse explosions ripped through the night in a way automatic gunfire never could: shook the ground with enough force that even high up in the cab, Bradford felt the power. Whatever hesitation the driver held, whatever decision he readied to make, was resolved by the bigger noise and the flash from behind. The driver jerked, shoved forward into the cab, and slammed the door behind him faster than Bradford imagined possible for a man of his girth.

Once behind the wheel, the driver released the brake and the truck crawled forward toward the chain-link gate, still closed. The men who'd been shooting were behind the truck. Bradford could see them in the side mirror, crumpled on the ground bracing for another explosion from the warehouse.

"Get the lights on," Bradford said. "And don't stop for the gate."

The driver didn't say anything, just reached out and powered on the lights, kept moving until the grille of the truck touched the gate, advancing until even from inside the cab Bradford could hear and feel the squeal of metal twisting under pressure, and then the rig was through and the wheels were on the street.

"Head north," Bradford said, and they swung wide with the impossible-to-hurry kind of slowness only massive trucks could conjure, the type of crawl that made movement feel like slugging through mud pits and created the sensation of sitting on a target in a firing range.

Far up the street came the flash of blue, red, and white—Bradford didn't hear the sirens, couldn't even clearly see the patrol cars, but they were coming. Into his mic he said, "Daddy's on the way. Party's over."

The driver turned to stare at him and after a long pause said, "Where to, boss?" And that was the question, *Where to?* The problem with Irving was that the city sat nearly dead center between Dallas and Forth Worth, surrounded by thick civilization on all sides with no fast way out of town in any direction. North was the best bet, but Bradford didn't want to waste time hauling ass out of the city if Logan wasn't in the truck.

"Take I-35 toward Denton," Bradford said. "That'll do for now."

The driver nodded, and as the truck picked up speed, switched gears.

Three patrol cars with sirens blaring blew past, and in the mirror Bradford watched the vehicles stop beyond the transport fence and their doors swing open. He had radio silence from Jahan and Walker, and that was a good thing. He'd only hear from them if there was trouble; if they got out clean, next contact would be a phone call.

"What's in the back of the truck?" Bradford said.

"The manifests are there on that clipboard, if you wan' 'em."

"That wasn't my question."

The driver glanced at Bradford again, at first blankly and then the fog lifted. "You saying what I'm hauling ain't what's on the manifest?"

"Exactly that."

The driver paused, then said, "What's it you think I got? Drugs?"

"People."

The driver let out a half-laugh that came more as an indication of spontaneous relief than humor. "Aw, man, no, not possible," he said. "We don't run up from Mexico. Down sometimes, but freight only goes one way."

"I wasn't talking about illegals."

Bradford stopped there because this line of discussion was pointless with an underling. "You know an out-of-the-way place to pull over, somewhere not too far outside the metroplex, somewhere that won't draw any attention?"

"I might," the driver said, "but you and that pop toy there make me real nervous. I need some guarantee you ain't planning to use it."

"If I was planning to kill people, those guys with the guns back at the depot would have been the first to go."

The driver switched gears again. "I suppose you have a point," he said, though his body showed signs of agitation, what Bradford expected in a person amped for fight or flight.

"Where were you headed with this load?" Bradford asked.

"Houston, same as always."

Bradford repeated the answer. "Same as always?" And then, "That the only place you ever go?"

"I run the smaller trucks all over the country, but with this rig, yeah, always Houston. Though before I come on, before Katrina, it was New Orleans."

"That doesn't create questions?"

The man shrugged. "I do my job, I don't ask whatfor."

"You have a name?"

"Dave Lockreed."

"Okay, Dave, listen. All I want right now is to get into the back of this truck. I don't want to hurt anyone, definitely don't want to kill anyone, and I'm not planning to steal anything. I'm convinced there's a person in the back, and I'm only here for that. I want to be done and out as quickly as possible, and all I'm asking is for you not to make this any harder than it has to be. Can you work with me on that?"

THEY WERE JUST beyond Lewisville when the call from Jahan came in, a brief swap of details that let Bradford know his team was safe and confirmed specifics for the proposed rendezvous point. With that settled, the remainder of the run north from DFW provided an opportunity to poke and prod at the driver's knowledge in a not-so-subtle attempt to fill informational gaps.

Lockreed, though a slow and cautious speaker, offered far more in his stop-start moments of rambling than Bradford fished for, a nervous stringing of words, talking for the sake of talking. Houston, as it turned out, was where Veers operated a second truck depot, a location that hadn't turned up in any of the war room's digging; a smaller office that, as far as Lockreed knew, handled import and export, a location that tied in well with Bradford's theories about why Veers operated in the way that it did, and because Houston had access to both sea and air, Bradford suspected this smaller, off-the-map arm of the Doll Maker's network was the primary gateway for moving his merchandise in and out of the country.

The meeting spot was a park just off the interstate beyond Denton: trees and grass, baseball diamonds, and soccer fields with a deserted parking lot in an area both quiet and sparsely populated.

Brakes hissed, then Bradford climbed down from the cab. Rounded to the rear of the truck while Lockreed did the same along the other side. At the truck's back end they stared at the door and the double bolts padlocked into place. "You got the keys to these things?" Bradford asked.

"Wish I did, normally would. Didn't get that sorted before the shooting started."

"Still no idea what's inside?"

The driver shook his head. "Not but what's on the manifest."

"What do you do when you get to Houston?"

"Back the truck in, hand over the papers and keys, get a signature, and leave."

"To where? In what?"

"Usually, there's a company car waiting. I put up in a nearby motel for the night, come back in the morning, and make the return trip, sometimes with freight, sometimes empty."

"But always with this exact trailer?"

Lockreed nodded.

"Nothing strange about that?"

The driver's posture sagged. "It's a job," he said. "Puts food on the table."

They waited in silence for a few minutes until Walker, in the Trooper, pulled up beside the rig. Jahan followed several car lengths behind.

Lights switched off and engines running, they stepped from the vehicles and stood beside Bradford. He motioned toward the padlocks. "Driver doesn't have the keys. Anyone have any PETN left?"

Jahan pulled primer cord from his pack. Wrapped and knotted a segment around the hook of each lock and let out a lead. Then all four stepped a few paces away. The explosives cut through the metal, knife to butter, and the pieces fell to either side. Bradford pushed the scraps out of the way, slid the bolts, and pulled the doors outward. With a flashlight beam roaming, they peered together into a darkened container filled with oversize boxes stacked nearly the height of the interior.

Walker sighed. "They couldn't make this shit any easier, could they?"

Bradford climbed up into the truck and Walker joined him.

Jahan said, "You want me to cuff the civie?"

Bradford said, "Nah, he's got nowhere to go," and then after a moment of staring at the boxes, "Hey, Dave, get in here and help us empty this thing."

Walker said, "There's got to be some pattern here. Some route to get to whatever is inside—makes no sense to have to load and unload all of this every single time."

"Maybe," Bradford said. "Do you see it?"

Walker shook her head.

"Jack?"

"I see a wall of cardboard and have a big target on my back. Can we get moving?"

Bradford reached for a box and shoved it in the driver's direction. The thing was heavy for being nothing but a prop. "Check out what's inside," he said. "Find out if it matches your manifest."

The document said children's furniture, and the boxes, heavy and unwieldy, held wooden pieces sandwiched between packaging material: to all appearances genuine cargo, and possibly truly intended for export. The four worked in sweaty silence, offloading enough of the freight to create space within the interior so that they could shuffle boxes from one place to the next, looking for they knew not what but expecting to recognize the thing when they found it.

Bradford was halfway to the front when the first sound of tapping, faint and nearly imperceptible, caught his attention. He held up a hand to stop movement, and within the silence the others also picked up what he had, though the sound had no obvious source and was faint enough that one might think the taps had been imagined.

The noise—if you could call it that—seemed loudest in the direction of the far front, so Bradford switched focus from moving boxes from one spot to the next to clearing a path straight through until he reached the front, and there he found nothing but the end of the container.

The tapping came again, louder than it had been before, the origin still no clearer than when they'd first heard it. In the narrow path, Jahan squeezed beyond Bradford, knelt, and placed his palm and ear to the wall. Waited for the tapping, and when it came, shook his head: no vibration.

In the disappointing silence, each inhale, each exhale, reverberated loudly enough to drown out the faint link to hope until the tapping returned, this time louder and unmistakably an SOS that came from everywhere and nowhere at the same time.

Finally Lockreed stated the obvious. "That can't come from one of the boxes," he said. "None of them is big enough to hold a whole person."

"False front, false floor, false ceiling," Walker said. "Those are our only options." After a moment of pause, without further discussion or consultation, they started moving freight again, faster and less cautiously than before, shoving boxes toward the rear and out the back without regard to how the merchandise fell or if packing burst, spurred on by the confirmation that somewhere in this truck was the score they'd set out to find.

When the container was finally empty and the ground outside littered, Bradford swept the flashlight beam from corner to corner and seam to seam, while Jahan knocked knuckles against the walls and floor, trying to find a change in pattern that would lead them to a hidden space.

The SOS repeated, and in an automatic response, they each turned to look at the ceiling, the direction from which the sound had seemed to come. "Can't be up there," Walker whispered. "It's gotta be front."

She begged the flashlight off Bradford, and using the light to guide her fingertips, ran her hand up along the front corner seam from floor to ceiling. Shook her head, backed up, and tried again. Finally she paused and said, "I got something. Jack, give me a hand." Pointed him to a spot a couple of feet away. "Press there," she said, and when he applied pressure at the same level she did, the panel clicked, moved inward an inch, and slid a few feet to the side.

The truck went silent, as if a vacuum had emptied the container of air.

Bradford fought the urge to push his way forward. Held back to allow Walker the moment she'd so rightfully earned, watched her face as she shone the light into the opening, and felt the disappointment when what lit up was not a hiding spot but another wall right behind where the first had been, this one with a narrow door. The shell of a self-contained room, installed behind the false wall, kept separate from the actual walls and floor of the semi by several inches of insulating material.

Walker motioned Jahan toward the lock. Said, "Det cord again?" and stepped out of his way. He knotted primer cord around this lock as he'd done on the one outside the truck.

The pieces severed. Halves fell to the floor. Walker reached forward, opened the door, and swung the light inward. The expression on her face told Bradford everything he needed to know and his breath caught in his throat.

Walker moved farther into the room and out of sight. Lockreed maneuvered forward ahead of Jahan, pushed his way in, only to turn on his heels and rush for the back of the truck.

Head out, he heaved and vomited.

Jahan peered in after Walker, threw a wary glance in Bradford's direction, and stepped aside to allow Bradford to squeeze into the interior of an area the width of the truck but less than three feet deep—a crawl space, if that. Vents led from the top of the space through to the roof of the trucking container, but even with the mild airflow, the interior was fetid with the smell of rot and decaying body fluid.

Walker shone the flashlight over the body, crumpled on a mat and twisted in a way the human form was never meant to bend. Wounds that had been hastily bound oozed pus from infection.

"Oh, Jesus," Walker whispered, and really, there wasn't any more to add. Logan's eyes were glassed over in a drugged stupor. Leaned up against the wall, he stared in a way that would have been slack-jawed had his head not been wrapped with filthy bandages. His wrist was tipped back, knuckles to wall, continuing the same plaintive SOS that had first alerted them to his presence.

The euphoria of finding Logan alive—if barely—was fast followed by the nightmare of figuring out how to safely move him. He needed immediate hospitalization at a facility big enough to handle multiple trauma, and with everything that had transpired at the depot they couldn't risk taking the truck directly to an emergency room.

Gagging against the stench, skirting urine, feces, blood, and vomit, Bradford moved behind Logan, knelt so his mouth was near Logan's ear and his chest supported Logan's head, and whispered the same shush of comfort a parent might use to calm a child from night terrors: They'd get him out of here, he'd be okay—had to be okay.

The mat, filthy as it was, became a means of transport.

Logan never cried out, never spoke at all, but as they worked him slowly out of the little room—inching forward along the floor, keeping movement as small as possible—the mixture of pain and gratitude came through the glassy gaze without the need for words.

In increments, they got the mat and his broken body through the door to the wider space of the semi's container, to where the air was fit to breathe and they could pause to strategize. The Capstone team huddled so Lockreed wouldn't overhear, but the move wasn't entirely necessary. Having pushed his way into the crawl space and seen the human cargo, then come bolting out again, the driver kept a deliberate distance.

Behind his back, they formed plans in decisive whispers.

Bradford left the truck and backed the Explorer to the rear of the semi so it would be easier to shift Logan from one vehicle to the next. Walker transferred the weapons cache entirely into the Trooper—she would return to Capstone and man the office while Jahan and Bradford continued across the state border with Logan. They'd take him to a hospital in Oklahoma City, which at this point wasn't a whole lot farther than Dallas, where it would be more difficult for anyone to connect Logan to the events in Texas. They wouldn't stay gone long, not with so many threads left untied.

Using blankets already in the Explorer and packaging from the boxes on the ground, Jahan formed a cushioned platform in the back of the SUV, and while he and Walker worked to get Logan settled, Bradford, in an attempt to cover their tracks, took Lockreed aside.

Next to the truck the driver paced, several slow steps forward and then back again, hands in his pockets, repeating the same question over and over, not to Bradford but a mumble to himself, "What do I do? What do I do?"

At a loss for words, Bradford let the man do his thing until, finally, frustrated with the irrational drama, he said, "Look, you really don't have a lot of options."

Lockreed stopped pacing. Turned toward Bradford's voice.

"First, you were at the scene of the shootout. Second, you've seen this—seen what you've been hauling. Your employers are going to know and they're going to want you dead. And, worse, even if they don't kill you, the authorities probably already consider you an accessory." Bradford paused. "Really, your best bet is to go to law enforcement. Get it out of the way, tell them exactly what happened tonight."

Lockreed pulled his hands out of his pockets and then shoved them back again. "But what about when they ask me about you? Who you are and where you went? Aren't you going to want to kill me, too?"

Bradford shook his head. "I'm not coming after you," he said. "Tell them the truth." He straightened and stepped toward the Explorer. "Tell them you have no idea."

twenty-five

BEYOND MONTEBRUNO, ITALY

Proof of life arrived in the same way news of death had come: a noise that jarred the quiet, an alert that lit the screen with blinding revelation. Munroe stared at the phone a long while, neither moving nor blinking. The Doll Maker had made his play, and now it was her turn.

The signal was weak and the site to which Lumani's text linked loaded slowly and incrementally, the status circle continuing its rounds, loading, loading, while inside Munroe's chest the fist gripped harder, tighter, fingers wrapped around her spine, crushing her heart so that the pain made breathing difficult. And the voices, always the voices, incanted to the pounding of her pulse, urging toward violence, until at last, fully accessible, the video file, freeze-framed, waited to be played.

Logan.

Truly alive.

The entire clip was barely a minute, but without a doubt he was living—or had been when the footage was shot—horribly battered, but still breathing: blond hair matted with dried blood, face swollen and mottled, green eyes the equivalent of olives in tomato juice. Given the camera angle, she couldn't see much of the room beyond the mat upon which he lay, but best guess said the space was narrow and the walls, if the sound could be trusted, were high and made of something other than drywall.

Logan, positioned at an odd angle, faced the camera, but his eyes weren't focused on it. "Michael," he said, and he paused in a struggle for air, and then again as if to remember. "A message for you," he said. His words were slurred and garbled, the distortion made even worse by the transmission. "They say you're in Italy, not Dallas," he said. "That you're in a car on a country road and you fought a man and hurt him worse than he hurt you. There's a girl beside you. They say these details are the proof you want."

He paused again, had that dazed in-and-out quality of pharmaceuticals she'd seen in years past. Turned his head away from the camera, gazing upward at something outside the frame's view until a noise that could have been speech drew his attention and he started again. "They say they'll take more life if you don't do what they want." With an effort, he shifted to face the camera, struggled to focus directly on the lens, and said, "Michael, listen. You do what you need to do."

The clip went dark and the connection to Logan became nothing more than a solid image waiting to be replayed. Munroe stared at the phone, and then in response to the night blindness, shut off the screen and closed her eyes. Emotion rushed in flash flood through her veins: hatred, grief, pain, and love.

Even in the face of torture and his own demise, Logan understood.

Do what you need to do.

Resolve etched and cracked. Threatened to shatter completely.

Logan was still alive.

She could still finish this job—deliver the package and save her brother.

No. If Logan could be freed, it would be Bradford—if he was still alive—who would have to save him. Mentally downshifting, she pushed aside the anguish. When this was all over, there would be time enough to grieve.

Do what you need to do.

Munroe exhaled. Pulled in another breath and held it long, and with each long draw, let go another portion of the present, bringing into its place the pure focus of assignment. If sacrificing Logan was the price to be paid to spare Neeva, it wasn't enough to merely save *her*. For every Neeva with powerful parents and for whom the media hounds were out sniffing scent, there were a hundred thousand other trafficked girls and women that the world, either through ignorance or indifference, wrote off or forgot altogether. No, if Logan was the price, then his blood would purchase more than one life, and sacrifices be damned, she would wait as long as possible, get as near the delivery point as possible, and from there take her chances.

THE STREETS OF Genoa at five in the morning were like the streets of many cities in the early pre-dawn: relatively quiet and mostly deserted. Lumani's route took them from rural roads directly into the populated areas and finally to the roadway that ran parallel to the ocean. Not the faster highway that tunneled through mountains and made a beeline for the French border, but the smaller provincial road, without tolls, that followed the curve of the coast.

In either direction the ocean was stippled with dots of light, spliced with harbors and coves where boats and yachts, from dinghy to the obscene, could slip in to anchor and then move on again. Pieces of mental strategy shifted again: Transfer Neeva from dry land into the belly of a yacht, and the girl would never be heard from again.

Dawn arrived by the time they'd passed Ventimiglia, the sun low on the horizon and the ocean's blue now distinguishable from the sky. The streets were still quiet, though it wouldn't be long before civilization began to stir, and it was helpful that Neeva had fallen asleep yet again. The final address in the array of texts dead-ended in Menton, a few kilometers beyond the French border.

Munroe reached the checkpoint, a setup similar to the small provincial outposts they'd passed when crossing from Croatia into Slovenia: a station with an overhang. She slowed the car, Lumani's documents on hand should they have to stop, but the exit and entry booths were empty and they passed into France with the same fanfare as crossing a street.

The phone on the console vibrated. Munroe picked it up, highlighted the text, and stared hard at the newest round of driving directions. Took her foot off the gas pedal, downshifted, and slowed, searching out an empty parallel space along the curb. She pulled the emergency brake and cut the engine. Neeva slept on, so Munroe removed the keys and stepped out of the car.

In rebellion she dialed, and Lumani answered on the second ring. She offered no hello, how are you, or *are you out of your fucking mind.* Instead she said, "It makes no sense to take her in there, there's no logic to a move like this."

"You're not here for opinion," Lumani replied. "You have a job to do, you follow instructions, and that's all."

Munroe dragged in a breath and pinched the bridge of her nose, pulled into the present and pushed past the exhaustion and emotional overload. With so little access to Lumani, every second mattered.

She drew him into her head and breathed him into her lungs.

"You're right," she said, voice softer, tone contrite. "You're right and I agree with you—I'm only here to do the job. And I think, like you, I just want this over. But tell me, Valon, from a professional standpoint, does this feel right to *you*? Having come so far, don't we risk things going to hell at the last minute?"

"It's not ideal," he said.

Munroe leaned low to check on Neeva and then said, "You have no choice either, do you?"

"Always the client's rules," Lumani replied. "There's nothing more to tell you than this is where we go. There will be more instructions when we reach the destination."

"But the price for failure is yours."

"Yes," he said, and the word was barely above a whisper.

She pulled his mind into her body, put his emotion in her chest.

"My delay forced this, didn't it?" she said.

"Only the daylight," he said.

"And because of my actions, if having to go in during the day creates failure, that failure will be yours."

"And yours," he added.

"There's a horrible frustration in having to pay the price for someone else's choices," she said. "I'm sorry for having brought repercussions down on you. If this delivery blows up on us, will you suffer badly?"

A long pause of silence, then he ended the call.

Munroe focused on the ground, processing. He'd given her what she needed to know, and she in turn had scattered seed that might lay fallow or might, if she was lucky, eventually sprout into saplings strong enough to split the hardened topsoil that kept him as the Doll Maker's doer.

Munroe's fingers tapped against the hood in contemplation. They were heading into the Principality of Monaco, which, at less than one square mile of land, was the world's second smallest and most densely populated country, tax haven and playground to the rich, best known for the Monte Carlo and the Formula One Grand Prix: a square mile of mountainside; tiny, winding, congested roads, of underground parking lots and tightly packed high-rises, all less than twenty minutes away along this coastal route.

Under the cover of darkness, the handoff might have made sense, but this early in the morning, taking Neeva into the heart of the city-state begged for attention and made something of a proverbial suicide mission out of what should have been a straightforward exchange, merchandise for payment.

Monaco.

Insanity.

It didn't take teenage years spent running guns and drugs across unmarked borders to know that the current arrangement wasn't the type of planning produced by a person or organization that wanted to guarantee a mission's success. This was a move that taunted and challenged authority to discover and stop it.

Instructions from the client.

Of course.

A bored, intelligent, sadistic, and very wealthy client: annoyed at the delay, toying with the criminals, playing games with them. Raising the ante. Setting them up for failure.

The drop was near Port Hercules, Monaco's deep-water port, where many of the world's largest private yachts home-berthed or visited. Where better to play with your pawns or taunt the governments of the world in a completely swollen ego sort of way—the fox walking blatantly into the chicken coop and daring the farmer to catch him—than to bring a highly visible trafficked woman into the country with the world's lowest crime rate and largest police force per capita, in broad daylight, and then silently make off with her?

Munroe reached for her pocket and retrieved the stolen phone. Her course of action was set, but before continuing, she hoped for news out of Dallas that might mute the inner voices and allow her to plunge fully into the task at hand.

She powered on the screen and winced. Battery—if barely—but no signal. Hurting against the unknown, voices running dialogue inside her head, Munroe shut off the phone for good. Needed to hold things together just long enough to receive the final set of instructions that would take her to the client.

She returned to the driver's seat. The engine's turnover, loud in the relative silence, brought Neeva's eyes open: a slow rolling out of sleep that had, by the time Munroe had gotten the vehicle halfway out of the parking spot, parsed quickly into full-blown panic. Neeva glanced from Munroe to the road, to the sidewalk, and to the road again, as if she'd spent hours planning an escape inside her head only to wake and find time and opportunity had flown. Still sleep stunned, the girl twisted and clawed at the door and the seat belt simultaneously, her body tensed to bolt and run.

Munroe snapped a hand on her arm. "Don't," she said. And then, when Neeva, wild-eyed, turned back to glare, to fight, Munroe tightened her grip and yanked her close. Through clenched teeth she said, "Don't do it. I'll find a way for you."

Whether or not the words meant anything to Neeva, the girl yanked back hard, got her free hand on the door latch, and snagged the handle; the door inched open. Unable to control Neeva and move the car forward at the same time, Munroe opted for both hands on Neeva, and a second later, resorted to using her full body.

She let the clutch and brake go.

The car jumped forward just enough to tap the vehicle in front.

She leveraged her grip on Neeva into a pivot. Clamped her second hand on Neeva's far shoulder, dragged a knee out from beneath the wheel, and punched Neeva's pelvis with the cap, her own weight and size overpowering Neeva's smaller frame, and still Neeva didn't stop. In the space of seconds, the girl bucked, clawed, bit, and finally screamed, bloodcurdling and vicious.

Few pedestrians were on the street, but it would only take one; houses with open windows, patios with open doors, just one curious bystander and this was over. In a move vile enough someone might die for it, Munroe leaned back and struck an open palm across Neeva's face.

In the shock of the blow, Neeva, eyes wide and blinking, gaped and went mute. "Shut up," Munroe hissed. "And stay put. I will find a way, okay?"

twenty-six

They entered Monaco at the principality's northernmost border without anything to mark the crossing but a change in signs and a sudden tightness in building density.

The GPS led them south along the coast, down pristine streets bordered by trees and beautiful landscaping, streets slowly filling with morning traffic; past the beach area of Larvotto; past a mix of grand architecture and block-style residential buildings making up in height what they couldn't grab in land; past innumerable CCTV cameras, toward the area of the Japanese Garden and specifically to an underground parking not far from their final destination.

It couldn't have been easy for Lumani to send them down— even if he had the connections necessary to tap into surveillance cameras—not with nooks and pillars and cars with which to play hide-and-seek with his nerves. But in a city-state where square footage consumed fortunes, street parking was nearly impossible to come by, and accessing the garages was the only way to get rid of the car and move the delivery forward.

Munroe pulled into the entry lane, took a ticket, and the beam lifted. Continued downward into a subterranean world reclaimed from the sea, well lit, and not yet filled with the day's haul of metal.

On cue, the phone beeped another alert.

She scanned the text, placed the phone in her lap, and took the vehicle past long rows of sporadically spaced cars, down another level, beyond many open spots, toward the areas farthest away from the choice parking that arriving drivers would fill first.

Cameras monitored the interior in the same way their counterparts did the streets above, and so Munroe continued at a crawl, searching out blind spots, and finally, as certain as she could be under the circumstances, pulled into a space next to a Pajero where at least the vehicle's height would shield something.

Turned off the ignition. This was the end.

The final instructions required going on foot, out in the open, in public. Munroe left the parking ticket in the glove box and car keys in the visor, as instructed, and while Neeva sat staring, clearly waiting for some piece of advice or news, grabbed the backpack from the backseat, pulled the GPS off the dash, and shoved the machine inside. Paused long enough to glance over Neeva.

The ripped tights had been replaced on the road toward Genoa, and although Neeva's eyes were puffy and she was developing dark circles beneath them, the makeup had been redone well enough that she looked presentable—stareworthy, but not in a beat-up domestic-abuse sort of way. Munroe reached for Neeva's hair, and when the girl winced, she stopped.

Said, "May I?"

Neeva held still.

Munroe fluffed up the curls, untwisting several that had wrapped around one another. Other than that, the hair, like nylon doll hair, was still perfect, and for all of the attention the getup would attract, it also provided a distraction; human nature would have observers try to make sense of the costume before noticing the person wearing it.

"You look good," Munroe said, and Neeva rolled her eyes.

Munroe reached low and popped the hood, felt beneath the seat for the lug wrench stowed so many hours ago, and left it on the floor between her feet. Then, deliberately and very slowly, so that she drew Neeva's attention to her movements, she placed Lumani's phone on the console, opened the driver's door, and said, "Let's go."

She made it around to the other side before Neeva had stepped fully to the pavement, took Neeva's hand, guided her away from the door, and shut it. With her arm around Neeva's shoulders, Munroe walked her several steps from the car and said, "We don't have time to talk and I really need you to listen, okay? I am not one of *them*. I'm going to find a way to get us out of this mess, but you *have* to do what I say. Don't try to run, because if you do, they will find you and I will be powerless to save you, you understand?"

"But what about your friend who will die?"

"That's my problem," Munroe said, her voice a whisper and speech running at hyperspeed, trying to cram into fifty seconds what should take much longer to say. "Right now we need to focus on staying alive. I can get us out of here, but only if you do what I tell you."

Neeva's head tipped down, just once.

"The sniper is out there somewhere watching us and we're also being followed by the guy who hit you last night. I need to know where he is before we do anything. I'm going to give you the phone, my shoes, and the backpack. I need you to start walking when I hand them to you."

Munroe turned Neeva, oriented her based on what she'd seen on the GPS prior to packing it up, faced her toward an exit. "In that direction is a stairwell. Take it up to ground level. The exit will open to a street that leads to a seawall. Follow the ocean—you'll see a big hotel and a tunnel that runs under the hotel. Anytime the path splits, keep left and as close to the ocean as possible—always follow the ocean. Walk slow and keep going until I find you."

"What if you don't come?"

"Then I'm dead. Just walk. Don't talk to anyone, don't make eye contact, and if anyone recognizes you, pretend you're a body double."

Another head tip.

"And I am not kidding, Neeva, if you run, or try to get away from me, you'll be doing me a favor by letting me wash my hands of you, but these men *will* capture you again. If you try to get help from someone else, people will die. You are not smarter than them. Not faster. Not stronger. I am your way to salvation. Understand?"

"Yes," Neeva said, and Munroe, in one long, drawn-out movement, loosened her grip on the girl's shoulders and turned her so that they were eye-to-eye. Searched her face, her expression, her body language, wanting and trying to read what went on behind the mask, and then let go of Neeva completely. Slipped off her shoes, put them in the backpack, and handed it over. If after this the girl still chose to flee, she did so fully aware of the cost, and Munroe's conscience was clear.

"If I haven't found you within fifteen minutes," Munroe said, "then you're on your own."

Neeva stared at Munroe's socks and then up again at her face. "Thank you," she said.

Munroe turned to the car, lifted the hood long enough to grab the rag she'd once used to wipe off engine fluids, and gently, quietly pressed the engine cover shut. Opened the driver's door and pulled out the phone that was already ringing.

She pressed talk and, before Lumani had a chance to speak, said, "It was an accident, I won't forget again."

"You need to get moving," he said, and because of what was missing in those five words a wave of relief washed over her. He didn't have visual contact, had no idea what she'd just done, and Arben or some other thug would be there soon.

"We're moving now," Munroe said, then paused and with a lowered voice that bordered on conspiratorial said, "Valon, is there anything I need to know? I can connect the dots. Things aren't what you'd planned. If there's going to be a double cross, if you're getting set up—if I'm getting set up—let me on your side, we can work this together."

As had been typical of the man-boy so far, he waited a long while, but this time he didn't hang up. "I can't," he said finally, "it's not possible."

So she ended the call.

Before Munroe shut the door for the final time, she reached to the floor and pulled out the wrench. Set it on the ground and turned to Neeva, who'd remained waiting and quiet. Munroe put the phone in Neeva's hand and a finger to her own lips. Pointed to her eye and then the exit, and with a slight wave, motioned the girl off.

Neeva took a few hesitant steps, past an empty space, continued beyond the nearest parked car, and then turned as if begging for reassurance.

Munroe waved her on farther.

Neeva nodded and gave a mock salute: camaraderie—or Stockholm syndrome. Whatever went on inside that girl's head was now completely beyond control, and with instinct rebelling against letting her go, Munroe remained in place, watching the rear of the departing costume as Neeva sashayed in slow motion toward the other side of the garage and out of sight.

Munroe turned to the adjacent Pajero, and with the cold wash of assignment taking over, slid beneath, elbows to the ground, head angled beside a rear tire. Body poised and ready, she waited.

Arben arrived within the minute driving a black Passat, the first Munroe had seen of his ride, tires cruising slowly past, while his head, visible through the window, swept from side to side as if searching out the Opel. He braked. Reversed slightly and then pulled into the spot directly on the other side of his target.

Arben opened his door, and from where Munroe lay, she had only a line to his feet. If he'd been smart and on his game, if he'd believed half the things Kate Breeden would have told the Doll Maker, he would have leaned down to check beneath the chassis. At least then he might have had a fighting chance.

Instead, he stepped from his vehicle to the Opel, opened the driver's door, and according to the sounds that followed, dropped the keys from the visor into his palm and presumably took the parking ticket as well. His pause was long enough to tuck them into a pocket or pouch, and then he shut the door and returned to his car.

Munroe slid out and in a crouch between the rear axles of the two vehicles, her body shielded by tires and trunk space, she stretched just high enough to observe him through the windows. He was in the driver's seat on the phone, apparently on the receiving end of a one-sided conversation.

Palms to the concrete, runner on her mark, Munroe closed her eyes. Arben would follow on foot, but with Neeva moving slowly and the assumption that the two were together, he held back, allowing a small lead time. Cold fed into her hands, fueling the drive of the hunt. The voices that had for the last several hours played as backdrop to rage hushed in peaceful anticipation.

Arben's door opened.

She picked up the lug wrench and rag.

His feet hit the concrete.

She moved to a crouch.

He stepped out of the car and turned his back.

She stood.

She came up behind him fast, and as if in response to instinct, or perhaps the rustle of her clothes or her feet on the ground, he began to turn.

But he was dead from the time he'd arrived in the garage.

Dead from the moment he'd laid hands on Neeva.

Dead from the moment he'd first touched Munroe.

All the rage, all the anger, all the hatred at everything the Doll Maker stood for, the pain over Noah's death and Logan's loss, came through on that first and only swing.

The lug socket of the wrench connected with Arben's temple in the same moment his face turned toward her. The force of the swing and the smack of the metal snapped his head to an unnatural angle, and his body, which had begun to pivot in Munroe's direction, did a time-lapse pause before he sprawled against his car's side and slid down.

Whether he was dead or not, she didn't care and didn't bother checking. He was out cold, blunt trauma, with not a lot of blood. All that mattered. Wrench to the ground, both hands on Arben's collar, she pulled him closer to the car and stripped him of his jacket. Found his weapon, retrieved it. Checked the magazine, checked the sound suppressor, which was already attached. Stashed the piece. Found his phone, the Opel keys, and the parking ticket. Pocketed them. Thumbed through his wallet and pulled out seventy euros in cash. Not much, but better than nothing. Found his keys, unlocked the door, and opened.

Released the lever of the driver's seat so that the back reclined nearly horizontal. In a crouch, she dragged him by the underarms to the driver's door and propped him up. Tossed the jacket, the rag, and the wrench into the car; climbed in after them; and then, half kneeling, half squatting on the seat, hands cupped beneath his arms again, inched him into the car; stressing over the dead weight of his body and the time it took to drag him inward; stressing over how far Neeva had already gone and how much was still left to do.

twenty-seven

Munroe pulled Arben's torso into the driver's seat of the Passat, shifted his legs under the steering wheel, closed his door, and positioned him so he reclined with the seat. Leaned his head so that he faced his own window. Weapon to his hand, to the side of the head she'd battered, rag between her fingers and all she touched, Munroe pulled the trigger.

The *pop-spit* spattered bone and blood, and like the snap of a rubber band against skin, provided the shock of release.

She didn't pause to examine the aftermath. Left behind the weapon and the temporary illusion of suicide that might, if she was lucky, buy her a fragment of time. Was out the passenger door with Arben's jacket and her two pieces of evidence before she'd fully contemplated the emotional cost of what she'd just done.

Still low to the ground between the cars, Munroe opened the Opel's unlocked door, wiped the wrench down for prints, shoved it under the seat, and closed the door. If Monaco's video surveillance had been intended to prevent crime before it could be accomplished, the city had failed miserably, but still open to debate was whether or not the kill had been observed in real time. The answer would determine how far she could get before this underground world exploded in noise and commotion.

Strategy against strategy in mental triage, Munroe pulled out Arben's phone. Thumbed through his recently used apps. Mixed in among a handful of games she found what she wanted. Opened. And there was Neeva, a little red beacon crawling along a close-cropped map, depersonalized into the equivalent of an object in a shooter game that might as well have had a detached floating label marked with dollar signs moving along with her.

Bearings set, adrenaline still coursing, Munroe moved in the direction of the exit, slipping between vehicles whenever possible, dodging camera angles to the best of her ability, until finally out on street level, she traced the path Neeva had walked, or at least something close based on the pulsating red light, moved quickly to catch up, but not so fast as to draw the additional attention a young man in slacks and jacket with bruises on his face running down the road without shoes would bring.

Munroe reached the seawall and followed the curve of the ocean in the direction of the port, where, in so small a space, was the world's most expensive collection of waterborne real estate. Only when she spotted the back of Neeva's costume and no longer needed digital eyes did she slow.

In this early-morning hour tourist traffic was still thin, and although the roads were full of cars, there were few pedestrians. Not only did Neeva in her costume stand out, so did the man who sat on the seawall fifty meters down: the segment in which Lumani, in his final text, had instructed Munroe to deliver the package.

Neeva had done well in dragging out the distance, and even now strolled casually, taking time to pause and gaze at the ocean as if she was one of those who kept house in a nearby apartment or belonged to one of the yachts ahead. The man on the wall, who'd been slowly turning his head from one end of the walk to the next, caught sight of the costume and stared intently in Neeva's direction, fixated upon her.

Oblivious, Neeva walked on.

The man was middle-aged. Soft. Insecure. Scared.

Another pawn.

Munroe quickened her pace. Searched out balconies and

approaching cars, moving ever forward, randomly lengthening and shortening the distance between herself and Neeva. Wherever Lumani hid, he had to be west of the ocean, and the sun, still lifting in its arc across the sky, would work against him.

Pulling in detail, counting seconds, Munroe risked falling into the capture zone and into the crosshairs of Lumani's rifle.

She needed to see the client. Observe him. Memorize him.

He'd be here.

Somewhere.

The type of man who'd set these events in motion wouldn't be content to have the pieces fall into place without him. He would want to be present, watching, reveling in his own brilliance, gloating over how sure, odds stacked against him, he was to capture his quarry—certain to escape unscathed because he'd positioned others to take the fall.

Neeva kept walking. If Munroe didn't stop her soon, she would reach the man on the wall and slip into whatever trap awaited. Munroe quickened her pace to close the gap and then, in a heartbeat of recognition, hesitated.

He was here.

The focus of desire, in deck shoes and a sweater, clean-cut and casual, approached the sidewalk from a diverted path, walking a little dog in Neeva's direction so that he might, if he wanted, draw close enough to intersect her trajectory. The man on the wall half stood in the presence of the newcomer and then, in a jerky movement, almost as if realizing he'd committed a faux pas and might as well have pointed out his master, sat down fully and returned his focus to Neeva.

There was nothing overly distinguishable about the man with the dog: early fifties, perhaps, average height, and fit body, as were many wealthy people; straight blond or silver hair, kept short; skin tanned and freckled. His presence wasn't the tell pointing to who he was, nor was it that he was one of few along the oceanfront, nor even that he studied Neeva with a curious smirk, as any passerby might, nor his posture or his stride. The tell, subtle and shameless, was his expression, which screamed of recognition.

His image burned inside Munroe's head: body shape, gait, ratio of limbs to torso, all of it etched onto a mental canvas. She sought out his eyes and he noticed her now, studying him, and averted his gaze while the narration of his body language turned a page and his lips lifted in a half-snarled grin, as if to say *I know who you are, and I win: game over.*

With his acknowledgment and his taunt, the euphoria that turned killing into a satisfied craving, demons battled and conquered, rose from the dead. Vision fading to gray and casting the target in vivid color, voices chanting, heartbeat quickening into the percussion of war, the urges sent her to the hunt. Lust for blood brought her to the tipping point beyond which there was no backing away from the kill. Panting, breathing against the pressure, Munroe pressed palms to her temples and physically pushed past the urges.

Logic against desire.

Strategy before action.

To release them now under the watchful eye of the city cameras was to seal her fate together with his. The client passed her, gaze locked on hers as he went, smirk still wide, the story continuing in his expression. He knew her. Somehow, he knew her.

Munroe reached Neeva and, still fighting the want, the craving, wrapped an arm protectively around the girl's waist. Neeva handed Munroe the phone and pointed at it, eyes wide as if to say, *It rang while you were gone.*

Munroe nodded. Let go of the girl, accepted the phone, and with all of the pent-up emotional energy that had gone unused in the client's wake, threw the phone out toward the ocean.

Munroe lifted the backpack off Neeva's shoulders and handed her Arben's jacket. "You did good," she said. "Put this on, it'll make your clothes less dramatic."

Neeva turned her nose up slightly. "Doubt it," she said, but took the jacket anyway, and while Munroe stepped back into her shoes, Neeva slipped into sleeves that went past her hands. The size added comedy to the getup, but the dull navy blue also covered so much of Neeva's dress that the vivid color all but vanished.

The man on the wall began to stand, then paused and sat again in apparent bafflement over a course of events that had nothing to do with what he seemed to expect.

Arben's phone rang.

Munroe ignored the jolt and shifted between Neeva and the wall, positioning herself so that she could observe the mark and gloat

over his reaction when he turned to watch the scheduled approach
and discovered plans had changed; she kept her arm around Neeva
and readied to cross the street against traffic when the moment arrived.

The client paused and turned back, and the quick flash of surprise that passed across his face phased into hostility. Munroe
waited for a break in traffic. Smiled beatifically while the voices
and the bloodlust urged her toward him, willed him closer, begged
for a viable excuse and the pretense of an accident for the sake of
cameras and passing cars so that the floodgates could release and
her torment be satisfied.

But the client didn't move. How could he, when the location,
with its cameras and high visibility, all meant to taunt authority
and possibly ensnare the Doll Maker's operation, now had the potential to be his own undoing? Eyes hard and lips pressed together,
his hand clenched around the leash so tightly that his knuckles
whitened.

Arben's phone rang again, reminder that Lumani, still out there,
was aware that things were askew. For whatever reason, he hadn't
yet taken a shot.

Munroe said, "We need to move; stay close."

Together they stepped off the sidewalk into the street. Munroe
guided the girl, skirting across lanes during intermittent gaps in
traffic. For a third time, the phone rang, and once more Munroe
ignored it.

From the other side of the road, she smiled at the client again,
imprinted his face again. He would die. On Munroe's life, she would
eventually see to it that he died, but for now she had robbed him
of his prize.

Munroe turned her back and prodded Neeva toward the tunnel.
They used the pedestrian passage beside the road and hurried back
in the direction they'd come.

At the garage entryway, Munroe scoped the distance and listened for sirens, searched out Lumani or any other person who
would set off the inner warning sensors. The lower level had filled
considerably in the minutes they'd been gone. Ignoring attention
from passersby, arm still around Neeva's waist, Munroe pushed the
girl forward until they reached the Opel.

Munroe pulled out from the parking spot and wound through

the ramps toward the exit. At street level came the first sound of sirens. They arrived too slowly to have been the result of Arben's murder being caught on camera and had certainly not come as a result of his body being discovered.

Parking ticket to machine, cash to machine, machine arm to the sky.

Seconds ticked along while the sirens grew louder.

Munroe ignored the itch along her skin that told her to run. Monaco wasn't more than three miles at its longest stretch, and they were about halfway in from the north. It would take them less than ten minutes to get beyond the judicial boundaries of the city-state. Notice would go out to the French police, but once outside the city proper, where every square foot was utilized and packed, there'd be a chance to hide.

"Are those sirens for us?" Neeva asked.

Munroe nodded.

"Oh my God," she said. "Michael, stop! Stop the car. They can help us." When Munroe's response was to check the mirrors and pull around a slower vehicle, Neeva grabbed Munroe's forearm and tugged.

The reaction to the physical contact was instant and brutal, and Munroe struck without thought. Pulled back before fully connecting, and Neeva stared wide-eyed at Munroe's hand frozen in space, angled toward her throat.

"You need to be careful about the grabby thing," Munroe said. She took her eyes off the road just long enough to glance at Neeva and added, "It's not personal."

"Stop the car, please," Neeva said. "Why won't you stop?"

"Right now, the police are not our friends."

"Of course they are," Neeva said. Her tone went from excited panic to pleading. "They'll know who I am, they can get me home."

Lights flashed in the rearview mirror.

Vehicles began to pull to the sides. "The sniper sent them," Munroe said.

The car in front of them slowed to move aside, and Munroe jumped ahead.

Like the one man running in a crowd of casual shoppers, she'd just clued them in to the chase. But now the road was clear. Munroe pressed foot to floor, and the Opel gave up speed reluctantly.

With a kidnapped girl at her side and a dead man in her wake, Lumani had to know she would avoid the law. He was forcing her to choose between evils: Allow capture and lose years of her life waiting for the authorities to sort out what had actually happened, while in the meantime Neeva was sprung and delivered. Or be flushed from hiding into a waiting net.

Munroe checked the rearview once more.

Confirmed again that Neeva's seat belt was fastened. Tight spaces and clearly defined roads be damned. The city had more than one way out.

twenty-eight

With every movement exacted in precise counterpoint to frustration and mounting anxiety, Lumani removed scope from rifle.

Twist. Breathe. Pack. Think.

If ever he hated Uncle, hated him to his core, this was that moment. So close. Within a minute this entire ordeal would have been over, and in that minute it suddenly wasn't. *The analysis is unassailable, Valon, the plan is perfect. If failure will be found, it can only come through faulty execution.*

Uncle the planner, Lumani the doer.

Clearly, the plan *wasn't* perfect, because the driver had just done what Uncle had said was unthinkable, impossible.

Lumani slid out of position.

He'd not wanted this assignment. Had begged off of it.

Capture the driver, yes; in spite of the warnings, he could deliver her to Zagreb and put her in Uncle's array. But the obligation of bringing the merchandise to the purchaser—he'd wanted nothing of it. Prior deliveries had been fraught with complications while the client toyed with his abettors, a veritable match of wits with Uncle that had twice nearly ended in disaster.

Now this third *was* a disaster.

At least two more men, Uncle. At least one more car, please.

No. The answer was no, made worse because the request challenged Uncle's infallibility, spoke of doubt in the great man's ability to predict so many moves in advance. Uncle had always been right.

Always. Until now.

Lumani had been given no room to refuse.

Uncle would hear nothing of logic or reason—weak excuses, he called them—and against Lumani's objection put the assignment with its high price for failure on his shoulders. "You are the weak spot," Uncle had said. Derision that cut like slivers of glass, disgust reserved for garbage rotting in the sun. "You, Valon. Always remember. You." And then pressing those slivers into Lumani's flesh: "Do this and I release you. You can take your money and your life and go to your parties and your whores. Don't think I'll spare you if you refuse."

Resentment smoldered, hatred keeping time with movement, perfect movement, as superstitious as it was mechanical, while he jogged the steps to his car.

He called Arben again and for the third time received no answer, which meant the man was dead and for this he felt nothing. Overconfident and arrogant, Arben hadn't heeded the warnings and so had brought an end upon himself. Lumani left a voice mail for the Michael woman on the off chance she took the time to listen. Beeped open the car and tossed the briefcase into the back.

No matter what Uncle claimed, the failure was not in the doing. The failure was in the planning, in the understanding, in the predicting. *You don't need extra men or extra cars, Valon, the choke hold is the reason she complies.* Yet a moment before delivery, the Michael woman had defied Uncle's prediction and diverted.

Failure that shouldn't be his to bear.

Lumani climbed behind the wheel. Revved the engine and backed out of the parking space with more noise than necessary.

Needed to calm. Needed to think.

Did she know about Logan's rescue? She couldn't. He'd listened for even the tiniest of chances that she'd somehow found a means of communication, for a signal of any kind, and had heard nothing, seen nothing. She couldn't know . . . could she? Lumani questioned himself. His judgment. His ability.

Uncle's voice chanted inside his head: *You are the weakest of them, Valon.*

She'd been parked alongside the country road in the dark when the rescue happened and still waited two hours for the footage—a lucky break that had been, filming before the mercenaries had come calling, though it had taken time to get the connections re-established and the clip uploaded. But if she knew her friend was safe, if she was going to run, why hadn't she done it sooner?

Lumani pulled into traffic. In the distance the sirens wailed and from them he felt a surge of pleasure. This part of the planning, which had been made on the go and was his alone, would be more successful than Uncle's so-called insights: When the Opel was flushed out, he would be waiting.

That the car had to be ambushed at all, that the driver was still alive, was an unforgivable failure. He was expected to make a re-taliatory kill and in a decisive second had chosen not to. Traffic and pedestrians that wouldn't have been present even an hour earlier meant that he didn't have a clean line of sight. He couldn't afford the margin of error.

Excuses, Uncle would say. In an endless maze of accusations and trains of thought jumping from one track to the next, logic would turn to absurdity, and always Lumani was to blame.

The injustice burned hot, burned angry.

No matter how successful he might be in fixing this, he'd still be held responsible—responsible for a failure that had not been his, for decisions that had not been his, for actions that had not been his.

Lumani dialed Tamás. Barked a command. Hung up.

A man's strength was defined and proven by the strength of his enemy. He would prove to himself that he would not be beaten.

Uncle be damned.

On the passenger seat the tablet blinked the red lights of the Opel's tracker, the Doll's tracker, the driver's tracker, all together in one movement like a big, happy, blended family. Lumani noted distance and kept time.

His earpiece, which had until now been silent, chirped with sound from the bug inside the Opel. "I know you can hear me, Valon, I know you're listening."

He swerved to avoid a car entering traffic. Was nearly to the border of the city, still a jump ahead of her. "I know your plans because I am *you*," she said. "I'm inside your head. You think you know what drives me, but you don't. You can't outthink me, and I *will* outrun you."

Lumani smiled, pleased. *A man's strength, defined by the strength of the opponent.* In response, he checked the tablet. Tamás was closing in from the other end of the city. She was between them, moving in his direction, and then, just as she'd done on the delivery, she detoured. Up. Toward the hills, away from the plan as if she'd read him. With so many directions in which she could turn, he didn't have the manpower to corner her.

He would let her run. Let her expend herself, and when she'd exhausted and slowed a bit, got to feeling safe, he would close in.

DALLAS, TEXAS

Bradford hit the call button and tried again. Maybe the fiftieth time in four hours, an unnecessary and worthless repetition, because somehow it made him feel better.

The first time had been right after he'd left the eighteen-wheeler and climbed into the Explorer. That call had gone directly to voice mail.

He'd left messages, sent texts, and without a response, kept trying, until finally he got a mechanized voice that he didn't need to understand to know that the number had been disconnected.

Munroe's handcuffs were off, and he had no way to communicate the news to her, no way to know if she was even still alive or if his contribution to the party had come too little or too late.

He pushed that thought aside. Logan was safe. That mattered on its own, regardless of whatever else played out, and from the *whatever else* followed the fear and he pushed that away, too.

If she *was* still alive, the most probable scenario was that she'd get ahold of another phone and call the voice drop again, but according to his frequent check-ins with Walker, that hadn't happened, either.

It was nearing four in the morning when Bradford pulled into the parking space beside the Trooper. He and Jahan had dozed in the emergency room after bringing Logan in, had waited around just long enough to ensure that he was stable before making the three-hour trip back to Dallas. Bradford had done the driving and now, blurry-eyed and sleep-deprived, made for the office.

The Capstone reception area was empty and low-lit when they stepped through the doors, three days' worth of boxes and mail delivery still cast to the side and ruining the carefully crafted image of the normally meticulous front room.

Jahan swiped his card and buzzed them through the panel. On the other side, Walker waited in the war room. She shook her head before Bradford could ask the question: Still no news out of Europe.

"Anything from Adams? Gonzalez?" he asked.

"There's a court date, but no updates. All continues as it was."

"Adams still in Houston?"

"Burning dollars, hanging around, feeling useless."

"Kate Breeden will make a move," Bradford said. "Trust me, the timing isn't coincidental." He paused. "What about Alexis? Tabitha? Have you checked them again?"

"Knocked on the door of one pretending I'd got the wrong address. Called the other, same story, and then about two hours ago Alexis called the office. Everything's normal."

"I don't like it."

"Just go sleep," she said. "There are a few minor things on the board, not anything you have to look at right away, and there's nothing more we can do here—not without news."

Bradford nodded and headed for his office, for the bedroll, for whatever sleep he could grab in the moments of silence, because even with Logan tucked away and out of state, this thing wasn't over yet, wasn't anywhere close to over.

Underneath the desk, he turned away from the world, sleep fell hard, drawing him fast and deep into a turbid blackness, where before he'd even fully stretched out, relief from feeling and relief from burnout cocooned him in silence and forgetfulness.

Was awakened just as suddenly, thrust into the middle of war: explosion, shaking and reverberation, shattering glass, crunching metal, and the smell—that indelible burning, acrid stench of unnatural death.

The survival brain that had lived through more firefights than he could count had him crawling down the hallway, bracing for a secondary explosion, moving closer to the cries for help, the cries of combat, the cries of the maimed and bleeding; dialing 911 as he went because halfway down the hall full awareness kicked in: He wasn't in a combat zone but the Capstone office; the rooms weren't dark but filled with daylight.

Silence followed the explosion, silence like a black hole that drew in and devoured everything. Bradford yelled for Jahan. For Walker. Heard her plaintive wail, a call for help, and moved toward the sound, toward the paneled reception door that had blown inward, the walls ripped and twisted. Skirted glass from the interior, shattered and littered across the carpet.

Sirens filled the background.

Walker's plea called to him, and through quicksand and over fire, he slogged in slow motion to the reception threshold and found her just beyond the door, on the floor, her head leaning against the wall of the desk.

Blood, so much blood.

On his knees, he reached for her, hands searching both tender and frantic, trying to find the source of the bleeding.

"FedEx package," she whispered.

"Shhhh," he said.

He tore her shirt and bared her skin. Gaped and stuffed the material into the largest hole.

Helpless. He was helpless.

Her skin was clammy. He reached for her wrist and checked her pulse.

"FedEx package," she said again.

Tenderly, he moved her so that she lay flat. Had nothing with which to elevate her feet. "Hang in here," he said. "Help is coming."

He leaned forward, searched beyond the desk for Jahan. Pulled back with images from another world, another life, flooding from every pore; unspeakable things seen and experienced, bodies charred and dismembered, combat memories shoved away and better left forgotten. Sweat and emotion coated his skin while Jahan—what was left of Jahan—unrecognizable to anyone unfamiliar with the nightmare that was war, held vigil at the front of the desk.

The smells. The blood. The wreckage.

Jahan, who had taken the full force of the explosion, would have died instantly.

Bradford tore off his jacket, laid it across Walker's chest. Loosened the snaps and belt at the waist of her cargo pants. Her blood covered his hands, his jeans. Her eyes were shut and he tapped her cheek. Held her jaw, turned her face toward his, screaming inside his head though his voice entered the world as authority without horror. "Samantha."

Her eyelids lifted slowly.

"Listen," he said.

She responded with another eye flutter.

"The sirens are downstairs. Do you hear them? Listen!"

Downstairs—they had to be downstairs by now.

Help was coming. Had to be coming.

"Here," she whispered, teeth chattering.

"Please," he said. "They're coming. Please hold on."

"Jack," she said. "Package."

"Shhhh," he said, and the background filled with thunder, peripheral vision with color. Boots against the silence. Rescue.

Hands pushed him away from Walker and he fought them. "ID!" he screamed. "Need to see ID!" Although the verbal replies didn't satisfy, they were enough for him to let go, to fade into the background while limbs and bodies blended into waves of patterns and Walker was lifted onto a stretcher.

Bradford followed out the door. Sat with her in the ambulance while activity rushed and blurred around him, a hurried and methodical fight to keep her alive. Stayed with her from ambulance to emergency room until finally hands pushed him back again and he was left staring at a threshold he could not cross, and blinded, was guided to the same waiting room that just four mornings earlier he and Walker had entered in their search for Munroe.

These were not the worst casualties he'd experienced; on a logical scale, a visual scale, a sensory scale, today couldn't come close to matching mass graves of decomposing bodies, or mutilated children, or IEDs and burning personnel carriers. But these were people he loved and had bled for, this was his own land, the office was his home away from home. These were not strangers, this was not the battlefield.

Bradford found a seat. Fell into it more than sat and stayed staring at the floor, air seeping into his lungs incrementally. He would not return to the office, not when only carnage awaited him. For now, this room was all he had: there was no place to go, no mission to accomplish. Everyone near him had, within the last four days, been ripped away, leaving in the gaping holes an empty numbness.

He needed to get out before he imploded. Had to get back to the garage and move the Trooper with its war chest before investigating bodies got too far into digging for whatever they hoped to find.

One foot in front of the other, more aimless than direct, Bradford left the waiting room for the outside world. Called for a taxi and then dialed Munroe again, desperate for her voice, for one ray of light in the darkness, afraid of what he might say if she did answer, afraid of himself and the inner deadening that pointed to a danger far more lethal than any rage he'd felt.

twenty-nine

Out of Monaco, up into the hills, roundabout to roundabout, Munroe headed away from the coast. The rearview offered no glimpse of Lumani, but she didn't need to see him to know that, like a shadow following the beacon, a shark circling for blood, he was out there. The danger wasn't in the running, the danger was in the stopping, and eventually she would have to stop.

They could find sanctuary if they stayed just one step ahead for a little while longer. In Nice, the closest sizable chunk of civilization beyond Monaco, there was an American consulate—not the same level of protection as an embassy, sovereign territory on foreign soil, with its Marines and high security, but safety nonetheless.

In Nice, Neeva could contact her parents, get a passport, and go home. In Nice, Munroe could contact Bradford. Find out about Logan. Regroup. Think. Sleep. God, she needed sleep. In Nice was a refuge, a place where, for a time, she could stop running, but she wouldn't be able to get there in the Opel. Not with the evidence that tied her to the murder in Monaco, a murder for which she wasn't willing to keep running for the rest of her life.

Scanning, hunting, Munroe scouted the area, time ticking off inside her head. At every turn, every junction, she opted for provincial signage and smaller roads until they were thoroughly into countryside. Neatly kept fields rose and fell with the rises and dips in the terrain. Farmhouses abutted the roadway, and traffic was sporadic at best.

A flash of red caught her attention, and she pulled the Opel off the road and followed a gravel track fifteen meters in, past laundry drying on the line and well-tended vegetable and flower gardens still in the young stage of early spring, to a courtyard between a three-story farmhouse and a building that was either storage or a barn. She stopped next to the motorbike that had caught her attention: the flash of color against the whitewashed wall.

Munroe shut off the engine. Waited for any sign of occupancy in the house, and when there was no rustling of curtains, no face peering from window or door, and no dogs coming to greet her, she got out of the car.

Down the road in either direction the quiet hum of nature replaced the traffic noise. Birds in a territorial screech flushed from a nearby berry bush, all of it a relative silence that made it easy to hear a car approach from far away, which meant neighbors who'd heard the Opel's engine would have taken the time to glance out windows; meant that no matter how secluded this particular set of buildings, someone had inevitably seen her pull in and was now curious.

Five minutes to be here and gone again, if she could find what she wanted.

Munroe leaned toward the car window, put finger to lips, and motioned Neeva to follow; strode across the gravel parking area and up the steps to the farmhouse door.

Peered through the glass; rapped on the frame; was answered by silence.

The predictability of human nature said that the keys to the motorbike were inside. Would be found someplace familiar and routine: an office desk, a kitchen drawer, a key rack, or a decorative bowl—a spot intended to spare the house owners the ordeal of always having to hunt them down.

Munroe tried the lock, and when the door swung inward, stepped in after it. Motioned for Neeva to wait on the threshold, a decision intended to keep egress clear, but especially to keep the girl from touching anything or getting underfoot.

The side entry into the house opened at the end of a long wood-paneled and runner-lined hallway. The air inside smelled of a mixture of wax and dust. Munroe peered down the hall, stopped short at the sight of several sets of keys hanging from a rack. Softly on the runner she moved inward to snag them and then, securing them, backtracked to the kitchen; searched through cupboards and shelves, conscious of every wasted second, requisitioning as she went: long-handled broom, bottle of vodka, bottle of cognac, large tub of flour, box of matches, and knife.

Returned to the side door and, arms full, nodded Neeva, with her inquisitive and unhelpful stare, out of the way. Munroe dumped the bounty on the ground beside the car. "Wait here," she said, and continued to the laundry lines. Tore off a dry bedsheet and brought it to Neeva. With her foot, Munroe nudged the knife toward the girl. "Cut strips," she said. "Lengthwise. As quickly as you can."

Neeva set to work without asking why, and Munroe strode toward the motorbike. Checked the tires. Tried the keys until she found the one that brought the machine to life. Noted the fuel level, then switched off the ignition and dropped the rest of the keys on the ground, where they'd be discovered easily enough. She had her way out, and a compromise between lost time and forensic evidence.

Munroe returned to the Opel. Dumped the bottles of alcohol over the seats and then took three of the strips Neeva had torn and cut. Knotted the material, and with time moving faster than her fingers, the strips became a braid.

She paused again to listen: No sound of traffic. No sign of Lumani. At least not yet. Her initial five minutes had come and gone, and although she understood his mind, his strategy, knew he was content to hold back and let her run, she also knew they'd lost the lead and he would begin to circle in for the kill.

Munroe removed the Opel's gas cap and used the broom handle to push most of the cloth into the tank. When the braid was soaked, she pulled it out and repeated the procedure with the other end. Reached into the back of the car to snag the backpack and tossed the bag to Neeva. Lowered the rear window on the Opel just enough to feed the wick far into the interior, place it on a puddle of alcohol. When it was set, she moved to the front.

From the driver's seat, she scattered the flour in the interior until it filled the air, then tossed it against the windows, over the dash, several kilos' worth of the stuff until the inside was full of dust. Dumped the container on the ground and shut the door. "Step back a few feet," she said, and when Neeva complied, she lit a match and set the wick alight at its center.

Took Neeva by the elbow and hurried her toward the bike.

The flame traveled in both directions, the dust explosion inside the car louder and flashier than the slower burn of the fuel in the gas tank, all told not enough to destroy the vehicle in an exciting ball of flame, but enough. Fibers and hair were gone and the fuel would continue to feed the fire and raise the surface temperature inside the car enough to warp plastic and rid it of any prints that were left.

Mouth agape, Neeva stared at the car.

"Flour can do that?" she said.

Munroe prodded her forward. "We're in a hurry," she said. "We need to go."

TWO-WHEELED VEHICLES WERE not created equal. The motorbike, closer to scooter than motorcycle, was a world away from the Ducati abandoned in Dallas, black-on-black with speed and torque and adrenaline rush, but in the moment, as a way of escape and of pushing closer to ending the madness, it was every bit as beautiful.

With the Opel billowing black smoke, Munroe revved away from the farmhouse, bike tires spitting gravel, instinct adjusting for the differences between the power with which she was familiar and this lesser thing.

Neeva squeezed hard and pressed her forehead into Munroe's shoulder.

Reaching the asphalt, Munroe gained speed and traction. Down the road to the left, in the direction they'd come, activity announced itself in flashes of color. Not Lumani, but neighbors, inevitably curious about the noise, the smoke. Munroe took the turn hard and Neeva yelped; they headed in the opposite direction of whatever was going on down the road.

Without access to the GPS, without a solid bearing on roads that twisted and wound in no specific direction, sporadic signs to tiny and unrecognizable towns became meaningless markers forcing them to wander toward the edge of lost until the roads became larger, the signage pointed to the familiar, and the refuge of Nice, which had begun to dissipate like a mirage, phased back into a solid, viable destination.

Into towns, along two-lane streets that ran through the heart of them, the journey segmented into one roundabout and junction to the next; curving with mountain ridges and through tunnels, traffic often backing up in long stretches behind slower-moving vehicles. Not once did Neeva lift her forehead from the shoulder she'd planted it against, and her squeeze tightened whenever Munroe pulled out of the traffic queue and straddled the line, weaving ahead of cars in a way that would have brought on aggression back home, but here was no different than the erratic riding of the many other mopeds and scooters on the road.

They couldn't move as fast as Lumani, not if he was driving anything similar to Arben's Passat, but by zigzagging and maneuvering, cutting through traffic, they would gain a time advantage nothing on four wheels ever could.

Downhill and up again, Munroe bought minutes, bought Neeva's life in increments, until finally the road wound steadily downward and they reached the city, and neared the coast with the same humidity and salt-tinged breeze that had caressed Monaco's air.

Like the boardwalk in San Diego or South Beach, the coastal avenue of Nice was green and palm-tree-lined, and even this early in the season was filled with locals and tourists alike, cyclists, pedestrians, and skaters, all threading along the walking paths. Once within the city Munroe knew the way without directions, could find the building that anyone else would be hard-pressed to locate without having been there before.

A stone's throw from the beach, and two doors down from a police station that filled the corner of the block, just far enough back from the ocean that the crowds were thinner, the consulate was housed three floors up in a nondescript office building. Only a small square plaque near the intercom buttons announced its presence. No flag. No sign. No nothing.

Munroe took the bike up onto the sidewalk. Thumb-punched the intercom for the consulate before she'd fully switched off the ignition. "Get off," she whispered to Neeva, and when the intercom hissed, she said, "American citizens, passport issues."

After a short delay, the door buzzed and Munroe stretched forward to grab it. "Hold it open," she said, and Neeva, still sliding off the seat, reached out, took the handle, and stood in the door frame.

Munroe set the kickstand. Left the key in the ignition and hoped against hope that someone would brave the police station and steal the bike. She took Neeva by the elbow, prodded her inside, and shut the door behind them.

With the thud, with the silence in the cool empty foyer, with only postal boxes and an elevator bank for company, one world ended and another began. Munroe slumped against the wall, and for the first time since she'd felt the sting on her thigh those many, many hours ago in Dallas, she truly breathed.

She had brought Neeva to safety.

Realization settled, and against the wall, eyes closed and thumb to the bridge of her nose, she allowed the first wave of relief to reach inside. From here, she could discharge her duty and plot her own way forward.

When she opened her eyes, Neeva, looking as tired and beat-up as Munroe felt, was studying her. Munroe straightened. Pushed off from the wall and nodded toward the elevator. "Up we go," she said.

THE ELEVATOR OPENED onto a cramped foyer with a door on either side. One led to the stairwell; the other, metal-reinforced and CCTV-monitored, to the consulate.

When they stepped off the elevator, a uniformed guard waited for them.

Asked for passports, Munroe offered a modified version of the truth and presented the person of Neeva Eckridge in their stead.

The guard left them. Disappeared behind the metal door. Returned a few moments later and opened the door wide. They moved from a small foyer to an even smaller entryway, made impossibly cramped by both an X-ray machine and a metal detector, and before allowing them into the consulate proper, the guard X-rayed the backpack and requested all electronics.

Munroe handed over the bag. "Just keep it all," she said. "I'll get it on my way out."

The consulate filled the entire floor of the narrow building and was itself not more than one large room, partitioned by false walls and windowed booths that made it possible for those in the waiting area to see, if not hear, most of what went on beyond the accessible spots.

A young couple sat on one of the couches. Munroe assumed newlyweds, from their body language, and their facial expressions guaranteed that they recognized Neeva. Were it not for cell phones having been commandeered by the guard, she would have bet thirty seconds before images of Neeva hit the social networks.

The consulate's one staff member called Neeva to the window, and after a rush of hushed conversation, motioned for her to return to the guard area and from there through the security door that would allow her on the other side of the partition.

Backing away from the window and the woman behind it, turning in the direction she'd been ushered, Neeva glanced at Munroe for reassurance.

Munroe nodded her on.

This was how it should be. The wheels would start spinning, the phones ringing, and the powers-that-be would throw their weight into Neeva's fight. As for herself, all Munroe wanted was a phone that could make international calls. She needed to contact Bradford, and surely the consulate had one, but until the issue with Neeva was settled, until Munroe had been vetted, she wouldn't bother asking to use it.

The last of Neeva's dress passed around the corner, and Munroe, depleted beyond empty and with nothing more to do than allow fate to run its course, turned toward the waiting area's smaller couch. Ignoring the accusatory stares from the couple and the disapproving look of the guard, she sat, shifting her head to the armrest, her knees dangling over the edge, let go, and fell hard into oblivion.

THE COUPLE LEFT. Others entered and were soon on their way again. Another staff member arrived to tend fully to Neeva: On the edge of sleep, Munroe was aware of all of these things, but she pushed them away and allowed time to pass and a dreamless darkness to consume her until finally the room was quiet.

She begged the use of a phone. The consulate staff member passed the handset under the glass and, on Munroe's behalf, punched in the number for Bradford's cell as Munroe recited it. The connection made, Munroe nodded her thanks, and while it rang, dread and desire mixed, swirling, within a beaker of conflicted emotion.

More than anything, she craved the soothing of Bradford's voice, craved to drop from the pressure and the pain, from death and the fractured reality of the present back to peace—the way things were when she was with him, the way they'd been before this nightmare had struck. But the call would also bring news of Logan, news she could not bear to hear, yet must.

Even accounting for the long distance connection, Bradford answered immediately.

"Michael?" he said, and that one word, her name on his lips, like fire deprived of oxygen, suffocated the adrenaline of rage and suffering, suppressed the voices and tremors rumbling in the background, and she fell instantly into a vacuum of nothingness.

"Me," she whispered.

"Hey," he whispered back.

Receiver in hand, the cord taut, she slid down the wall and sat on the floor.

"Did you ever get my messages?" she said. "Were you able to find Logan?"

"We got them and we found him."

The air went out of her. She closed her eyes, breathing in the words she'd feared she'd never hear. "Thank you," she said. Paused. "Thank you," she whispered again. And then: "I've seen some nasty video footage. How is he?" When Bradford hesitated, she said, "Please tell me."

"They fucked him up pretty bad," Bradford said. "He's hospitalized right now—kept sedated for the time being. He's going to need reconstructive surgery at some point, but it's hard to get information because I'm not a relative."

She drank in air, one long, drawn-out breath following another. Decompression.

Logan was safe, and the joy of that fact washed over her.

She'd given him up for dead to do what she had to do, and somehow, in the midst of everything, running blind and without options, she'd brought Neeva to safety *and* Logan was still alive.

He might be damaged, but he was, unbelievably, alive.

She wanted to shout. To dance. To scream *Fuck you* to Lumani, who by now was certainly hidden in some enclave where he could target the consulate entrance. But her reaction remained muted as she stayed sitting, one hand pressed into the carpet, fingers playing with the fibers. "If you contact Charity, she might be able to help," Munroe said. "She holds a medical power of attorney for him." Charity, keeper of secrets from Logan's previous life and mother of his daughter—a child Munroe had risked her life to save.

"How are you?" Bradford asked.

"I'm okay," Munroe said. "In one piece—no bullet holes. I'm at the consulate in Nice, and I've brought Neeva Eckridge with me."

Bradford waited, and then said, "How *are you*?"

With the unspoken and valid concerns, her smile faded and she searched for words to properly give meaning and context to what he truly wanted to know.

"They killed Noah," she said, and on the other end of the line Bradford swore unintelligibly. She lowered her voice and added, "Truthfully, I'm not well." They both knew she wasn't referring to mourning.

"Africa?" he asked.

"Not as bad," she said, and then after a heartbeat, "Miles, I'll be okay, I promise. As soon as I fix things on this end, I *will* be okay."

"Argentina?" he asked.

She sighed and half-smiled over her failed attempt to get him to let the subject go. "No nightmares yet," she said. "Just the darkness, and it fades quickly."

"I worry," he said.

"I know," she whispered.

"Do you need help getting home?"

"Soon," she said. "I have unfinished business, but I think there might be an APB out for me. Is there any chance Jack could poke around? See what's out there?"

There was a long pause, the kind of pause even the worst delay on a horrible international line couldn't account for.

"Jack's dead," Bradford said finally.

She'd anticipated something like this and steeled against it, and yet the news still hit hard and overwhelmingly, the rawness inside made worse by Bradford's having fussed over her while giving no clue to the depth of his own cruel anguish.

"How did it happen?" she whispered.

"Explosion at the office," he said.

"And Samantha?"

"ICU. It's touch-and-go."

"Oh, God, Miles," she said. "I am so sorry."

"We both have unfinished business," he said, and his tone hardened, shifted from emotional to professional, almost as if he'd wiped his eyes and straightened his spine. He said, "What do you need, Michael?"

She hesitated, cautious of her wording. In a U.S. consulate, speaking on one of their landlines, which, even if not tapped, was still one of the least opportune places to discuss forged documents and guns and explosives. "I need everything," she said. "Do you know a guy?"

"You're in Nice?"

"Yeah," she said. "Nice. You can pull from my emergency reserve, all of it if necessary—it's no good to me if I'm dead. Can you work that?"

"Call me back in an hour," he said. "I'll let you know what I've got."

Munroe nodded to empty space, abhorring the idea of getting off the phone, of being separated from him again when what she wanted more than anything was to crawl into his arms and feel peace once more, to forget the moment. "An hour," she said, and added the words she wished she'd had the chance to say before she'd been ripped away. "And I love you."

"I love you, too," he said. "Always." And so ended the call.

Without moving from the floor or leaning back against the wall, Munroe reached her arm up to the desk and groped until she found the hole under the glass. Shoved the receiver inward and then slowly stood. Needed to step outside into the hall for a bit, needed to be alone.

In the small security room she collected her things. "I'm just going to the foyer," she said. "I'll be back in about ten minutes." The guard nodded.

Munroe turned and the side door opened. Neeva stood in the doorway, still in the doll clothes, still in the jacket, feet together and hands folded and looking more haggard than she had when they'd first arrived. "You probably want quiet," she said. "Could I have just a few minutes?"

Munroe hesitated and then motioned Neeva on ahead.

The metal door shut loud behind them.

"Was that your boyfriend?" Neeva asked, and Munroe nodded. Didn't want to go into any detail or explanation, didn't really want to talk at all.

Neeva clasped her hands together and then separated them. Shifted from foot to foot. Munroe understood the body language. They'd shared almost exactly twenty-four hours, most of that time as prisoners in a car—the kind of experience that made it awkward to say good-bye, made it feel as if there should be some formal ceremony to acknowledge the moment.

Munroe said, "Did you reach your parents?"

Neeva smiled. "They cried a lot," she said. "I cried a lot, too. Everyone says I'm really lucky. They talk about you like you're some sort of hero but like secretly you're in trouble or something."

"I probably am," Munroe said. "So." Paused. "What happens for you now?"

Neeva turned and looked toward the metal door. "They've called the FBI. They're arranging for a passport from the embassy in Marseilles. After that, flights and stuff."

"The pretty boy is still out there," Munroe said.

"They know. They said they can keep me safe and get me home." She sighed. "My dad said they're going to put me into protective custody, but I don't know if that's enough."

Munroe shrugged. "Hard to say." She slid down the wall and stretched her legs. Tipped her head back and up in Neeva's direction. "Anything that makes it more difficult is going to help."

"What about you?" Neeva asked.

"I've got a few things to take care of, someone's got to end this mess. Where I'm going, that type of protection wouldn't do me much good."

"Thank you," Neeva said.

"It's not just for you," Munroe said. The door opened and the guard asked Neeva to step inside to take a call.

Arben's phone, which had remained in the backpack, went off with a text alert. Neeva, who had begun to walk toward the door, froze. Blanched. Caught Munroe's eye with that deer-in-the-headlights look. They both knew the sound, the harbinger of evil. To the guard Neeva said, "Give me just a minute."

Munroe didn't move.

"Are you going to find out what it is?" Neeva asked.

Munroe pulled the phone out of the bag and turned on the screen. The text had come from Lumani's number, and in a Pavlovian reaction, her stomach churned. She didn't want to look, didn't want to hurt anymore. Wanted to put off whatever news this was until it didn't matter.

The Doll Maker's words mocked her: *There are others who matter to you.*

Voices in her head rose in chorus, a damning reply to the men who were the cause of this turmoil. *If you had let them live, I would not kill you.*

Munroe pushed the scripture back.

The image loaded, and in response to the visual of yet another life taken from her, her throat burned and her eyes smarted.

Neeva remained motionless, her face reflecting the horror. "Who is it this time?" she whispered, and when Munroe's only answer was to take the back off the phone and remove the battery, Neeva said, "What do they want?"

Munroe tossed the pieces of the phone into the pack and, without truly seeing, looked up at Neeva. "They want you," Munroe whispered. "Just as they always have."

thirty

The consulate waiting room had long since emptied, and in an un-abashed land grab, Munroe stretched out on the longer couch, one arm draped over her face, the other by her side. An hour until she could contact Bradford, an hour for the Doll Maker's latest trick to turn around and around inside her stomach, feeding and nourish-ing the cancerous hatred that poisoned her.

She hovered above the mental abyss, kept from falling by force of will. Shut out the world by descending into darkness, the closest she could get to putting herself into suspended animation while she waited for time to pass, waited to take matters into her own hands and either through her own death or someone else's put an end to this misery forever.

Conversation between Neeva and the office staff continued be-yond the walls, more of the same constant attention that filtered out as an indecipherable murmur and made it easy to imagine rounds of e-mail, one person confiding in the next until inexplicably news of Neeva's surfacing leaked and Internet headlines swirled with rumors and everyone with an opinion became an instant expert. Neeva could return to her life, to some sense of normalcy, and this time she'd have a wave of media at her back, cresting her celebrity status higher.

Munroe was glad for the girl. At least Neeva's story had ended happily, and now she could turn her back on that chapter to focus fully on what she must do next. At an hour to the minute, she sat up. Stepped to the glass and knocked for attention. Begged for the use of the line once more, and although the staff member, courteous and professional, obliged, Munroe understood from nuance the inconvenience her presence created.

She didn't need whispers and surreptitious glances to know that by bringing Neeva to the consulate she'd raised unanswerable questions about her own role. So the staff, with no authority to detain and question her, focused entirely on Neeva, politely providing Munroe with what she needed to sort out her own plans and then left her alone.

The woman put the handset beneath the glass and dialed.

Unlike before, Bradford didn't immediately answer, and Munroe counted rings. The inner pressure that had been kept in check, one soothing pull of oxygen at a time, amped exponentially higher with each long tone—fear of losing yet another part of what mattered— a pounding tempo that built, frenetic and maddening—proof, if she ever needed it, that she walked the razor edge of sanity—until the line finally connected and Bradford, breathless, as if he'd run for the phone, said, "I'm here."

The internal pressure released, collapsed into temporary calm.

"I've got you set," he said, "but the closest I could manage was Milan. Can you get into Italy?"

Munroe closed her eyes and sighed. More driving. More time wasted.

"Yes," she said. "I can do it."

"I haven't been able to find an alert out for you yet," he said. "Doesn't mean it's not there, just means I haven't found it. Do you have access to e-mail?"

The waiting room had a computer that the consulate staff would connect to the Internet if that was what she needed. "I can get to my race-or-die account," she said.

"I'll send you general directions. It'll get you started. You'll need to contact me from Italy for the rest of the details. I'm sorry about that." He paused. "Do you have any money on you?"

"About seventy euros," she said. "It's enough to get me to Milan." She hesitated. "Miles, they have Alexis."

Bradford was silent a long second. "I was afraid it would happen," he said. "I tried to protect her. When you disappeared, we started digging and pulled a match on some of the information in the Burbank files. I went to Kate hoping she might have some idea of what was going on. She's still facilitating, Michael, even from behind bars, only now it's not for you but against you. She sees this as her magnum opus. Payback, she said. She's had an appeal running through the courts—her next court date is in a few days—and although I don't think she expects you to survive what she's put into play, no matter how things turn out, I think she's planning to disappear. I've got a team keeping an eye on things so we don't lose track of her."

Munroe drew in the words. Plotted through them, then said, "They're threatening to replace Neeva with Alexis if I don't get Neeva back to them." Paused. "But it gets worse." She outlined the logic, the analysis behind her fears regarding the client, the fate she expected either girl to be thrown to, and when she was finished, she shut her eyes against the pain. "They're forcing me to choose who lives or dies," she said. "And the result of not choosing is the same as making the decision itself."

"What will you do?" he said.

"Stay the course," she said. "If it's not Neeva, not Alexis, it will be Tabitha, or you, or someone else. It's not going to end, Miles, unless someone ends it." Munroe drew another long breath. "The image they sent me was taken in front of her home in daylight. Find her for me, Miles—please, if you're able. It's an unfair burden to place on you, and I'm sorry. It's the only way I can let everything go. I need you to free me so that I can do what I need to do."

"I'll give everything I've got," he said. "My friend will have a phone for you. I want you to call me when you get it." She understood what was left unspoken: call him so they could speak freely.

"I promise."

"I love you," he said.

"Always," she whispered.

She returned the handset beneath the glass and sat for a while, running circles around the effort she'd made to protect Alexis over the years, all of it gone to waste. Could count on one hand the people she'd allowed to become that close to her: Logan, Bradford, Kate Breeden, and a couple of male friends—long-forgotten—whom she'd brought home to her sister Tabitha's house for shock value during the worst of her inability to integrate into suburban American life.

They had been rough, her early years in the United States.

As a surprise to missionary parents who believed they were finished with child rearing, she hadn't exactly been wanted. She'd been six when her closest sibling, more like a father than a brother, turned eighteen and left Africa for home. There were two sisters before him who'd been old enough to remain in Dallas when their parents had moved to Cameroon, and until Munroe, just shy of her eighteenth birthday, had showed up unannounced on Tabitha's doorstep in the United States, whatever familial bond that existed had been based entirely on sporadic photographs and occasional mail that arrived until she was fourteen and had abandoned home for good.

Munroe wasn't so much the black sheep of the family as a nonexistent child who'd given up trying to belong to sisters she'd never known and a brother who'd abandoned her; had given up trying to earn parental approval in favor of carving her own niche on Cameroonian soil until, at seventeen, violence sent her running to a country that held no attachment but a passport and strangers she called family.

Moving into Tabitha's house had meant living with a woman old enough to be her mother, who'd welcomed her because of who she was and resented her for everything she wasn't; a woman whose eldest daughter, Alexis, was the closest Munroe ever had to a real sister, and now the Doll Maker had her.

Munroe stood. As with Logan, she would abandon what she wanted most to do what needed to be done. Wouldn't bother with getting Bradford's e-mail, she knew where she was going, and Internet access here at the consulate or not, she'd still have to find a way to get the details once she was in Italy.

If Neeva had been alone, Munroe would have stopped to say good-bye, but under the circumstances she preferred not to invite the additional attention doing so would attract. In the security area, she retrieved the backpack again with the maps, the tape, the GPS, the pieces of Arben's phone, and everything else she'd dumped into it before abandoning the Opel.

Passed back through the metal detector—the only way out of the consulate's one exit—but before she got to the foyer, the side door opened and Neeva was there.

The girl followed her to the elevator. "You're leaving?" she asked.

"Yeah," Munroe said, and passed up the elevator for the stairwell.

Neeva didn't stop. "I need to talk to you," she said.

"Now's not a good time, Neeva."

The girl followed down the flight of stairs. "It's important."

On the second-floor landing, Munroe paused. Turned so that she was eye-to-eye with Neeva, who was a few steps behind. "Go back," she said. "I'll e-mail; you can talk to me later."

Neeva was beside Munroe now. "I want to come with you."

Munroe paused midstep, Neeva's words like cymbals crashing inside her head, was noise that kept reverberating and drowned out everything else. Hissed, "Are you out of your mind?" Moved another two stairs down and stopped again. Turned again. "I just risked my life and the lives of people I love to get you to a safe place. Get away from me. You have your shot at freedom. Go home."

One floor up, the door to the stairwell opened and the guard, who'd apparently followed Neeva out, leaned over. Seeing the two in a standoff, the woman trotted a half-flight down and peered around. "Neeva?" she asked. "Is everything all right?"

The tone was friendly enough, but her facial expression and body language betrayed the protective animosity Munroe had felt since their arrival. Neeva turned to the guard, and Munroe, unwilling to endure the ludicrousness of the conversation, used the break in focus to keep going, two steps at a time.

Neeva ignored the woman's question and followed Munroe.

On the ground floor, Munroe pushed through the door to the lobby, was halfway to the main entry when Neeva popped out behind her saying, "Michael, please let me come with you."

Munroe said, "Go back."

Neeva hurried to catch up. "I won't," she said—that same goddamn stubbornness and refusal to quit that had made the first half of the drive from Zagreb so much trouble.

Munroe spun around. Nearly collided with the girl. "What the hell is wrong with you? Do you have any idea the risks I've taken to get you here? People have died for you and you finally have a chance to get out of this mess. Go. Go back. Be free. Live life."

Neeva crossed her arms. Said, "No."

"Get the hell back up those stairs or I'll drag you in by your hair."

"You wouldn't," Neeva said, chin out and defiant. "Not with the consulate people up there, staring at you, secretly wondering if you had something to do with my kidnapping. You're smarter than that."

"Fuck you," Munroe said. "I'm done being responsible for your life." She turned her back and stepped from the cool, silent interior of the lobby to the noise and life of the streets outside.

Neeva did likewise, and the pounding inside Munroe's chest upticked to a dizzying tempo. Noah had died and she'd risked Logan's life to get Neeva to a place safe from the Doll Maker, safe so she could discharge all responsibility, cut loose from the puppet strings, and put an end to the madness.

Insanity.

Lumani was out there somewhere—not just Lumani. If he'd had anyone local, then he'd possibly pulled together reinforcements during their hours inside the consulate, would be waiting and watching for an opportunity, and here she was again, tracking device saying *Come and get me,* and Neeva exposed and out on the street in the open, as if the entire ordeal of the previous twenty-four hours, the death and the suffering, had been for nothing.

Munroe stared at the empty space where the motorbike had been. Stolen or reclaimed, she'd never know. The back of her neck prickled with the unmistakable feeling of being watched. Her gaze shifted to the park across the street and from there to the nearby buildings. She strode away from the consulate, in the direction away from the coast. At the nearest cross street, Munroe took a sharp turn, and at the next street another, each directional change chosen at the last second, a form of mental coin toss, while her eyes ran a continuous scan along rooftops, balconies, windows, and streets for a sign of the shooter.

Whatever her pace, Neeva kept up. Not at Munroe's side, or even as a shadow at her elbow, but with the timed rhythm of a determined tracker, following a few feet behind, just beyond the edge of her peripheral vision. Munroe didn't turn, never stopped to gauge how close she kept but could feel her, tugging at the threads of awareness.

This was the path to madness, to death. Made no sense at all, served no purpose. Enraged her sense of justice and fairness. Made a mockery of the life expended and the choices made. They passed an empty apartment doorway, and Munroe turned and grabbed Neeva. Shoved her into the nook. Fisted the jacket at Neeva's throat, and, teeth clenched, pushed her against the wall. "They will kill you," Munroe said.

Chin out, still defiant, Neeva said, "We all die"—a paraphrase of the words Munroe had quoted in the aftermath of the fight with Arben—"it's really just a question of what deals the final blow."

"No," Munroe said. She tightened her grip on Neeva's clothing and pushed her harder against the wall so that her head knocked back. "You don't fucking understand. They're not just going to kill you. That man with the dog, the one in Monaco, he's a psychopathic sadist. He's going to carve you up in pieces and take his sweet time doing it—he's not going to *just* kill you, he's going to torture you for his own gratification, he's going to get off on making you bleed and suffer. Do you get that?" Shoved again. Harder. Angrier. "Right now, me standing here, having this moronic conversation with you, ups the chance someone else is going to die exactly like that."

Neeva pushed back. "No, you don't understand," she said. "I see what you don't see."

Munroe dropped the backpack, kicked it down a step, lowered her voice, and said, "What the hell are you talking about?"

"I am not the stupid silver-spoon spoiled rich kid you think I am," Neeva said, and she, too, lowered her voice, stopped pushing, and Munroe relaxed her grip. Neeva slipped down the wall slightly so that she stood straight again.

"I know you don't like me," Neeva said. Her words were rushed whispers, as though she was afraid she wouldn't have time to finish what she'd followed all this way to say. "You think I don't understand what saving me cost you and that I'm throwing away a chance to live. I'm not stupid and ungrateful. You saved me, right? But people died because you saved me. I don't know why they want me so bad, but I saw your face when you got that text. You don't have to tell me, but I *know*. Someone else is dead or is going to die because of me. How many will it take?" Neeva paused; her voice caught and she looked up into Munroe's face. "It's not right—one life for all those others."

The image of Noah, like a mirage rising from the desert, his body on the ground, darkened holes in his forehead, danced in Munroe's vision, and teeth clenched, she said, "It would have been really helpful if you would've reached that conclusion twenty fucking hours ago."

"I didn't understand twenty hours ago," Neeva said. "Didn't get what was going on—didn't see it until after we were inside the consulate and they started telling me some of the stuff they knew, and then that text came, and I saw your face and . . ." Neeva stopped. Pleaded. "How was I supposed to know?"

Munroe bit back spite and anger and venom. Food to a starving man, she wanted what Neeva offered yet couldn't take it. "You've fought too hard to just roll over now," Munroe said. "You want to live."

Tears welled in Neeva's eyes. "Yes," she whispered. "I want to live so bad—I want life more than anything else on earth."

"Then why are you doing this?" Munroe said. "I got you to safety." Paused. Whispered, "I fucking got you to safety. Against everything I wanted, against everything I am. I gave up everything to get you there. And now you just throw it away?"

"I didn't know. I didn't know what it cost you. I thought you were just like *them*—the people who stole me."

"You'd willingly turn yourself over to these people, this"—Munroe spat out the word—*"animal?"*

Neeva's cheeks flushed and she shook her head. "I-I . . . no. Not that. You're plotting something. You're going to get back at them, I know it. The men who took me, they still want me, so I thought maybe you could use me. Like as part of a trap or as a bargaining chip in your plan—like bait."

Munroe let go of Neeva's jacket. "God, you are so naive," she said. "You left the safety of the consulate for *that*? You are young and stupid and clueless, and I despise and adore you for it."

"Can you, though? Can you use me as bait and would it do any good?"

Munroe checked the street in both directions. They'd already stayed still longer than was prudent; needed to keep moving. Munroe took Neeva's biceps and turned her toward the sidewalk. "You know what happens to bait when you fish?"

Neeva stared at her blankly.

Munroe sighed and picked up the backpack. "This isn't Hollywood, Neeva. This isn't a movie set. In real life, the bait dies."

"But this is all so fucked up," Neeva said. "That *they* can just steal women and sell them—they do whatever they want, take whatever they want, and nobody does anything to stop them. But I heard you. You're planning. You're actually going to do something about it. I know how dangerous these people are, and I hate them, and I have a chance to make a difference. I can help you."

Munroe stared at her for a moment, wasting precious seconds, trying to understand the underlying thought processes that had made Neeva follow her, trying to grasp what Neeva *really* wanted, but in the end she had no reply, so she walked on in silence while Neeva stayed beside her, legs working overtime to keep up with Munroe's long stride.

Whether or not she wanted Neeva along was irrelevant now. She didn't have the time or the inclination to return her to the consulate, and she couldn't leave her to wander back on her own just so Lumani could pick her up en route. "We'll have to get you a hat," Munroe said, "and some different clothes." Once more she lowered her voice to a whisper. "And I can't promise to keep you safe. I have other priorities now."

"This was my decision," Neeva whispered back. "I'll be responsible for me." She hesitated. "But you'll do the best you can, right?"

"Yeah," Munroe said. "The best I can to keep you safe, but you're better off scared."

"Of course I'm scared."

"Good. At least you're not entirely insane. Odds are ten to one we'll both be fish food by the end of tomorrow."

Munroe checked over her shoulder. Along both sides of the street. Crossed it. Neeva said, "Well, you wouldn't be doing whatever it is you're doing if you didn't think you'd succeed."

Munroe stopped midstep, stood just long enough to stare hard at Neeva. "You're wrong," she said, then continued walking again.

"I'm doing this because I don't have a choice. Even if everything had gone the way it was supposed to, even if I had delivered you like they wanted, the people I love would never be safe as long as I'm alive. If I traded you now, they'd still kill me—so I'm dead either way."

Munroe hunted for transportation along the side streets of Nice. Here the pedestrian traffic was lighter and those who took note of their passing fewer, but even off the main streets and busy walkways, the occasional passerby turned to stare at Neeva and her odd getup, which worked as much as a distraction from her face, and as such a disguise, as it did a beacon.

Neeva, seemingly oblivious as to the liability she was to Munroe, continued on, head up and shoulders back. Irritated by the girl's ignorance, Munroe nudged her. "Keep your chin down, eyes to the sidewalk," she said, "Unless you're *trying* to be recognized and stopped."

Neeva dropped her head, and Munroe skirted her around yet another corner to another street, keeping the trail as random and unpredictable as possible so that Lumani would be forced to follow and couldn't, even with reinforcements, set an ambush.

Down one more block, around a corner, and finally, on a narrow street with cars parked only on one side, their tires up against the curb to leave a single lane for two-way traffic, Munroe found what she wanted: a vehicle plain enough to garner little attention, new enough to be considered reliable, old enough to still be hotwired.

And it was unlocked.

Through the window, Munroe checked the fuel gauge. Three-quarters of a tank. She pulled the roll of tape from the backpack, ripped off a strip with her teeth, and tossed the tape and the pack at Neeva. "Get in the back," Munroe said. "Keep an eye out—let me know if anyone curious or angry heads this way."

"We're going to steal a car out in the open?"

Munroe opened the front passenger door and pointed with a head motion. "Consulate's about a kilometer that way. Just start walking. Pretty Boy will be by shortly to give you a lift."

Neeva climbed into the back.

Munroe checked the emergency brake and set the car in neutral. Lay across the floorboards and, head beneath the steering wheel, removed the plastic cover beneath the mechanism, searched for the wires that would take her home, and said, "This makes you an accomplice—no longer an innocent victim. The people in the consulate saw you walk out and follow me on your own, without coercion."

"Why do you keep trying to scare me off?" Neeva said. "I understand the consequences."

Munroe pulled at the wires. "Just checking," she said, "making sure you know there's a path between death and freedom, and it might not be a happy place, either."

Neeva huffed in reply, and with the piece of tape stuck to her forehead, Munroe used her nails and teeth to pinch and strip. She'd have been faster with more experience, but it'd been a while since she and Logan, still young and stupid, had played anarchists with other people's cars.

The ignition caught. Munroe taped the exposed wires and scooted out from beneath the seat and got behind the wheel. Leaned over to shut the passenger door, then put the car in gear. If they were lucky, they wouldn't need to stop between here and Milan, might not have to go through this process again, and with the border only forty minutes away along the highway—a route they could take now that Munroe was certain Neeva wouldn't be banging on windows and screaming for help from passing cars and tollbooth operators—odds were good that they'd be in Italy before the car was reported stolen.

Munroe checked for traffic and pulled onto the road. To Neeva she said, "If you throw that bag all the way to the back, you can come up front."

Neeva tossed the backpack behind the rear bench and squeezed between the two front seats, jacket and doll dress tangling as she dragged herself forward. "I really think new clothes would be a good idea," she said, then settled and buckled in. "Why do you keep avoiding the backpack?"

Munroe checked the rearview. Lumani was out there, she knew it, knew he knew she knew, and his continued invisibility added to the pressure inside her head. She turned onto a main street and followed instinct toward signage, and the signage toward the highway. Glanced at Neeva and found the girl staring, waiting for something.

"What?"

"The backpack—why do you avoid it?"

"The phone has a tracker and a bug in it. I pulled the battery, but just in case."

Neeva's forehead creased, and the same girl, who while dodging killers and kidnappers would, if given half a chance, have pranced down the streets of Nice with her head held high, glared at Munroe accusingly, as if she'd been betrayed. "Why do you still have it?" she said.

"Now you're an expert, too?"

Neeva crossed her arms and stared at her lap.

Munroe said, "It's the only way I have to communicate with them—I have a few things to sort out before I can get rid of it. Listen, you chose to come along, uninvited, so if you're going to stick around, you need to zip it and let me lead. If you question me every step of the way, I'll give you back just to get rid of you. I need quiet right now."

"I was just asking," Neeva said.

"And you're still annoying me," Munroe said. "I'm not your friend. Just because I saved your life doesn't make me a nice person. I didn't do it for you, I did it for my own reasons—just like what you're doing here isn't for me but for yours. So since we're stuck with the phone for now, the plan is to move fast, stay a step ahead, and avoid saying anything that allows them an advantage. Get it?"

Neeva nodded. "Not stupid," she said, and despite herself, Munroe smiled.

"Good," she said. "And when we do get a real phone, you need to call your parents."

"And tell them what?"

"For starters, that you weren't re-kidnapped, because it'd certainly make my life a hell of a lot easier if my face isn't on every other television, right next to yours. And since you won't be on the flight they booked, they probably deserve to know the reasons why."

Neeva sighed. "It's not going to be a pleasant conversation."

"Welcome to the world of difficult choices. You're doing a brave thing, Neeva, but it only counts if the ones you love know you're doing it of your own free will."

THE HIGHWAY OUT of Nice took them along the coast farther inland than the regional roads, a scenic straight shot into Italy that bypassed border control, cut through tunnels, skipped towns, and made a mockery of the wasted time it had taken to drive the opposite direction.

Munroe stuck to the highway only until they diverted past Genoa, and the beauty and grandeur of the coast and the mountains and the tunnels phased into a bland industrial flatness. She used Arben's money to pay the toll and exit the highway. Smaller roads meant slower going, but they also meant that Lumani, in whatever powerful vehicle he drove, wouldn't be able to overtake them on speed alone.

Neeva broke the silence. "What happened to the scarface guy?" she said.

Munroe glanced sideways but didn't answer.

"At the consulate you said the pretty boy was still out here," Neeva said. "And you said *he* and *him* as if there was only ever one. So what happened to the other? Did he follow us into the garage?"

"There are some subjects better left alone," Munroe said.

Neeva stared at her hands. "I'm in this of my own free will, so I kinda earned the right to know."

"He's dead," Munroe said, and Neeva nodded, satisfied.

THEY APPROACHED MILAN from the south, following signs toward the city center until they were thoroughly into a mix of civilization and Munroe's focus changed to locating the metro. She continued through a residential area of apartment blocks and dead-ended at Famagosta, a station with not much more to it than a large bus exchange and several parking garages. Took the car up a ramp. Found an empty spot, switched off the ignition, and abandoned the vehicle.

The metro station, down a long level, was clean and well lit, with frequent trains running into the heart of Milan. Munroe purchased tickets at a vending machine, the price, at one euro per trip, shockingly low. Gusts of hot air blew out from the tunnel, propagating the stale smell of burned metal, hydraulic fluid, and machine oil—the universal underground fragrance that belonged only to the tracks. She kept her arm linked in Neeva's, boyfriend to girlfriend, and as in Monaco and Nice, passersby paused or did a double-take when they caught sight of the costume, but this time Neeva kept her chin down, and from the smirks and sometimes outright staring, it was evident that people focused so much on the clothes that they failed to take notice of who wore the outfit.

Neeva whispered, "Won't he follow us in?"

Munroe shook her head. Lumani would be an idiot to attempt to track them through the subway, not only because of the cameras and security, but because of how easily he could miss them by even one train. She said, "He'll wait for us to surface and follow from there."

They rode the line to Milan's central station, where, as it was now nearing the end of the workday, the building bustled with early twinges of rush-hour traffic. They transferred up a level, and yet another, to the main lobby of the station, a high-domed hall, one long side of which led to the tracks for the distance and high-speed lines, and the other to the outside. Through this part of the station, travelers, national and international, fed in and out of the city by the hundreds of thousands each day.

Neeva twisted around, her face turned upward, eyes wide in wonder at what was said by some to be the most beautiful station in the world, and tripped. Munroe caught her. "Sightseeing is going to get you killed, okay? Focus."

Outside the station, streets were trash-strewn, narrow, and congested with traffic, and Munroe searched out the storefronts for what she knew had to be nearby. Came at last to what she wanted:

a small shop sandwiched among a strip of mom-and-pop stores, glass windows entirely filled with colorful phone-card and travel advertisements that touted rates to mostly third-world destinations; a business that provided the means to make cheap international calls and Internet access by the minute.

Inside, Munroe set Neeva by the front, where she could watch the street from the cracks between the window posters, and handed her the backpack. "If you see someone familiar," she said, "don't try to be brave. It sounds stupid because I won't be far from the door, but they can move fast. Scream '*fuoco*' with everything you've got. Noise is your friend."

Neeva mouthed the word and nodded.

"And don't step into the open doorway. If he's watching, he'll just as easily take you with a tranquilizer and carry you off."

Another nod.

Munroe turned to the nearby counter, where an elderly man, the business's only apparent employee, took Munroe's money while casting an occasional stare in Neeva's direction.

The phone booths closest to Neeva were occupied, so Munroe took what was available, trying to keep an eye on the girl while she punched in a seemingly endless stream of numbers and codes to dial Bradford's number. He answered on the first ring.

"Hey," he said. "Where are you?"

"Milan," she said.

"You okay?"

"Yes, but I've got to make this quick because I've not only got a tail, I've got Neeva with me, too."

"You what?"

"I'll explain it as soon as I've got more time."

"I need your address," he said, and she read the details off the receipt.

In an exchange of business, without any of the emotional undertone that had punctuated their previous conversations, Bradford ran through step-by-step directions that Munroe jotted down; an address she dare not put into the phone's browser or plug into the GPS in case that, too, transmitted details back to Lumani.

"Your guy needs to know I have a tail," Munroe said.

"Can you shake it?"

"They're like a bedbug infestation."

"I'll warn him," Bradford said, and Munroe heard the smile in his voice. "Be safe."

"My very best," she said.

Neeva still stared out the window when Munroe approached, and the old man still studied Neeva.

"Anything?" Munroe asked, and Neeva shook her head.

A clothing shop three doors down toward the train station displayed discount signs in the windows, and Munroe walked Neeva to it and stepped inside. Counted out most of what was left of Arben's money, found an oversize long-sleeved shirt that could replace Arben's jacket and a stylish hat Neeva could use to tuck her hair underneath.

Although the two pieces didn't entirely erase the ridiculousness of Neeva's getup, combined they helped to make her clothing more of a choice, and by implication far less attention-garnering.

"We'll get you something else later," Munroe said. "For now this is all I've got money for."

"It works," Neeva said.

They returned to the station and Munroe searched for storage lockers, found none, and so followed the signs for *Deposito bagagli*, the manned luggage depot where for a fee baggage could be screened and left behind. She stopped when she saw the line, five people deep. Turned a slow circle, scanning shops and people, searching faces for the curious and familiar. Shrugged off the backpack. Opened it long enough to pull out the tape, phone, and travel documents. Shoved everything, including the tape, bulky and uncomfortable, inside her jacket, then with a subtle re-check of surroundings, pushed the pack and the remainder of its contents into a garbage bag.

Neeva's mouth opened and her lips formed a question, but she stopped before the words came out. Munroe took her elbow and pointed her toward the escalators. "Keep walking," she said.

If she could have, Munroe would have left Neeva at the station and returned to collect her when business was finished. Partners in general added complications, inevitably had to be protected and typically got in the way. Neeva, in particular, and under these circumstances, with her lack of training and childlike trust, made for an exceptional burden.

But she couldn't risk the separation.

Not even running decoy.

If Lumani was even half the predator and a fraction the strategist she assumed him to be, he would know this stop at the station and the sudden movement of another tracker was his prey, masking scent. To be certain, he'd be forced to check out all leads and it would cost him time, and that was all she'd done by abandoning the backpack and the equipment: purchased time.

Munroe looped from the upper level, wound through crowds, down again to the track they'd just used, returning in the direction from which they'd come. Reached the platform, and with Neeva sliding back against a tiled wall in order to catch her breath, Munroe scanned faces, waiting for the mechanical announcement and the hiss down the tracks. The approaching roar, the squeal of brakes meant another ride, another chance at freedom.

Waiting passengers approached the doors, and Munroe maneuvered Neeva into the thick of the crowd, stepping to the side to allow those within to exit. Near the stairs on the opposite platform, Munroe caught the first sign of familiar. Recognition came first in a flash of color and a glint, as if light had reflected off metal or an oversize briefcase.

Munroe stepped onto the train and, hand on Neeva's shoulder, guided the girl behind standing passengers, but the move wouldn't have made any difference. Lumani stared at Munroe through the glass and on his face was a gloating smile. The train began to move and he touched an index finger to his forehead and tipped it toward her.

"Was that him?" Neeva said. "Pretty Boy?"

Munroe nodded.

Pulled the pieces of Arben's phone from her pockets. Put the battery in and powered the device on.

"Are you worried?"

"Not yet," Munroe whispered, and Neeva, taking the cue, kept silent.

Another text waited when the phone finally booted. Another picture, of Alexis, this time naked, blindfolded, and spread-eagled against a concrete floor. Munroe clenched her teeth and deleted the image. To focus on anything other than the moment would mean mistakes, would mean death, and by default allow innumerable other girls to fall into the same fate as Neeva and Alexis. She would stay the course.

Warm and uninvited, Neeva's hand touched Munroe's arm.

Munroe tensed.

Neeva withdrew. "Sorry," she said. "I forgot."

Munroe nodded and forced a pained smile of acknowledgment, scrolled to the phone contacts, and, with paper and pen she'd taken from the phone shop, wrote down Lumani's and the Doll Maker's numbers. Then, with the phone still on, Munroe dropped it into the jacket pocket of the woman standing next to her.

thirty-two

They rode in silence to Cadorna and left the station for the streets and the plaza that led to the buses and trams, an open-air square, clean and colorful with bright sculptured art. To the left, touristic and inviting, rose the massive walls of the Sforzesco castle, and Munroe went in the opposite direction, navigating through pedestrian traffic with the directions Bradford had given, for several minutes along a street lined with trees still bright green with young leaves.

Munroe double-checked the address on her paper and stopped at a gelato store that stood contrastingly spare and modern against the grand colonial structure it inhabited. Inside, she found a seat for Neeva and, in an attempt at normalcy and in acknowledgment of the hunger that gnawed at her own insides, reached into her pocket for the last of the euros to buy Neeva something to eat. She caught the eye of the man behind the register.

He was deceptively young-looking, though Munroe placed him in midthirties, tiny and wiry, and not at all what stereotype might suggest one of Bradford's connections would look like. But in his focused interest, his unwillingness to drop his gaze, there was no mistaking that he'd recognized Munroe, if not Neeva, when she'd first walked through the door.

Without breaking eye contact with her new admirer, Munroe

handed Neeva the cash. "If you're hungry," she said. "But don't leave the shop. And if you see Pretty Boy, or anyone else who looks familiar, same instructions as last time."

Neeva nodded and Munroe moved toward the register. The aproned man motioned one of the employees to take his place. He stepped away from the counter, not so obvious as to be noticeable to the random observer, and definitely not to Neeva, who, money in hand, was already headed to the cold glass cases, but enough that Munroe understood she'd been invited inward.

He exited the room through a swinging door not far from the register and Munroe followed. He turned only once to confirm her presence and led the way down a narrow hall that wrapped into an L, past a cold room and a small kitchen, to another door, which, contrary to everything else about the shop, had a keypad and a biometric scanner.

He placed his thumb against the pad and the door clicked open.

The room was walk-in-closet-size with bare walls and a bare desk. The door shut behind Munroe of its own accord, and the aproned man turned to face her. "I'm told you have a tail," he said, and his English was spoken with an unmistakable hint of small-town Texas.

"Yes," she replied, and out of habit scanned the walls and seams of the windowless room, taking measurements, calculating where she assumed the faux walls ended and the real room began. "I'm ahead by at least five minutes," she said. "I'll drop into a few other places for the sake of appearances."

He reached beside the bare metal desk. Picked up a briefcase, laid it flat on the desktop, popped it open, and turned it toward her.

Munroe examined the contents. Two Israeli Jericho 9 mms. Two spare magazines. Eight 50-round boxes of 9 mm ammunition. An envelope. Six blocks of dollar and euro bills, bound and stacked. Cell phone. Charger. Pocketknife. Taser.

God, she loved Bradford. Only he could have, without any explanation on her part, anticipated her moves in advance. Munroe pulled the roll of tape and Lumani's travel documents from her jacket and dumped them into the briefcase.

She looked up to find the aproned man studying her the way she'd studied the room. "Whoever you are," he said, "Miles just pulled in a large favor for you—you'd better be worth it."

"It's well earned," she said, and the nameless man dropped the briefcase lid, pushed it shut, then handed the case to her.

"Do you have another bag?" she said. "Something easier to carry, that won't attract as much attention?"

"You're on foot?"

Munroe nodded.

"In the staff room," he said, tipping his head in the direction he'd intended. She followed him out again to the room next door, where he pulled a satchel from a cubbyhole and dumped its contents on the floor. "This'll have to do," he said. "Unless"—he glanced at her again from head to toe—"you want a purse."

"This is fine," she said.

He held the satchel open while she transferred the items from one bag to the other. "Miles referred to you as a 'she,'" he said.

Munroe shoved the phone into her jacket pocket. Took one of the handguns back out. Released the magazine, pulled the slide, snapped the magazine back into place. As soon as she had a moment she'd strip the weapons down, reassemble, and reload, but for now this would have to do.

"I am a she," she said.

She slipped the Jericho underneath her jacket at the small of her back.

The aproned man said, "I see," and he motioned to the door. "Questions, but no time." She followed him out.

"I need a clothing store," she said. "Something away from the metro—doesn't have to be big."

They moved through the swinging door back into the shop.

"Take a right on your way out and just keep walking," he said.

"Someone's probably going to come looking for me," she said. "I really do apologize."

He smiled—the first spontaneous facial expression he'd offered. "I'm not worried about it, might even be a good thing."

When Munroe returned to the main room, Neeva was sitting at a table eating chocolate gelato from a half-finished large cup. She paused when Munroe approached.

"Take the food," Munroe said. "We've gotta go."

Neeva half stood and, with the cup in her hand, hesitated. "It's not disposable," she said. Munroe took Neeva's elbow and guided her upward so that Neeva had no choice but to stand upright.

"Take it anyway, we need to move."

Neeva put the glass on the table and, with head down and no protest, followed Munroe to the door. There, with another scan up and down the street, Munroe slipped back in among the pedestrian traffic.

"Why did we go there?" Neeva said. "Not for food."

"Money," Munroe said. "Options." And left it at that.

They'd need to move quickly to turn this stop into one of many so that Lumani, knowing she was working toward a plan, would be forced to check each lead in his own attempt to put the pieces together and try to jump ahead of her.

Another several minutes of walking and Munroe spotted a clothing store. While perhaps not specifically the one the aproned man had in mind, it would suffice.

Inside, she pulled items off of racks, held them up to Neeva for size, and draped them over Neeva's outstretched arm until she'd combined two full sets of clothing for the girl and another for herself, then headed toward the checkout—they didn't bother trying anything on for fit because they didn't have the time, but once the items had been paid for, she tore tags off several pieces and sent Neeva to the changing room.

"Take off everything you're wearing," she said. "Down to your bra and panties—leave nothing that came from the bad people—bring it all to me because I need it."

Neeva grimaced. "Even the panties? I've been wearing this stuff for two days."

"Everything," Munroe said.

"What about the shoes?"

"That's our next stop."

Years in a job that required the ability to blend seamlessly from one environment to the next had taught Munroe well in regard to clothing. The human subconscious filtered out the familiar, and as such, the fastest way to become invisible in any city was to acquire and wear what could be had locally.

Neeva returned from the dressing room and handed Munroe a ball of textured color, and Munroe stuffed the lump into the shopping bag. The new outfit, combined with hat and sunglasses, had effectively turned Neeva into one in a crowd. Munroe nodded approvingly.

"What about you?" Neeva said.

"No time, we need to keep moving."

"I thought you got rid of the tracker."

"I got rid of some of them," Munroe said. She took Neeva's arm and nudged her toward the door.

"So they're still following us?"

"I hope so," Munroe said. Heat along her neck, like breath, a finely attuned sense long developed by hunting and hiding, told her Lumani was close.

Imagined or not, she could feel him, watching, breathing in her ear.

Out of the store and down a side street, flattened against the wall, heart slowing into the reptilian calm of narrowed focus, Munroe waited, watching traffic, finally spotting a vehicle, which, although only one of many, was traveling particularly slow.

She saw no faces, only the shadows of two people in the front. Couldn't know if the car belonged to Lumani or one of his people, only that intuition had spoken, and she had learned through long, hard experience to trust her instinct and allow the inner tempo to lead where logic failed.

THEY FOUND A shoe store and repeated the procedure, allowing no time to dally, and were on their way again in minutes with directions from the shopkeeper for a grocery store, where along aisles a tenth the size of what she'd have found in Dallas, Munroe filled a basket haphazardly and at random with packaged food and bottled drinks.

Outside Munroe handed two of the bags to Neeva. "I know you're tired, but you're going to have to help me carry some of this stuff," she said, "just a couple more stops and we can rest."

Last came a drugstore, where Munroe searched out the closest items she could find to hair wax, eye pencils, and lip products. Added hydrogen peroxide, nail polish, and mascara and grabbed a backpack off a circular rack—a shopping foray that would have made most males proud: items procured with indifferent efficiency. Neeva grabbed soap, shaving cream, and a packet of razors and held them up for approval before adding them to the pile.

From the drugstore Munroe led a zigzagged course toward the nearest tramline, reaching the bus-stop-size platform at the same time a streetcar arrived. Didn't matter where the tram was headed, only that they would move away from the area faster than they could if they remained on foot.

The doors hissed shut and Munroe studied passersby through the windows. Caught sight of a familiar figure—not Lumani, Arben the second, the nameless silent man who'd been with them in the cells—running, so foolishly running, as if to say *Here I am, notice me*, through the crowds.

He'd clearly not spotted them, as he had headed for the tramline as if following a map, as if he'd known where to look. Then missing the tram, he turned from the platform to the street, and the car Munroe had spotted earlier slowed only long enough for the man to climb into the passenger seat.

thirty-three

The tram stopped at a light, and Lumani's car, pointed in the wrong direction, was forced by traffic to continue on its way. With Bradford's phone, Munroe utilized online maps and based on location searched out nearby hotels.

Eye on the traffic, she waited another stop and then, last minute, nudged Neeva toward the door and maneuvered to be last off the tram. Left Neeva's old shoes on the floor by the feet of an elderly man as they moved off, and if anyone noticed the subtle deposit, no one called attention to it.

They'd only traveled four stops, but because of the direction and route, and the ebb and flow of traffic, Munroe had gained more time. They moved on foot again, following the directions from her phone, the streets darker now, the lights reluctantly turning on to replace the fading daylight.

The hotel, when she found it, was a boutique establishment, modern and clean and upscale, with a proprietor who gladly accepted cash, courtesy of the aproned man, and travel documents, courtesy of Lumani. He didn't question the absence of luggage and led them up one floor and down a short hall to their room. Opened the door courteously, and when Neeva entered, Munroe stopped in the hallway to tip the man but, more specifically, to prevent the potential loss of innocent life that her presence might cause, to warn him, to caution against those who would undoubtedly come hunting for her. The man looked at her quizzically and then turned to go.

Munroe entered the room and closed the door. Neeva stood quietly with eyebrows raised, as if saying *What now?* but what came out of her mouth was "You speak a lot of languages."

Munroe nodded. "I do." She shed the weight of the bags onto the bed and dumped out the contents of the satchel.

Neeva stared, mouth agape, and Munroe held up one of the firearms. "You know how to handle one of these?"

Neeva nodded. Munroe released the magazine and checked the chamber. Tossed an empty magazine at Neeva, then handed the gun to her. "Show me. I don't want to wind up with a bullet in the back of my head."

Neeva snapped the magazine into place, ratcheted the slide, and taking a wide stance, two-handed, as if she'd spent considerable hours at a firing range, pointed the weapon at the window and pulled the trigger for the click.

Munroe handed her a box of ammunition, then turned toward the room's one window along the far short wall and approached from the side, peering out with a quick glance and retreat, an instant assessment of potential threat. The room was one floor up, fronted by a small garden and a wide street that faced three- and four-story buildings. Not much available for a sniper's hide, but if one was to be had, Lumani would certainly find it.

Staying away from the window, Munroe tugged the drapes closed. The room went black and Neeva flipped on a light.

"Keep it off," Munroe said. "We don't want to cast shadows."

"Were you trained by the CIA or, like, some military special thing or other?"

Munroe smiled. "No." Picked up the second empty magazine and, until her eyes adjusted to the dark, loaded bullets by feel.

Neeva said, "How do you speak so many languages and know about the things you know? How did you get this"—she paused— "stuff?"

Munroe tapped the magazine to seat the bullets, pulled the weapon from her waistband, and swapped out magazines. "It's a long story," she said. She put the contents of the satchel back in the bag and moved everything to the floor.

The one bed in the room was queen-size and welcoming, and her nearness to it, and the darkness, heightened the gravity of the need for sleep. She pulled back the linens, shoved the mattress off the bed, and propped it, like an A-frame, up against the wall near the bathroom door. "I need your help moving the desk," she said.

Calculating trajectory and strategy, Munroe pointed and mapped with her fingers so that Neeva understood, and together they rearranged the pieces. "Will they come for us?" Neeva said.

"They have to," Munroe answered. "Every change of direction we've made, we've dropped a tracker and kept on. They know we know we're being followed, so for us to stop moving is counterintuitive. They won't know if our bread-crumb trail was just a way to lead them to a trick where we pretend to be holed up but we've really dumped the rest of the trackers and split. They'll have to come to find out."

"So you want them to come?"

"Yes."

"And when they do?"

Munroe ignored the question and pulled the ball of the doll dress and the rest of Neeva's clothes from the bag, shook out the dress, and laid it flat atop the empty bed frame. "What are you doing?" Neeva asked.

"Teasing them," Munroe said.

Her fingers hunted among the folds and seams for the small electronic piece she knew she'd find eventually. Grimaced when she grabbed hold of the plastic and used her teeth to cut through the threads that kept the strip fastened between layers of clothing. And then, having freed the device, held it out for Neeva to examine. "It sends a signal so they can locate you."

When Neeva handed the thin piece back, Munroe took it to the bathroom and flushed it down the toilet.

Now came the waiting. Could be half an hour or thirty hours; the move was Lumani's to make and she hated that this gave him the advantage. She was a hunter, not a hider, a predator not prey; hers was meant to be the position of seeking, discovering, gathering information, and controlling the elements.

Not this.

And this was all she had.

In the bathroom, where there were no windows, Munroe unscrewed all but one bulb, and this she allowed as their only source of light. Unwilling to shut the door and chance being cut off from the main room if the attack came sooner than expected, she stripped out of the Doll Maker's collared button-down and T-shirt, and Neeva stared at her in a way that defied all rules of common etiquette. Finally the girl turned away.

From beneath the tight sports bra, Munroe pulled at the bandage that wrapped her chest. Drew the length out until she was free, balled the elastic up, and tossed it in the garbage. At the sink, she ran cold water, then using the hotel's small bar of soap and a hand towel, washed her torso and arms, her face, neck, and hair.

She needed a shower. Desperately. But couldn't risk getting caught compromised when the hunters arrived, and even this was pushing her luck.

Munroe stepped from the bathroom, towel around her neck, and Neeva stared slack-jawed. Munroe didn't need to follow her line of sight to understand the reaction. The scars were ugly, and there were many, always prompting questions to which she rarely provided a truthful explanation.

"If you want to use the bathroom, now's a good time," Munroe said. "I have no idea how long we'll be waiting, so if you're hungry, help yourself to the food, too."

Neeva nodded, silence instead of conversation, avoidance instead of questions, while she rummaged through the shopping bags, pulled out a few items. All the way from one side of the bed to the bathroom door, with the same stupefied lack of etiquette, her eyes remained on Munroe's torso. "I might be a while," she said, and Munroe answered with a dismissive wave.

When Neeva had shut herself inside, and Munroe no longer had a gawking audience or light for that matter, she stripped down and removed every bit of the Doll Maker's clothing in the same way she'd had Neeva remove her own in the clothing store. Redressed in the items she'd purchased: boots, black cargo pants, and a black camisole layered beneath the jacket she'd kept with her since Dallas. As long as the jacket was zipped, the outfit remained if not quite androgynous, not exactly gendered, either, and would allow her flexibility when the time came to move again. At the moment, returning to being female was the better bet considering every visual record of her movement over the last forty-eight hours would show her as male.

Clothing, hair, shoes, accessories: these were props, visual cues, that people used to filter information and make instant assessments out of random connections, to categorize and assign value to those who populated their world. And layered beneath the props for sight came those for smell, and hearing, and more, that sense of intangibility that allowed people to read nuance and body language and interpret what the other senses didn't grasp directly; cues that together formed a picture that matched perceptions based on expectations and that, when adjusted one way or the other, filtered past the gatekeepers of the mind, allowing Munroe to become whatever she needed to be.

THE WATER IN the bathroom ran long and the sounds of Neeva messing about filtered beneath the door. Munroe pulled the pocketknife from the satchel, sat on the frame of the bed, flipped the blade open, and stared at her hands. This knife, like all knives when she picked them up, became a living thing, and like all blades in her hands when the voices were alive and the darkness nibbled at the edges of sanity, this one, too, begged to be used. Not on the soles of her shoes, as she worked it now, probing until the heels gave way, but to be used on those who tormented. To cut, the way she'd been cut, and to make others suffer for the pain they inflicted.

Munroe folded the blade and pocketed the knife.

In the hollowed-out segments of each shoe, Munroe found two more tracking devices. She pulled them out and palmed them. Took paper from the desk and folded it into a makeshift envelope. Dropped the trackers inside and shoved the packet into a pocket. These were the last of them, and when they were dumped, she and Neeva could effectively disappear. Lumani had to know this. Had to feel the pressure. Even if he assumed this stop at the hotel was a feint or, in terms of the chessboard inside her head, a *decoy:* a move that lured a piece into an unfavorable position, he had to act, had no choice, the issue was only when he'd come, not if.

The water in the bathroom continued running, and so Munroe

lay on the floor beside the upright mattress. With her body horizontal, exhaustion settled heavy, thick and blanketing, threatening to submit her fully to sleep against her will.

Taking the phone from her pocket, she dialed Bradford, the fulfillment of her promise, and in the seconds that it rang, her eyes closed of their own accord, only to open reluctantly when he came on the line.

"How are you?" he asked, and she heard in his voice the same worn-down fatigue that she felt.

"I'm okay," she said.

Questions about Alexis, Logan, and Samantha were foremost on her mind, but to ask for news would only add to Bradford's burden and so she left them untouched. "I got another image of Alexis," she said. "A concrete floor and a fairly large space."

"How long ago?"

"A couple of hours or so, but who knows when it was taken."

"I'll get to her," he said. "It's slower work now. I do have backup but not much, and I have to be careful in covering my tracks so I don't face"—he paused—"local complications. But I know where she is."

Elation tugged at Munroe's thoughts. She sat up. Hugged her knees.

"Talk to me," Bradford said. "You've got Neeva with you. Are you about to play capture the flag with the traffickers?"

"Sounds bad," she said, "but, yes, that's what it amounts to."

She walked him through the events that had put Neeva back into her custody, the offer the girl had presented, the steps she'd taken so far to stay ahead of Lumani, and the reasons why she now waited for him to find her. When she'd stopped and silence ensued, she could hear in Bradford's sigh the words of caution and warning he would never say. He moved instead to the topic they'd both danced around: the darkness.

"I've got a handle on it," she said. "I promise you, it's not like Africa. I'm tempted, you know, the urges are pretty strong, to seek him out in retribution for what he's done to me and Logan, and I may yet. But on my own terms. Consciously."

"What do you know of the client?" Bradford asked.

"Wealthy, male, and a regular. He's paid for several girls from this trafficking organization, but this isn't the only operation, so there might be other victims—less famous ones, you know?—cheaper. He could have a place or even several places where he stashes his purchases long-term, but I think it's more likely each girl replaces the one that came before."

"And the torture aspect?"

"I can't be certain," she said. "But it's the only way everything makes sense—rules I've had to follow, the way he toys with the traffickers—he fits the profile. I could be wrong. I could be projecting my own past onto the present, but it doesn't really matter—he's no less evil if instead of torturing and killing these girls, he's pimping them out or collecting them and keeping them locked away. He's not going to stop, Miles. Even if I take this organization apart piece by piece, this guy will find a way to feed his addiction."

The running water from the bathroom had shut off for a while, but Neeva was still inside and far too quiet. Munroe stood and knocked on the door.

"You okay in there?"

"Just a few more minutes," Neeva said.

A heartbeat of silence and then Bradford continued the conversation. "Your client couldn't have been the only customer."

"No," she said. "But he is one, and he's one I can find."

"Is there any way I could convince you to wait? Just buy me a little time so I can get to Alexis. We can sort through options when we have a chance to breathe."

"Even if this never involved me or mine, you or yours, being this close, knowing what I know ..." When her sentence faded, Bradford finished it for her.

"Knowing what you know, you can't just walk away," he said. "But I had to try."

"I know," she whispered. "I'll finish this, and I'll live through it."

"Don't make promises like that. You only tempt fate." He was quiet for a moment, as if resigned and letting go. Finally he said, "Regardless of what happens, I understand why you have to do it."

"Thank you," she said.

Munroe stared at the phone a long while before putting it away, and fearing that to lie down would mean falling into a deep sleep, she pulled hair product from the bag and, with practiced fingers, ran the paste through short strands, tugging and spiking, and turning what had been boy into what now went either way. Without a mirror, she continued with black eyeliner and then heavy mascara, and was painting her short nails black by the time Neeva opened the bathroom door.

thirty-four

In the low light coming from the bathroom, both women stared at each other: Neeva at what had been added, Munroe at what had been taken away.

"You look different," Neeva said.

"So do you."

Younger. More helpless. Tinier, if such a thing was possible.

"Trying to wash out the curls only gave me a clown wig," Neeva said. "I figured this was better than being reminded of *them* every time I looked in a mirror." She lowered her eyes. "What do you think?"

"Kind of gives you an emaciated concentration-camp-survivor look," Munroe said. "Or maybe chemo."

Neeva half smiled and her cheeks flushed. "It's sort of a disguise."

Munroe stood, secured the weapon in her waistband. Ran her palm over Neeva's shaved head. "I'll help you with the spots you missed," she said.

Munroe put Neeva's head over the sink and, with razor in hand, worked over the stubbled patches. Said, "Why'd you do the identity change before heading to Hollywood? You have a good relationship with your parents, so it's not like you were running away or anything."

Munroe shut off the water, handed Neeva a towel. Neeva rubbed a hand over her head and smiled. "It's smooth," she said, and then her expression changed. "My mom was always really good about keeping me out of the limelight, not using us kids as chips in her politics."

Neeva dropped the towel into the sink. "We weren't part of the whole stage, stumping for votes as part of the wholesome family image, but I still saw what happens when people know your name and your face. They constantly twisted what my mom said or did to turn opinions and projections into truths, but where it got totally crazy was how they did it to the rest of my family, who didn't even have anything to do with anything."

Neeva slid down the wall and stretched her legs out so that her feet nearly touched Munroe's. "There's no such thing as truth, that's what I learned," she said. "Only opinions people want you to believe as truth." She ran a hand against her scalp once more and smiled again. "I knew that once I got work in Hollywood, everything about me would become public property and I'd have to deal with that same issue. I didn't want the movies and the roles I took to impact my mother's career—didn't want to worry that my potty mouth or late-night partying would become her politics or that my own talent would be smothered by her shadow. I just wanted to be me without the baggage, so I changed my name, invented a past, and started clean."

Munroe said, "Funny how that decision came full circle."

"What do you mean?"

Munroe stood and, hand outstretched for Neeva to follow, led her back to the bedroom and out of the confining space, where it had been harder to keep attuned to the sounds in the hallway and the street. She listened and, certain that things were still as they should be, said, "The same baggage you tried to save yourself and your family from is pretty much what saved you now—all the media attention, the speculation, put your face on every TV in the world."

Neeva sat on the floor beside the mattress. "I guess," she said, and Munroe tossed a package of cookies and a bottle of juice in her direction.

Neeva touched the mattress. "Why is this here?"

"So when the shooting starts and I shove you into the bathroom, I can put another layer of protection between you and the bullets."

"I thought I was here to help."

"You won't be much help if you're dead."

"But what about you?"

Munroe joined Neeva on the floor. Placed herself so that the room's one window was ahead on the opposite wall and the hallway door between her and Neeva. Unlike American construction, which relied heavily on drywall to partition rooms and often used hollow doors, this hotel was European and old, which meant stone and solid wood—meant that unless Lumani or Arben Number Two, or anyone else who might be with them, intended to blow the place up, they'd be coming through one of those two openings.

Munroe put the Jericho on the floor, took a cookie out of Neeva's package. "Like I told you, if I don't get them first, then I'm dead either way, so it doesn't much matter."

"Who did that to you?" Neeva said, and she moved to touch Munroe's torso but stopped with her hand hovering in the air above the jacket.

Those who dared to ask about the scars inevitably used questions framed in the context of what and how, but Neeva had cut to the heart of the question with who. Munroe glanced at her, one victim of violence to another. Neeva withdrew her hand and, like a wounded child, went back to the cookies.

"It was a long time ago," Munroe said. "Done over the course of a few years by a man quite similar to the one who put the purchase price out for you."

"Do you ever think about trying to get even?"

"He's dead now."

Neeva stopped chewing and very slowly swallowed. "Did *you* kill him?"

"Yes," Munroe said, mimicking the slow speech, "I did."

"Was it difficult to get away with it?"

Munroe shifted, shoulder to the wall, so that she stared fully at the girl. Measured and deliberate, she said, "It was a long time ago, in a place most people don't know exists. Why all the questions, Neeva?"

Neeva shrugged. "Sometimes I think about how it would feel."

"Revenge is best left to fantasy," Munroe said. "It feels better there. In real life you can eventually learn to deal with the pain and trauma, learn to cope on some level, you know? But you can never undo death, and even if you think they deserve it, killing doesn't take away your pain, just puts you on dangerous ground that can collapse out from beneath you at any time."

"You did it."

Munroe stared at her a moment longer, thoughts running in a melee that amounted to *My point exactly*, but she said, "I did. Partially out of revenge and partially to save my life and the lives of future victims, but even if it had been entirely to settle a score, that means I, of all people, should *know*."

Without meeting Munroe's eyes, Neeva nibbled on a cookie, said, "Would you take it back if you could?"

"I wouldn't, but that doesn't mean I haven't paid a price."

Neeva huffed. "Well, I still think people like this doll guy and the Pretty Boy, people like them, will never learn or ever stop unless someone goes up against them, fight fire with fire, you know? Someone has to teach them."

"The problem with fighting fire with fire is that you can get burned and you risk becoming like them."

"Has that happened to you?"

"It has at times," Munroe said, and shifted back against the wall, forearms resting on bent knees, and stared across the room at the curtained window.

Neeva tilted sideways and tipped her head so that she rested against Munroe's shoulder. "I like you, Michael," she said, "even if sometimes you don't like yourself a whole lot."

Munroe smiled, leaned over, and kissed the smooth top of Neeva's head. "Thank you," she said, and after a pause, "What happened to the one who hurt you?"

"Nobody knows," Neeva said. "They never found him."

Munroe understood, then, what had driven Neeva to leave the safety of the consulate. The offer to give herself up as bait was more than just an exchange of one life for many lives. Neeva's actions were those of trauma victim refusing to be the victim again—revenge surrogacy, insistence on playing an active role in what happened next. She rested her cheek where her kiss had met smooth skin.

"How do you know about the man with the dog?" Neeva asked. "Who he is and what he has planned?"

"I don't know who he is," Munroe said, "only what he represents."

"So you're guessing?"

Munroe shrugged Neeva off her shoulder and placed her hands, fingers splayed, across her abdomen. "There are these. The man with the dog is just another version of the psychopath with the knife." She turned to Neeva. "He paid to have you kidnapped so he could own you as a slave. Do the details of why or what for make a difference?"

"Not really," Neeva said. "I mean, sort of, in terms of physical pain and the idea of murder, they do. But people like the doll guy who sells women and the dog guy who buys women, and other guys who, say, rape women, or maybe don't go as far as violent rape but treat women like objects instead of people—sure, there's a difference in the level of crime, but it's all the same thing, where women become a canvas for throwing emotional baggage, Jackson Pollock style."

Munroe said, "Those are some pretty big thoughts for such a little person."

Neeva's face clouded. Her mouth shut, then opened again. "Was that a joke?"

Munroe flicked a finger against Neeva's nose. "Yes," she said. "It's called dry humor. You should try it sometime."

Neeva smiled. Slumped back against the wall. "This doll-guy situation is an extreme of what I deal with in everyday life," she said. "Where men believe that what they want I want, and they project that on to me and then blame me, curse me, when I don't respond the way they've fantasized, like it's some personal attack on them, like they're entitled to something. Doll guy and dog guy and rape guy, the dangerous ones, they just go a step further and take it anyway. Then they blame you and the way you look for what they did. What's worse is that a lot of the time, society blames you, too."

Munroe put her arm around Neeva and moved the girl's head back onto her shoulder. "You are way too young and innocent to be forced to understand these types of things," she said.

"I'm not as innocent as you think I am."

"And apparently not quite as naive."

Neeva pulled her head off Munroe's shoulder and shifted to her knees, hands on her thighs, eyes happy and smile wide, then pumped a fist and whispered, "Yessss."

The smile and simple joy were infectious to the point that Munroe, in spite of circumstances, couldn't help but smile in return—a smile that faded fast in the wake of a barely perceptible tap against the door handle. Not the movement of the door being tried but a gentle rocking of the latch in its holder as if the wood had only been touched or brushed against.

Munroe's hand moved to the weapon on the floor. Fight-or-flight instinct would have her unload the magazine into the door and push on after the hunter, but the same wood and stone that protected her also protected him.

Focus never leaving the hallway door, she turned slightly so that her mouth was to Neeva's ear and whispered, "Go to the bathroom. Lock yourself inside. I don't care what you hear, or what you think is going on out here, don't come out till I call for you."

Neeva, who'd been oblivious, turned to follow Munroe's line of sight and, staring wide-eyed, whispered, "Are they here? I want to help."

"You're here. That's the help. I need you alive. Get your gun. Go."

Neeva reached for the weapon that lay in the shadow between mattress and wall, low-crawled to the bathroom, and with a near silent click shut herself inside, taking the light with her. Munroe closed her eyes, allowing fingers, hands, and senses to work where sight failed, and shifted the mattress so that it straddled the bathroom door.

thirty five

The door handle moved again. Subtle. Audible only because Munroe anticipated the movement. With the Jericho aimed toward where she expected a body and the two spare magazines shoved tight against her waistband, Munroe moved the few steps to the desk. The heavy side faced out where it could provide the most benefit in shielding her body from whatever came through the door, and she kept behind the furniture, one knee to the floor, hands on the desktop for control.

Silence ticked along until the next subtle rocking of the latch against metal.

But the door didn't open, which she would have expected by now if the person on the other side had even a modicum of lock picking skills. Munroe leaned out to scan the floor. Had it been she on the other side, had the equipment been available, she would have run a camera under the door to confirm the location of the room's occupants, and if she hadn't had the equipment, she would have waited until the dead of night, when people slept the deepest, would have used stealth to enter and dispatch. But no hair-thin wire snaked in silhouette to the sliver of light beneath the door, and so she braced for an explosion that never came.

Instead, another subtle tap arrived, and less than a minute later still another, louder and more obvious: each new noise, like scratching at the door, was an invitation welcoming the curious to approach and discover, a juvenile trick encouraging the strategist to overanalyze. If the hunter was lucky, tapping might bring someone like Neeva closer, but Neeva wasn't alone, and Munroe wasn't stupid, and Lumani knew this.

Another tap.

The man-boy had sent an underling to flush her out.

Strategy to strategy, Munroe mentally placed herself on the other side, stood in the hall facing the door, blocked off from her quarry but so close she could feel them, hoping for some sound, some giveaway to point in the right direction so as not to immediately walk into the line of fire; sweating each protracted second because she'd already attracted attention coming into the hotel and couldn't wait long in the hallway.

She understood. Stretched out and snagged a bag of food, pulled it toward her, and right hand still steady on the desk, removed four of the small juice bottles. Left-handed, she tossed them in a patterned succession toward the door, the closest she could get to imitating footsteps with what she had.

Whatever the hunter wanted—noise, vibration, shadow—he'd received the cue. The door blew inward; an explosion neither small nor controlled. Light from the hallway flooded the room. Dust and haze and smoke filled the hole where the door had been.

Time slowed. Movement filtered into her brain in incremental gaps. The door lay in thirds, one part braced against the foot of the bed, the others strewn across the floor. Ears ringing, eyes smarting, Munroe emptied half the magazine in a diagonal across the hole, placing bullets where she imagined an enemy she couldn't see, shots that thundered back in recoil, noise that masked the spit of return fire, which came not angled down from a standing man, but up from off the floor, splintering the desk, sending fragments flying.

He was rolling. Crawling. Moving toward the desk.

She went up, slid over the top to avoid his line of fire, hands first, counting rounds, giving up precision to protect her head, hoping for a hit to his legs, groin, face, something unprotected, because bullets to his chest didn't appear to stop him.

Behind her, stone shattered, spitting shards.

Beneath her, wood chunked off.

The slide across the desk continued, a slow-motion eruption of noise and fragments. She dumped onto the floor behind her target, swapping magazines as she went, that frustrating swap that stole seconds and slowed her down, and happened only as quickly as it did because of long practice.

Fired again until the click.

Released the second magazine and, wasting more time, loaded the spare while crawling forward. Pulled the slide and, all or nothing, continued around the desk, shooting hand leading the way. And then, after another six rounds, the realization dawned that the return fire had stopped.

She paused to deafening silence. Ears useless.

From her position, she could see the edge of the enemy boot.

She fired into it.

Nothing.

Moved to her knees. Inched toward the empty door frame.

Head out once and back.

Nothing.

Again and back.

Nothing.

Stood and stepped into the hallway.

A door opened, and the amped-up adrenaline took her within a hair of firing. Wide eyes in a wizened face spotted her or maybe the gun.

The door slammed.

Idiots. People were idiots. Why? Why did they have to risk a look?

Munroe spun, ears still deaf, eyes burning.

Lumani was near. Maybe not in the hallway, but close.

If he'd sent Arben Two to flush her out, then he was here—in a hide watching the exit or in the hotel itself.

Munroe stepped back into the room, kept low to avoid casting a shadow on the window drapes. Paused at the body on her way to the bathroom.

He'd been hit several times. Two in the chest, slugs nestled into his vest, one in the calf. Maybe that's why he'd fallen, but a random shot had killed him, had to have been one she'd taken while on the floor, had gone up through his chin and out the side of his head. He was missing an eye and part of his face.

Munroe knelt to examine his weapon: HK USP .45 Tactical with a suppressor. Wanted to take the gun but wouldn't, wanted his vest as well, but it would require too much time and effort to get the thing off him, and so she shoved aside the mattress and knocked on the bathroom door.

"Neeva, come on out," Munroe said. "We need to move quickly."

The door opened a crack and Neeva peeked out from it.

"Let's go," Munroe said, and she reached for the packed bags beside the bed.

Neeva said, "You've been hit," and she pointed at Munroe's thigh, where tears ripped into the pants outlined blood and flesh, and surrounding the holes, wetness seeped and stained the cloth a darker color.

Munroe paused and glanced down, feeling for the first time what she hadn't during the rush of adrenaline. Droplets ran from her leg onto the floor.

"And your face," Neeva said, and Munroe swiped her free hand across her forehead, her cheek, and drew it away bloody.

"Give me a second," Munroe said, and moved past Neeva into the bathroom. Didn't have time for this crap. Needed to get out before Lumani closed in, but escaping the hotel alive wouldn't do much good if she was going to bleed out fifteen minutes down the road.

With Neeva watching, she unzipped and pulled down the pants.

"In the bag is a bottle of peroxide and the roll of duct tape," Munroe said. Peroxide she would have used on her hair if Neeva hadn't taken so damn long in the bathroom. "Get those for me, will you? And quickly please. We need to go."

Neeva jerked back, as if from a trance, turned for the bags, and rummaged through items from the drugstore. While Neeva busied herself, Munroe examined the wounds: two from shards of stone, one massive splinter that might as well have been a dagger, and one from a bullet that had grazed her thigh and lodged elsewhere. She gritted her teeth and pulled the largest of the chunks from her leg above the knee. Ran water and soaked the towel, irrigating the wounds as best as she could given the passing time, then pressed the towel as a compress.

Seconds counted.

Neeva placed the items on the closed toilet lid, and Munroe tore at the packaging. "Get that open," she said, and when Neeva handed the hydrogen peroxide back, Munroe dumped it on the open wounds. Took a dry washcloth, wadded it in place against the largest bleeder, and wrapped it with duct tape. It would be enough, would have to hold until she could get a better look.

The pain she could block out, that was the easy part, and it had nothing to do with being tough or a badass and everything to do with how she'd gotten through those nights in the jungle with the knife coming at her time and again.

Block it out. Push past it. And then kill.

Munroe tossed the tape at Neeva. "Pack it up," she said. "We're moving."

She'd also taken hits to her chest and abdomen—those she'd felt, like a punch in the gut that sucked air out of her and would most likely leave bruises, would keep her sore for a while—hits that should have torn holes through her torso and created massive trauma. In this she'd had the advantage. She'd had reason to expect the hunter would wear body armor and had adjusted during the firefight to compensate. He, on the other hand, had had no idea.

She wouldn't bother searching for the slugs, they'd be there waiting, nestled between the leather and the repellent lining durable enough to protect vital organs from an assault rifle. Miguel Caballero, the Armani of armor. They'd been stupid to let her keep the jacket, and now the stupidity had cost them.

Munroe pulled her pants back up, zipped, and stepped from the bathroom. Grabbed the satchel and the bags from beside the bed, handed the bags to Neeva, and moved on toward the hallway. The time for battle dressing had stolen two minutes.

At the hole in the wall Munroe paused. In the far-off distance, as expected, came the sirens. If Lumani had been inside the hotel, he would have struck after the firefight, during the moment of weakness, before she'd had a chance to gather her wits and get upright again. But even knowing this she moved with caution, taking another peek out into the hallway—a quick scan front and back before continuing on.

The hotel had two exits on the ground floor: the one they'd entered off the street to the front and the other directly opposite, down a long hallway to a dining room and then the back that opened onto a walled-in garden. The layout was crap as far as an escape went, but it had probably worked to their advantage. The building had but one exit, Lumani would be there with his rifle and so had allowed his henchman to come up alone.

Munroe motioned Neeva to the stairs and down half a floor. They stopped on the small landing. Munroe turned on the phone and located the preset for Lumani's number.

Made the call.

No Lumani, only a mechanized woman's voice in French and then the tone for voice mail. Munroe hung up, dialed again. To Neeva, she said, "I need you to start crying."

Neeva said, "Wha'?"

"A man just tried to kill you. You're an actress, I need a fit of hysterics—but without any noise until we head down the stairs. Can you do it?"

Neeva nodded.

Munroe dialed Lumani again. More French.

Hang up. Repeat.

Repeat.

On the fifth attempt, Lumani answered.

"Did you hear the shooting?" Munroe said. She spoke in English.

He didn't ask who she was, sounded neither surprised to hear from her nor disappointed. "I heard," he said. "Since you call me, I assume it's Tamás who is the dead one."

Ah, so Tamás was the name for Arben Two.

"You don't sound angry," she said.

She could hear the inaudible shrug. "This will be a problem for me because his incompetence becomes my failure."

"Your problem, you fix it," Munroe said, quoting the Doll Maker.

"Yes," he said, and his tone had a bite. "I've taken fault for him more than once. I won't cry that he's gone."

"Can you see the police? How far away are they?"

"There's traffic, maybe two minutes."

"I'm bleeding," she said.

"I'm sorry to hear it."

"Not really," she said. "It saves you the trouble. The plan was never to let me go, you would have killed me the moment your delivery was successful."

The sirens were louder, would be at the hotel soon.

"You are waiting for me, Valon, you and your rifle. Are you here to kill me or to take back your merchandise?"

"Both," he said, and then paused. "Did you know about Logan? Did you know before you ran?"

"No," she said.

"Does he mean nothing to you?"

She heard pain in his voice.

"He means everything to me," Munroe said. "But you overestimated my ability to bear the impossible. There's no winning for me no matter what I do."

"It was not me," he said. "Was not me that made the decisions. I follow rules, just like you."

The sirens were outside in the front of the hotel now.

"Not like me," she said. "Everyone has a choice. Even when there's a gun to your head you still have a choice. I made my choice, and you, Valon, you don't have a gun to your head."

Munroe hung up. Turned to Neeva. Her cheeks were flushed, her skin mottled and red, her eyes puffy and swollen, and tears ran down her face.

"Now you can start screaming," Munroe whispered.

They took the stairs at a near run, heading toward the front door with Neeva in hysterics, the two of them nearly colliding with the first of the police officers who had come in cautious and guarded through the front door.

"Upstairs," Munroe yelled. English first. Then Italian. "Upstairs, upstairs, the man with the gun is upstairs."

thirty-six

Without moving his eye from the scope, Lumani returned the phone to his pocket, drew a breath, and tried to block out the sting. He shouldn't care, had no reason to care what she said.

Prove himself stronger and smarter than his opponent. Reclaim the package. Kill what stood in his way. Succeed in the mission. These were the things that mattered. She, with her words and her strategy, was not a person but an obstacle and a challenge. She was prey. Formidable prey, but prey nonetheless. Yet it pleased him to speak with her, and it puzzled him that it should. Perhaps like a cat playing with the mouse: entertainment before food, although the food had just bit him, and this he didn't like.

Lumani lay prone against the wooden bench, off which he'd tossed cushions and dragged from the living area, propped on his forearms, rifle on a bipod, the scope and muzzle continuing out between gauzy curtains that hung over open balcony doors four stories up and at an angle to the hotel. He had a clear shot of the entrance—the only way his prey would be able to reach the street—and she would be a fool to wait inside with the police on their way in.

She could have left the last of the trackers in an empty room and jumped the garden wall or gone out a window, while, like a fool, he waited her out, but his predator's instinct had said that she remained in the hotel.

Feeling the trap, he'd sent Tamás. Now Tamás was dead, and instead of flushing her, as Lumani had intended, he was left second-guessing, watching the entrance while police cars circled, forced to wait out instinct in the hide he'd accessed by bullying the old lady who'd been home when he'd come knocking.

She was in the kitchen now, secured to a chair with her own tablecloth and quieted with a freshly laundered dish towel in her mouth.

He might eventually kill her. Or he might not.

He was not a thug like the others, brutes who couldn't adapt to situations as they unfolded. He was not useless overdeveloped muscle who took pleasure in the screams and the crying and the fear, who felt manliness in unearned respect or felt nothing at all. His job was the capture, and he was a professional to whom killing was occasionally a part of the work: messy but necessary, preferably executed from the business end of a rifle where he wasn't forced to touch the dead.

The screaming sirens were in front now, four cars with engines running and lights flashing, uniforms approaching the front door with far less precaution than he would have deemed prudent. She would need to exit the hotel soon unless she planned to be taken into custody because of Tamás's death.

In anticipation of the hit, Lumani rested his index finger alongside the trigger guard, controlling his breathing so his heartbeat didn't pulse heavy through his fingers, his hands, his shoulder, and knock off his aim.

Onlookers, summoned by the sirens like zombies to the living, gathered from apartments and shops, curious, stupid, stupid people with their cell phone cameras waiting to catch some action to send to friends or post online, lucky people because Tamás had gone in to blow down doors and not the entire building.

Sirens. Police. Crowds. And still no sign of his prey.

Questions and self-doubt percolated and mixed into a potent cocktail.

He couldn't afford another failure.

Inside his head, the sparklers tickled, the collapse was there at the edge of his senses, creeping closer because of the need for sleep and the ongoing lack of success. Soon. Soon enough he could lock himself into a hotel room for days and pump toxins and chemicals into his system in a form of rapturous release from the pressure of perfection and the agony of rejection and nonexistence.

But not yet.

Lumani took his eye off the scope.

The window of opportunity was closing. He risked the streets being cordoned off, risked getting caught in a random photograph posted on the Internet, risked visual proof that tied him to the scene when the police came around for witnesses.

He inched backward, drawing the rifle with him. Froze.

The prey and the package barreled through the door, huddled together and covered in dust as if they'd escaped a bomb blast. Eye returned to the scope, Lumani followed them and drew in the magnified version: Michael, bleeding as she'd said, from her face and legs. She limped and yelled about a shooter, switching between perfect English and broken Italian, words that he read on her lips. Her clothes were different. Everything was different. And the package—good God—worthless now, emaciated and hairless.

Officers who hadn't yet entered the hotel ushered the women away from the door, victims to safety, and once they were away from the door, the curious and the crowds drew nearer so that Michael's head dipped and dodged between others', limiting his line of fire.

Lumani's lips twisted into a vicious smile. She'd waited to use the police and the crowds as diversion and deflection; she'd timed this to limit his ability to take the shot. He snorted. As if *that* would make any difference.

Crosshairs on the target, Lumani calculated, deliberated, waited through the movement. Exhaled slow and measured. And then Michael turned, leaned beyond the brown hair on the head that separated her from him, and stared straight at him. Finger to her temple and thumb in the air, mock gun to her own head, she pulled an imaginary trigger.

His heart reacted as if physically tagged.

Another slow breath in countermeasure and he moved his finger from trigger guard to trigger. So little pressure to send the death.

But his hand shook. The crowd parted slightly. Michael's back was toward him again and she, with the bald girl at her side, moved slowly away from the hotel.

So little pressure.

He could make the hit.

He could end the life of this person who, by her very existence, proved his own worthlessness, who had with no effort earned Uncle's approving affection.

If he could calm.

But his heart continued to beat heavy and he felt the thud in his fingers. The kind of beating that wouldn't be stilled by breathing or lack of breath.

Confused, he pushed back the panic at this new imperfection.

No.

Not imperfection, this was strength. For the first time in memory, the kill wasn't business. This was personal, and this beating was passion warming: the first sensation of what it meant to desire the death of another for pleasure.

More sirens wailed from far down the street.

Lumani drew backward. Disassembled the rifle and packed it up. Returned to the kitchen, a room with barely the floor space for the tiny table and two chairs tucked to its sides: a room built for the lonely. The woman was in the center of the area, bound as he'd left her, but the cloth was out of her mouth; she'd found a way to rid herself of the gag but hadn't called out or raised the alarm—a wise choice that had kept him from having to permanently silence her.

Her chin raised when he stood in the doorway, face haloed with short curly hair clearly dyed to hide the gray. He imagined that she, in her independent solitude, might be a grandmother; wondered what it must feel like to have a pillowy mother figure with the warmth and care and universal acceptance mothers were said to provide. He envied the imagined offspring.

The woman stared up at him with soft rheumy eyes while he deliberated eliminating this witness as a professional should, then he stepped into the room and patted the old woman on her head—a form of affection, he thought, to this mother of sorts. His movement came jerky and awkward and not at all familiar to what he expected a touch to an old woman should be.

Lumani blocked the apartment door open on his way out so that when he was gone, she could call for help. This was like the people who paid money to . . . What was the American word? Offset? Yes, to offset a carbon footprint for their wasteful lifestyles. He had paid in professionalism for the pursuit of death. No matter that it was passion for watching another die that spurred him on now, he was not like Arben and Tamás. To prove his point, he had allowed the old woman to live, and now he would go kill Michael.

thirty-seven

Munroe guided Neeva through the crowd of onlookers, gatherers who'd arrived in the wake of the sirens and lights, past the police cars. There were others, too—fellow hotel patrons who, after the shooting ended, and realizing the police had arrived, had also made their dash for freedom, adding to the confusion and the crowds.

They continued along the sidewalk, away from the hotel, Munroe waiting for the instant death that might or might not come and caring not one way or the other. One bullet and the pain would stop. But the death never came.

And so Munroe moved Neeva onward, more quickly now that they were beyond the police. Additional sirens called from down another street, undoubtedly summoned as backup after the first on scene had experienced the guests pouring out and seen the hotel proprietor on the floor of the lobby. She didn't think the owner was dead, although they'd passed through too quickly to confirm—for conscience's sake, she hoped he was still alive.

Neeva, by her side, legs moving twice as quickly as Munroe's, continued to sob. Munroe said, "You can stop crying now," and from one breath to the next, the tears dried up.

As she had done so many times in the past hours, Munroe turned down streets at random, moving slower this time not only to accommodate Neeva but also her own weakening, stopping occasionally to ask strangers for directions to the nearest metro, only to deliberately head off course, doing the mental math: trying to avoid making a beeline for her destination without taking so long to get there that Lumani was able to project her plan and arrive before she did.

One more phase and she could stop. This last strategic play meant, at least for the night, that the constant movement and the adrenaline spikes would be over, meant she could sleep.

The metro station led off the street and to the underground. If Lumani followed, and Munroe expected he would, he would be methodical and slow. She'd picked off two of his men in one day, and he'd be concerned about avoiding strategic errors, although why he hadn't taken the shot outside the hotel puzzled her.

The train arrived, and with rush hour long past, they found seats easily. Munroe caught stares from two passengers across the aisle and swiped at her forehead. Neeva handed her a washcloth that she'd apparently taken from the hotel, and Munroe tamped down the blood.

To Neeva she said, "Are you still willing to go through with your plan—to be used as bait?"

The girl didn't answer immediately, and Munroe switched on the cell phone. "I can't guarantee this will work," she said. "And there's the possibility we only half fail—that you end up getting taken and I can't get you back. I need to know you've seriously weighed the consequences and I'm not gambling with your life without your consent."

Neeva stared at the floor a long while and then looked up. "I understand the consequences," she said, "and yes, I'm still willing."

Munroe reached for Neeva's hand. Squeezed it. "I'll do everything I can to keep you safe," she said, and when Neeva smiled in reply, Munroe turned to the phone and worked as quickly as the spotty cell signal would allow, utilizing credit card numbers she'd had and memorized for years, setting the steps out in advance that would get them to the end of the night.

"Okay, then," Munroe whispered, and she dialed Lumani.

When he answered, she said, "I want to make a trade."

A heartbeat of pause, then Lumani said, "You'll give up the package?"

"I can't protect her," Munroe said. "I'm bleeding. Weakening. You'll take her from me, anyway. But I want the girl in the United States freed as was the original offer."

"That was before you killed Tamás."

"I still want it."

"I'll do what I can."

"No guarantees?" she said.

"I can't. But like you said, I'll take her from you, anyway."

"Why didn't you shoot?" she said.

"The timing wasn't right."

"You want me dead," she said.

"Yes, badly."

"I'm going to leave her at a restaurant for you to pick up," she said. "I won't be there."

"I'll still find you."

"Possibly, but not tonight."

"Where will you put her?" he said.

"I'll call you when I figure it out."

THE TAXI MUNROE had arranged for was waiting at the station when they arrived, and the transfer from train to platform to stairs to car made seamlessly. Munroe gave the driver the name of the hotel she'd booked across town and, seated in the comfort of the backseat, fought the body's command to drift to sleep—sleep Neeva quickly succumbed to.

Buildings rose like silent sentinels standing guard along the way, their facades framed and shadowed by streetlights, casting an otherworldly impression over sidewalks alive with pedestrian traffic. Munroe studied the eateries, searching for one that would abet her purpose, and when she found it, signaled the driver to pull over.

Her instructions were simple. Drive around the block at least once, and upon the return, idle down the street with the meter running. "When it's time to leave," she said, "it might be with two sleeping people, and I'll probably need your help." She waved a wad of cash. "Assuming you're available."

The driver's smile widened and he nodded. "Yes, available," he said.

Munroe nudged Neeva, and the girl came awake grudgingly. "It's time," she said, and Neeva scooted out of the taxi with her.

The restaurant filled a corner, the front well lit and inviting, but the side street mainly in shadow, and most of the tables set out under awnings along the fronting still empty.

Munroe called Lumani, and although she suspected he wasn't far away, she gave him the coordinates. She placed Neeva at the table in a corner, in a chair whose back faced the windowless side of the restaurant, and left all of the bags but the satchel at her feet.

Munroe pulled the trackers and the handmade envelope from her pocket. Scribbled a fake address on it. Neeva forced a smile, but reflective of the stress and exhaustion, the gesture came out crooked. Munroe said, "I promise." And with a kiss on the top of the girl's head, walked away.

The journey wasn't long. Several meters along the length of the building, into the shadows, far enough away from the restaurant patio that she wasn't visible beyond the lights but still close enough that she could see the back of Neeva's head.

A group of two men and a woman walked in Munroe's direction, and Munroe called out to them, offered a hundred euros if they'd take the envelope and drop it into the nearest mailbox for her.

Their expressions were a mix of suspicion and curiosity, but money, the world's most common language, was one they spoke well, and so they took the envelope and the cash and continued along their way until their laughter and playful banter faded with them.

In the shadows, Munroe waited, her back to the wall, time continuing its slow march forward while her glance roved from Neeva to what she could see of the sidewalk and the pedestrians who filled the night.

In place of the Jericho, she held the taser. Double-checked the safety, reconfirmed the battery power. The moments passed, and eventually Neeva was forced to order a meal to retain her seat, but still no Lumani.

He'd seen the blood. He'd seen the limp. He was running on nervous fumes and exhaustion the same way she was, and he wanted the package. He had to show. And even if he took Neeva down from afar, he'd still have to come in close for the pickup. Even if he'd driven by once—twice—to confirm Neeva was truly alone, Munroe should have caught sight of him by now.

Consumed by the silence, by Lumani's absence, by exhaustion, and entirely focused on trying to spot him on the street and in the crowds, she nearly missed the cues of approach from behind. Didn't hear him, didn't see him slinking through the shadows from the opposite direction until almost too late.

She turned. Caught a glimpse of him. Of the handgun.

Exhaustion became energy. Weakness became strength.

He was still in the range between far enough to miss and close enough to hit.

He stopped suddenly when she turned. Drew, and so did she; he fired and the slug hit her square in the chest. The force threw her backward onto the ground, and when he approached to fire again, she aimed the laser sight at his neck.

Pulled.

Threads of voltage sent him into spasms.

Hurting, trying to breathe, Munroe forced herself up from the ground and closed the distance. Kicked the gun out of reach; it was another HK USP .45 Tactical, same as what Tamás and Arben had used. Let go of the taser and put the Jericho to Lumani's forehead.

With a boot on his chest, she used her free hand to search for the syringe he surely carried. Found it. Jabbed it into his thigh. Waited with the gun to his head until his eyes shut and his jaw went slack. Punched him just to be sure. The sedative would have been measured to heavily dose Neeva and her nearly half-weight to his, but at this point, what the fuck ever.

A group of pedestrians on the other side of the street had watched the entire scene. Munroe waved them on. "It's official business," she said, and whether they believed her or not, they moved on. Human nature was always more inclined to apathy, to avoiding involvement, to seeing things as someone else's problem. People were easy like that.

Munroe called to Neeva, though it took several attempts, each louder than the last, to capture the girl's attention. Neeva, as Munroe had been, was so entirely focused on pretending to eat and act naturally while studying pedestrians that she'd filtered out the noise from behind. When the girl finally heard the call, she put money on the table and brought the bags, then, spotting Lumani on the ground, smiled. Had no idea that because of Munroe's slipup they'd both come perilously close to disaster.

Munroe blinked back the exhaustion. God, she needed sleep.

Soon. Almost. Another hour at the most and she could collapse.

Munroe gave Neeva a strained smile. "Good job," she said, and dialed the taxi driver. When he answered, she called him around for pickup.

That Neeva was still awake was a bonus Munroe hadn't counted on, and so together, with one of Lumani's arms draped over Munroe's shoulders and Neeva propping him up more with her head than shoulders, they walked him to the curb. To the occasional passersby who stopped to gawk, Munroe said, "Too much wine," which inevitably elicited snickers.

Inside the cab, Munroe handed the driver half the cash she'd offered and said, "The rest when we reach the hotel." Switching to English, she said to Neeva, "We need to get him naked."

By the time they arrived at the hotel, through something of a maneuver in the small backseat, they'd stripped Lumani down and then Munroe, having confirmed the pants and shirt were free of trackers, put them back on. The shoes, jacket, belt, and everything else he'd worn and carried on him she'd rolled into a ball, and they'd stopped along the way so that she could dispose of them.

With another portion of cash handed over to the driver, he didn't question the many requests for turns and false starts. They traveled aimlessly along random streets. Stopped and waited. Moved to parking garages and waited more, and although Munroe expected a tail, she found none. Throughout, the taxi driver paid attention but said nothing but *grazie* when at last he parked at the curb outside the hotel and Munroe handed him the last of the money. "I have more," Munroe said. "Wait and I will return."

To Neeva: "I'll be right back."

Taking Lumani into the hotel, unconscious and barely clothed, was one thing, putting him on display and babying him through the check-in procedure another, and so she entered the hotel alone, scoped the lobby and the elevator area to place the cameras and security, and then returning to the front desk, secured the keys.

At the taxi, Munroe and Neeva inched Lumani out, and with his arm draped over her shoulders and his body sagging, Munroe handed the driver another payment. "Don't return for any of the items we threw away," she said. "Not even the phone or the watch—

there are evil people looking for those pieces, and if you carry even one of them, you'll invite death to your family."

The driver gazed at her quizzically and she said, "You have enough money to make up for any value you might get out of going back for them. Please just believe me."

He nodded.

"I'll keep your number," she said. "I may need your help again." So he smiled and waved before driving off, and she stared after him, hoping he'd follow through—not just for his own sake, but for hers.

Munroe turned from the diminishing taillights toward the bright hotel entrance. With Neeva's help, she juggled carrying bags and walking Lumani through the front door, a slightly more attention-gathering process than it had been getting him from the back of the restaurant into the taxi.

This hotel, unlike the boutique one that had served her purpose earlier in the evening, was a European version of an American chain, which made it easier to blend in and hide. The twenty-four-hour front desk rotated shifts, and employees and guests passed through the cycle in numbers great enough to make this one odd incident just another curiosity.

From lobby to elevator, past curious hotel personnel and guests, Munroe tossed out the occasional sarcastic comment poking fun at Lumani and eliciting smiles as they continued on, up several floors, down a hall, and finally, into the seclusion of the room.

Munroe shifted furniture, and when she'd cleared the space she needed, she stripped Lumani out of his clothes again and then maneuvered him into the desk chair with its back wedged into a corner. With the roll of tape, she bound him—ankles, knees, wrists, elbows, shoulders, and torso—so that he took on the shape of the chair and could not, through accident or effort, tip it over. The sedative wouldn't be enough to keep him under for long, but he was as sleep-deprived as she was, and she expected him to be out a while. She didn't tape his mouth for fear of suffocating him, and because in any case what noise he made would surely alert her before anyone else.

Duct tape. Perfect weapon; so many uses. With her work done, Munroe took a step back and tossed what little was left of the roll onto the desk.

Munroe sighed. Glanced at Neeva, who'd fallen asleep as soon as Munroe had gotten Lumani in the chair. Sat on the room's one bed and took off her shoes. Lay back and darkness descended.

TAPPING PULLED MUNROE from the deep. Subtle random thuds that paused and continued on, eager and frenetic, only to pause again. Without moving, without changing the rhythm of her breathing, she opened her eyes just enough to observe and for a minute or two lay still, while Lumani twisted in the chair, straining at the bonds, throwing himself forward and occasionally inching the chair away from the wall.

Neeva slept on.

Munroe opened her eyes fully, waited until Lumani had finished thrashing. Smiled at the shock on his face and the sudden freeze when his eyes locked onto hers and he realized she'd been watching him.

"What do you want with me?" he said.

Munroe sat. Stretched. The clock on the desk told her six hours had passed since she'd dropped into oblivion, and the darkness on the other side of the curtains, that dawn had not yet arrived.

She stood. Pulled the last bottle of water from the grocery bag. Opened it and, standing in front of him, staring at him, took a long, drawn-out swig.

She wiped a hand across her mouth.

Placed the bottle on a side table, close enough that had he not been secured to the chair, he could have reached out and taken it.

Pulled the taser from the bag and rewound the electrode wires she'd had no time to deal with when hustling him from the street into the taxi. With the probes back in place, she set the taser on the desk within his line of sight.

He studied her intently now.

She fished through the satchel for another gas cartridge, shook it for him to observe, and then slowly, deliberately, each movement exaggerated for staged effect, swapped old cartridge for new. Facing him, she sat on the edge of the bed with a box of ammunition and reloaded bullets into the two spare magazines she'd not yet had time to refill.

Swapped out the half-empty one for a full one.

Reloaded the third as well.

"Where's your rifle?" she said.

"In my car."

"Where's your car?"

"It *was* not far from the restaurant where I was *supposed* to pick up the girl."

"Oh, yes," she said. "You are definitely the wounded party here." Loaded the last magazine. "You didn't have keys in your pockets."

"I had a driver."

She raised her eyebrows. "Another one?"

He shrugged.

Munroe stood. Picked up the taser. Casual and nonchalant, she aimed the laser toward his chest and fired.

thirty-eight

For the second time between sunset and sunrise, the electrodes worked their magic. Lumani flailed and twitched, this time naked and bound, and what should have been satisfying in some small way left Munroe hollow.

When the current had ended, she leaned over and removed the probes. When Lumani had caught his breath, she stared down at his thighs and pointed the taser at his groin. "Next one goes there," she said.

"What do you want from me?" he said. When she didn't answer, he tugged at the bonds, manic and frantic. The chair rocked and the back legs tipped off the ground, and when finally he'd spent his energy, he said, "Why didn't you kill me?"

"I might still," she said. "But right now you're worth more to me alive. I can't decide whether the value is in trying to trade you for the girl in the United States or use you for information."

"Can I have clothes?" he said. "This is inhumane."

Munroe stepped closer. Knelt so she was eye-to-eye and tapped the taser against her thigh. "When I douse you with cold water so you can't breathe, when I shove wide objects up your ass, when I beat you while you're bound and helpless or stand by and laugh while someone else does, when I pull out your teeth and slaughter your family members, then we can talk about inhumane."

Lumani fought the bonds and the chair again. Twisted. Shook. Grimaced and snarled, and finally out of breath, he glared at her. "I don't do those things," he said.

Munroe stood and moved several paces back. Behind her, the covers on the bed rustled, and without turning she knew Neeva had woken, had sat up and was watching. "You do those things," Munroe said. "You do them every time you bring another girl through your uncle's doors." She paused. "Who killed Noah? Was it you?"

He said, "Noah?"

"The Moroccan. The punishment when Neeva ran."

"Not me," Lumani said. "My counterpart."

"How did you find him—the Moroccan?"

"The same way we found you," he said.

"The woman in prison?"

Lumani nodded, and his confirmation felt like a savage knife slice followed by an injection of painkillers. She drew a long breath past the pain for the morphine: For what it was worth, Logan hadn't been tortured for the information, yet even sequestered in prison and cut off from the world, Breeden had found a way to dig and probe and follow Munroe's movements; with nothing but time, endless time, what else did a person have but reason and motive to plot revenge?

Munroe cursed her own weakness, the failure to anticipate, the failure to watch her back. If anyone was to blame in this scenario, it was she. She should have known better.

She turned back to Lumani. "Was Noah dead from the beginning?" she said. "Before this even started, killed ahead of time just so you could have that image available in case you needed some sick card to play to control me?"

Lumani raised his eyes to hers. "I don't know," he said. "It's possible, but I truly don't know. That is a question for someone else to answer."

"How many counterparts do you have?" she said.

"There are three of us," he said. "But I am the . . ." His voice caught, and his sentence failed.

"The best?" Munroe said, finishing it for him. "You should be proud." She turned to Neeva. "You want revenge? Want to know what it feels like? You can't kill him, but if you think it'll do you any good, have at him."

Neeva scooted off the bed and Munroe dug through the satchel, pulled out the pocketknife. Flicked the blade open, all four inches of it, and even as small as the knife was, the weight of the metal in her palm became soothing, calming: a familiar lullaby of death that put the world at ease.

Neeva said, "Use this?"

Munroe said, "Yes."

"What about the taser?" Neeva said. "Or maybe the gun. I could shoot him in the leg."

"No," Munroe said. "If you want to know what it really feels like, then you do it personal and close. Anything else is cheap and easy."

Neeva took the knife. Gingerly. The way someone unfamiliar with handling a gun might take such a weapon: two-fingered from the base, like it might morph into a snake, might coil and bite. And then, with a toss of her head and her posture straight, Neeva grasped the handle firmly, strode around the bed to Lumani, and stood in front of him for a long while, looking from the knife to him and back to the knife again, as if analyzing what she truly felt and determining what course she would steer.

Lumani's jaw clenched and his gaze hardened, as if he braced for a pain he was too proud to plead against.

"You're the guy who kidnapped me, aren't you?" Neeva said.

Lumani held stoic and didn't reply.

"I could cut you," Neeva said. "I'm not scared, and it wouldn't bother me to see you suffer. But I want to talk to you. So, you choose. Cut or talk?"

"I was one of them," Lumani said.

"And this is what you do for a living? Kidnap girls?"

His head jerked up defensively. "It's not a living," he said. "It's a requirement, and I never touch the girls."

"Oh, so that makes you better than the rest of them?" Neeva returned to staring at the knife. Pointed the blade down toward Lumani's thigh. There her hand hovered with the point of metal barely touching him, and she said, "Who dies?"

"I don't understand."

"Who dies if you don't follow through on your requirement?"

He lowered his eyes.

"You're an asshole," Neeva said. "You turn innocent girls into human cattle and you still find a way to feel sorry for yourself. You should feel guilty, not make excuses for why it's not your fault."

Neeva's hand gripped the knife handle harder, tighter, until her knuckles whitened. And then she jabbed the blade down into Lumani's thigh and jerked: a three-quarter-inch penetration, easy. Maybe an inch. To the side of his leg, missing bone, striking soft tissue.

Had to hurt.

Lumani screamed and Neeva pulled the knife out. Stood staring at the blood on the blade while the wound began to weep. Munroe stepped forward and slowly, almost tenderly, took the knife from Neeva's hand. "Do you feel better?" she said.

"A little."

Lumani swore and rocked the chair, teeth gritted, hands clenched tightly around the ends of the arm handles.

"Do you want more?" Munroe said.

"Telling him he's an asshole felt better than cutting him."

Munroe handed her back the knife. "Go get a washcloth and bring it to me. Then wash off the knife," she said. "Make sure you do a good job—those are your fingerprints and his blood, and we're in Italy, not the United States."

Neeva took the handle between forefinger and thumb and left for the bathroom, returned briefly with the cloth and left again.

Munroe picked up the tape from the desk. Put the towel over Lumani's wound and used the last of the roll to hold it in place. Knelt so she was eye-to-eye with him once more. "I'd like the names of your counterparts," she said. "And I'd like you to explain everything you know about the way your uncle operates, both here and in the United States. I want to know about the clients and I want to know the structure of the organization."

Lumani, breathing shallow, broke off eye contact and stared at the floor.

Munroe stood and returned to the bed. Sat on it and studied him, while from the bathroom the sound of water flowing continued.

Threats of pain, death, even Neeva with the knife, weren't what poked at his psyche. He wasn't afraid of those things and they would never be enough to overcome the needs that drove him.

The water in the bathroom shut off and Neeva returned, knife wrapped in a towel. "Just put it in the bag," Munroe said, and she pulled out the phone. Dialed the Doll Maker. Set the call to speaker.

At six in the morning she didn't expect an immediate answer, especially not when dialing for the first time from an unknown number, but the line was picked up and the voice, clearly woken from sleep and unmistakably him, said *"Kush?"*

"Your missing friend," Munroe replied, speaking in English for Neeva's benefit. She could hear the shift, the crinkle against the phone that indicated movement.

"Such a tricky one," the Doll Maker said. "The problem you were meant to fix, you've only made worse."

"Your punishments didn't fit the crime, so I've taken matters into my own hands."

"My philosophy is so simple," he said, voice lilting, no longer sleepy, and clearly amused. "You break it and so you break, too."

"So, congratulations, I broke," she said. "And now, because of that, there's a whole lot more broken. What are you going to do? Destroy the whole world?"

"You called me," he said. "Do you have a proposal or are you a woman wasting time with useless chatter?"

"I will trade your Valon for the girl you currently hold in Texas."

The spontaneous laughter was loud enough to carry across the room, and Lumani raised his eyes in response.

"If you have him—and I ascertain you must since he's been missing for some time—then you can do me a favor and dispose of him. The girl in Texas, she has value, might fetch a fair price on the market, but Valon is a failure and worthless to me."

"Are you absolutely sure?" Munroe said. "Because that isn't a bluff you can take back. If you know anything about me, you know I have no problem, no conscience or hesitation, in killing people like you. He's caused me considerable grief, so if you won't trade him, then he's worthless to me and I will kill him."

"Do as you wish," the Doll Maker said.

"In that case, I'm willing to offer you your multimillion-dollar package for a girl nobody will miss," Munroe said. "That should be an appealing trade."

"I've seen the state of the merchandise," he said. "She is damaged. Worthless."

"That's fine," Munroe said. "I know who we're dealing with and delivering to, I saw him in Monaco. I'm wounded, I need hospitalization, Logan is free, and I no longer have a need for your merchandise. I have to rid myself of evidence and I'm sure he'd be happy to take her for a lesser price. Hair grows back fairly quickly. I'll deal with him myself and keep the fee, which means no Valon for future captures, no payment—not even to recoup your losses—and no me. You lose, you lose, and you lose."

The Doll Maker waited a long silence before speaking again. "What, then, my tricky friend," he said, "is the benefit to you in delivering the doll to me?"

"There will be less blood on my hands."

"Ah, so you do care for them after all," he said. "Fine, I will take the doll and give you your niece. Bring her to me."

"I need time to set it up with my backup to be sure you deliver on your end."

"My word is good."

"Then you should have no problem with my arrangements. I'll bring the merchandise to you and call when I am ready. And really, what do you want with Valon?"

"Do as you wish," he said. "I have no need for him."

Munroe put down the phone and turned to Lumani. She'd suspected the direction the conversation would run, but never to the extreme it had, and the pain etched on Lumani's face was deeper than what had surfaced when Neeva had cut him. In spite of circumstances, Munroe hurt on his behalf.

She stood and reached for the bottle of water. Uncapped it and put plastic to Lumani's mouth. He drank and kept drinking until the bottle was empty. Water dribbled down his chin, and though he tried to force it back, water also escaped, just barely, and only once, from his eyes.

Munroe returned to sitting on the bed, then leaned forward and faced him. Said nothing and neither did he, until the silence in the room became palpable. From behind, Neeva, inching toward Munroe, said, "Are we going to kill him?"

"I don't think we have to," Munroe said.

Oblivious to the undercurrents that drove the silence, the thoughts that went unspoken, Neeva said, "Well, we can't trade him, and he won't want to tell us what we want to know. He'll just make noise and call attention to us. He's a killer and a criminal *and* a total dick. What's the use in keeping him alive?"

"Will you talk?" Munroe said to Lumani. "What does he offer that you can't find elsewhere? He'll never love you—no matter what he promises. He's not capable of giving you what you crave."

"He has at times," Lumani said.

"Just a game to him. An amusement, a way to control you."

Lumani lowered his eyes, and Munroe, offering him a way out from the emotional devastation that verbalizing and facing such an internalized worthlessness and shame would cause, said, "What hold does he have on you?"

"I have no life without him," Lumani said. "Since I was four, he has taken me under his care—spent years and hundreds of thousands of dollars on training—money I owed him and had to pay back as the price for my own freedom."

"You've earned it back, but you still work for him."

"There's a bank account somewhere, money I've earned—"

"Blood money," Neeva interrupted.

Munroe raised a hand to hush her.

"I've seen the statements," he said. "It's not a small amount. He's promised to release it many times. Always one last job and then I am free. And, I think, if that money was really ever mine, I think he's taking the account as payment for the merchandise," Lumani paused, then whispered, "and terminating me."

"You don't need that money," Munroe said. "You're young. Well traveled. Speak several languages. And maybe not as smart or as good as you think you are, but smart enough, good enough. You can start over just about anywhere."

"With what? My rifle?"

"Point taken," Munroe said. "But everyone starts somewhere. I started with nothing. It's not easy, but it's possible if you want it badly enough."

"You are a killer," he said. "No better than me."

"I didn't know we were comparing," she said, "and frankly, terms like better or worse are meaningless to people like us." She jabbed a finger to his chest, and he flinched. "But I do own up to my actions instead of finding someone else to blame, and until you get that sorted out for yourself, you're just a stupid dumb sheep. You have potential, Valon. A life. Don't squander what you have chasing an illusion." She paused for effect. "You have options and you're a fool if you don't at least examine them."

He shrugged, his expression empty. "What do you want to know?" he said. "If it is reasonable, I'll tell you."

Without turning, Munroe said, "Neeva, check what food is left, will you?"

Neeva rummaged through the bag. To Lumani, Munroe said, "Are there reinforcements on the way?"

"They arrived last night."

"How many?"

"Two more."

"Before or after you came for Neeva?"

"After," he said, and then, reluctant and perfunctory, "They were en route, couldn't get to me before the exchange. I was to return to the car and then to rendezvous. Had they gotten into town sooner, we wouldn't be here right now."

Munroe shrugged. "Maybe, maybe not. Are they looking for you right now?"

Lumani stared at the floor. Not the gaze of contemplation but of searching. "I don't know," he said finally. "If they are looking for me, I believe that it is only to eliminate loose ends. They're certainly out for her, for you. To kill you."

"What about your driver?"

"I was lying," he said. "I left the keys in a magnetic case under the vehicle's carriage. That's how we operate, so someone else can come get the vehicle if we don't return to it. My wallet is there also, and ID."

Neeva stood by Munroe, last packet of crackers in her hand. Munroe took the package, opened it, and placed a cracker in Lumani's mouth. He chewed. She handed cash to Neeva. "Do you think you can find painkillers in the gift store? We'll need another couple bottles of water as well."

"I'll manage," Neeva said. "I assume I can spend the change."

Munroe nodded and, without glancing back, said, "Wear your sunglasses and hat."

"Got 'em," Neeva said, and she left.

thirty-nine

Alone with Lumani, Munroe stepped to the bathroom, returned with a towel, and draped it over his legs in a concession to his modesty. She squatted again, looked at him eye-to-eye, and this time Lumani didn't challenge or avoid her gaze, although gradually his focus moved from her face to her torso and he stared at the jacket.

"I hit you," he said. "And you got right back up."

She stood so that the jacket straightened. Ran her hand along the leather and paused at the hole near her heart. Allowed him to see it, then spread her fingers and ran them along the front, pausing at each of the hits she'd taken from Tamás.

"Fashionable armor," he said. "Those pieces are very expensive."

She nodded.

"I should have demanded the jacket from the beginning," he said, "together with everything else."

"You would have had to kill me first," she said, and with show-and-tell over, knelt, and whispered, "Tell me what you know about the organization, Valon—and about the client who purchased Neeva."

"May I eat first?" he said.

"After. I'd like to hear what you have to say before Neeva gets back."

"They're looking for her," he said, "she might never come back."

"You're not tracked and we weren't followed."

He sighed. "I want you to help me in exchange," he said.

"What do you want?"

"Something. Anything. A place to go or a way to survive. I have the clothes I was wearing, and that is all. No bank account, no home to return to, nothing. At this point, I am a beggar in the street."

She nodded. "I'll do what I can."

"Tell me something first," he said. "I want to know what you told her. When the girl was running and you chased her onto the restaurant patio. One moment she is screaming and fighting and then instantly silent, so easily controlled. What were your words, what did you say?"

"I told her the truth," Munroe said.

Lumani stared at her quizzically. "Truth?"

"Yes, truth. I described, quite graphically, what would happen if she did manage to get free, and I told her I was the lesser of two evils."

Lumani smiled, almost blushed. "All right," he said, and then began a monologue that started in Monrovia and worked its way westward, across Europe, into the United States, and back again: an intricate web of safe houses like the one in Zagreb, transport routes and schedules, a network that pumped a regular flow of young girls from impoverished eastern European countries, and some from South America, into the arms of willing buyers. A business for which demand was always high and the cost of merchandise cheap.

And then there were the clients from the upper echelon, those to whom Lumani and his near-equal counterpart had been assigned, their jobs to secure specific targets, the man with the dog just one of a dozen or more who picked their girls like clothes from a catalogue and paid handsomely for the privilege. Lumani referred to him as Mr. Hollywood, not for the client's looks but for his proclivity for actresses: Bollywood, Hong Kong, and now Neeva from the United States, his picks always rising film stars, always sensual, always tiny and childlike.

None of the detail was in and of itself enough to build a complete picture of the organization or to understand entirely who the many men were that kept the Doll Maker in business, but it was enough for a start. Munroe jotted notes on hotel stationery and occasionally interrupted with a question, but once he began, Lumani needed little prodding, and they continued until footsteps from the hallway arrested Munroe's attention. She straightened and moved from the desk to the door, hand on her weapon, waiting for the knock, and when it came in the pattern she expected, Munroe let Neeva in.

Neeva dumped an armful of items on the bed, glanced at Lumani, and said, "Did he tell us anything useful?"

"Some," Munroe replied, and fished for the small box of paracetamol. Took a bottle of water from the pile of items. Popped four blisters in the pack and downed them, popped another four and offered them to Lumani. He opened his mouth without being asked. She gave him the pills and water, then fed him crackers until the packet she'd previously opened was empty.

To Neeva, Munroe said, "I'm stepping out for a few minutes. Whatever you need to do before we go, do it now." Nodded toward Lumani. "You can talk to him, ignore him, whatever, just don't go near him, okay? And if you get the itch to kill him while I'm gone, don't, because I will disappear and leave you to take the fall."

Neeva rolled her eyes. "I'm not going to kill him," she said.

Munroe stepped into the hallway, closed the door. Strode past doors and recessed lighting to the end of the hall, and there, with her back to the wall, slid to the floor, stretched her legs forward, and tipped her head up to the ceiling.

Detox.

Quiet.

Solitude.

An attempt to survive, to push beyond the anguish of the living and the voices in her head, which though muted, had not left her since Noah's death. Blocking them out could only go on so long before the darkness overtook her, as glimpses did now that she'd had a chance to breathe.

Logan was saved, but he'd never be the same.

Samantha alive . . . for now.

Noah was dead.

Jack was dead.

Alexis might also die or be sold on the slave market.

And her relationship with Bradford, which had somehow allowed them to juggle the disparities of their work and this hellish life and still find peace, was, for all practical purposes, over. Through no fault of his and no fault of hers, they could never go back to the way things had been.

In the acceptance of so much was such unspeakable pain that for the first time, the urges compelled Munroe not to fight, but in an act of self-preservation to get up and walk, to keep on walking until she reached a place where she was truly alone, and humanity with all its evils ceased to exist. In the quiet, in the silence of the empty hall, no longer able to turn off the emotion or shut it down, Munroe allowed the hurt, the gnawing ache that consumed her, to pass through.

How long she sat, she didn't know, breathing, feeling, allowing herself to simply be, while hotel guests came and went and occasionally did a double-take, and when the moment finally arrived that she felt strong enough to once more push herself off the floor and continue what had to be done, she pulled the phone from her pocket and dialed Bradford.

LUMANI RAISED CHIN from chest when Munroe stepped through the door, and Neeva was on the bed watching TV.

"Anything about us?" Munroe said.

"There's lots about me, but I haven't seen anything about you yet," Neeva replied. "You took a long time, where were you?"

Munroe tossed her the phone. "Call your parents. Please. You can go into the hall if you want privacy, but stay right outside the door, okay?"

Neeva stared at the phone, snatched the key card off the nightstand, and scooted off the bed. Stepped out the door. With Lumani watching, Munroe unzipped her pants and took them off. Examined the deepest cut on her leg. The area was raw and red but not yet showing a lot of infection. She needed to get the wound properly cleaned and stitched up, but couldn't until this ordeal was over. Munroe doused the area with peroxide again, put a clean hand towel over the spot, and used the same tape to hold the mess in place. Pants back on and five minutes in, Munroe stood and knocked on the hallway door.

Lumani said, "Does it hurt? The wound, does it hurt?"

Munroe didn't turn toward him. "Does yours?" she said.

"Yes," he replied. "But I prefer the physical pain. I appreciate the distraction."

Munroe tested the batteries on the taser and glanced at him over her shoulder. "The pain on the inside is what keeps you human," she said. "Never forget that."

In the wait for Neeva, she unloaded and reloaded the magazines. Seated the bullets, and finally, with these items and most of the euros, she filled the pockets of her cargo pants so that what was left to carry was easily divided between the satchel and the backpack.

The key card was swiped and Neeva stepped back inside, her eyes red and puffy. She gave the phone back and Munroe waited a beat to see if she'd need to play therapist, but when Neeva offered nothing, Munroe handed her the satchel. "Give me three minutes," she said.

Neeva raised an eyebrow but didn't question her, and when she'd left the room again, Munroe turned to Lumani. "I'm leaving money, your clothes, and food and water," she said. "I hope to be back within thirty-six hours. Forty-eight at the most, but I expect you'll be free before then."

Lumani said, "Will you use the information I gave you to kill my uncle?"

"Possibly."

"If you don't, he will kill you or have you killed."

"It's you I'm concerned about," she said. "Do you have a reason to hunt me?"

"Yes." He stared at the floor, at her feet. "I have a reason," he said. Looked at her face. "But no motivation."

"You may one day find the motivation," she said, and then knelt so she could better see his face. "Even if you're successful in hunting me, killing me, it won't make you more of a man, won't earn you the acceptance you're looking for—not from him, not from yourself."

"I never loved him, never worshipped him," he said.

She stood, strode to the door, turned back, and in a whisper just loud enough to carry across the space, said, "I, too, once danced on marionette strings to earn the affection and approval of a man who would never be capable of giving it. You have a lifetime of options ahead of you. If that's what you choose."

Munroe stepped into the hall, put the Do Not Disturb sign on the door handle, and shut Lumani in behind her. He'd be free by the time she returned—if she returned—of this, she had no doubt.

And like the randomness of life's chaos, the decision to let him live was a coin toss. Just as she currently fought to get out from under the weight of her decision to allow Kate Breeden to live, so she might also one day again find herself in Lumani's crosshairs. All she could do was walk the narrow line between instinct and conscience and hope for the best.

forty

Bradford exchanged his jacket for a service technician's shirt: gray, grimy, and still bearing another man's sweat—at least he assumed the stink belonged to Roger, the name stitched in red letters above his pecs. Another man's shirt, another man's pheromones—a simple illusion for a simple plan: He would walk in the front door, take the girl, and walk back out with her.

Bradford handed the Explorer keys to Andre Adams, swapping them for the keys to the panel van Adams had parked behind him. The utility vehicle, acquired on short order, white, dirty, ladder-topped, and by virtue of its everyday commonness nearly invisible, would serve its purpose just fine.

It was six in the early evening and they were still hours away from the handoff Munroe had arranged. The details called for a parking-lot rendezvous at eight in the morning Zagreb time, one in the morning local, but with the area lit up like the Fourth of July, with trucks coming and going around the clock, and new shifts in and out of the port facilities at all hours, time of day meant little, and there was no such thing as true night.

If Bradford had been in Dallas when the arrangements had been made, he would have needed every one of those precious hours to pull some kind of strategy together. But he hadn't been in Dallas; he'd been in Houston.

It hadn't been difficult to figure this one out. The Doll Maker people knew Bradford was still alive, knew he was hungry and hunting, and they would want Alexis off the grid, somewhere beyond his Dallas reach. But since he was dealing with foot soldiers short on resources, he expected they'd fall back on familiar and convenient.

When Munroe had begged him for help, he'd gotten off one call and made another, to Adams, already in Houston, burning through cash, waiting to see what moves Kate Breeden might make. Bradford sent him to the address taken from the eighteen-wheeler's freight manifests and then, going with his gut, pulled Rick Gonzalez up from Gatesville to temporarily man the Capstone office and left town. Was already halfway to Harris County by the time Adams called back with an assessment and pictures of the property.

While the traffickers were still waiting for instructions, he'd already been inside their crawl space. This time he'd gotten to the battlefield first; this time he knew what he was up against. This time there were no employees to worry about, only the criminals. He'd debated calling in the police, getting a SWAT team to handle the rescue, but couldn't figure out how to do it without implicating himself in the shit storm he'd already started, or a way to ensure that a raid didn't occur too soon or, God forbid, too late or not at all.

No. He'd get Alexis, but not by throwing away Jack's life and possibly Sam's as well, just so the scum could spend a day behind bars before posting bail and disappearing like their counterpart trash up north had done after the firefight. The playing field was different now; the stakes had changed and the only way to make sure this got done right was to do it himself.

THE BUILDING WAS warehouse style with straight lines, constructed of concrete and corrugated metal, and ran the length of the entire block. Veers had the end suite, and the other companies in the building ranged from light manufacturing to storage. This address, unlike the others, was leased instead of owned, so it made sense now why the location had never shown up in any of the war room's searches.

The back portion of the property was larger than the warehouse, a fenced lot mostly filled with containers, a place where trucks loaded and offloaded cargo, all of this within an industrial zone just south of I-10 and slightly north of one of the many facilities that comprised the Port of Houston's twenty-five-mile stretch along the Houston Ship Channel.

A transport business like Veers fit right in—disappeared entirely.

Bradford backed the van into one of the few parking spots that fronted the building and stepped into the warm spring air, heavy with moisture and fragranced with chemicals and petroleum, courtesy of the area's refineries. The Explorer passed in front of him: Adams on his way to the end of the block, to the gated open area in back, an area the doll people couldn't protect because it wasn't their property. Bradford pulled a duffel bag out and then a tool chest, and with a clipboard tucked under his arm, laminate ID hooked onto his pocket under ROGER, picked up the heavy stuff and strode to the front door.

Didn't bother to find out if it was locked; it was.

A tremor reached out from beyond the glass: Adams blowing charges on the back door. A thirty-second pause, enough time for defenses to go up, for rounds to be fired, and then came the concussion that Bradford could hear even from here: the first in a series of flash-bangs tossed in through the hole.

Beneath this oversize roof the effects wouldn't be as devastating as if this had been a living room or bedroom, but if Adams had managed to get the grenades anywhere near the men inside, then they would feel as if the Jolly Green Giant had just stormed through the door and smacked both hands upside their ears, and a ten-car pileup was having a party inside their heads.

Disorienting. Nauseating. Painful.

Bradford drove toolbox to the door.

He was tired. He was pissed off. He was coming for blood.

Stepped through the hole in the glass.

Set down the toolbox and pulled a loaded tactical vest and an MP5 submachine gun from the duffel. Snapped into the vest and, adrenaline amping, slapped the 100-round Beta C-Mag drum into place. Felt the concussion of another grenade, incredibly loud even from here. Counted seconds.

Another went off.

With images from the main room playing out in his mind's eye, he strode forward through a standard industrial-carpeted hallway, past standard offices with standard office equipment and furniture, toward the back, which was not standard by any means: Under the high ceiling three smaller prefabs waited.

Soundproofed and insulated, they were windowless sheds, padlocked and up on cinder blocks, larger versions of the truck's crawlspace in which they'd found Logan.

Bradford rounded the hallway corner into the warehouse. The two-man contingent, in a form of disoriented retreat from the gaping hole and the light and the noise, fired suppressed semiautomatics toward the rear of the building, squandering ammunition on shots that went wide and scattered while they stumbled toward the sheds; headed toward the human shield as Bradford expected they would.

His throat burned in recognition of a face he'd seen before, had broken before, a face that hadn't been there when he'd scouted the location; recognition accompanied by his promise to Walker to take out the trash after they'd gotten Logan. Bradford moved forward, finger to the trigger, firing a staccato of controlled bursts.

The warehouse man and his partner dropped. Rolled. Emptied magazines at him, still too far away for accuracy, and then backup magazines. Bradford continued forward until the drum was empty and the room went battle-deaf silent.

The smell of war filled his airways. Fireworks. Fear. Death.

Bodies on the floor, punched full of holes.

An enemy who might have had a fighting chance if they'd had the ability to think ahead, to strategize, to prepare for the possibility he might arrive already knowing their traps and their weapons.

He with the biggest guns wins.

Bradford moved to the nearest man. Kicked him.

Dead.

Stepped to the warehouse guy, drowning in his own blood. The weapon that had been in his hand was a foot away, and Bradford toed it completely beyond reach. The man could have it if he was willing to die for the effort.

Bradford gazed down at him, then with time bolting wild, turned and strode toward the middle storage shed, the one he'd watched from the crawl space. Checked the door for wires, for any sign of explosive rigging, and, finding none, pulled a length of primer cord from the vest, wrapped, knotted, sliced, and in a maneuver getting old really fast, set it alight.

ON A MATTRESS, bound with tape at the wrists and ankles, in torn and dirty clothes, lay Alexis Jameson—part-time medical transcriptionist, single mother of a two-year-old—crying out from pain, from fear, turning from the light as if to escape it.

She didn't bear any signs of the brutalization Logan had endured—no broken bones that Bradford could see, though from the bruises and the marks she'd clearly been brutalized in other ways. Battle readiness kicked in again; the push of war survival that stamped down emotion, the relief of numbness so that he didn't have to feel.

He took a step inside and paused. Had expected to find Alexis in this holding cell, hadn't expected to find another on the opposite side, staring up at him in terror. Blond, brown-eyed, she was young—sixteen or seventeen—unbound and in much better physical condition. Arms around her knees, she rocked.

Bradford moved toward Alexis, whose cries had become screams, and her turn from the light into a frantic struggle to crawl away from him, as if she couldn't see him or had no memory of who he was. "Hey," he whispered, and she said, "No, no, no."

He knelt. "I'm not going to hurt you," he whispered. "I promise I'm not going to hurt you. I came to take you away from this place, to put you somewhere safe."

Alexis responded to the tone, to the words, if not the face; stopped trying to crawl away. Didn't move.

"You'll be okay," he whispered. Moved closer. "I'm going to touch you," he said. "I'm going to put my hands on your arms and legs, so I can move you. I won't hurt you. I promise."

Alexis flinched but didn't fight, and he drew her close to him. Picked her up and carried her outside into the warehouse. The blond one followed, jabbering, yammering words he couldn't understand, tugging at his sleeve until finally through sign language and tears and very broken English, she communicated that there were others in the sheds.

Bradford hesitated. Swore. This hadn't been part of the plan.

The delay in dealing with other girls, in finding a way out for them, too, could mean the difference between getting caught or not, arrested for murder or not. But he couldn't leave them like bags of unwanted belongings beside a Goodwill container.

He yelled for Adams.

Through the opening in the back wall, the former Marine materialized. He, too, paused when he saw the blond girl. Bradford moved toward him. "Take her," he said, and transferred Alexis, like an overgrown child, from one pair of arms to one stronger.

Hands free, Bradford pulled paper from the vest and scribbled Tabitha's married name, her number. "This is her mother," he said. "Call her. I don't care what bullshit story you have to make up, just make sure she knows her daughter's been traumatized. Find out what she wants to do." He paused. "And then, whenever you know what that is, call me. No. Don't wait that long. Call me as soon as you know you're safe and then call her mother."

Adams nodded, then was gone.

INCLUDING THE BLOND one, three foreign girls had been contained in the prefabs, pretty and young in a long-legged, fresh-faced sort of way, each a modern version of the goose that laid the golden egg: feed it, house it, pimp it out, and the money would keep on coming.

They would soon show up on Craigslist and other online meet-up sites, touting themselves as *young* and *new in town,* looking for a good time, forced by their owners to pass themselves off as willing prostitutes and call girls, full of smiles and lies and fabricated pasts.

Not knowing what else to do, he motioned the girls toward the office area, motioned them to wait, and assuming they understood, he turned from them to the nearest fallen enemy, grabbed him by the collar, dead and deadweight, and dragged him into the middle shed.

The warehouse man was still alive, if barely, each breath rattling with a gurgle. Bradford stood over him, one leg on either side of his body, watching the man shake in the way the battlefield near-dead often did. Pain. Shock. Whatever. Waited just long enough for the man's eyes to focus and then gave him a big toothy grin. Grabbed the man by the arm and, smearing blood behind him, dragged him, too, into the shed and left him there.

The girls were in the hallway when Bradford reached it, crowded into one another like a small herd of frightened sheep, staring wide-eyed at his approach. He wanted to feel pity, sympathy, but battle numbness, the logistics of war, the frustration of the moment, over-rode the ability to care. He'd been in the warehouse six minutes already. Far too long. He strode past them toward the front of the building. Dumped the vest, the gun, and the drum into the duffel, picked up the toolbox, and went out through the broken glass door, the girls following.

He'd intended the van to be a way to transport Alexis and, un-sure what her condition might be, had put a mattress in the back. This was where the girls sat. Bradford shut them inside. Got the van moving away from the building and once he was far, far down the road, certain he hadn't been followed, he pulled over.

His phone rang.

Adams. Safe. En route to Dallas.

Before he could follow Adams, he needed to find a way to help the helpless; he couldn't just put the girls on the street and wish them well. He left the front and slipped into the back. It took a while, but utilizing maps from the Internet on his phone, he grad-ually understood that they were from Moldova, one of the many pieces split off from the former USSR.

Another Internet search and the best he could turn up locally was a consulate for the Russian federation. He didn't know if taking them there would be the equivalent of dropping an American stuck in Thailand on the doorstep of the Canadian embassy, but at least at the consulate there was a better chance of someone understanding their language, their story, and able to communicate on their behalf to those who could help. Not much, but all he had, and so he put the van into gear and began the drive.

For now, at least for this moment, he'd won.

The police would come, they'd find the bodies, they'd find plenty of evidence. They'd have to dig for answers and would hopefully discover the same threads the war room had uncovered. Whatever law enforcement didn't eventually get to, Bradford would, over time. But that was more than he could worry about right now. He'd taken out the garbage on Walker's behalf. He'd found Alexis and she was on her way to safety. Now he could focus on Michael.

forty-one

MILAN, ITALY

Hands in her jacket pockets, Munroe stepped from the bistro and scanned the main hall of Milan Central below, searching for a danger she might not recognize even if spotted.

She'd left Neeva behind, tucked away at a rear table with her back to the room so that it would be impossible for someone to recognize the girl in passing and equally difficult for Neeva to give away her own nervousness through eye contact and jumpy behavior. Two thousand euros, the phone, and a set of instructions were the insurance on the off chance Munroe didn't make it back.

A final glance over the crowds and Munroe headed down the stairs and through the bustle of the station toward the ticket counters, fighting the limp that marked her as an anomaly.

According to Lumani—assuming he'd told the truth—two more of his people had arrived in town last night, and they'd be searching; there could be two, or more, or none at all, but regardless, the Doll Maker knew she was on her way back to Zagreb with Neeva, and no matter how small the needle of her person or how big the haystack of Milan, there weren't *that* many ways to get there.

Traveling by road would have been ideal for slipping between the cracks, and had Munroe been alone, she'd have offered cash to a random driver and hitched a ride, but Neeva as a travel companion made that impossible. Stealing another car and attempting to cross Italy and outside the Schengen Area borders without proper papers was out of the question, and carrying weapons ruled out flying. The Doll Maker's people, if they were worth anything, had to play these possibilities.

Munroe waited in line, waited for the telltale hair rise of warning, but there was no incident, and with the next train still some hours away, she returned to Neeva with tickets in hand.

They punctuated the wait in the bistro with sparse conversation: Munroe with her back to the wall and face to the door, drinking far too much caffeine; Neeva picking at her food, pretending to have an appetite and to smile in order to mask a fatigue deeper than what had been there the day before, until finally their departure time rolled around and they had to move again.

Munroe lingered until it was nearly too late to board, holding back on the platform, searching for what was out of place, that inability of the truly focused to hide concentration, for faces that sought out other faces instead of travel schedules and compartment numbers—searching for those who were alone and headed in no obvious direction, and only when she saw none of this did she lead Neeva to the train, walking the long length of many cars to their first-class berth.

Had it been she giving chase, she would have skipped this uncertainty and focused manpower on the arrival, knowing eventually she would have to show. But this was the disadvantage of the hunted: always running, chasing monsters from shadows, never able to rest or predict from which direction the blow would come. Inside the berth, Munroe sat with her back to the window, legs stretched out along empty seats, Jericho in her hand between leg and cushion. Time drew on. The assassins never came, and after an uneventful change of trains in Venice, she relaxed and eventually, even against her own guard, fell into fitful sleep until Bradford called.

THEY PASSED THROUGH immigration at the Croatian border and the train arrived in Zagreb in the wee morning hours while the streets were still dark and the city slept. A few people waited on the platform when they disembarked, and among them were two whose manner and posture set off Munroe's warning instinct.

Munroe kept close to departing passengers, alert for ambush, and not wasting time or energy with words, used her body to herd and corral Neeva, keeping the girl hemmed in among the others: camouflage in numbers as they moved from platform into Glavni Kolodvor, Zagreb's main railway station.

The building, small and almost provincial after the scope and size of Milan Central, still carried historical grandeur in its architecture, a throwback to days of glory when Zagreb, like Belgrade, Prague, and Budapest, had been a stop along the Orient Express. Not entirely deserted, the station was quiet and the sense of threat made worse by the early-morning dark and the wide area of open space outside the station.

Against the urge to run, Munroe nudged Neeva slightly faster. The sound of pursuit also picked up, but whoever kept behind them never closed the distance.

Outside, a small line of taxis waited. The shadow kept back far enough that even pointedly turning and staring in his direction, Munroe couldn't see him.

He was a scout. Not here to kill but to report.

Bradford's call and the news he'd delivered while they were in transit, confirmation that he'd recovered Alexis, had changed the dynamics. The Doll Maker had to wonder if she would show, and if so, if Neeva would be along—he'd need to know to plot his strategy and rearrange his pawns.

So now he knew.

The hotel was a short ride away and at the reception desk Munroe presented their documents and filled out paperwork, paid cash, and received the key for their room. They made their way to the elevator, and headed up, only to reach the sixth floor and turn around for the lobby by way of the stairs. With her arm looped in Neeva's, Munroe led the girl through the hotel's side exit, to nowhere in particular, along sidewalks similar to the ones she'd experienced outside the Doll Maker's building less than a week earlier.

They were in the old city, the same general part of town where his safe house stood, where tidy streets formed a matrix of blocks built out of old three- and four-story buildings with elaborate stone facades and closed-off archways, which inevitably led to courtyards in the same way the Doll Maker's building had.

"What was that about?" Neeva said.

"We can't stay there, it's not safe."

The Doll Maker knew she was here, knew she'd have to hole up somewhere, had the names on the documents she carried, probably had the license plate and car details of the taxi itself. Now he had something to play with, something to plan and keep busy around.

"Where do we go, then?"

Munroe paused. Nudged Neeva into an arched doorway and turned to face her. "We're waiting out the night," she said, "and then after that there's no more 'we.' I'm taking you to the U.S. embassy so that you can get home."

"You can't," Neeva said. "I'm here to help you."

"You have helped. You've been a tremendous help. The entire reason you came along was to use yourself as a bargaining chip, and you've served your purpose, but there's nothing to trade you for anymore."

"What about that person?" Neeva's voice went up a notch. "Whoever was in the text?"

"She's been rescued."

Neeva stared at the ground. "Okay," she said. "I understand that. But I still want to be part of whatever comes next."

"What's the point? You put your life on the line—bravely—but now it's over and you can go home and start living again."

"I can shoot. I've got eyes. I can watch your back."

Munroe smiled and shook her head. "You'll be one more person I'll have to worry about."

Neeva crossed her arms, and the old Neeva, the Neeva who'd spat and lunged at her, who'd sworn and fought and run, the hellion in the little girl's body, resurfaced. "You're going to have to drag me kicking and screaming all the way to the embassy and I'm pretty sure that's way more trouble than I'm worth."

"Come on," Munroe said. "After everything we've been through? Don't be a brat. I know you understand the reasons why. You might not like them, but if you were in my shoes you'd do the same thing."

"I didn't *just* come along to offer myself as a trade," Neeva said. "That was only part of it." She glanced up, looked Munroe full in the face. "Sure, you have your reasons, but after everything we've been through, you have no right to take this from me."

"Take *what* from you?"

"Revenge."

"Holy fuck, Neeva. I thought you'd got that out of your system."

"I've earned this," Neeva said. "I've been loyal, I haven't questioned, I've kept quiet, and I've done everything you've asked me to. I haven't caused any problems. I've earned it."

"Earned what? What exactly do you think I'm going off to do?"

"Kill the head guy," Neeva said. "I know that's what you're going to do."

"And if I am?"

"I want to be a part of that. I want to see him die."

"No."

"You can't take that from me."

"I can and I will."

"I'll follow right after you."

"You're pissing me off," Munroe said.

"Look," Neeva said. "I've waited years for law enforcement, my therapist, somebody, anybody, to make sense of things that happened. I'm tired of being helpless." She paused, took a deep breath. "And I'm tired of being scared. Either let me come along so I can prove myself and be your partner like I've been so far and take what help I can offer, or fight me and waste time and energy and resources."

"Or I could kill you and get that out of the way now and save him the trouble."

Neeva rolled her eyes. "Whatever."

"What the hell is it with your need for revenge? How can seeing him dead possibly mean that much to you? I'll take a picture. You can post it on your bedroom ceiling and stare at it when you drift off at night."

"You're missing the point," Neeva said. "You—with your scars and your killings—should know better than anyone, and instead you're playing like you're dumb or something. You know exactly what I want, and exactly why."

"Neeva, it's senseless. I'm going into this knowing I'm probably not going to come out of it alive, I might not even be able to get the guy, but I have to do this, I have no choice. You have a choice. Don't throw away your life."

"I've never wanted anything so badly as I want to finally be able to *do* something to *someone* who's hurt me."

"They might kill me and take you. Have you thought about that?

That you not only don't get your revenge but have to suffer through the aftermath for your stupidity?"

Neeva shrugged.

"You've got fucked-up priorities," Munroe said.

"You're one to talk."

Munroe straightened. "You're a liability, Neeva. If you weren't with me right now, he'd already be dead."

Neeva stood taller, up on the balls of her feet. "If I wasn't with you right now, the people you love would already be dead."

Munroe sighed. Took a step backward, out of the archway and onto the sidewalk. "I don't have the energy to argue with you," she said. Pulled the phone out of her pocket, turned, and began walking. "If you're not smart enough to preserve your own life, I'm not going to waste mine trying to talk you out of being an idiot."

MUNROE DIDN'T HAVE an address for the goldwork building, but on the drive out she'd gotten a feel for how the location related to the area. Knew what she was looking for and the general idea of where she wanted to go, and with a taxi driver doing the navigating, it wasn't difficult to find her way back.

The sky, still dark when the driver deposited them one street over from their destination, had begun the shift from black to deep purple, and waiting for the dawn, Munroe walked the block, pacing lighted and quiet sidewalks that gave off a feeling of quaint and small-town safety.

Neeva, ever silent, kept beside her. No questions, no conversation, they continued in this way until Munroe came full circle and paused opposite the two jewelry storefronts to the sides of the archway in which Lumani had stood smirking in her rearview mirror.

She continued to the end of the block, found a nook within a doorway in which to wait for the sun, and when she sat, Neeva sat, too. "When I move," Munroe said finally, "I won't have time to explain. You either stay with me or you don't, but if you're left behind, you're on your own."

"I'll be fine," Neeva said, and Munroe, focused entirely on the Doll Maker's building and the storefront windows, didn't reply.

More than once in the drawn-out wait, the skin along the back of Munroe's neck itched and tingled in the telltale sensation of being watched, but although her gaze sought out windows and rooftops and down the streets for some visual evidence, she found nothing to confirm it. If this was Lumani, if he'd gotten free and made it here this quickly, if he spotted her now through his scope, she welcomed him to take the shot he hadn't in Milan, welcomed him to end things forever. But time ticked on.

The sun had fully crested the horizon, had begun its ascent in the sky, when the first opportunity to breach the Doll Maker's building arrived in the form of a wide-shouldered, middle-aged woman in sensible shoes. She was at first, by all appearances, just one of the ever-increasing number of pedestrians heading to work, but she slowed in front of the nearest jewelry store and reached inside her purse.

Munroe was up and off the steps before the woman's hand had fully traveled back out, was across the street by the time the keys were in her hand. Was behind the woman when the key was inserted into the lock and had the Jericho to the woman's head as soon as the door opened.

forty-two

The woman with the keys and sensible shoes opened her mouth to scream, and in the gap of silence between shock and sound, Munroe's other hand wrapped around the woman's face. The shrieking came, and continued to come, but muted, while the woman chomped at Munroe's fingers and clawed with her nails, and Munroe, once more amped up on adrenaline, struck with the gun—a hard crack against the woman's head.

For a moment the woman stopped struggling, and Munroe, shifting so her back was to the interior and her eyes to the street, worked the woman into the store. Neeva crossed the single-lane road casually as if she owned it, caught the door before it fully shut, then followed them inside and, without Munroe asking, removed the keys, relocked the door, and pulled the second handgun from the satchel.

She waved the weapon in the woman's face theatrically, and with the realization that there were two to her one, the wide-shouldered woman, like many people when confronted by stress and overwhelmed by fear, shut down in a form of self-preservation. Behind Munroe's hand she blabbered incoherently and then lost bladder control.

Neeva stared at the puddle on the floor.

Munroe said, "See if you can find the key to the back door."

Neeva jangled the keys and muttered, "Yes, she *can* be useful."

Ignoring her, Munroe whispered in the woman's ear, cycling through languages until she struck recognition with Hungarian. Because of the strange wiring inside her head and the recordings she'd been force-fed, she had extensive knowledge of the language but limited colloquial ability, and so communicated her lack of intent to harm as best as she could.

The woman nodded frantically, but Munroe couldn't risk releasing her mouth and because of this, frustration set in. This woman, if Munroe meant to keep her alive, was going to be a problem.

From the back of the store Neeva said, "Found it."

"Don't open it," Munroe said. "Come here and help me look for something to stuff in her mouth."

"I thought you work alone," Neeva said.

"Just shut up and do it," Munroe said, and Neeva smiled a fake smile before stepping behind the counter and rummaging through shelving and several boxes on the floor.

Munroe motioned for the woman to go behind the other display counter and to sit. *"Nem akarlak bántani,"* she said, "and I want you to live." This was true. She'd come to kill the Doll Maker, to cut off the head of the organization, and the arms, and possibly the feet. But this woman—she couldn't know if this woman was a bystander like the many who worked with gold in the main room, possibly here through no choice of her own, or if she was a player in the game.

Neeva said, "I found some box-wrapping stuff and some newspaper."

"Good enough."

The woman sat as instructed. Munroe wadded paper and stuffed it into her mouth, then with a roll of twine worked a thick figure-eight around the woman's wrists, leading the twine down to her ankles, where she repeated the procedure. Not struggle-proof, but the bonds would buy time, save the woman from raising an alarm, and prevent Munroe from having to kill unnecessarily.

Four minutes in and the shop was still quiet.

Munroe straightened and stepped out from behind the counter, then slipped beyond Neeva to the rear door. Checked along the frame for any sign of security, any alarm that might be triggered by opening it, and finding nothing, turned the key. Inched the door inward, peered around the corner.

The large room was quiet, still empty of the worker bees who would, she expected, arrive soon for the daily grind. The lack of light filtering out from the Doll Maker's lair was incongruous and surprising. Every time Munroe had passed through the main room, his light had been on, almost as if he lived in that doll-filled office like some esoteric hermit.

At the far back the large steel door stood open, and beside the door a guard sat on a metal folding chair, awake but only in the way of one who'd sat alone for far too long: eyes open but mind unengaged. Munroe motioned Neeva closer, then signaled that she should hold the door open.

Had there been no guard, Munroe would have taken Neeva inside, headed down to the prison for a quick look-see, and then returned to lie in wait in the Doll Maker's office. But a guard indicated prisoners, and prisoners were innocent life with which evil would barter freedom or, worse, use as a control mechanism.

Munroe tucked the Jericho away and pulled the pocketknife from the largest of the cargo pockets. Metal on skin, release to anxiety, warm in her hands like blood fresh from the vein. She slipped inside, low to the ground, creeping between desks and the narrow hallways they formed. Paused occasionally to stretch a hand up in search of loose items and snagged prizes: pencil, ceramic cup, lump of wax. Collected them and moved on until she'd slunk fully across the expanse of the work floor, stopping behind a plywood wall that formed half a cubicle, close enough to the seated guard that even in the soft early light filtering through the windows, she could see the acne scars that marked his cheeks.

Munroe tossed the ball of wax across the empty aisle so that it tapped against the wall of one of the offices. The noise was soft and the guard took no notice of the muted thud that would have caused a more worthy man to look.

She tried again with the pencil. His head jerked up at the clack of wood against the wall, and his shoulders straightened. She willed him forward. Didn't necessarily need him to pass her way, just wanted him off the chair and on his feet, away from the wall, so she wasn't making the equivalent of an unarmed suicide lunge at a target with all of the advantage.

But the guard didn't move and he was burning her time.

Munroe palmed the cup. If this didn't pull the man forward, she'd be forced to shoot him and in the process draw the attention of whatever security was in the building—either upstairs in the apartments above or downstairs in the prison.

She rolled the mug, bowling style, down the concrete floor behind her, and at this, the guard finally stood. He tapped on the metal door, a signal, she supposed, to whoever remained down in the pit.

Weapon in hand, an HK USP .45 Tactical just as the rest of the Doll Maker's men had carried, as if it were part of some de facto bad-guy standard issue, he proceeded forward in search of the noise source. Passed along the half-wall behind Munroe, and she remained crouched beneath a desk, gauging distance and time by his footsteps, his breathing.

Munroe kept count of his paces, waiting until he'd fully passed before shifting her crouch to face him. Focus, pure and feral, tamped down the weakness of compassion and the predator resurfaced. She closed her eyes. Pulled in air through slow long breaths, drew down to the primal nature that had for days begged to be released, allowed the instinct that built layer upon layer and night after night in the jungle to assume control.

The subtle tap of his boots against the floor marked his location on the map inside her head. Step by step, turn by turn, she tracked him.

The guard bent for the cup and his shooting hand extended carelessly toward the floor. Munroe slid from beneath the desk, and as silent as in times past, like the mamba, swiftest of snakes, she struck his wrist. Twisted and sliced, paring through skin, vein, and tendon.

His weapon fell.

The guard bellowed.

She reached for the gun.

He spun toward the attack.

She rose up and fired.

Double tap to the head, the weapon's roar silenced by the suppressor like screams choked into whispers.

The man's bellow halted before it had fully begun. He dropped.

She paused long enough to stare at open and lifeless eyes and body twisted and crumpled on the stone floor, discarded like a sack of garbage—garbage with two rosebuds seeping from a pale pink forehead, wrist bleeding into a puddle on the floor: an ugly replica of Noah's death.

From below came a question in Albanian. Munroe dropped her voice an octave and, drawing on a language from long ago, yelled back, *"Minjtë!"* Too many words and the dialect and accent might be wrong. No answer and he would come hunting.

From below came a guffaw.

Close enough.

Carrying the dead man's gun, Munroe worked backward toward Neeva, the weapon held two-handed and aimed toward the empty prison stairs.

When she was within whispering distance, Munroe hissed for Neeva's attention, got her to block open the gold-shop door and follow her into the main room. Not because she owed Neeva anything, not because she wanted her help, but because she couldn't afford to get cut off from her and have her used against her the way the prisoners downstairs might be.

For the third time in nearly twice as many minutes, Munroe crossed the wide floor space, this time quickly and without fear of being seen, to get to the stairs and down before the dead man's counterpart got curious and headed up. Detoured around the body for Neeva's benefit, reached the stairway, and there Neeva froze.

Munroe started down, paused at Neeva's hesitation, and motioned her to follow. But the girl wouldn't move. Color drained from her cheeks and she shook her head. Munroe fought back the anger.

Liability.

There were times when all the bravery in the world couldn't compensate for trauma and flashbacks.

Liability.

It wouldn't be easy walking down these stairs and returning to the smell of bleach and mold. Wouldn't be easy to descend, knowing that once underground she was helpless against the metal door being locked in place, shutting her away forever. Munroe had to do it, even against her own foreboding, but Neeva didn't.

Liability.

Two fingers to her own eyes and then to the room at large, Munroe set Neeva to keep watch. Motioned to the weapon, then to the room again.

Shoot to protect.

Neeva nodded.

Munroe blocked out the frustration. The anger. Had to focus on the now. Headed down several stairs with quiet foot placement that wouldn't alert the guard to her presence. Listened for pacing, breathing, clothes rustling, and keys clinking, but heard nothing. She didn't need to peer around the corner to know where he was, she'd seen it a half-dozen times during her time in this hell. Didn't need to worry about hitting an innocent with stray bullets, because whoever was being held captive in this dungeon was locked away behind stone and steel.

Munroe turned and did a quick double-check on Neeva, whose back was to her, Jericho two-fisted and pointed toward the floor. Drew a breath, ran down the remaining stairs, and skirted the corner, firing, counting rounds, moving steadily closer, until the clip in the .45 was empty. She drew the Jericho and charged the remaining distance.

The guard had managed to unholster his weapon. Had managed to draw and get off three shots but had never made it fully out of a sitting position. He tried now, crumpled between chair and wall, to lift the weapon and fire. She stomped on his hand. Took the gun and, in a single movement, put his own weapon to his forehead and pulled the trigger. Tucked the Jericho back into her waistband and ripped the ring of keys off his belt loop.

forty-three

With the dead guard's key ring in hand, Munroe started toward the nearest cell in the underground prison. Tried keys until she found the right one. Unlocked and slid the bar free. The cell was empty, and the air filled with the same fetid stench that had been there when Neeva was inside.

She strode to the next. Unlocked it. Slid the door wide and on the mat was huddled a wretch of a child, nine, maybe ten at the most, in rags, clawing away from the door as if it might somehow be possible to become part of the walls.

Inside Munroe's head a chorus of voices ruptured and broke free. Rage unbridled and blinding tore from her core, and her heart pounded heavy in a beat entirely different from the adrenaline rush of battle. The lust for blood, the thirst for violence, unquenchable, unspeakable: the killer fully arisen from a deep sleep; voices rising, chanting, demanding.

I have removed the bounds of the people.

Munroe turned from the doorway, found the key for the third cell, and opened this, too.

I have robbed their treasures.

Two more girls inside this one, teenagers, fifteen or sixteen, seated on the filthy pad that passed as a bed, staring silently, arms wrapped around their knees.

I have put down the inhabitants like a valiant man.

Munroe cycled through languages with the teenagers, and having exhausted her repertoire of anything that might be understood in Europe, switched to hand signals, motioning the girls toward her.

They didn't move.

She put the gun on the floor and raised her hands. Motioned again.

One of them slid off the mat and scooted forward. Munroe nudged the weapon out the door with her heel, kept her hands in the air, and backed out of the room. The girl followed.

By the strength of my hand I have done it.

Munroe pointed down the hall to the dead guard, then to herself, to the gun. The girl's face lit into a huge smile, and chattering animatedly, she turned to the other. The second girl stood and nearly ran to the door. Munroe showed them to the previous cell where the child still huddled on the mat. The braver of the two entered, knelt, and began to talk with the girl, and when once more language became a barrier, she tried to pick up the child and the little girl screamed.

And that was when Munroe first heard the noise above: another scream, this one from someone older, more mature, followed by Munroe's name and gunfire. Scooping the second guard's .45 off the floor, she ran for the stairs.

Shouts. Scuffling.

Metal door shutting.

She raced the steps three at a go. Hit the door full force before it had shut, pushing it open some, although strength and momentum were dulled by the uphill climb. She shoved hard, and whoever was on the other side let go and the door swung fully open.

Munroe stood in the doorway, a clear target for anyone who wanted to take a shot, but nobody did. The Doll Maker sat on a chair near the closest desk, leaning back and smiling. He shook his finger at Munroe. "Oh, my crafty friend," he said. "Thank you for bringing me this gift."

To Munroe's left, beside the door, was a man she'd not seen before, who, like Arben and Tamás, appeared to be nothing more than an interchangeable part in the Doll Maker's machine. Beside the Doll Maker was Neeva, gun to her head, arms pinned behind her back, held in place by yet another part of the machinery.

Liability.

Like a bad case of déjà vu, she'd seen this scene play out a hundred times since the moment Neeva insisted on following her out of the consulate. A dozen arguments, untold energy toward keeping the girl from this exact scenario, and here they were.

Neeva, her expression devastated and panicked, mouthed *I'm sorry.*

Munroe took a step out of the doorway. If there were more machinery parts here, she didn't see them, and the numbers made sense considering they tended to work and travel in packs of two.

The teenagers, who had remained in the whitewashed hall when she'd blown past, crept up the stairs behind her, as if they understood they had one chance at escape and she was it. They flanked behind her now.

With the dead guard's weapon in her right hand, Munroe pulled the Jericho from the small of her back. She trained one toward the Doll Maker and the other on the thug beside the door. Sidestepped fully out of the doorway so that her back was to a wall.

The Doll Maker flicked a finger in the direction of the thug beside the door, and the man lunged, grabbed the wrist of one of the girls, and yanked her out into the room. The girl shrieked and began to cry, trying to fight. He put the gun to her head the way the other had his to Neeva, and so the young girl stood there, sobbing, docile, scared.

"Put the guns down," the Doll Maker said. "A smart one like you knows there is no way out of here."

"Perhaps," Munroe said. "But I don't have to die alone."

He shrugged. "So you kill me maybe. You kill one of my men maybe. You kill two innocents definitely. What do you gain?"

Munroe stepped away from the wall but kept her back guarded. Moved closer to him, running the odds, the speed, the numbers.

"You won't kill them," Munroe said. "They're too valuable. Worth more to you alive, more difficult to replace than your gorillas."

The Doll Maker turned to gaze at Neeva for a half-second. "This one, yes," he said. "But those ones, and the baby down in the chamber, they are cheap and very easy to replace. There will be more tomorrow."

He stood and stepped next to Neeva, his own lack of height emphasized by the way he didn't tower over her as his thug did. Glanced at her up and down and then said over his shoulder to Munroe, "I think those girls are worth more to you than they are to me."

While his back was turned, Munroe took another slow step toward him, and within the heartbeat of that movement, the Doll Maker grabbed Neeva and pulled her into him. He took the gun from his man and held it to Neeva's temple. Squeezed her cheeks and turned her to face Munroe. There were tears in her eyes and her lips kept saying, *I'm sorry, I'm sorry.*

He said, "None of them are valuable to me if I am dead, so yes, I will kill even this one, if necessary. Don't take another step."

Munroe stopped moving.

The Doll Maker nodded to the man from whom he'd taken Neeva, and he made for the stairs, for the second teenager who until now had stood transfixed, frozen in fear. She turned, screaming, running back down the way she'd come, and he chased and caught her. Dragged her back up the stairs by her hair while she flailed; scraped and bloodied as concrete and stone tore at her clothes and her skin. He kicked her, again and again, and she balled into the fetal position, screaming and pleading, trying to protect her head and her stomach.

The seconds passed incrementally, as if time slowed to near standstill, and but for the heartbeat thudding in Munroe's ears, sound ceased to exist. Within the pulsing wash, one beat to the next, flashed odds and strategy.

To kill the kicking man and put an end to the madness, she'd have one shot and be forced to use her left hand; the odds were not good.

Move against move.

With that first round fired, the girl would die, possibly Neeva as well.

Weapons would turn on her. She would die. And then the teenager, and the child in the cell, and God knew who else.

Blood in her ears. Rushing. Maddening.

Decisions. Choices.

My soul chooses strangling, and death rather than my life.

She'd come this far knowing she walked into a trap. Come this far knowing she'd had a good run at life, and if it ended now, she was okay with that. She said, "Stop."

The Doll Maker laughed but repeated the command in Albanian, and the man stopped kicking, and the girl on the floor lay sobbing, matted hair covering her face. Neeva bit on her lip and her expression hardened, face taut and focused as if she ran the same scenario, the same odds, the same probabilities and came to the same conclusion as Munroe.

The Doll Maker cackled again, as if he'd triumphed. "You are weak," he said. "Exploitable, and only dangerous in your element when you are in control—so easy to read and manipulate because you lack the ability to make difficult decisions. A good man would have killed these women first so there would be no sword over his head and then come after me. You? You're worthless."

As a cloud vanishes and is gone, so one who goes down to the grave does not return.

"Kill me," Munroe said. "I know you want to."

"Of all the merchandise in this room," he said, "you are the most valuable, you are most highly prized. Delivering you—even drugged—I earn ten times what this girl would fetch thanks to the enemies you have made these past days."

"I would kill myself first," she said.

"You are not capable of that, either."

Neeva said, "Take the shot, Michael, please take the shot."

The Doll Maker jabbed Neeva in the side and she winced.

"If I surrender what do I buy?"

"You buy four," he said. "Those little pigs and this one here. I let them all go."

"Let them go now," she said. "And then I surrender."

Neeva screamed, "No!" and the Doll Maker punched her again.

"I am not a fool," he said. "You first, then the girls."

"Let the replaceable ones go first."

The Doll Maker smirked. "Where would they go? I put them on the street, they are found, and eventually the police are at my door. No. When I let them go, I let them go where they are no trouble to me."

"Then we're at an impasse."

The Doll Maker barked a command. The thug from whom the Doll Maker had taken the gun pulled a second weapon from beneath his shirt. Before he'd fully aimed the muzzle at the prostrate girl, Munroe yelled, "No!" and the Doll Maker halted the killing. "It is your choice," he said.

Munroe said nothing, processing, trying to find a way out of an unwinnable situation, where even taking her own life would only propagate evil.

"I will not wait long," the Doll Maker said.

If she surrendered, she'd have no way to enforce compliance, but without surrender an immediate execution would take place.

As if reading her thoughts, he said, "Ten seconds and the girl dies."

Neeva screamed, "Take the shot!" and once more the Doll Maker hit her, this time hard enough that the sound carried, and even from this distance Munroe could see her tears.

The Doll Maker counted, moving directly from two to seven. On eight, Munroe began to lower. Neeva screamed again, and once more time slowed, filtering movement and events in increments, life defined in jerky strobe-light motion.

The man by the metal door, his gun to the teenager's head. Yanking her hair, jerking her tear-stained face upward, laughing in her ear. The girl on the floor. Huddled. The thug beside her with his weapon pointed at her, index finger stroking the outside of the trigger guard, face turned to the Doll Maker, eyes expectant and happy, waiting for the command. The Doll Maker pulling Neeva tighter. Smiling. Gloating. Jamming the muzzle of the gun against her ear. A whisper of movement on the far side of the room that could as easily have been from a draft as from a shadow, costing a half-second distraction in which the Doll Maker's voice, stretched out and distorted, reached the number nine.

Munroe dropped one knee to the floor.

Neeva screamed, "No!" She rose on the balls of her feet so that her cheek aligned with the Doll Maker's and her body pressed into him, tensed and shifted. Her right hand reached for the hand that held the gun to her own head, her left hand reached for his head. Not frantic. Deliberate . . . focused . . . determined, full of intent and eyes set hard.

His smile faded.

Her finger curled around the trigger.

And then an explosion of blood and bone that terminated life twice over.

Neeva and the Doll Maker fell together, slapping against desk and chair, pinball and ragdoll, collapsing finally, crooked and bent, arms and legs entwined.

IN THE TIME it took to blink, to register and understand, Munroe dropped the Jericho. Raised both hands to the .45 and, still kneeling, fired at the nearest man, the closest replaceable part in the Doll Maker's machine: rapid pulls that emptied the magazine and sent his body jerking, falling, full deadweight onto the teenager on the floor. Turned from him to his counterpart, time held captive in that same fractured breath, the moment distilled into screams and violence, while the first man fell and the second raised his head, hesitating in the choice between killing his hostage and human shield or returning fire.

His weapon moved from the hostage to Munroe.

She dropped the .45. Scooped the Jericho. His gun leveled at the same time hers did. He knew she wouldn't fire—not as long as he held the hostage as a shield—and she knew his aim and control would be off because he was forced to shoot one-handed to maintain his hold on a moving body.

Munroe braced for the hits. Hoped to be lucky enough to take the bullets in her torso where the jacket could still protect, where the odds of him connecting to the same spot another bullet had already struck were slim; and in that breath of resignation came another spray of red mist, from the man's head, death that had not come from her.

Time, which had until now been held taut and captive, cut loose, unspooling like the snap of an overstrained cable. The thug collapsed, leaving the hostage standing alone, screaming, trying to escape from liquid and death, as if she might, by crawling out of her own skin, be let free of the moment. Her shock and terror chorused with that of the girl on the ground, all of this a deafening noise that penetrated Munroe's senses for the first time.

Like a runner off the starting block, Munroe bolted through the maze of desks and passageways, catty-corner across the room to where she'd spotted that shadow of movement.

The space was empty.

She turned a slow circle. Scanning, searching, while the cries and wails of the teenagers filled the cavernous room in an echoed bounce-back.

By the foot of a chair she found a single ejected shell.

She reached for the metal piece, anger coursing.

He'd found his way from Milan. Had been here. Could have ended it all by killing the man who'd caused so much suffering but had instead allowed Neeva to die and, in what he would have seen as a noble gesture, saved Munroe's life, taking from her any chance of peace. He could have killed his uncle. Put an end to the suffering. He'd had the power to let Neeva live and had not used it, and Munroe hated him for it.

She'd allowed him life, had given him a chance, but not for this. *Not for this.*

Munroe pocketed the casing as a memento, and before recrossing the room she peered into the gold shop. The woman behind the counter was dead, slumped against the wall with a single hole in her head.

AT THE METAL door to the dungeon, Munroe bypassed the teenagers, who, with the glassy-eyed daze of shock, attempted to wipe blood and body fluids off their hands and faces but only smeared and streaked them, making matters worse.

She motioned for them to follow her down to where she could hose them off, but they refused, and she didn't force the issue.

The Doll Maker was dead. Four more of his thugs were dead. The lady in the gold shop was dead, but the gold workers would still come and there could be more of the Doll Maker's army on the way. She wanted to get away before they arrived.

Downstairs, the child had stepped out of the cell and into the hall and Munroe found her staring at the dead guard. She flinched when Munroe approached, and so Munroe kept still, held out her hand, and gradually the child turned and reached for her fingers.

She led the little girl upstairs to the office with the dolls, where the child's eyes lit up in response to the multitude of toys upon the shelves. Munroe picked up a life-size replica and handed it to her. Motioned for her to sit, and while the child stroked the hair and dress with nearly the same reverence as the Doll Maker had once shown, Munroe tore through the drawers, searching for papers, for electronics, anything that might provide information on who the Doll Maker was or how he ran the operation.

She found nothing.

The teenagers came to the room and paused in the doorway.

Munroe hesitated. Stopped searching and stood upright, stepped around the desk and stretched out her hand for the child in the seat. When the girl scooted off and her feet met the ground, Munroe led her to the doorway, placed her hand in the hand of one of the older ones, and then took money from her pocket. Handed them each nearly a thousand euros and escorted them to the outside door, where they stood, a macabre sight, blinking in the early sunlight: the entire exchange and all intent communicated without words, without language.

Munroe waited until the girls had walked half the block and then shut the door, burdened with wanting to see their fate through, but that was beyond her. They would have to find their own way, would hopefully find the police, find someone who spoke their language, someone to whom they could tell their story and eventually lead truthseekers back to this place of evil. Barring that, and perhaps on top of that, she'd track down a local AP or Reuters correspondent and feed enough information for someone who truly wanted a story to find one.

Munroe returned slowly, cautiously to where Neeva lay.

Stood over her.

Knelt.

The girl's eyes were closed, her face, untouched by the carnage, was placid. If Munroe searched for it, a smile lay beneath the calm, and in death, even without any hair, Neeva looked every inch the doll that this insanity had tried to make her. Her near-final words tumbled over and over inside Munroe's head until she finally spit them out in a whisper to purge them: *I never wanted anything so badly as I want to finally be able to do something to someone who's hurt me.*

With the floor hard against her knees, Munroe leaned forward to untangle Neeva from the Doll Maker's arms and then she stopped. It felt a violation of everything sacred to leave her there, enmeshed in this travesty, but it was the way things had to be. Without disturbing the scene, Munroe stretched out farther and pressed her lips to Neeva's forehead.

By the strength of my hand I have done it.

"In death, maybe peace," she whispered, and stood.

Turned her back on the scene and headed to the front, to the gold shop door, dialing Bradford as she walked away.

forty-four

DALLAS, TEXAS

Munroe stepped from carpeted Jetway into carpeted terminal with nothing for luggage but the satchel filled with the few items she'd accumulated in the week since Neeva's death.

She'd been in the United States for two days and was only now returning to Dallas, to the closest thing she had to home. Hadn't spoken to or heard from Bradford in the several hours since she'd texted the information for her connecting flight out of Denver, but he'd be waiting, she knew, on the other side of the revolving doors.

After leaving Neeva, after calling Bradford and letting him know she was alive and coming home, she'd placed a call to the Reuters office in Zagreb, allowed twenty minutes, then followed with a second to the American embassy.

The news of the bloody scene spread quickly along the wires, and before long, visuals made it to televisions across the globe. In the absence of detail, speculation ran high, and with the graphic images accompanying Neeva's discovery, it would be several weeks at least before the frenzy died.

With the death of the Doll Maker and so many of his lieutenants, his right-hand man vanished, and the dismantling of the U.S.-based side of operations, it would be a while, if ever, before the organization got back into the business—although, in a world that funneled billions of dollars into the war on drugs and only a pittance to combat the invisible, safer, and more profitable business of moving human chattel, with traffickers and slave owners risking so little in providing women to feed rapacious appetites, there would be others—there would always be others—to take up the slack.

Munroe had taken the first train to Ljubljana, and there waited out the tedious and time-consuming aspects of reporting a stolen passport and gathering documentation to acquire a new one—a real one. And once she had it, had caught the first flight back to the United States.

She'd bypassed Dallas for Aspen, where the Tisdale parents were staying; had arrived unannounced. Cautious, guarded, they'd welcomed her into their home, and in their formal living room, separated by an oversize coffee table, she had laid out the details of what had happened after Neeva skipped from the consulate in Nice; told them of the trafficking network and why Neeva had been kidnapped; detailed the reasons their daughter had chosen the path she had. What she offered was a small consolation, if any, for the loss of a child, but the details of Neeva's revenge, details the media and the world would never have, were all she'd had to give.

The Tisdale parents, seated together on the sofa, leaned into each other with as much poise as circumstances allowed. Judith had done much of the talking, perhaps not so much an exchange of truth but an unburdening in the way a patient might to a therapist. Filled in the gaps, the specifics Neeva had dodged around, the horrors of the brutal attack that had taken place when the girl was fourteen, and the ways in which this had transformed her life and logic.

Having delivered what she'd come to offer, having listened to a mother's tears, Munroe made the return to Dallas. She spotted Bradford through the glass before she reached the door: leaning back against a near wall, arms crossed and body relaxed, with only the movement of his eyes to reveal how focused he was on what went on around him—so typically Bradford that she wanted to laugh for nothing more than the relief that she was here again and weep, knowing the relief wouldn't last.

She pushed through the door and he smiled. Studied her, watched her. After she took several long strides he straightened off the wall to meet her halfway. The world continued on—suitcases and shoes, announcements and baggage carousel alarms, a congestion of people—while he wrapped his arms around her, put her head to his shoulder, and held her there for a long, long time.

At last she raised her head, drew in a breath, and said, "Let's go."

That's when she first noticed the stricken look on Bradford's face, the one he'd masked so well in his smile of greeting.

"What's wrong?" she said. "Logan? Samantha? Alexis?"

He shook his head. "Nothing like that. It can wait."

"I don't think so," she said, but in response, he put his hand to the small of her back and guided her toward the exit and the parking garage.

"Please tell me," she said.

"I will, but I want to take you home first."

Home.

Munroe didn't press Bradford for more details. If for just this one day she could have peace in place of the anxiety, if just for today she had a home, she'd wait for whatever he had to say. Side by side, steps in sync, they walked in silence to Bradford's truck.

HOME WAS NORTH, outside the metro area, where land was still plentiful and towns were still towns and the urban sprawl hadn't yet overrun the miles, although the sprawl was definitely creeping in. Home was a five-bedroom ranch-style house, recently built to Bradford's specs, set on fifteen acres. And because Bradford spent more time away from home than in it, home was cared for by a full-time housekeeper and her husband, both of whom had been with Bradford for years and who now lived in a smaller place of their own at the back of the property.

Bradford pulled into the half-circle drive that fronted the house, and Felecia opened the front door before they'd reached it. She smiled at Munroe and welcomed her back, and Bradford waited only long enough for the niceties before playfully nudging Munroe along toward the bedroom. Once across the threshold, he picked her up, shut the door with his foot, and tossed her onto the bed.

Munroe laughed, and he smiled and stood, studying her.

"What?" she said.

"It's good to see you laughing."

"You worry too much," she said.

He knelt on the bed. Leaned over her. "I don't think I worry enough," he said. "And, God, I missed you."

In the room, time lost meaning, and all the words left unspoken, all the fears pushed down, and the anguish and the heartache, the losses and the pain, faded away for those hours that the outside world ceased to exist.

They stood in the kitchen, the island between them, sipping wine and picking at the food on a tray that Felecia had prepared.

Munroe said, "So are you going to tell me?"

Bradford poured another glass. Didn't ask for clarification; they both knew what she meant. He said, "I've lost track of Kate."

Munroe stopped with a cracker halfway into her mouth. "She's out of prison?"

"After the explosion at the office I had to call on my guys for help in running things so I could get to Alexis . . ." He paused and let the rest of the explanation falter.

She put fingers to his cheek. "Don't beat yourself up over it."

"I hate knowing she's the only one who's walked away from this a winner."

With a glass of wine in one hand and his hand in the other, Munroe tugged Bradford back toward the bedroom. "She hasn't won yet, and if she does win at all, it'll be a Pyrrhic victory."

Bradford paused and his expression shadowed. He pulled her back and held her tight. Whispered, "Don't say it, okay? I know what's coming and I don't want to hear it. Not tonight. Tomorrow maybe, but not tonight."

He wasn't talking about Kate Breeden. They both knew that Munroe could only bear so much pain and loss before coming completely undone. She needed time away, time to heal, and she could only do that by returning to who she was: the lone operative, shut down and shut off.

Munroe set the glass on an end table, wrapped her arms around his neck, and kissed him. She truly loved him; always would. She smiled and fought back the sadness, glad in a way that she was spared from having to say good-bye, from uttering the words she never wanted to speak—although, in truth, there would never really be a good-bye, because if this was where home was, then like a homing pigeon she'd return, and Bradford had to know it, just as he also knew her reasons for leaving.

It wouldn't happen tonight, or tomorrow, she still had things to do here. Needed to visit Alexis; should probably make an effort to call on most of her family and would, when she was ready. What she wanted most, needed most, was to see Logan, to look into his eyes and beg forgiveness for all he'd suffered because of her, and because of this she had time—*they* had time—before the inevitable.

RICHARDSON, TEXAS

The midnight air was still, the coolness of night made deeper by the damp of recent rain. The condo, set toward the back of the complex and away from street traffic and the rush of tires against wet pavement, sat in an area that had, over the past three hours, turned eerily quiet.

In a darkened nook, invisible in the night, Munroe watched and waited. Over the hours and with the deepening evening, neighbors had returned home, and some, as evidenced by the limited lighting, had already gone to bed.

A hunter in a blind, she'd marked time by cars and open doors, by curtains drawn and lights on and off, shadows that reached the streets, and sometimes by people, unaware of what was so easily seen from the other side of the glass.

And still, she waited.

Munroe had asked Bradford for a weapon, searched through the plastic locker he'd offered, and taken what she wanted. Had borrowed his truck with no promise of when she'd return and hadn't told him where she was going.

He didn't ask, but he knew—had to know.

The ground was cold and Munroe shifted, one uncomfortable position into another. She had no doubt that Breeden would eventually return to this apartment, a little hideaway Munroe had discovered years ago and about which she'd kept silent—although when Breeden would return, and how often, was a mystery.

During Breeden's prison tenure, while her house went into foreclosure and her car was repossessed, the mortgage on the condo continued to be paid and the utilities kept on. Something waited here, something Breeden needed or wanted; something called her back. If nothing else, this one-bedroom unit was the only sanctuary Breeden had—a roof over her head, a place out of the cold—a temporary home while she regrouped and moved on to whatever she planned next.

The midnight quiet drew long and the scent of woodsmoke spoke to the erratic Texas weather that could still bring a solid freeze in early spring. The occasional set of headlights turned down the lane, disappearing into garages or under carports, but the condo remained as it had been: dark and unoccupied; beckoning.

It was a delightful temptation to enter ahead, to lie in wait in the dark of the rooms, away from the elements and the chance of prying eyes, but she had no idea what was on the other side, what preparations Breeden may have made to give notice of intrusion, and was cautious of warning her off.

More time passed, damp and quiet, the dangerous kind of quiet with thoughts and memories and the voices running dialogue inside her head, voices that had still not been silenced even after the Doll Maker's death; had not allowed her a return to the peace she'd had before the madness began.

It was folly to think that by finishing tonight what should have been finished so many nights ago she'd find quiet once again, but the thought was there, and it phased into others far darker, far needier. Those in turn were replaced by images of a dungeon and children, of Logan and Neeva, of Jack and Sam, of Noah, and her own words of caution to Neeva: *Revenge is best left to fantasy.*

There was always a price to pay.

Another set of lights pulled into the lane and continued into the slot reserved for Breeden's unit. Half expecting a decoy in Breeden's place, Munroe was instead taken by the gaunt frame that clipped a rapid pace in her direction. Even in the dark, it was apparent that Breeden had drastically aged since Munroe had last seen her. Gone was the poise, the champagne bubbles, and twenty-five pounds of the good life, replaced by a haggard severity.

With measured patience and a predator's instinct, Munroe waited for Breeden to pass, waited for her to fish keys out of her purse, watched as she ran a finger along the upper doorjamb and fiddled with what Munroe could only assume was a wire.

Munroe stood.

Death and the loss of these past weeks called for closure.

The righteous will rejoice when he sees the vengeance.

Inside her chest the war drum tapped.

He will wash his feet in the blood of the wicked.

Moved forward, black against the night, shadow to the stairwell lights, focused entirely on Breeden's posture, Breeden's breathing, Breeden's spine. And then, very nearly at Breeden's side, Munroe put the muzzle of the gun to Breeden's head and said, "Hello again, Kate."

forty-five

DALLAS, TEXAS
FIVE MONTHS LATER

A quarter of a mile of gravel separated the blacktop county road from Bradford's front door; a quarter of a mile between foyer and mailbox. For the most part, the distance was meaningless. He wasn't home often enough to worry about collecting the mail—Felecia did that for him, and anything urgent was sent to Capstone's office.

But today he was home, and so Bradford swung the truck off the blacktop, along the shoulder, to collect what lay within the box and spare Felecia the trip. Paper gripped between his fingers, he tossed the stack onto the passenger's seat, and not until he was around the back of the house, parked in the garage and leaning over to collect the meager bounty of inserts and magazines, flyers and envelopes, did he catch sight of the handwriting that stopped his breath cold.

One leg already outside the truck, he reversed, sat back down, and stared at the envelope: plain, white, and from both the shape and the stamp clearly not from the U.S. There was no return address, but his own name and address were written in an unmistakable print that quickened his pulse and set his fingers shaking.

Bradford tore into the side of the envelope with his teeth—enough to get a finger into the crease and slit the edge open.

Inside was a single sheet of paper. A newspaper clipping in a foreign language, printed in a script he didn't understand—most probably Cyrillic, although for which country, he wasn't sure—and he didn't care, didn't need to know. Because although the words were meaningless, the accompanying photograph, in all its newspaper-quality graininess, told him everything.

Charred and gutted, with only enough of the hull left intact to keep from tipping below the waterline, a very large yacht listed off some Mediterranean-looking coastline.

Bradford stared at the clipping a long while, smile widening the longer he sat, happy in a way that defied words, until finally he laughed out loud.

ACKNOWLEDGMENTS

Without the help of many who love me, this story would never have seen the light of day—and certainly not in the polished format it is in now, so to my children, who begrudgingly allow me to work, and to my family and friends, who don't take it personally when I drop off the map for months at a time, thank you for still being there when I surface for air.

To all of my wonderful teammates within Crown Publishers, thank you for your tireless efforts on my behalf. A particular shoutout to Zack Wagman, my editor, who forced me to think far harder than I wanted to, and my publicist, Sarah Breivogel, who I'm convinced knows the secrets of magic.

To the individual who helped me get the Croatian and Hungarian details right (at least I hope I got them right) and who didn't want to be named, you have my appreciation.

And last, my agent, Anne Hawkins, to whom I owe my entire career and at least half of my sanity: you have become my champion, confidante, therapist, surrogate family, and wonderful friend. I wish every author could be as fortunate as I have been to have you in my life. Thank you.

ALSO BY TAYLOR STEVENS

The Innocent

Taylor Stevens

Eight years ago, a man walked five-year-old Hannah out the front doors of her school and spirited her over the Mexican border, taking her into the world of a cult known as The Chosen.

Now, after years of searching, childhood survivors of the group have found the girl in Argentina. But getting her out is a whole new challenge.

For the rescue they need someone who is brilliant, fearless and utterly ruthless.

They need Vanessa Michael Munroe.

Because the only way to get Hannah out is for Munroe to go in …

OUT NOW IN EBOOK

Out in Arrow paperback in Summer 2014

arrow books

Bones of the Lost

Kathy Reichs

The body of a teenage girl is discovered along a desolate highway on the outskirts of Charlotte. Inside her purse is the ID card of a local businessman who died in a fire months earlier.

Who was the girl? And was she murdered?

Dr Temperance Brennan, Forensic Anthropologist, must find the answers. She soon learns that a Gulf War veteran stands accused of smuggling artefacts into the country. Could there be a connection between the two cases?

Convinced that the girl's death was no accident, Tempe soon finds herself at the centre of a conspiracy that extends from South America to Afghanistan. But to find justice for the dead, she must be more courageous – and take more extreme action – than ever before.

OUT NOW IN PAPERBACK AND EBOOK

arrow books

ALSO AVAILABLE IN ARROW

Bones Are Forever

Kathy Reichs

A newborn baby is found wedged in a vanity cabinet in a rundown apartment near Montreal.

Dr Temperance Brennan, forensic anthropologist to the province of Quebec, is brought in to investigate. While there, she discovers the mummified remains of two more babies within the same room.

Shocked and distressed, Tempe must use all her skills and inner strength to focus on the facts. But when the autopsies reveal that the children died of unnatural causes, the hunt for the mother – a young woman with a seedy past and at least three aliases – is on.

The trail leads Tempe to Yellowknife, a cold, desolate diamond-mining town on the edge of the Arctic Circle, where her quest for the truth only throws up more questions, more secrets, and more dead bodies.

Taking risks and working alone, Tempe refuses to give up until she has discovered why the babies died. But in such a hostile environment, can she avoid being the next victim?

OUT NOW IN PAPERBACK AND EBOOK

arrow books

ALSO AVAILABLE IN ARROW

Déjà Dead

Kathy Reichs

The Number One Bestseller

The bones of a woman are discovered in the grounds of an abandoned monastery. The case is given to Dr Temperance Brennan of the Laboratoire de Medecine Legale in Montreal: 'too decomposed for standard autopsy. Request anthropological expertise. My case. ' Brennan becomes convinced that a serial killer is at work, despite the deep cynicism of Detective Claudel who heads the investigation. Dr. Brennan's forensic expertise and contacts at Quantico finally convince him otherwise, but only after the body count has grown and the lives of those closest to her are more than just endangered.

'Better than Patricia Cornwell'
Express on Sunday

'A guaranteed sleep-deterrent. Genuinely thrilling'
Literary Review

arrow books

Monday Mourning

Kathy Reichs

**Three skeletons are found in the basement of a
pizza parlour.**

**The building is old, with a colourful past, and Homicide
Detective Luc Claudel dismisses the remains as historic.
Not his case, not his concern . . .**

But forensic anthropologist Tempe Brennan has her doubts.
Something about the bones of the three young women suggests
a different message: murder. A cold case, but Claudel's case
nonetheless.

Brennan is in Montreal to testify as an expert witness at a trial.
Digging up more bones was not on her agenda. And to make
matters worse, her sometime-lover Detective Andrew Ryan
disappears just as Tempe is beginning to trust him.

Soon Tempe finds herself drawn ever deeper into a web of evil
from which there may be no escape: three women have
disappeared, never to return. And Tempe may be next . . .

'Reichs is not just "as good as" Cornwell, she has become the
finer writer'
Daily Express

'Terrific'
Independent on Sunday

arrow books

Siege

Simon Kernick

LONDON. THE STANHOPE HOTEL, PARK LANE. 16.00

A normal afternoon.

THE MANAGER

Newly engaged Elena Serenko has just made the life-changing decision to quit her job and start a new life in Australia.

THE GUESTS

Upstairs, a young woman waits for her lover; a visiting family prepare for an evening out; and a sick man contemplates his own mortality.

THE ASSASSIN

High up amongst the penthouse suites, a skilled and dangerous killer is hunting a quarry who's eluded him for far too long.

THE SIEGE

What none of them know is that a group of ruthless gunmen are about to burst into the Stanhope, shooting indiscriminately, and seizing hostages.

As darkness falls and the gunmen become increasingly violent, only one thing matters.

Who will survive?

'Expertly plotted ... fast and furious'
Daily Mail

OUT NOW IN PAPERBACK AND EBOOK

arrow books

ALSO AVAILABLE IN ARROW

Ultimatum

Simon Kernick

THE THREAT

8am: an explosion blasts through a cafe in Central London.

THE ULTIMATUM

Minutes later, a call from an unknown terror group warns that a far greater attack will be launched in 12 hours' time.

THE PRISONER

William Garrett, AKA Fox, is awaiting trial for mass murder. He claims he can name the bombers. But only at a price.

THE CLOCK IS TICKING

It's a terrifying race against time for DI Mike Bolt and DC Tina Boyd as they chase their targets across the city in a desperate bid to stop a major atrocity - before it's too late ...

'More gripping than action man's hands'
Mail on Sunday

'Brilliant ... a tense, action-packed read'
Sunday Mirror

OUT NOW IN PAPERBACK AND EBOOK

arrow books

dead
good

*For all of you who find
a crime story irresistible.*

Discover the very best crime and thriller books on our
dedicated website – hand-picked by our editorial team
so you have tailored recommendations to help you
choose what to read next.

We'll introduce you to our favourite authors and the
brightest new talent. Read exclusive interviews and
specially commissioned features on everything from the
best classic crime to our top ten TV detectives, join live
webchats and speak to authors directly.

Plus our monthly book competition offers you the
chance to win the latest crime fiction, and there are
DVD box sets and digital devices to be won too.

Sign up for our newsletter at
www.deadgoodbooks.co.uk/signup

Join the conversation on: